A Royal
DANCE

He makes all things beautiful
in its time!
Linda Ferguson
His Little Butterfly

A Royal Dance

The Lion and the Butterfly
BOOK ONE

LINDA FERGERSON

A Royal Dance

Published by Carpenter's Son Publishing, Franklin, Tennessee.

Published in association with Larry Carpenter of Christian Book Services, LLC. www.christianbookservices.com

Cover illustrated by Rachelle Williams

Edited by Lori Martinsek

Cover and Interior Layout Design by Adept Content Solutions

Printed in the United States of America

978-1-946889-21-8

Dedication

To my loving husband, Steve,
>   Without your continued support, I would have quit writing.

To my three adopted sons, Samuel, Stephen, Joshua,
>   I pray you cherish this gift as much as I cherish you.

To my mother and father who gave me life,
>   You are the greatest!

To all those friends who prayed, encouraged, and stayed with me to
>   the end,
>   Thank you!

To my Father in heaven, who spoke this book into my destiny,
>   I am amazed at your faithfulness. You never gave up on me,
>   even when I ran for years from your call to write!

To my precious Jesus, who danced with me in those dark moments,
>   I love you!

To the Holy Spirit, who guided me through the confusion,
>   Your quiet whisper has become a cherished treasure.

Contents

Acknowledgments

I want to acknowledge Royalene Doyle, my first editor on this project. Without her early encouragement, I would have run away from this project. It seemed so impossible.

I also want to acknowledge Hope Flinchbaugh and her editing team at Hope Editors. Without Hope's vision to see this writing project as a novel, her selfless time and patience in training me, along with her content editing expertise and that of her copy editor, Pamela Brossman, this novel would never have happened.

Finally, I want to acknowledge my best friend, confidant, and prayer warrior, Judy Ackerman. She always believed in God's call on my life to write and never gave up on encouraging me forward. Her journalistic expertise was invaluable.

Prologue

In the Beginning

From the beginning of time he loathed her. Why was she the center of attention? True, she was unique and different from the man, and that intrigued him at first. But who was this creature? Was she destined to replace his previous position with God? And such beauty!

God created the world with his words. He formed the man from dust. But this one—this one was created from the side of the man. There's something about her. . . .

"It is not good that man lives alone," the Creator said. Was that it? A creature made for the man? Or was there more? He guessed the latter.

Her fiery love and innocent worship of the Creator reminded him of his own ridiculous adoration at the beginning of his high, heavenly career. He was such an idiot to exalt the Creator. That was a long time ago, of course, and these days he much preferred being the one in charge—the one exalted and adored. But then *she* came along. Every time she opened her mouth heavenward he wanted to shut it! Every time Adam looked at her with that dreamy look on his face, he knew:

she would become his greatest enemy, the ultimate challenger to his throne. *No one must know that I fear her. I fear her even more than the man. Just look at the effect she has on both of them!*

Whatever the Creator had in mind when he made her—whatever purpose, whatever destiny—it must be stopped. And so he watched them, looking for his opportunity to shake their beliefs and make them fall. Really, his greatest pleasure would be to watch them die, but he would never tell them that, of course. They barely knew he existed. And so he watched them closely.

After feeding the fish one morning, he heard the man speak to his wife. "The Creator does not want us to eat of the Tree of Knowing Good and Evil," he said. "If we do, we will die."

Her eyes widened. "I don't want to die."

Ah, she did not hear directly from the Creator, but from man. I can use that to my advantage.

The dark angel summoned his scrawny scribe to write down on a scroll the four words he would use in his strategy. Yes, it would take but four words to cast doubt on both the Creator and the man.

"Write this down," he commanded. "Write these four words—*did God really say?*" Then he laughed fiendishly and slapped his scribe on the back in his delight for wickedness. She would disobey—of this he was certain. Then the Creator will have no choice but to kill them, and that will be the end of the woman and the man. Destiny will be aborted!

Day after day he watched until he found her in a moment of vulnerability, when the man was not nearby. Quickly, he entered and possessed the most colorful, beautiful reptile creature he could find in order to attract the woman and deceive her. She looked his way! Then, from the mouth of the bejeweled serpent he asked, "Did God *really* say not to eat of the Tree of Knowing Good and Evil?"

Doubt! Oh, how he treasured that look of doubt in her eyes! Doubt and accusation would serve him well, he thought. The woman listened to the doubt and sinned. She ate from the Tree of Knowing Good and Evil, and she convinced Adam to join her in her doubt and disobedience.

The dark angel swirled and twirled with slithering delight inside the serpent. "Two for one!" he exclaimed. "Now they will both die!"

He laughed fiendishly again and waited to see the Creator destroy his adored family.

At sundown, the Creator came and found the man and woman, ashamed and hiding. The serpent recoiled at the compassionate look in the Creator's eyes.

Death came. Blood was shed. Not their blood, though, but that of an innocent animal! The serpent screamed, "No!" and slithered away behind a bush and watched as the Creator clothed them with the animal's skin.

Then the Creator roared like an angry lion and the possessed serpent froze! He knew the judgement awaited. Down he fell at the Creator's words, squirming on the ground—cursed by God himself to slink in the dust, not rule on a throne.

"How dare the Creator say her seed will crush my head!" he later scoffed. "We'll see about that! She'll never rule over me. I'll—I'll kill her seed!" *But how?*

After some thought he again summoned his gloomy scribe. "Write this down. I will use the Creator's own curse. He said that the man will rule over her, and I will use that to my advantage. I will entice the man to smash her until she grovels in darkness at my feet, both her and her seed. Then this world will not belong to the Creator or the man and woman. The earth will be *MINE!*"

Chapter 1

AD 20, Jerusalem

The Feast of Shavuot

U neasiness churned in Jacob's belly this spring Sivan morning. He hated that the Romans called the month of Sivan May after Maia their earth goddess. Too many false gods and goddesses in the land. Trouble lie ahead. He knew it. Why else would he have lost his appetite and felt so jittery? Certain darkness, like a claw, gripped his thoughts.

He shook his head and tried to clear his mind, then stepped onto the cobblestone street and wrapped a protective arm around Abigail, his wife, great with child, a month past her due date. Taking her for a walk, like the midwife suggested, may help the baby to come and might rid him of a sense of impending doom. The ornate iron courtyard gate creaked behind them and closed itself on its own and latched.

Jacob breathed in the fruity fragrance of the neighbor's palm plums. The sun, not yet high overhead, shined through the trees, and the cool morning breeze on his face soothed his troubled thoughts. Before crossing the street, they waited for a young Jewish man and his donkey to pass. The beast, laden with decorative baskets and loaves of bread, no doubt to sell in the street booths in the lower city, plodded along like it led a king's procession. A white lamb, leashed to its bridle, trotted behind. While they waited, Abigail placed her hand on her large abdomen and then took his arm.

Her swollen face, flushed from the heat, troubled Jacob. Wisps of dark, damp hair escaped her radiyd, the long shawl that covered her head and wrapped around her shoulders. Her beauty, in the past, turned the heads of a number of Roman soldiers. Even in her present condition, Jacob felt the urgency to protect her from their stares.

He directed her across the street and up the hill a few paces to the wall—the perfect place to look over the city of Jerusalem. Because of the unusually warm day, he chose to stop beneath a jujube tree to give his wife the shade she needed from the heat of the rising sun. From there, he looked down at the celebrations beginning in the streets of Jerusalem. The Feast of Shavuot, called Pentecost by the Greeks and Romans, drew all Jewish men to make the mandatory journey once a year to bring their firstfruits wheat harvest offering to the temple priests. This year, the joyful celebration unnerved him.

Jacob glared at the cruel Roman legionaries, some with horses, all with spears and shields, sprinkled among the pilgrims coming in the gates. Jewish zealots, ready to fight and take back the kingdom from Rome, mingled in the crowds unnoticed by the soldiers, and Jacob saw his neighbor, no doubt a zealot by his talk of late, creep past the gate, gather in the shadows, and whisper to a group of Jewish men in tattered and torn robes. Restless, Jacob shuffled to the other foot and placed his hand on the wall.

Abigail stood beside him, much quieter than he, and pointed out a few of their neighbors on the streets below. They carried their firstfruits baskets and gathered with the thousands of pilgrims that flooded Jerusalem for the celebration. Later, Jacob would descend to the lower city and greet incoming travelers before ascending the Temple Mount with his own offering. He longed to see Yeshua, his friend and tradesman, who came from Nazareth to Jerusalem every feast day.

"Jacob, look," said Abigail. She pointed to the Jericho Road outside the distant East Gate of Jerusalem. Swirls of dust rose behind the advancing soldiers as they rode in uniform around the Mount of Olives. More soldiers. Soon they would enter Jerusalem and, as always, disquiet her citizens. Abigail gripped his arm more tightly.

"Such a world our child will be born into."

"Mashiach ben David, come soon and restore the kingdom to your people," Jacob's voice sounded louder than he intended.

He looked down at Abigail's sweaty face, more swollen today than yesterday, wiped her brow with his sleeve, and hid his concerns behind long, thick lashes that winked a loving response to her beautiful dimpled smile. Her small-boned, five-foot-three-inch frame might be too fragile and tiny to deliver. She flinched just a little and grabbed his hand, her skin soft against his rough callouses.

"Feel," she said. "Our baby is active today." He allowed her to place his hand on her abdomen and rubbed his full beard with his other, then chuckled.

"It is time, my son, to be born," he said with authority. Then he bent over, both hands on his knees, and stared at her wide girth as though the child could hear him clearly and no doubt obey his every word.

"If King David can be born on Shavuot, it is good enough for you. No more delay."

He looked up at his wife and followed her eyes to the small, purple butterfly that flittered above their heads for a few seconds then landed on the thick stone wall.

"Jacob," Abigail said, a shyness in her tone, "will you be disappointed if the baby is a girl?"

His eyes danced. "He kicks like a boy."

Abigail sighed deeply.

Jacob added, "I will be pleased with any child."

A loud scuffle turned their attention back to the streets below. Procurator Gratus's legions bumped and shoved Jewish pilgrims that lined the larger road coming into Jerusalem, the soldier's authority not given by YHWH, but by the tyrant, Caesar, whose hatred of the Jews grew more and more each day.

A young boy somehow separated from his family and looked up at them, mesmerized by their shiny armor and their helmet's red plumes. Without provocation, the legionary crashed his shield into the boy's head. The soldier lifted his chin and laughed at the youngster who tumbled to the dusty ground. Streaks of crimson soaked into the boy's cloak. A woman screamed and ran with haste and recovered the child before another soldier on horseback trampled him.

Jacob's jaw tightened and he straightened his broad shoulders. The muscles of his immense six-foot stature tensed. He clenched his fists, ready to fight and take revenge for the boy's injustice. *Vermin! Shove MY boy aside and see what happens!* he thought.

The sun reflected off the gold Aquila, the eagle atop the Roman standard that led the three legions, and blinded him for a moment. He squinted and turned his eyes away and looked down at his beautiful Abigail. She waited beside him, tears in her eyes, the boy bloodied from the shield of a cruel soldier a more traumatic sight to a woman about to give birth. He forced himself to dismiss the scenes below from his mind and concentrate on her.

"Shall we return?" he asked. She took his arm again, and he led her back inside the safety of his walled, white-marbled villa, an inheritance from his late father. As a child, when his father brought him here from his other home in Tarsus, this villa turned into his enchanted castle where he could be anything he wanted to be. He won every sword fight and never backed down from Goliath, his sling and stones in hand. His enchanted castle now belonged to him and his beautiful Abigail.

Even though their elite, Roman-styled villa looked like a small fortress at the very top of Mount Zion, he often wondered about bringing a child, a son, he hoped, into the hostile climate that ruled the streets of Jerusalem. Better here than the Judean hills around the city where the Roman savages killed every man, woman, and child in several of the villages—an attempt to squelch allegiance to the zealots.

"Mashiach ben David, come soon and restore the kingdom to your people," he spoke again, this time pleading for his child's sake.

They latched the iron gate behind them, turned left, and followed the blue-and-white-tiled walkway in front of their villa lined with the pomegranate bushes that his mother planted. She died a few years before his father's disappearance, and he took comfort that the red blossoms against the dark green leaves still bloomed. The gurgling fountain in the center of the courtyard provided the perfect place to cool off on such hot days. Its purple and blue tiles sparkled in the sunlight. He opened the bronze garden gate. Abigail pulled his arm, and her quick breathing told him she needed to be in the shade. Jacob seated her on the bench underneath an olive tree and called the servant girl to bring her a glass of water.

The thought of his child needing to hide in an enchanted castle to find acceptance grieved him. Outsiders regarded his dwelling as his enormous Roman inheritance from his father. It sat among the broad avenues laid out in an orderly pattern like the elegant cities of Greece and Rome in Jerusalem's upper city. The rich and powerful Jewish families who lived in this part of the city at least pretended to honor him.

His father, a Jew's Jew and a descendant from the tribe of Judah who settled in Tarsus, Cilicia, bought his way into Roman citizenship, something most Jews shunned. Although Saul from Tarsus, a noble Jew with Roman citizenship, gained the Jewish leaders' favor, Jacob feared their rejection and never divulged his Roman citizenship. He remembered the mocking stares from his Jewish friends in the synagogues of Tarsus. How he grieved when his father, a Roman tribune, never returned. The rabbis cared little about what happened to a Roman tribune, so he hid his grief; then after his mother died, he ran away to Jerusalem to find acceptance.

He attended Rabban Gamaliel's rabbinical school started by Gamaliel's grandfather, Hillel, the Elder of the Sanhedrin, the highest court in Jerusalem. There Jacob learned, along with 500 other students, a deeper understanding of the Torah. He became a Pharisee, a doctor of the law. No Jew would mock him again or question his allegiance to his Jewish faith because of his father, the tribune.

He rejected his inherited third name, the Roman cognomen Regulus, which meant little king or prince, and embraced his Jewish bloodline, Jacob from the tribe of Judah. Here in Jerusalem no one knew of his father's Roman connections—not even his wife. How could he tell her?

He wiped the sweat from his face and imagined his father yelling orders from horseback, a sight he'd seen numerous times in Jerusalem, especially at times like today when legionaries swarmed the city at the Feast of Shavuot. They guarded like vultures, ready to swarm in and stamp out all zealot uprisings as well as anyone else that happened to be in the way. Of late, he toyed with the idea of helping the zealots achieve their goals. Perhaps he could help them in some way, but not now—not when his wife and child needed him the most.

The servant girl brought the water, and Jacob took the cloth that was draped over her arm and dipped it in the courtyard fountain. He placed the cool, wet cloth in Abigail's hands and sat beside her as she dabbed her face and neck.

"Does the midwife have the birthing room ready?"

"Yes, Chaya has been ready since Pesach. She's asked YHWH that the death angel pass over our home like it did for those in Egypt years ago," Abigail sighed. "The servants helped me prepare a birthing room here as well—just in case."

Jacob smiled. "It is good to be prepared, no?"

Abigail nodded. "Chaya is well worth the money we are paying her. My friend Ramona told me that she and her family consider her to be the best midwife in Jerusalem. But right now her mind is on other things. Her son is restless and wants to get back home. Do you remember Timon?"

Jacob nodded and crossed his legs in front of him.

"He misses the children in the lower city," Abigail said. "An orphan is not readily accepted here in the upper city among the wealthy Sadducees and rich merchants."

Jacob knew too well the ins and outs of surviving among your peers as an orphan child in Jerusalem.

"The children shun him?" he asked.

"The upper classes heckle him quite a bit." Abigail sat up and rubbed the small of her back.

"I like that boy," said Jacob. "How old is he now?"

"Ten," Abigail answered. A smile played at the corner of her mouth. "But he behaves more like fifteen."

Jacob nodded. "I see you like him, Abigail. Well, if Chaya agrees, I will take him with me into the lower city to greet the pilgrims and ascend the Temple Mount and offer our firstfruits to YHWH."

Abigail looked at Jacob gratefully. "You would do that for Timon? A boy who is not your own?"

"Of course." Jacob smiled down at his wife, her face red and perspiring. He prayed that her time would come soon, touched her abdomen again, felt movement and a slight bulge protrude under his hand. "YHWH has blessed us this year. It won't be long before we dedicate our child to him in the temple. What happened to Timon's father?"

"He abandoned him after his mother died while birthing him. Chaya, a childless widow, took pity and raised him as her own. It has not been easy for either of them."

Jacob shook his head and sighed, "I remember well what it is like to be fatherless."

***

The stench of animal droppings and human feces permeated the air as Jacob and Timon trekked down through the narrow pathways that led to the lower city. The lower section's main cobblestone streets branched off into various dirt pathways that wove between the one-room limestone dwellings, yellow-brown from years of sun and wind. The more fortunate ones in the lower city had a small courtyard and second floor. Jacob slowed his pace so Timon, whose long, dark curls shone in the sun, could keep up. At times the children yelled from the roofs at him and waved.

"You are loved," Jacob said and patted his back.

Timon smiled up at Jacob. "I teach them to target shoot with the sling and stone."

Jacob chuckled. "A marksman, eh? A skill that may come in handy if the Romans have their way. Come, this way."

Jacob stopped at the small olive grove that was shaded and elevated just enough to get a good view of the incoming travelers. "I'm looking for a friend from Nazareth, a carpenter. Every feast he comes to Jerusalem and we share trade secrets and talk of the Torah into the night."

Many hot travelers gathered in the coolness of the olive garden. Jacob and Timon found rest on a large, high rock under the rustling leaves of an old olive tree. Jacob scanned the open marketplace below for his friend. In the distance, groups of pilgrims came by the thousands, the line as far as the eye could see. Closer, just outside the gate, he saw the lines of festive travelers waiting their turn to cleanse in the mikvot bath before entering the city and paying the taxes—the horrendous Roman taxes. No one enters the gates without paying. Cohorts guarded the publicans' collection. He saw one slip a soldier some coins. The toothless soldier grinned and looked away while the publican dropped several coins in his own pouch.

"Scum!" he muttered under his breath.

Timon looked up at him, the question in his eyes.

"Timon, they know every Jewish man is required by our law to come to Jerusalem for the feasts. If they don't, they become morally unclean and become an outcast, destined to be landless and poor all his days. They take advantage of our obedience to YHWH to line their own pockets." Jacob shook his head in disgust and picked up his decorated basket that held loaves of bread, his firstfruit offering.

"There's my friend," he said and pointed, "the man with the colorful, striped robe and all the children pulling on him." The man swung a little boy high into the air and caught him. The boy giggled deep from his belly, and all the other children begged to be thrown into the air, too. Timon laughed.

Jacob looked down, smiled, and patted his head. "Yes, he knows how to have fun, especially with the children. I've never seen so much joy in one man. He knows how to make everyone feel loved—genuine love. It flows from his smile and encompasses all that he says and does. Come, I want you to meet him."

Timon jumped off the rock and ran ahead of Jacob down the last slope, around the bend, and stepped into the open marketplace. From there, he pointed to the travelers that entered the Water Gate and then to the man in the stripped robe that played with the children. Jacob grinned at his enthusiasm. In spite of the Roman soldiers' presence and taxes, he felt the festive spirit of his fellow Jews that made the journey from all across the Roman Empire.

The flutes' melodies resounded above the many languages being spoken by the different people groups entering the gate, all Jews from various countries and regions where they had been dispersed after Babylon's captivity. Over 400 years and Mashiach had not come to restore the kingdom. Jacob sighed. How much longer?

His friend, Yeshua, stood among the skilled artisans of Jerusalem, who greeted the newcomers. These craftsmen, the distillers of expensive oils and perfumes, master tailors, silk merchants, gold and silversmiths, dealers in ivory, incense, and precious stones, owned shops in the upper market with its Roman-style arcade.

"My turn!" a little girl cried, her arms held up to Yeshua. He scooped up the little girl and two others beside her. They threw their heads back laughing until Yeshua tweaked their noses and put them down.

Jacob noted the artisans' smug repulsion to Yeshua's kindness to the children, an act they no doubt considered below their status—a reminder of why Jacob enjoyed the marketplace in the lower city as opposed to the artisans' bazaars in the upper city.

"Is all well with you?" Jacob asked Yeshua, then grabbed both shoulders and offered a kiss of peace on his cheek.

"Shalom, cowdh," Yeshua answered. Jacob considered it a great honor to be called cowdh by Yeshua. It meant he considered him an intimate friend, one he reclines with in face-to-face communion. Over the last few years they grew to know each other well and talked many times into the late hours of the night about the Torah and the coming Mashiach—and the future.

"Jacob, look," Timon interrupted and pointed toward the Water Gate's high arch, its gates swung wide.

A group of rich Jews from Egypt entered beneath it with their gold- and silver-lined baskets that held their bikkurim offering of fruit and bread to take to the temple. An ox with its horns glazed with gold and a crown of olive branches on its head led the procession.

"Our legs are standing in your gates, O Jerusalem," the men cried in the Demotic Egyptian language.

The artisans, who stood around Yeshua, greeted the new visitors.

"Our brethren, the inhabitants of Egypt, you have come in peace."

Yeshua moved off to the side to get out of the line of traffic and kicked a stone back and forth with two of the older boys.

"Humph," said one of artisans. "This is a gate, not a play yard."

Yeshua looked at the man and smiled. He held his eyes and smiled until the man looked uncomfortable and looked away.

More and more groups streamed into the gate. The Jewish leaders even greeted the poor with less decorated wicker baskets of peeled willow branches. The crowds, so large that they looked like a river moving uphill, poured into the city, each with their eyes toward the temple court where they would present their grain offerings and unblemished lambs to the priests.

Jacob nodded to Yeshua to follow, tapped Timon on the shoulder, nodded to him, too, and slipped behind the artisans. Yeshua sent the children back to their families and followed.

The two friends were of the same tall stature, about six feet, but Jacob was of a brawny, large build and Yeshua of a medium frame. Jacob's eyes were green with a blue rim, not like Yeshua's blue eyes typical of the descendants of the tribe of Judah. When he was a boy in Tarsus, many voiced their doubts that Jacob's bloodline was pure, partly because of the eye color and partly because his father was a Roman tribune. Many a night his mother nursed his blackened and bruised eye because of it. Since his move to Jerusalem and his training with Gamaliel, no one dared question him now.

Yeshua's hair and beard were a lighter brown than his own black hair and beard. In keeping with the law in Leviticus to not cut the hair on the temples, both men wore pe'ots or sidelocks, their heads covered with a pe'er or linen turban, in contrast to the keffiyeh headdress that many around them wore. Both wore the lightweight linen kethoneth tunic with a colorful addereth cloak over it instead of the meil, the more common, less colorful cloak worn by most in the marketplace. Yeshua wore the expensive chagowr girdle that Jacob gave him, a sign of great honor, while Jacob wore the more common ezowr girdle. Hundreds dressed like them, but just as many hundreds dressed in clean but tattered and threadbare meils.

Jacob wondered again why his friend never married. Yeshua was not notably handsome, but surely his special way with children and his righteous character would attract the most beautiful Jewish women.

"Yeshua, this is Timon, my midwife's son."

"Midwife?" the corner of Yeshua's mouth tipped up. "YHWH's blessed you with increase, your own firstfruits offering, eh," he said and chuckled, then gave attention to Timon, who stared up at the two men. Jacob noticed the admiration in his eyes.

"Timon, are you a carpenter like Jacob perhaps?" Yeshua asked.

Timon appeared to be tongue-tied.

"I see a desire to learn in your eyes," Yeshua added as he ruffled the boy's hair. Timon nodded and smiled and Yeshua added, "Indeed you will be a good carpenter." Then he grasped Jacob's shoulders with both hands. "You should apprentice this young man. I see a future for him and you."

"Your wisdom has never failed me yet," Jacob answered and turned to Timon. "How do you feel about being my apprentice?" He noticed shiny, white teeth between a smile that spread from ear to ear.

Jacob tipped the boy's chin upward. "I take it that is a grin of approval?"

Timon's strong nod jerked his chin from Jacob's hand. He wasn't much for words. Perhaps he could draw him out as they worked together. Why hadn't I thought of teaching him before?

"Jacob," an older man with a long, white beard hollered and waved, an unusual strength in his voice for someone his age. A younger man yelled Jacob's name from another direction. One after another, men in the marketplace began to migrate toward the trio.

"It is obvious they have great respect for you," Yeshua said to Jacob. "One day you will show them the way." He noticed the seriousness in Yeshua's eyes and wondered what he meant.

"Shalom," they greeted. "May we accompany you to the temple?" Each had their own basket in hand with two loaves of bread.

"Of course," Jacob answered and they all turned and began their ascent to the temple. By the time the introductions were made, they reached the baker's table. Yeshua had not yet purchased his bread, so Jacob waited with him.

Yeshua dropped a few shekels in the baker's palm, then raised an adorned basket filled with his firstfruits offering to his shoulders. The man handed back the coins.

"I share my bread with you freely."

"YHWH bless you," Yeshua said with a jovial tone and huge smile. Jacob slapped him on the back.

"You are favored, my cowdh," he said, then lifted the older man's basket to his other shoulder. The elder gentleman grinned.

"Toda. Has your wife given you a son, yet?"

"Today, I pray. No better time than Shavuot, King David's birth," Jacob responded. A flash of Abigail's swollen face passed before his eyes and his heartbeat quickened. He stopped, pulled Timon around, and bent over to talk to him as they walked.

"Timon, I was going to take you to the temple for the sacrifices, but I have a favor to ask of you." The ten-year-old boy gazed into Jacob's eyes with rapt attention.

"Return to my home. If there is any sign that my son is being born, come and get me. I will be in the temple courts. Will you do that for me?"

"Yes," Timon said with eagerness in his voice. "You can trust me. When the time comes, I'll run as fast as the wind."

Chapter 2

J acob laughed. In Yeshua's jovial company, he forgot for a while his troubled thoughts of Roman occupation, false gods, and his child's birth. The men, baskets on their shoulders, waited in line to give their offerings to the priest. They stopped at the money changers and bought their lambs, two each, and held them on ropes in one hand. Simultaneously, they recited from the Tehillim, "Praise the Lord!"

Just then, Yeshua threw his head back in joyful exuberance. "Praise YHWH in his sanctuary." Jacob and his friends' deep voices echoed his enthusiasm: "Let everything that has breath praise the Lord! Praise the Lord!" Their laughing voices trailed off at the sight of the skinned lambs that hung before them. The priests had caught blood in silver bowls then let the carcass hang until ready to be given back for the feast, drained of all blood. Fresh blood dripped on the steps and mixed with that of previous sacrifices earlier in the day.

Jacob paid little attention to the Levites' response in song from the Tehillim: "I will extol you, O Lord, for you have drawn me up. .

. .” Their words faded into the background noises of flutes, laughing children, and mews of lambs. His thoughts settled now on his beautiful Abigail. He smelled the stench of dried blood in the air and longed to be home with her and imagined their feast together, his newborn son in his arms. In the distance, dark clouds gathered, but the sun's rays broke through and shined on his lifted face.

"Blemished!" He heard the voice of his friend, Caiaphas, who had recently become the high priest. Jacob looked at the temple worker beside Caiaphas and watched him push the lamb away from the old man who ascended ahead of them up the Temple Mount. Caiaphas yelled, "Buy another one. This one's unacceptable." The older man stumbled.

Jacob frowned at Caiaphas's rudeness. "This isn't the man I knew from Gamaliel's school," he said quietly to Yeshua. "He has changed since becoming high priest."

Yeshua dropped his basket and lamb's ropes then rushed ahead to help the older gentleman down the steps. Jacob saw fire in Yeshua's eyes as he stepped back in line ahead of him, Yeshua's hand under the old man's forearm.

"I have heard the priests are lining their own pockets with the money from the sale of extra lambs," Jacob said to his friends in line with him. He picked up Yeshua's offering basket and lambs' ropes, his eyes now on Yeshua's back.

Jacob smiled. "If my son shows such love and honor to the elders, I will be satisfied," he murmured to himself.

When they reached the money changers' table, Jacob watched as Yeshua escorted the man to the purchasing tables. He nearly lost sight of him as people shuffled forward and sideways to the various tables. By the time he could see Yeshua again, he saw the exchange of Roman coins for shekels, and they moved to the end where the lambs were penned in a makeshift stable right there in the courtyard. The temple worker handed the old man a lamb and extended his open palm for payment in silver shekels. Yeshua rubbed his hand over the animal, examined it, and gave it back. The scorned worker protested, but Yeshua held his ground and they gave him another one. It was at that moment that Jacob noticed the old man bump into the table and put his hands out in front of him. Immediately the man pulled a stick out of his robe and tapped the ground beside him.

"Why, he's blind!" Jacob whispered.

Yeshua's six-foot frame towered over the man, whose thin frail back was bent, not allowing him to stand upright. A Roman soldier, who scoured the crowd for rebel rousers, knocked the older gentleman aside in his brusque effort to pass him. Jacob tensed, his desire to fight Romans stirred. He could see between the heads of the many people in front of him. Yeshua glowered at the soldier's back, his arm still underneath the man's forearm. He tugged on the rope for the lamb to follow and smiled down as he said something to the older man. The blind man crimped his neck to look up, and an appreciative smile spread wide between his moustache and scraggly white beard.

Jacob followed Yeshua as he helped the blind man up the steep steps with the new lamb. Several priests were there, with Caiaphas in the middle. Each priest took the firstfruit bread offering of the worshipper and raised it up in all four directions and handed it back to the worshipper, then took the lambs and made the blood sacrifice. Caiaphas stared down at the three of them, a pompous lift to his chin.

He does not appear to be the same man I shared Passover seder meals with in the past, thought Jacob. Still, as Caiaphas's friend, he wished to at least voice a kind rebuke in an attempt to call his attention to the way he handled himself.

Jacob leaned over the table and whispered, "Rome is attempting to corrupt you, my friend."

Caiaphas ignored Jacob and rubbed his hands over the animal. He looked with disdain at the blind man bent over and unable to look up. "This lamb is not . . ." he started to pronounce, then Yeshua stepped up beside the old man and glared at Caiaphas. Jacob looked from one man to the other. Their eyes locked, and it appeared a challenge was underway.

Caiaphas rubbed his fingers through his beard, then swung around. His black robe swished in the air as he climbed a few steps higher, then turned back and looked down.

"The lamb is accepted," he added. His dark, beady eyes peered through tiny slits, his eyelids half shut. Jacob breathed a sigh of relief.

***

People lingered—the threadbare poor, strangers dressed in a myriad of colorful turbans and keyffiyehs, mixed with the Levites dressed in their holy robes of blue and white. Jacob smelled the roasted lamb and his stomach rumbled. The communal meal would begin soon. His friends remained at the high priest's table, waiting to give their bread and lamb offerings to Caiaphas who seemed distracted with something else going on behind him.

Atop the flat temple roof in the distance he saw the gleam of the sun against the shofar and the priests readying themselves. Soon it would blast the call to all the poor, the strangers and the Levites, a signal to join in the feast at hand. He slapped Yeshua's back and turned to the blind man and tapped his shoulder.

"Will you feast with us at my house?" he asked.

"No, I will stay here, in the temple courts. I've waited many years for Mashiach ben David. Tonight may be the night he comes to restore the kingdom to us," he answered. Jacob looked at Yeshua and noticed his grim expression.

"He will come soon," Yeshua said, and Jacob followed as Yeshua led the man to a safe place in the shadows.

"Don't concern yourself with me," the old man said. "This is the day the poor, the blind, and the maimed are fed, their bellies full of roasted lamb and bread," the old man said.

Just then, Jacob heard the voice of a young boy call his name and looked across the temple courtyard and scanned the crowd.

"Timon!" he said and glanced back at Yeshua. "I may have a son!" The youngster rushed up, breathless, and stood in front of the men.

"My wife?" Jacob asked.

"She is in danger and the baby, too."

Jacob's ears rang and his heartbeat pounded in the side of his head. With trembling hands, he squeezed his temples.

"I was afraid this would happen. I should not have left her."

"Go!" Yeshua said. "I will stay here with our new friend. I will look for you later."

Timon pulled on Jacob's hand.

"My mother said to tell you to hurry! I have never seen her so worried about a birth. Please, come!"

Yeshua grasped Jacob's shoulder and reached into his own cloak. "Fear not! She will live," he said and placed a wooden object in his palm. Jacob felt Yeshua's rough, calloused fingers wrap around his own fingers and enclose them.

"Come, Jacob," Timon continued to pull. "I am fast. I can keep up with you. Let's go before it is too late."

***

Jacob swept into the birthing room connected to his bedroom and slid to a stop, his hand on the lintel. Abigail grasped the rope that dangled above the birthing bed and squeezed, knuckles white. "Ay-YAAAAH!" she cried out. She gazed up into the midwife's eyes for assurance.

Chaya glanced up and saw Jacob. She motioned for him to step outside the room.

"I am so glad you are here."

Jacob's stomach churned. With an earnest expression on her face, she directed him to step farther outside into the courtyard.

"The baby wouldn't turn, although I've tried again and again. The child is bent at the waist, knees crossed. What I thought was the head was the bottom."

Abigail cried out again, and Jacob started to go inside the room. Chaya stopped him. "Not now, you are too upset. She will sense your fears."

"You will not tell me what I can do with my own wife," he countered.

"All right, if you must watch, stay in the corner out of sight," she said as she ran upstairs and ducked back inside the shadowy room. With a swift, long gait, Jacob followed. A sense of helplessness draped around his thoughts when he entered the room. He stopped and backed up until he hit the wall in the dark corner.

Chaya's soothing voice calmed him a bit as she wrung a cloth in the bowl of water and spoke to his wife. As soon as she wiped the perspiration from Abigail's ashen face, Jacob noticed his wife's writhing subside and she closed her eyes. Lifeless, she looked dead. *No! Please, YHWH. No!* Chaya wiped a strand of hair back from her face.

"Abigail, you are doing well," she encouraged her. "Your body will tell you when it is time to push."

Again Abigail cried out, squeezed her eyes shut, and tried to stifle her pain. Relief flooded Jacob's body. *She's alive!*

"Breathe, Abigail! Breathe!"

Quickly, the midwife checked her abdomen.

Jacob wiped the sweat from his brow and noticed Chaya's beads of sweat blend with silent tears that ran down her cheeks. She turned her back to his wife and wiped her face with her sleeve. Jacob started to move toward Abigail, but Chaya stepped in his way and motioned for him to go outside again. He felt like retching and needed air, so he relented and stepped outside with her.

After they both caught their breath, Chaya turned to speak to Jacob.

"Please know this, Jacob, like every Hebrew midwife, my highest joy is to aid mothers in the process of bringing new life into the world. It is my deepest sorrow when something like this goes wrong. I have experienced this scenario before and I must be honest with you. I cannot save the baby," she whispered. "I will try to save Abigail, but most likely both will die. I am sorry."

Abigail cried out again and the midwife left Jacob to go to her side. Jacob stood in the doorway and watched, a sickness swooped over his whole body. One of Abigail's hands gripped the rope while the other dangled. Chaya grasped the limp hand. Instantly, the hand tightened in the midwife's grasp, fingers digging deep into the flesh.

As he watched Chaya push on his wife's abdomen to expel the baby, the dark whispers of doom he had sensed in the early morning hours gripped Jacob again. The negative words of the other women in the room hung in the air. Chaya signaled them to be silent and then motioned for them to get out of the room.

Resisting the urge to run away, Jacob stepped around the doorway, slid to the floor in the darkened corner, and hid his face between his knees When he found the courage to look up, Chaya was bent over Abigail.

"Don't worry. There is a purpose for this child," she encouraged his wife. He saw two dimples form through her grimace and a smile spread across Abigail's unblemished face. So charming—even now! Her beauty was undeniable, even with her long, jet-black hair, disheveled and wet from perspiration.

Abigail's long, thick lashes blinked back tears. Courage and determination that Jacob had not seen in any other woman dimmed in her dark, round eyes. They begged for relief!

Jacob noticed her grip loosen. *Don't give up Abigail. Keep fighting. I cannot lose you and the baby.*

A shadow moved across his face, and he looked up and saw Chaya's assistant in the doorway. "A man named Yeshua is here to see you," she said.

Jacob turned onto his knees, pushed himself up, and followed her outside. He constrained his sobs until he stumbled down the stairs into the courtyard, Yeshua at his side. He felt Yeshua's strong hand steady him.

At the fountain, he crumbled to his knees. His hands over his face and mouth, his muffled groans poured out in convulsing sobs. He tried to stop. Abigail must not hear. He felt a hand on his back and then Yeshua was beside him, crying out to YHWH, too.

"They're dying," he said to Yeshua when their prayers were finished. Jacob heard another cry from Abigail and covered his head with his arms. "Why, Yeshua? Why?"

"The Torah says, 'in pain you shall bring forth children.' They will not die. Your wife shall bring forth the child."

"It would take a miracle."

"YHWH is a miracle-working God," Yeshua said. "Come, let's sit in the garden while we wait for your miracle." Jacob let Yeshua help him up. He immediately went to the gurgling fountain and splashed cool water from the overflow on his swollen eyes. He raised his face up and let the breeze blow through his black beard, down his neck, and into his tunic.

Yeshua stooped over inside the open garden gate, searching for something in the pomegranate bushes. His shoulder-length, brown hair glistened in the sun as his head bobbed in and out of the bushes. Finally he motioned for Jacob to join him.

"Come look at this chrysalis."

Jacob sighed deeply and approached with a skeptical arch to his brow. In honor of his friend's wisdom, he leaned down and stuck his head in the bushes, too. Yeshua pointed to a dark, oblong structure that hung from the branch.

"Tap this," he said, "and feel the hard outer covering." Jacob felt foolish, like a child again, but he touched the hard structure. Then the two men stood up face-to-face. "This new creation is protected. From the outside, it doesn't look like YHWH is working, but inside, in the dark, he is shaping something beautiful." Jacob heard another cry, this one long and shrill. "Don't be afraid, Jacob," Yeshua comforted. "YHWH is working. They are protected under the covering of his hand."

Jacob nodded. A peace settled on him and stayed even after Yeshua left. He walked through the garden alone and prayed to his God.

"They are yours. They have always been yours, YHWH," he said. "I take my hands off. I trust them to your care. Have your way." Each time he circled the courtyard, he looked for the chrysalis and heard Yeshua's words. *From the outside, it doesn't look like YHWH is working, but inside, in the dark, he is shaping something beautiful.* "Yes, YHWH, let it be so." The sun descended behind the dark clouds and a soft pink glow radiated through the branches of the olive trees.

"Jacob." He heard Timon's voice behind him and turned. "My mother wants you to come. It's time for you to see your wife." He took a deep breath, closed his eyes, and exhaled.

"Tell her I'll be right there."

***

The orange glow of the setting sun shined through the window on Abigail's face. Her eyes were closed, her skin pale and ashen in color. Jacob's eyes widened. *Is she dead?* Lying in her arms was a bundle wrapped in the traditional swaddling cloths. The baby's face was ashen like his wife, but eyes open, large and shining with life. He knelt beside Abigail, dropped his head in her lap, and shook with sobs. Chaya whispered in his ear.

"Sir, she lives."

He felt Abigail stir, raised himself up to see her fingers move, but also saw she was too weak to raise her hand.

"A boy?" he asked, placing his hand on the baby's head. Abigail tucked the child closer to her chest.

"No, it's a girl. Are you disappointed?"

Jacob took the tiny infant and cuddled her in his strong arms and gazed directly into the baby's large, round, blue-rimmed green eyes. "My daughter, I love you." He glanced up at his wife. "Who am I to question the Creator's choice? I could not be more thankful. Just a few minutes ago I thought you were both dead. YHWH granted you both life. A miracle! And I will forever give him glory!" He snuggled the baby close to his chest in one arm and knelt beside his wife. "Abigail, Abigail! How I love you!" With that, Jacob released his pent-up tension in joyful tears as she stroked his dark hair and whispered, "It's all right, Jacob. YHWH was with us. It's all right."

After some time, Jacob kissed his wife's forehead and kissed his baby's cheek. He felt Chaya's presence behind him. Now finished cleaning up the afterbirth, she smiled down upon them all and folded more swaddling cloths for later use.

"Thank you, Chaya," he said, then rose from his wife's bedside, sat on the chair beside her bed, and held his daughter in front of him. His face beamed with pride.

"Who is this daughter of the tribe of Judah? Who is this little miracle birthed from heaven?" He heard the scuffle of feet outside the door and looked up.

Yeshua stood under the lintel, his arm around Timon, both with twinkles in their eyes and lopsided grins.

"Is it a boy?" Timon asked.

"No, she's a girl. I think we will call her Jerusha. Is that a good name, Mother?" He smiled as he said the word "mother" and shifted his tiny daughter in the crook of his arm.

"What does it mean?"

"It means inheritance," Yeshua offered, "Your special treasure from heaven." He walked over to Jacob and reached out his fist with something enclosed in it.

"You dropped this in the garden." Jacob shifted the baby into the other arm, opened his palm, and Yeshua placed the hidden object in his hand. In the rush to get home to his wife, Jacob had tucked Yeshua's gift inside his robe without looking at it. He glanced down. He saw a butterfly carved in the middle of the round, decorative acacia piece.

"What does this mean?"

"Whatever happens, Jacob, YHWH makes all things beautiful in its time."

Chapter 3

AD 28

Eight Years Later

Jacob filed the edge of the small bench in front of him until it was as smooth as skin. It didn't seem fair that a man would enjoy his work so much, and even more so since Jerusha's arrival. Of course, he could work in his shop, but he preferred his family garden, surrounded by a spacious and ornate courtyard. Why work indoors on a day like today? The fragrant orange and red blossoms of the pomegranate bushes attracted a myriad of colorful butterflies that flew like colored jewels. The fig and olive trees provided shade, and the fragrance from the grapevines that hugged the courtyard columns filled his senses.

There wasn't a wealthy man in the world that enjoyed greater treasures, of that he was sure; especially when he watched his Jerusha dance, her tiny bare feet twirling around and around, her long, shiny, black hair bouncing with every step. *I must watch out for her. Those emerald green eyes surrounded by a rim of dark blue sapphire will attract many a young man's eye.* That thought worried him a bit. Like her mother, she was blessed with that dimpled smile that melts hearts.

The black mole on her right cheek, her "beauty mark," as he told her, is the Creator's special touch that distinguished her as his Jerusha. Deep in thought, Jacob vowed to make sure his little jewel knew that she came from the royal line of Judah. He knew because of his eye color and her eye color that many would accuse her of not being a true Hebrew of Hebrews. She must never think of herself as less. Her bloodline was pure.

"Look, Father!" Jerusha skipped off across the large flat stones toward the largest pomegranate bush and lifted her finger near the wing of the highest butterfly. The bright yellow butterfly, trimmed in black, flitted onto his daughter's finger. Jacob shook his head. She had a way with those butterflies—a gift from God, for sure.

Jerusha kissed the tips of the wings and sent her little friend back into the sky. She picked a red blossom from the bush and presented it to him. He took the small flower and placed it in his daughter's long, black, wavy hair, right behind her ear. Her eyes still shone, wide as saucers, as they did on the day of her birth. He set the bench down and inspected it. The right side needed a bit more filing, so he picked it up and began on the other side.

"Jerusha, never forget who you are," he said.

"Who am I, Father?"

"My little lioness, you are royalty from the tribe of Judah. You will dance before the King one day."

He touched her chin gently and set the small stool upside down on his lap.

She fingered one of the tzitzits that hung from the corners of his robe that lay on the bench and ran off to chase a butterfly, then just as quickly returned, out of breath. Her hair went every which way.

"Father, I love you. I never want to leave you. I want to go wherever you go." She watched as his steady hands worked on a different object that had caught her curiosity.

"What are you making?"

"You will see," he told her. "This wood is special—from the acacia tree. That is the same wood that was used to make the ark of the covenant."

She slipped off the bench and caught the shavings in her fingers as they fell to the stone courtyard floor.

"It smells good," she said, placing the shavings near her nose.

Jacob looked away from his work momentarily and grinned.

"What is so funny?" she asked.

"Oh, nothing," he said, as he dabbed at the dust smeared across her cheeks and removed the spiral wood shavings that hung from her lips.

"Father, look!" Jerusha pointed to a purple butterfly that fluttered near her father's face. She jumped up. With her tiny finger she reached out to touch it. "Why does the purple butterfly always fly away?" she asked.

"The flight of the butterfly is a mystery. It never looks like it knows where it is going. Our Creator has placed within it, though, the ability to always arrive at its destination."

Jacob spied an object lesson in the pomegranate bush and got up from his work.

"Come and look at this chrysalis," he said, motioning to her.

She skipped over to see. "What is that?" she asked.

"This is the place the Creator uses to mold and shape the butterfly. It is safe inside its dark world with this hard outer shell. When the time is right, it begins to work its way out. If you ever see a butterfly coming out of the chrysalis, do not help it, or it will die. It must do it on its own to gain the strength to fly and navigate after its entry into this world."

The little girl scrunched her brow. "It must be hard for the butterfly."

"It is a miracle. Just like you," he said, and tweaked her nose. "Look!" he said, pointing across the garden. Her eyes brightened at the flurry of butterflies in a rainbow of colors scattered before her among the bushes. She chased them, as he knew she would, and Jacob went back to his work.

In time, she tired of chasing the butterflies and returned to him. "Tell me a story, Father," she asked.

Her mind was a deep well waiting to be filled, and Jacob took great joy in being her teacher as well as her father. His rich, deep voice took her on another adventure into the past.

This time he told her about the acacia wood and the ark of the covenant—how it housed the law and how his presence hovered over the mercy seat, even causing the Philistine's god, Dagon, to fall before it. He dropped his tools at that part and embellished the fall of Dagon with exaggerated arm actions like he'd done so many times.

He told her how the water parted before the ark when they crossed the Jordan River into the Promised Land. He wanted her to envision the glory that filled the temple when the ark was placed in the Holy of Holies.

He told her about King David and how he danced before the ark as it was carried into Jerusalem. Of course, she "danced like David" and the simple, flat courtyard stones became the long, wide streets of Jerusalem under her feet. She stopped.

"Where is the ark now?" she asked.

"No one knows. It disappeared after the Babylonian captivity."

"Does YHWH still dwell with us?"

"It is a mystery. The high priest goes once a year into the Holy of Holies. If he does not prepare himself properly, he could die while in there. He needs to wash his body with water, dress in holy garments, and present the sin offering, the blood of a bull for himself and a goat for the people. Without holiness, without the shedding of blood, no man can stand in YHWH's presence."

Jacob put down the wooden object he worked on, lifted Jerusha onto his lap, and continued, "The scriptures have prophesied of a coming King. Many believe it is Yeshua. I am beginning to believe he is the One, too. He speaks with authority, shows compassion through healing the sick, and the people seem to love him."

Jacob paused and turned his daughter's face toward him. "For now just know that the pendant I am making is to remind you of all that I have taught. The words on the back are what the priests said before they moved the ark, which carried YHWH's presence. Sometime soon, he will return and restore the kingdom. In the years ahead, you will need the promise of these words and the stories that I have spoken to unravel the mysteries you will face in your journey."

"A journey?" asked Jerusha. "I am going on a journey?"

"Something like that," he answered.

She jumped down from the bench. Jacob looked up.

"Abigail."

"Come see what Father is making," Jerusha said.

Abigail scowled in reply.

"What is wrong?" Jacob heard Jerusha ask and look at her mother. He picked her up and sat her on his lap.

"I need to talk to your father—alone," she said. "Please leave us."

Jerusha glanced up at Jacob and slipped off his lap and scampered past Abigail to the garden gate. Jacob saw her stop and look back over her shoulder. He winked.

"You know the high priest does not approve of Yeshua," Abigail said. "He may be your friend, but it is dangerous for us if you continue to pursue his false teaching. Just the other day I overheard Caiaphas talking to another priest about arresting him. They want this heresy stopped."

"You visited Caiaphas's without me?"

"Numerous times," she answered. Jacob raised an eyebrow. "He spends much time at Herod's palace. Jerusha and I fetched Chaya to help with a servant's birth and another time his wife was sick and we spent several days there helping nurse her back to health," she continued. "You have been gone so much following those heretics or you would have known that *and* that your daughter is enamored with his son, Efah. She hopes you choose him as her betrothed."

Jacob scrunched up his face. "She is too young to be thinking about such things."

"She thinks he is handsome. I have watched her giggle in embarrassment when he looks her way."

"Not that pompous—" he hesitated. "Oh, never mind what I think of him. Timon shows more potential, but we have awhile before we need to make that choice."

"Timon is an orphan. Our daughter deserves better."

"I am an orphan," he said with inflection in his voice. "Do you think that I am not good enough to be her father?" He rose and moved around behind her and embraced her, his arms wrapped tight and his nose snuggled into her neck.

"Oh, Jacob, stop with this ironic banter. You know I love you and she adores you. Of course you are good enough. That is not the point," her words softened.

"Then what is the point?" he whispered.

"That you stop following Yeshua. He is dangerous." She broke his arms loose.

"What if he is the Mashiach we have been waiting for?"

"You are so stubborn," she yelled and turned her back. "He is just a common man from Nazareth. Did you hear that he turned over the money changers table in the temple? If he was destined to be our King, Caiaphas would know."

Jacob heard Jerusha's sandals on the stone walkway and looked over at the garden entrance just in time to see her slide around the corner and grab a low hanging olive branch to stop.

"They are coming!" she said, her eyes wide open with fright.

"Who?"

"The soldiers! They are coming to get us. I saw them."

"What?" Abigail exclaimed.

In three large steps Jacob was at Jerusha's side, swooped her up in his arms, and headed for the courtyard entrance. He heard Abigail's footsteps, turned, and waited for her to catch up. They hid behind the thorny jujube tree, its yellow-green fruit not yet a ripened red, and listened to the screams from down the hill. The clatter of footsteps grew louder and louder. Jacob felt the warmth of Jerusha's breath on his neck.

"They are coming to get us," she whispered. He looked down at Abigail. Her eyes shot fiery darts. He tried to wrap his arm around her, but she pushed it away.

"We are not zealots!" the man yelled as the Roman soldiers dragged him past and down the hill.

"Save your lies for Prefect Pilate and be glad we are not taking your wife and son." The soldier yanked him away from his little son, who clung to his robe and cried. A young woman ran to pick him up out of the dust, both crying out to the prisoner that they loved him.

Sickened, Jacob closed his eyes and held his hand over the back of Jerusha's head.

"Do not be afraid, Jerusha. They are not after us," he said and stepped out of their hiding place.

Abigail took Jerusha from his arms, placed her feet on the ground and took her hand. They walked side by side into the walled courtyard. Jacob saw Abigail turn her head and stare back at him, an angry glower behind her long, dark lashes. He knew what she was thinking and wondered if she may be right. He had to find out. Sometime soon he would leave again and find Yeshua. He must know if he was the One.

Chapter 4

Jerusha walked with purpose, her steps steady and strong. It took awhile to descend the winding path to her father's workshop in the lower city. She carried a basket on her hip, her morning chore, and a meal for Father and Timon in their workshop. Father left every morning before sunrise. She looked forward to this time with him. The grapes that covered the bread and overflowed the edges bounced with every step. The sun warmed her waist-long, black, wavy hair and took the chill off the early morning mist that had soaked into her cloak.

Although she was only eight years old, her father's instruction to her that she was royalty was not wasted. She knew within her spirit that YHWH had a destiny for her life, one of significance. One day she'd know this King father talked about and offer him a reverent dance. On days like today when she was too busy to practice, she danced the steps in her mind and imagined twirling with arms uplifted. Every king deserved a bow, especially at the end of a performance!

Distracted by a child's squeal in the distance, her thoughts of grandeur faded and she saw Father's friend Yeshua with some men under an olive tree at the far side of the market. She liked him. He made her feel special. Father said he might be *the One.*

She nodded her head up and down at that thought. He would make a good king, one that would like her dance. And he would be pleased if she married the high priest's son. That's what she needed to talk to Father about today. A royal daughter needs a royal husband. Father might think she's too young to think of these things, but she must convince him otherwise.

Jerusha crinkled up her nose. The stench in this poor section of the lower city was so much stronger than the upper city where they kept the wide, cobblestone pathways clean of rubbish and excrement. She took note of the children who played in the streets, many of them orphans, dirty and unkempt. *Thank you, YHWH, that I am not like them, fatherless and poor.*

Many ran to Yeshua, who held an infant on his lap, surrounded by little urchins with torn and tattered cloaks. If she wasn't so set on her meeting with Father, she would be tempted to join them. Whenever Yeshua visited her house to see Father, he made time for her.

He frowned at the men who tried to shoo the children away. Jerusha chuckled. She saw that same look on Yeshua's face when she was at the temple with Father. He laughs with the children one day then glares at the priests the next. She crinkled her brow in deep thought. Maybe he would not like her to marry the high priest's son after all?

As she rounded the last bend in the narrow pathway she saw Father in the distant tent workshop, his broad, muscular shoulders bent over a piece of wood. Timon, almost as tall as him and every bit as muscular, sawed the board with vigor. She waited for the donkey loaded with water pots to pass, then scurried around the lone sheep that wandered in the open marketplace and headed for his shop at the end of the row of vendors.

"Jerusha!" She heard Efah's voice call and glanced at the group of boys gathered at the other end of the vendors. She played coy and ignored the handsome fifteen-year-old and continued walking. *He must not know how much I care. It is not proper for a young girl to show affection toward boys.* She pulled her radiyd over her head.

Father looked up and waved. He stopped holding the board without telling Timon, and it fell on Timon's shins. He yelped and hopped on one foot while Father apologized. She covered her giggle with her hand. Timon, a handsome eighteen-year-old, felt more like a brother.

The marketplace was beginning to fill with traders from the east. A camel mewled. It decided to sit in the middle of the market between her and Father's shop. Its owner pulled on the bridle and whacked its rump to no avail. Whew! He smelled. She squeezed her nose shut, scampered around the lazy beast, and dodged a few stray goats, then gasped for breath as she straightened the grapes in the basket. She knew Father would be hungry. The basket drooped again, her arm achy and tired. Just a few more steps between meandering traders and donkeys and she stood at the shop entrance, the large dark flap rolled up. The cool morning breeze whipped the edges of the tent.

Glad to get rid of the extra weight on her arm, she walked past the men to a long piece of acacia laid across two wooden boxes in the back, brushed the shavings to the ground, and placed the basket on the makeshift table. When she turned, she saw Father squatted with arms open wide and ran full speed into his embrace. He lifted her high in the air and swung her around. Her radiyd fell to the ground and let her shiny, black hair fly out behind as he whirled her around and around and around. With each twirl, she giggled louder.

"Father, stop," she squealed between giggles.

"Are you sure?" he asked.

"Yes, yes," she squeaked. When he finally put her feet on the ground, she staggered with arms outstretched to keep her balance, but bumped against the tent wall. Father bought the best material in the empire for his tent. The cilicium, woven of black goat's hair from the mountains of Tarsus, would hold her weight.

This makeshift tent that could easily be taken down and moved was Father's favorite place to work, except in the garden at home. It was not like the fancy shops in the upper city, but spacious for a tent. The larger tools such as mallets, bowdrils, and saws hung on the back wall.

She sat on a stool near the front and watched them work. The aprons around their groins held chisels, hones, and bradawls. They had shed their cloaks long ago and worked in sleeveless tunics, the sweat soaking through the material on their backs. Each pulled the end of the saw. The perspiration on their flexed muscles glistened from the sun's rays that came through the rolled front flap.

"Father, we need to talk!" she yelled loud enough to be heard over the sawing. He pulled one last time. A board dropped and he wiped the sweat with a soft cloth sticking out of his apron pocket. Timon stared at her with a lopsided grin while Father picked up the board. She looked down at her toes that had slid over the end of her sandals and listened to Father address his apprentice.

"I am taking my daughter to the olive grove up the hill."

Jerusha smiled, happy to get her father's full attention.

"I know you can handle it, Timon," said Jacob. "You are doing excellent work now." She looked up to see Father remove his tool apron, slip something in the girdle on his waist, and grab some fruit, bread, and a goatskin water bottle, then motion for her to follow.

She took two steps for each of his one, but bounced along beside him with a joyful heart.

"Now what do you want to talk about?" Father asked as he lifted her onto a large, flat rock under an old olive tree, its trunk twisted and misshaped with branches that hung over their heads. She settled her hands in her lap and looked up, determined to persuade him.

"Well, Father, I am in love," she said with as much of an adult tone as her eight-year-old self could muster. She lifted her chin and gazed into his eyes. "It is time we talked of my betrothal." He arched his brows and tipped the corner of his mouth, so she lifted her chin a little more, wiggled her shoulders, and tried to look grown up. He took her hand.

"My little lioness, you are much too young to know true romantic love or talk of being betrothed."

"Father," she started to argue and he touched her mouth with his finger.

"If it is true love, you will still love him at an appropriate time to pursue a betrothal, like six or seven years from now," he said with a slight chuckle.

She saw him fiddle with the leather girdle and pull out a wooden pendant and dangle it before her on a leather strap.

"It is odd—I just finished this piece this morning before Timon arrived for work. This is for you, from me, the one that loves you more than you can know." He laid the lion-shaped object carefully in the palm of her hand. In its mane, engraved in a gold inlay, were the words, *Lion of the Tribe of Judah*, in Hebrew.

Her jaw dropped at its beauty, and she watched him flip it over. On the back, engraved in the same way were the words, *Arise, Lord. Let your enemies be scattered. Let all who hate you flee before you*, in Hebrew. She looked up at him and pieces of light bounced off his face from the sun's rays reflecting off the gold.

At that moment he appeared majestic like the lion she held in her hand. Suddenly the fascination she felt for Efah dimmed in comparison to the love she felt for Father. He lifted his beautiful creation up, placed the leather cord around her neck, and straightened the pendant over her chest.

"Jerusha, you are royalty from the tribe of Judah. The acacia represents the ark that carried YHWH's presence. The words on the back represent his promise to come one day, destroy our enemies, and set up his kingdom. Never forget who you are."

She threw her arms around his neck, hugged it tight, and savored his manly fragrance, her head nestled in the side of his full beard. When she let loose, she noticed a glistening rim in his eyes, and he rubbed his nose with his sleeve.

"I won't forget, Father. I will always remember what you told me. I will always love you. I will always be your little lioness."

***

The next morning Jerusha skipped in a brief dance around the corner into the sunny garden. The deep green leaves of the pomegranate bushes shone against the red blossoms, and she stopped momentarily to look for a chrysalis in the branches of the largest bush. She heard Father's whistle and peeked out to see him coming toward her, his arms laden with fresh acacia pieces. Father is always creating something new.

"What are you making now, Father?" she asked, and skipped along behind.

"Wouldn't you like to know," he said and dropped the load to tweak her nose. She laughed.

"I know you'll tell me," she said. "We have no secrets."

"That's true. No secrets between you and me." Jerusha heard her mother call from the gate.

"I'm going with Mother to Herod's palace today. Maybe I will get to see Efah. He and his father spend so much time there. Do you think he will be there?" She watched Father's face sour. "Don't worry, Father. I love you more than him." That brought back the twinkle in his eyes.

"Jerusha," her mother called, "hurry! I'm waiting on you." The little one wrapped her arms around her father's waist and held tight. She felt his fingers comb through her hair and off she went to join her mother at the courtyard gate.

The pendant her father made from the acacia wood hung around Jerusha's neck. She touched it occasionally as she danced along the pathway next to Mother. Light filtered through the limbs of the tree-lined path and reflected in her eyes. She glanced down at sparkles from the sun's rays that bounced off the gold crown in the majestic lion's mane on her hand.

A new melody formed in her mind as she skipped along and quoted the words she had memorized from the pendant's back.

She never felt more alive—so vibrant—so content. She stopped for a moment, bent down, and slipped off her sandals. There! That's better! Who can dance with sandals on their feet? She held her sandals in one hand and spread her arms out. The sleeves of her robe flapped in the wind, and she flew like a butterfly to catch up with her mother.

"Jerusha, why do you have your sandals off? Everyone is going to think we are mourning."

Jerusha twirled around, her face uplifted to the azure blue sky.

"I am royalty. Sandals get in the way of my dance to the King." She imagined singing to the One on the throne, her father watching with a broad smile.

"Arise, Lord!" she sang. "Let your enemies be scattered. Let all who hate you flee before you."

She spun around in delight, but her countenance fell when she saw the Roman soldiers in the shadows to her right. They seemed so close and towered above her with their hands on their swords. Their eyes were steady and unmoving, fixed firmly on the target of young Jewish menwho gathered in the open space between the temple and the high priest's palace. She stopped and fumbled to replace her sandals.

"Keep moving!" her mother ordered, her voice high-pitched and anxious. "Don't let them see you looking at them. The temple guards will protect us. We must hurry."

Her mother grasped her hand. "Stay close," she instructed the servants accompanying them. They slipped behind a large group of worshippers entering the temple and avoided the gaze of the soldiers. Jerusha stared at the crippled beggar who sat at the temple gate and yelled for alms. She had seen him before when Father took her and mother to the temple.

"Mother, let us give him some shekels."

Abigail took a few silver coins from her girdle and handed them to Jerusha.

"Here, run fast and come back. We are late. Besides, I do not want you to get in the middle of a skirmish with the soldiers and the zealots." With the coins wrapped tight in her tiny fingers, she ran fast and dropped them in his tin cup. At the sound of the tinkle, he looked her way.

"Toda, my child. May YHWH bless you."

"You!" A soldier pointed in her direction. "Stop!" She dodged in and out of the many people gathering to enter the temple and glanced back. He grabbed another child in a tattered and worn cloak, probably an orphan that stole bread from the soldiers.

A short time later, Jerusha looked up at Herod's palace. She would be safe there. *If Efah is here, he will not let anything happen to me.* The arched brow of the one whose protection she trusted most flashed across her conscious mind. *Father does not like Efah. Why?* The guards recognized her mother and opened the large ornate door for their entrance.

Jerusha saw Efah come down the stairs to greet them. Of course! He saw the soldiers and came to protect her. She closed her eyes and felt a tingling in her stomach, a sure sign of her love for him. Caiaphas came around the corner to greet them, too. Jerusha noticed that he wasn't dressed in his priest clothing. Instead he wore a blue silk tunic beneath a jeweled cloak. She didn't care why he dressed in fancy clothes, her eyes were on Efah. So handsome!

She felt a rush of air on her cheek as Caiaphas swept by, took her mother's arm, and escorted her out of the room.

"Prepare us a meal," he said to his servants over his shoulder. "Efah, I trust you will entertain Jerusha until we eat," he added. She watched her mother smile up at Caiaphas as they continued down the portico, then stop and look back.

"Jerusha, wait for me in the garden. We won't be long," she said, then smiled up at Caiaphas. Time with Efah. Jerusha's heart beat fast. What more could she ask?

One of her servants started to follow her and Efah into the garden, but Efah stopped him and asked that he attend to the meal like the other servants.

"It's not proper for a young lady to be alone with a young boy without an attendant," the servant responded.

Jerusha smiled. "It will be all right." Reluctantly, the servant turned to obey Efah's request but stopped at the corner to look back. Jerusha saw and waved him on. "He's my friend."

After the servant disappeared down the portico, Efah invited her to walk with him in the garden. His tall, fifteen-year-old muscular shoulders towered above her, and she looked up at his handsome face, square chin, and high cheekbones. Proud that he wanted to be with her, she walked beside him and felt like a queen. After all, his father belonged to the Sanhedrin. Everyone admired the Sanhedrin!

"Come," he said when they reached the back wall. "I want to show you something."

They rounded the corner, out of sight from anyone who would enter the garden.

"Come, see my special place," he asked. She wondered if his special place had chrysalises on the branches for them to watch and stopped beside a pomegranate bush. She leaned her head into the branches to see what she could find and felt his presence come from behind. He pulled her close and whispered things in her ear. Ugly things. Things she had never heard before.

Is this love? Innocently, she obeyed his request to expose the most private part of her body to his touch. His touch released silent choking and gagging in her throat. Fear speared her stomach. She didn't resist.

Suddenly, he pushed her to the ground.

"Ouch," she cried. "What are you doing? You are hurting me."

He put his hand over her mouth. "Not so loud."

She wanted to get away, but she was frozen, stuck to the ground, dirty, and ashamed. The words, "Don't do that," stuck in her throat as she yielded herself to him. Why, she wondered, had she given in to his touches when every fiber of her being screamed, "Stop!"

At that moment, she heard sounds coming from the other side of the garden. He jumped up. "If you tell what happened," he threatened, "I'll deny it. Whom do you think they'll believe? You or the son of the high priest? My father has great power."

He straightened his clothes and walked away, leaving her on the ground bloodied, bruised, and broken. Somehow, she managed to straighten her clothes, control the tears and hide the pain from mother. She had no other choice.

***

That night she tossed and turned in her bed, unable to sleep. The moonbeams streamed across her face lighting the darkened room. She pulled the covers over her head. *I hate myself. No one can love me now.* Deeper, deeper, deeper, she spiraled and tumbled. Strand after strand of itchy yarn wrapped around her body, trapping her inside a ball intertwined with a sticky substance that clung to her skin. "Help! Someone help me!" she cried. Her words, swallowed by a hidden monster, produced no echo, no vibration, no sound. There were no shadows. It was too dark for shadows.

Stuck, unable to move, she squeezed her eyes shut, afraid of what she might see. Her heart pounded. Sweat ran down her face. Flailing her hands and feet in every direction, trying to fight her way out, she grasped an object in the sticky substance above her head. She pulled it free, and clutched it to her breast, her fingers digging into the lion's mane. The words on her father's pendant penetrated the fog in her mind, *Arise, Lord. Let your enemies be scattered. Let all who hate you flee before you.* Somehow she managed to open her eyes. Terror-stricken, she scanned the darkness. In the far distance to her right, above her head, she noticed a faint light.

She shuddered, pulled the blanket over her head, and tried to hide from the invisible monster that seemed to be waiting to grab her. The once-soft cover scratched and itched against her face. Sunlight filtered through the fabric and warmed her body. Perspiration ran down her face and arms. This little lioness from the tribe of Judah, this one destined for royalty, cowered in darkness afraid to face a new day.

Chapter 5

In the months that followed, she dreaded every time Mother insisted she come with her to Herod's Palace. Why did they have to go there so often? Each time, Efah would find a reason to get her alone in the garden.

"Don't scream," he'd whisper. "If they find out what we are doing, no man will ever want you for his bride."

She believed his lies and submitted to his touches. For comfort, she would grasp the pendant Father gave her, close her eyes, and pray to YHWH. *Where are you? Am I not worthy of your attention? Am I too dirty for your Holy presence?*

Week after week she waited, groping for some sign of his presence, some sign that he had not forgotten her. In time, the dream she had of dancing before the King, like David, faded. She knew that she had become too tainted, too sullied by the encounters she had with Efah in the garden. YHWH had surely rejected her.

Her secret also kept her away from the one man whose company she enjoyed most. Father must not know. Ashamed, she no longer trusted anyone, not even him. Although she missed sitting with him, watching him work, and listening to his stories, especially the ones about the ark of the covenant, she no longer followed him everywhere like she had done in the past. She was no longer worthy.

It did not matter anyway. Father was gone a lot. Every time he left, Jerusha saw a glare in her mother's eyes, the same angry glare she had when he talked about Yeshua being the Mashiach. Father seemed more and more convinced he was the One.

Dancing felt different. When Jerusha opened her arms and tried to twirl around, her weighted arms just plopped at her side. She tripped and fell in the bushes. She was not sure if it was because she no longer felt worthy to dance or because mother seemed so unhappy with Father. Her feet just would not move like they did before the sadness set into her bones.

Months had gone by since her first encounter with Efah. She fought hatred, but how could she hate the one she wanted to marry? She did, though. He threatened to tell everyone she was a bad girl and deserved to be stoned. She had no idea what that meant, but his tone scared her. More than anything else, she did not want Father to know what she had done. She knew it was wrong, but Efah wouldn't stop— and Mother insisted she go with her every week to Herod's palace.

Jerusha saw a sadness in Father's eyes, too, and she knew that he missed their times together. *I miss you too, Father. I just can't dance anymore. I can't.*

Her mother seemed almost happy some days, usually when they were going to the palace. Her words to Father were cross, but sometimes she hummed a tune while she made dinner. One day, Mother sent her outside to collect the grapes in the basket.

"I'll pick the high ones later, Jerusha. Be sure to gather all the ones close to the ground. We'll take them as a gift to Caiaphas this week."

Jerusha's stomach tightened. She hated the trips to the palace. Picking grapes to take to that place, to Efah and Caiaphas, ignited a fire in her belly, but she had to obey and she put the basket over her arm and went outside.

"Jerusha!" her father called. She looked up. Father sat at his workbench in the garden, his muscular arms bulged through his tunic as he banged on a large beam, his latest project. He never wore his robe with tzitzits on the corners when he was working. He usually folded it neatly on his workbench where Jerusha played with the tzitzits. The blue knotted tassels fascinated her. She obeyed Father and came, hoping again to be able to touch the eight stranded cords.

"Come here, little one," he said. He touched her chin and then made an exaggerated frown.

"This is my Jerusha," he said. He contorted his face until Jerusha had to laugh.

"Father, my face cannot look that bad. And I do not have a big, black beard like you do!"

He tweaked her nose. "You are right about that, Jerusha. You do not. Now would not my little girl look hilarious in a black beard?"

Jerusha smiled then looked down.

"Yes, Father," she answered, the laughter gone from her tone. He lifted her chin.

"What is it, Jerusha? What has stolen the smile of my royal daughter? What has taken the dance from your feet?"

She turned her face away, unwilling to talk to him or look in his eyes. He placed his hand on her head with the gentle strength of one whose hands can carve delicate wooden pendants.

"My daughter," he said, "do not forget who you are. You are from the tribe of Judah. You are royalty. You will dance before the King one day." She looked down. He placed his other hand over hers, the one holding the tassel. Her sweaty fingers gripped the cords. "These blue tzitzits that you so dearly love to touch are a reminder of who you are."

At first, her heart leapt inside. She wanted so much to melt in his embrace and cry out, "Aba! Aba!" His hands with strong, thick fingers that had held her close and wiped her tears awakened the memory of the familiar love and protection that came to the innocent little girl from yesteryear, but that flash of security disappeared as soon as it came.

It had been less than a year since her first humiliating encounter with the son of the high priest. She was sure now that she would never be loved again the way Father loved her in the past. *It's too late! If you knew. If you only knew. I shouldn't have let him touch me. I'm not royalty. If you only knew, you'd never call me that again.*

Unable to accept his love, she slipped from his lap and ran away with his words ringing through her mind. *You're royalty! You're royalty! You're royalty!*

"No! No! No!" she hollered, her basket still on the bench beside the robe with the blue tzitzits.

She stopped at the corner behind the pomegranate bush and looked back. She saw him wrap the robe around his shoulders and grip the tzitzits. Tears coursed down his cheeks. "I'm sorry, Father."

***

A few months later, Jerusha waded ankle deep in the cool water. Her toes slipped against the smooth-stoned bed of the Siloam pool. She balanced her teetering body with outstretched arms and waited for the daily roar of water to gush forth. The long, winding cave above her head stored the only water supply of the city—the Gihon Spring. The gentle gurgles refreshed her tired and achy feet.

She had walked with Father from one booth to another in the marketplace while he bought the flour, oil, and fish for Shabbat. Jerusha envisioned the stuffed fish and challot on the table with the wine goblet and the two new lamps that Father bought. Mother said she could help light them this time. "We must have enough oil to last through tomorrow when the first stars appear," he had said. "These lamps and wicks are perfect."

Jacob knelt on one knee, the goatskin bottle next to his side, the neck tipped to allow the fresh mayim to flow easily into the small opening at the end. He stood with the bulging bottle. "That should be enough water," he said and placed it on the donkey next to the wine skin filled with new wine. "It was a successful day at market. Abigail will be pleased."

Suddenly, the water gushed forth from the rock cave above and splashed into the pool. The living fountain sparkled like diamonds in the bright sun overhead. Jerusha jumped and giggled with delight. The rushing flow climbed higher and higher, almost to her knees. Father grabbed her under the arms and pulled her out. He sat her next to him on the smooth ledge of a large, flat rock that faced the spring. She breathed in his manly scent and laid her head on his arm.

"Jerusha," he said and cupped her chin in his palm, "some may mock you for not having dark brown eyes, but remember your bloodline is pure. Those emerald eyes—those unusual emerald eyes with the deep blue rims around them are special." She wondered why it would be so important what color eyes someone had, but when she spied several white wildflowers that grew in the crack next to Father, she forgot about her concerns.

"Look, we can give those to Mother for our table tonight. She will be pleased."

"Indeed, she will," he said and reached over, picked the flowers, and handed them to Jerusha. He took a cloth from the bags on the donkey and wet it in the pool and gave it to Jerusha. "Here. Wrap this around the flowers to keep them fresh." She watched his large, weatherworn hands pick up her leather sandals that sat on the ledge and slip them onto her feet, her toes cold from the icy water.

"Do you want to ride the donkey?"

Jerusha's feet felt better now, but she didn't want to walk anymore. "Yes!"

Father tossed her lightly up in the air and over onto the donkey's back.

"Here, let me put those flowers in a safe place until we get home." She watched him arrange them in a small, clay pot that stuck out of a bag on the donkey's back, then the two started home, up the dusty path. The donkey rocked back and forth, left and right, lumpy and bumpy all loaded down with food and tools. The dust from the road tickled her nose. Jerusha sneezed and scratched it. The donkey bowed his head down to the ground and sniffed the dirt. Father tapped him again on the rump to keep him moving.

"Go on," he gently ordered.

Jerusha heard a commotion up ahead. A crowd of people rushed across the road, shouting with stones in their hands. Jerusha and Father froze.

"Whore!"

"Adulteress!"

A woman screamed, "No! Please! Have mercy!"

Jerusha gasped and slid off the side of the donkey.

"Father!" She cried out. Her heart pounded in her chest. "What are the people doing?"

"I wish I would have not taken this path into the city," he whispered into her hair. "YHWH, help us." Even Father sounded scared.

The woman screamed again, obviously terrified. Two men with stones in their hands pushed the woman to a cliff. Someone shoved Jerusha from behind, and she quickly found herself swept away with the crowd. Someone's elbow hit her nose. She touched it with her fingers and a wet, crimson liquid dripped down her lip.

"Father!" she screamed and reached back for his hand. The donkey snorted and jumped. His back feet kicked high, and Father held the rope tight and tried to calm him. His face disappeared from Jerusha's sight as more people came between him and her trembling body. Bumped along by the crowd, she found herself precariously close to the edge of a cliff. She heard the woman's cries for mercy echo across the valley. Everywhere Jerusha looked, the men, who towered above, had stones in their hands. Then she saw her, the woman, pressed by the crowd to the precipice, nowhere to go but down onto the jagged rocks below.

The crowd, mostly men's voices, yelled.

"Harlot!"

"Jezebel," one man screeched, his fist in the air, clutching a stone. Jerusha felt sweat run down her back, but she shivered. The woman tried to run to the right, then left. Each time, a man with a stone blocked her path. One of them spit on her while another sneered. Jerusha covered her ears with the cloth of her bloodied radiyd and looked for her father, her eyes darting back and forth. There in the midst of the crowd was Efah. A claw grabbed her stomach and twisted it until she felt like her insides were yanked to her throat. At that moment, some men dressed in priest's robes simultaneously shoved the woman over the edge. Jerusha squeezed her eyes shut and looked away. When she blinked them open again, Efah glared at her.

"No! No! No!" she screamed in horror and started to rock back and forth against the crowd, certain that Efah would tell everyone that she was a bad girl and push her over the cliff, too. Suddenly a strong arm enveloped her and swooped her up. Father! She buried her head in his robe and released her fear, the sobs drowned out by the mob's shouts.

Her father put his hand on her head and turned the other way so she could not see anymore. But nothing could keep her from hearing the woman's cries and the thud of the rocks that pounded her flesh.

"My little lioness was not meant to see or hear such things," she heard him say. When she stopped crying, he let her down and quickly buried her face in his chest and covered her head with his robe. The roughness of his robe against her face awakened the heart-pounding terror she felt while tangled in the thick, yarn-like webs wrapped around her body while sleeping. Her white-knuckled fingers gripped Father's robe.

She peeked out from under his covering to see faces all around. Efah looked down in disgust at the woman's body below.

Gradually, Father was able to lead them away from the jeering crowd and back to the donkey, who surprisingly stayed where he left it. Finally, alone with Father, Jerusha loosened her grip on his robe, and he lifted her onto the beast's back. He poured a small amount of water from the goatskin container onto a soft cloth that he pulled from his girdle and dabbed at her bloodied nose and lip.

"I'm so sorry we got separated," he said. "This is all my fault. I should have paid more attention and gotten you away sooner." Jerusha rubbed the smeared blood and sniffles from her nose with her sleeve.

"Ouch!" she glanced up into her father's pain-filled eyes.

"Oh, Father, I am all right. I am tough. I am your little lioness," she said and wrapped her arms around his neck and squeezed tight. After awhile, she released her grip and slid to the ground.

"Who is Jezebel?"

"She was a queen many years ago who did evil in the sight of the Lord."

"What did she do?" Father took her hand in his and led her and the donkey up the path.

"She persuaded her husband to have a man killed and take his vineyard."

"Why do they call THAT woman Jezebel? Is that her name?"

"No, Jerusha, they call her that because she has persuaded men to do wrong." Father's brow tightened together, a sign for her to be careful what she said next.

"What did she persuade them to do?"

"You ask too many questions."

"Please, Father. I don't understand such hatred." He stopped, knelt down in front of her and looked straight into her eyes.

"Not all men have such hatred." He then picked her up and carried her in his arms the rest of the way home.

**

Jerusha was relieved to be home—far away from the screams of the Jezebel woman. She watched as Father presented the flowers. Mother smiled slightly—just slightly. Jerusha felt the air leave her chest and her shoulders slump. *She's not happy, even when we are together for Shabbat. Well, at least I don't have to go to the priest's palace today.* Cheered by that thought, she escaped into the other room and changed into her favorite tunic, the one Mother made with blue stitches around the neck, and prepared herself for Shabbat.

Just as the sun began to set in the west, Mother called, "Come and light the lamps."

Jerusha rushed around the corner and stopped just inside the courtyard. The white flowers, so beautiful, sat in the middle of the table along with the challot, wine goblet and stuffed fish. Abigail greeted her.

"Shabbat Shalom." Her mother's dimpled grin spread across her perfectly shaped face. *She is so beautiful. Even the tunic, robe, and head covering couldn't hide her well-endowed womanly curves. I hope someday I am as pretty as Mother.* The rosy pink sunset in the distance accented the pieces of her shiny, black hair that she had allowed to hang loosely outside her veil. Her mother's blemish-free skin radiated in the dusky light. Jerusha touched her own face and covered the black mole. The ugly, black mole. A purple butterfly flitted in front of mother, landed on the white flowers, and drew Jerusha's attention to the table.

"Oh, Mother, the table is so beautiful, just like you."

She heard Father's strong, deep voice behind her. "Yes, she is."

At the sound of his voice, Mother's grin faded. Jerusha's shoulders drooped. *Why is she so unhappy with father?*

That night, after they returned from the synagogue, Jerusha followed Father into the courtyard garden. The soft breeze blew her hair. It blew Father's robe, too, and snagged it on the pomegranate branch. While loosening his robe from the snag, he noticed the fully ripened fruit and picked a pomegranate from the branch.

Jerusha hesitated—she had to catch that purple butterfly sipping juices from the lower branches. Done! She ran awkwardly toward Father, her purple treasure in her hands in front of her. She scooted back on Father's bench and watched him cut the red, rough outer skin of the fruit with a knife. He laid it open on the bench. Jerusha lifted her hands to the sky and let the butterfly go. Then she pointed to the seeds and began to count.

"One, two, three . . . oh, Father," she giggled, "I'm not sure which ones I counted."

He laughed. "Here, let's just eat them," he said, handing her one half.

"It's so de-li-cious," she said and slurped the juice and ground the seeds between her teeth.

"Oh, how big you are getting," he answered and wiped the juice from her chin with red-stained fingers. Jerusha felt his touch linger. "I won't see you for a while," he said. "Tomorrow, after Shabbat ends, I am leaving on another trip."

"I will miss you," she said earnestly.

"You will miss *me?*" He pointed to himself, shrugged his muscular shoulders, and scrunched up his long nose.

"Yes, silly," she said. The sound of her giggle vibrated across the courtyard and mixed with the song thrush's night melody.

"And I you." He stood up. "Come here."

Jerusha lifted her arms, and her father grabbed her and twirled her around and around, her long, black hair flying behind. He stopped and held her close. This time she enjoyed his embrace. It felt so different than Efah's. She wanted to tell him her secret. They had no secrets in the past, but this secret must be kept. *He can't find out,* she thought and pushed on his chest. *He won't love me anymore if he knew.*

"Put me down," she said.

"Jerusha, what's wrong?" he asked and loosened his embrace.

She slid off his lap. When she felt the cold stones beneath her feet, she ran back toward the house. At the iron gate, she hesitated—turned around. Her father was watching. She smiled for his sake. She would miss him.

Chapter 6

"Yeshua breaks the Sabbath!" the chief priest yelled. "He calls
YHWH his own Father, making himself equal to YHWH!"
Jacob tied his packed donkey to the post outside, stepped over the
threshold of the synagogue, and slipped unnoticed onto the narrow
limestone slab seat attached to the wall closest to the door. A chief
priest, one whom Jacob knew from Gamaliel's school, stood in the
front, a scroll in his hands, the eyes of every man on him.

Jacob came for the daily Torah reading before leaving the city to
find Yeshua. After his talk with Jerusha the night before, he hoped
to hear comforting words from the scripture, not this hate speech
about his good friend. Irritable and impatient with such nonsense that
interrupted his quest for answers concerning his daughter, he stood
and addressed the priest.

"Why do you speak of Yeshua like he is your enemy? His wisdom
shines in darkness. He is kind and loving. How does he break the
Sabbath?" Jacob spoke with strength and conviction, his words
controlled and steady.

"He heals on the Sabbath, and it is known that his disciples picked corn and ate on the Sabbath," the priest spewed his answer and spun around to get another scroll, an apparent dismissal of Jacob.

Backing down to any man, especially the pompous priests that paraded in the market such as this one who interrupted his honest quest for truth with his arrogant judgments and babble, made his belly churn. He stood his ground. A Pharisee himself, he knew the law.

"Is it a crime to heal?" he countered. The crowd that sat around him, many of them his dear friends, stirred. One neighbor, for whom Jacob made a beautiful bench free of charge, rose and stood beside him.

"He is right. I agree with Jacob. Yeshua does nothing but good. I believe he could be the Mashiach we have waited for these many years." Others nodded and piped up with the same sentiments: "He delivered my son from an evil spirit. How can that be wrong?" He raised my daughter from the dead. Only someone with power from YHWH can raise the dead."

Jacob sat down and another of Gamaliel's students who had a cordial friendship with him leaned over and whispered, "Be careful how much you defend him. Your friend, Yeshua, is not liked by the priests. He outfoxed many Pharisees who have challenged him in public. They do not take kindly to being repudiated in front of the people. The Sadducees hate him. I have heard they plot to kill him."

Jacob had no idea how disliked Yeshua had become by the religious leaders, another reason to make this trip, even though he hated leaving again his beautiful Abigail and precious Jerusha. He patted the man on the back and stood.

"Thank you for the warning, my friend. I will heed your words and make my departure now."

While the dispute continued, he slipped back outside and untied his donkey. His sources told him that he would find Yeshua near Tiberias on the Sea of Galilee, so he left the city and headed north. With his donkey loaded with a few tools, food, and water, he mixed in with the tradesmen caravan leaving for the north country, too. On the long journey, he sat around campfires with other carpenters and conversed with them about Yeshua and what they had seen and heard.

Most were convinced that he truly was their long-awaited King. Some mocked and laughed about the idea.

With Abigail's concerns in his mind and the priest's comments about the Sabbath, Jacob wondered if the mockers were right. His relationship with Yeshua sure had been trouble for him with his wife. Maybe he was wrong. A few miracles meant nothing. The magicians of the east did those, too. Friend or no friend, he would not let their friendship tear his family apart.

Yeshua made his rebellion plain when he threw the money changer's tables over in the temple court. Of course, Jacob could not blame him for that—the scoundrels cheated the people and lined their own pockets. Could Yeshua be a zealot, ready to overthrow Rome and help take back their land? No, he never seemed like a fighter, although he stared down Caiaphas in defense of the blind man. Jacob contemplated this. He wanted to think the best, but for Abigail's sake, this may be his last trip.

Of course, if Yeshua was the Mashiach, when he set up his kingdom, Abigail would come around. If that is true, Jacob's love and patience must prevail until then. *Mashiach ben David, where are you? Who are you?* He warmed at the thought of his little Jerusha dancing a holy dance before the true Mashiach, not like the seductive dance of the daughter of Herodias before King Herod. Then he remembered the last time he saw his daughter and how she pushed against him and wanted down, then ran away, no dance in her feet or joy in her steps. What has happened to his little jewel?

Traveling gave him too much time to ponder on things, and more and more his feelings toward Yeshua changed. How could a simple carpenter from Nazareth be a king?

Three days later, tired and dusty from his long journey, he separated from the caravan and went east up Mount Arbel outside Tiberias. He knew Yeshua's habit of climbing the Mount of Olives outside Jerusalem to pray and thought he might find him high on the mountain away from the hustle and bustle of those who gathered to dip in the hot mineral springs of the regional capital built by Herod Antipas. Yeshua desired quiet time alone. But where? *YHWH, show me the way.*

As he climbed higher, he heard the mutterings of people ahead. He rounded the rocky cliff and saw hundreds, maybe thousands, of people, men, women, and children seated in family groups on the hillside and figured they followed Yeshua. Tying his donkey to a branch, he sought the cool shade of an old twisted olive tree. A young boy ran through the tall grass down the hill, weaving in and out among the crowd, yelling over and over.

"Yeshua healed my crippled leg! He healed my crippled leg!" Jacob smiled at the boy's youthful innocence and thought of his Jerusha. *What has happened to my little girl? So sober these days. I must pursue this matter with her when I get back.*

Yeshua's jovial laughter in the distance drew Jacob's attention to search uphill, and he scanned the crowd. There! Sitting with his disciples, Peter, Philip, and his other followers at the top of the small incline, Yeshua laughed and conversed with his young disciples. Jacob yanked on the donkey's rope and meandered between the family groups that sat on the ground.

How he longed for his family to be with him, but Abigail never wanted to go. If Yeshua proves not to be the Mashiach, Jacob feared he might need to walk away from that friendship for his marriage's sake. More and more Abigail distanced herself these days, pouty and quiet. Only after her visits to Herod's palace did she seem more content. When he neared the place where Yeshua sat, his friend waved and motioned to him.

"Jacob, my cowdh, come!" Yeshua yelled from a short distance. Being called an intimate friend by Yeshua shamed Jacob for thinking of cutting off their friendship. "You look tired and hungry like all these who have come out to hear my teachings." Peter ran toward Jacob, greeted him, and took the donkey's rope and led the donkey up the steep incline behind Jacob. Jacob's feet ached and when Philip offered him his seat, a rock with a folded cloak on it, and he plopped down with a grin spread wide across his face.

"I am grateful for your hospitality, Philip. It has been a long journey."

"Here, drink," Philip offered a goatskin filled with water. Jacob tipped his head back and poured the water into his dry mouth. Only a few drops fell to the ground.

"Philip, where are we to buy bread that my friend and all these may eat?" Yeshua asked.

Philip checked with Judas, who had the money bag and shrugged.

"Two hundred denarii worth of bread is not sufficient for them."

Jacob watched the young boy who cried that his leg had been healed come up the hill with a basket in his hands. Peter stopped him.

"I have come to give my lunch to Yeshua. He healed my leg. I want him to have my lunch so he will not go hungry."

"This boy has five barley loaves and two fish, but what is this among so many people?" Peter handed the basket to Yeshua. "He says he wants you to have it so you will not go hungry." Yeshua stood, touched the boy's head, and scanned the crowd.

"Tell the people to sit down," he said as he lifted the loaves of bread to heaven and blessed them, then tore a piece and gave it to the boy who waited beside him. "Here, take some fish, too."

"But I wanted you to eat. Will there be enough?"

"Yes, yes, there will be enough. Because of your giving heart, my father will take the little you offer and multiply it for the multitudes." He handed a piece of bread and fish to Jacob. "Eat, my cowdh, my special friend from Jerusalem. You will need the nourishment for your journey."

Thoughts of past meals with Yeshua flashed through Jacob's mind. With Jerusha on his lap and Abigail at his side, Jacob would converse with him about common things, like chrysalises, butterflies, and the clouds that signaled a storm. Would a king speak so simply that even a child understood?

Jerusha loved Yeshua's stories, sometimes even more than the ones Jacob told. She hung on Yeshua's every word, just like these people. Even though their stomachs cried to be fed, they stayed on this hot, dry mountainside and listened.

His eyes followed Yeshua as he moved from one group to the other and gave them bread and fish. Where did it come from? Every time he tore some off, more appeared in his hand for the next person. How can this be happening? He's just a simple carpenter. Yeshua laughed and enjoyed the pleasure he saw in their eyes as he fed them one by one.

Working his way back up the hill, he gave instructions for his disciples to gather up the leftovers. Peter threw Jacob a basket, too.

"Here, Jacob, help us." When Jacob passed the basket from group to group, he heard their excited whispers. One said, "Let's make him our king." Another youngster added, "If he can feed five thousand with two fish and five barley loaves, he can help us overthrow the Romans." Still another said, "Then we will be free from Roman tyranny. He must be the promised Mashiach, the anointed One."

Jacob and the disciples gathered twelve baskets of fragments, but when they turned to head back uphill to show Yeshua, he had made his way up higher away from the crowd.

"He always withdraws when he senses the people are ready to overtake him and make him king," Peter said, and he encouraged the people to disperse.

"Why? If he is the One promised in the scripture, why not allow the people to crown him king?"

Peter stared off into the distance.

"Many seek him because of the signs he does. They do not seek him for who he is."

"Who is he?"

"He is the anointed One, the Christos, the Son of the Living God, YHWH. No one can come to him, unless the Father draws him. Yeshua will not commit himself to anyone who does not truly believe. If their motive is to have a kingdom of this world, then he withdraws."

Untying his donkey from the bush, Jacob walked with the twelve disciples down the mountainside and pondered Peter's words. By the time they reached the Sea of Galilee, the sun caste an orange glow across the clear waters that lapped at the pebbled shore. They sat around the fire and ate of the extra fragments of bread and fish and talked of the miracle they saw that day.

"We are crossing the sea tonight in a boat to Capernaum. Do you want to go with us?" Peter asked Jacob.

"No. Tonight, I need to stay here and talk to YHWH of the miracle I saw today and what it means. Maybe I will see you tomorrow in Capernaum." He watched them wade into the water waist deep, their robes tucked in their girdles, shove the boat off the shoreline, jump in, and row away, the sound of the steady slap of their oars gradually getting softer and softer as they moved farther out to sea.

By the flickering firelight, Jacob unwrapped a parchment that he had drawn from the bag on the donkey earlier along with a quill and started to write,

My Dearest Abigail and Jerusha,

I miss you both so much. It will not be long before I am home. I have so many things to tell you . . .

Chapter 7

The dark, black sky rumbled in the distance. Lightning flashed on the horizon and lit the familiar pathway up the steep hill. His weary donkey balked and sat with his back legs spraddled wide. The load on his back started to slide down.

"Come on, ole boy. We are almost home," Jacob urged him on, yanking on the rope to no avail. He almost lost his turban in the wind—his lantern blew out earlier and a torch was out of the question.

"If I could light a fire under you, I would, you old stubborn beast," he said while he straightened the pack on the tired animal, then gave him a little shove from behind. The lightening flashed again and startled the donkey, and he jumped to his feet and trotted a few feet in front of Jacob. He caught the rope and they both moved at a quicker pace.

When Jacob saw the large gate to his dwelling up ahead, he shook off the exhaustion—he was nearly home now. At least this time he returned with all of his questions answered. Abigail and Jerusha must know—Yeshua was indeed Mashiach ben David.

The gifts for his wife and daughter were tucked in a dry pocket on the side bag of the donkey, but the greatest gift was that he found the Mashiach. *Jerusha will be so excited to dance before his throne.* One thought troubled him, though. He said he'd be killed and after three days be resurrected. It must be then that he sets up his kingdom. He says it's not of this world, though. Resurrected from the dead! What kind of a glorious kingdom will it be?

Knowing his daughter's favorite color was purple because she always pointed first to the purple butterflies and hardly noticed the blue, yellow, or orange ones, he was excited to see her reaction to the purple cloth he bought for her and Abigail. Purple for royalty. The King had come. He must find a way to convince Abigail about Yeshua. No, he must be patient and let the father draw her, like he did for me. Jacob sighed. Certain they were asleep by now, the good news and gifts will have to wait until morning.

A gust of wind blew the unlatched gate open. It banged repeatedly against the stone wall and created dust whirls in the night air. He closed it behind him. This time it stayed latched. He jiggled it twice to make sure. All but the stable servants would be asleep by now. Jacob pulled the bags off the donkey and slung them over his shoulder, then led the tired animal around the right side of his home to the stable. His servant met him and fed and watered her and would bed her down for the night. A wind gust blew his cloak upward as he returned to the house and walked up the path to the courtyard. How he missed his favorite workbench. He placed the bags in his workshop. He would unpack them tomorrow. Tomorrow—would Abigail be as pleased as Jerusha with the purple cloth?

The fragrance of the pomegranate's red blossoms welcomed him home. Flashes of lightening revealed that the servants had done a good job trimming back the vines and keeping the water fountain clear of debris. He wondered how his vegetable garden was doing. That would have to wait until tomorrow, too.

Glad to be back, he sat for a while on the bench and rested. The thunder rumbled in the distance. The land needed a soft rain, one that allowed it a chance to drink deeply. He lifted his face. Plop! He felt the first cool drops on his dust-covered brow. The rain increased and instead of running for cover, he let it wash over his whole body.

Refreshing. After awhile, he dragged his tired, achy body up from the bench, stepped out of the dirty puddles around his feet, and entered the dark dwelling. He slipped off his soggy leather sandals and crept quietly down the corridor. The bedchamber door creaked. He winced. Abigail gasped. Even in the darkness, he saw them, there in the shadowy lamp light, in his bed, both naked. One was his wife. One was Caiaphas.

Stunned, he froze in the doorway. His tall, immense stature cast eerie, dark shadows across the bed.

"What are you doing here?" his voice boomed and joined the now boisterous thunder.

He didn't wait for an answer. Instead, he turned and stomped back down the corridor and outside. Oh, how he wanted to choke the words out of him. As he left the courtyard, he slammed the gate, too hard this time to stay shut.

So this is why she spent so much time at Herod's palace. Why hadn't he seen it before tonight? He stopped in an alcove and waited. He must calm down. Spewing angry words that he might regret later would solve nothing. As the storm slowed, he watched Caiaphas slink off into the darkness and disappear. He loved Abigail, but his mind burned with revenge. *If I bring accusations against them, the Sanhedrin will have no choice but to follow the law and stone them. They would find a way to protect him from being accused, though, that slimy hypocritical snake! It's the woman that pays!*

His heart sunk at the thought of her being stoned. Sobs threatened to erupt. He choked them back and moved with clenched fists toward his dwelling. With every step, his mind screamed, *Why?* He creaked the door open again. She stood in front of the window—now dressed—her silhouette against the darkened sky. He waited in silence and hoped she would plead for forgiveness. Instead, she just turned her back and clenched the blanket tighter. The cool mist blew through her long, black hair and hit him in the face.

After an uncomfortable silence, he spoke. "Why did you do this?"

"Because you are never home." Her words drifted out the window across the city. "You are always off somewhere following that insane Yeshua who teaches blasphemy." She turned and faced him. "Our daughter and I would be better off living as the high priest's servants than living with you. The people you follow will get us all killed." Her voice trembled. He saw the fear in her eyes.

The throbbing in his neck slowed. The tension in his shoulders eased and he unclenched his fists. "I will be back," he said with a gruffer tone than he intended.

***

Jacob was out of breath by the time he reached the majestic palace built by Herod that ran along the city's western wall. Its immense structure towered high above his head, an ominous sign that foretold the authority that lay inside. He knew Caiaphas no doubt ran back there to gloat and hide.

The coward!

When he slowed down to a walk, he could hear the bronze fountains gurgling. Fresh rain waters dripped from the silver green leaves of the olive trees that lined the tiled garden paths. He glanced up at the porticos that wound around luxurious pools on the grounds that connected the two main buildings, Agrippa and Caesar. He shook his head at the extravagance. Jacob questioned how much the luxuries and power of being the high priest had changed his childhood friend.

Scum! Traitor!

Lightning flashed and illumined the white marble retainer, forty-five cubits high.

Jacob made no effort to quiet his long strides up the steps to the priest's quarters. He cared little that Rome's praetorian guard resided there during Jewish feasts to keep the Jews under control. No concern of his tonight.

A palace guard stepped out of the shadows and planted himself directly in Jacob's path.

"Halt!"

"I know him," another one said, a friend of Caiaphas. "Let him pass."

Jacob had seen this guard numerous times since his friend's rise to power, many times with Abigail and Jerusha. He quickly passed both of them, bounded up the stairs, and pounded on the cedar door.

The porter slid back the small wooden opening and peeked out with dark, beady eyes. "Come back. It is late. The high priest sleeps," he said.

"You are lying—" Jacob stopped himself. His fight was not with a porter. Aware his entrance depended on this frightened servant, he continued. "He is not asleep—he will see me. And he will see me tonight!"

"Go away!" the porter replied and slammed the door shut, but Jacob caught it and pushed back.

"I will see him," the high priest's voice echoed from a distant, spacious room with high ceilings that absorbed its vibrations. The words sounded muffled. "Open the door. Escort him to my chambers."

Jacob's wet sandals squeaked on the jewel-tiled floor. He followed the porter down a colonnade lined with well-manicured pomegranate bushes and flowering shrubs. The damp air carried a foul odor mixed with frankincense. He stopped and waited.

When the porter opened a huge door into the spacious room, Jacob hesitated a few seconds and composed himself before he stepped inside. In the corner a fire burned. Its flames bounced like yellow and orange spears on the wall opposite the door. Caiaphas sat on an elaborate gold seat with jewels that outlined the high back. His weight sank into the soft, red velvet cushion. Like a king on his throne, he dismissed the porter with a wave of his hand.

Arrogant. Pompous traitor.

After the large wooden door with gold-covered reliefs creaked shut behind him, Jacob approached. In the corner black smoke wound to the ceiling, like an ominous snake. To Jacob, its incense smelled like poison in the air.

Caiaphas stood, *not* dressed in the attire he wore in Jacob's bedroom but in his impressive black robe. His religious garment that swooshed to his movements gave an appearance of righteousness, not like the look in his eyes that revealed a blackened evil heart full of hate and cruelty.

"Why do you bother me so late at night?"

Nauseated by the image of this "holy man" in bed with his wife, Jacob shouted.

"Don't act innocent with me! You know why I am here. YOU!" He pointed and advanced toward the priest. "You were my friend. We ate together. We attended Gamaliel's school together. I trusted you!"

"What are you talking about, Jacob? We *are* friends."

"You sicken me. You have a wife. Leave mine alone!"

Caiaphas's lips curved in a sly infuriating smile.

"Your wife made no objection to my presence."

Jacob grabbed the man's heavy, ornate robe and jerked him close. The priest's scar, hidden beneath his bushy brow, twitched.

"I don't care *who* you are. If you so much as look at my wife, I will wait until you are alone—and priest or no priest—friend or no friend—I will—I will leave you with more than a scarred brow," his words echoed.

"Now, Jacob," Caiaphas spoke with a smooth tongue. "You wouldn't want to be charged for striking the high priest, now, would you? You can't depend on your friend Yeshua to save you. He will never rule as King, the blasphemer."

Jacob loosened his grip slightly, his eyes locked on the scar. He trembled with rage. But Caiaphas's words made him think about Yeshua and consider for the first time how he would have him respond. Caiaphas smirked and removed his robe from Jacob's hands.

Temptation, beyond any temptation he ever felt, pulled on Jacob—he would be justified to strike any other man he caught in bed with his wife. But this man—this man was worse—the high priest of all men, breaking the Torah, adultery none-the-less, to please his own flesh.

Jacob whirled around so that Caiaphas could not see his expression. He looked skyward and restrained himself. He knew what the Torah commanded, "You shall not revile God, nor curse your ruler." Threaten? Strike him? Never! He knew the consequences—death by stoning or at the least flogged with thirty-nine lashes. For the moment, he yielded to the teachings under which they both were trained—Rabbi Gamaliel's teachings, the man he and Caiaphas studied with in the synagogue.

Caiaphas touted Jacob. "Your wife is beautiful and may I say—attentive."

Jacob whipped around again, fists readied.

"You pig! You coward, hiding behind your high position!" He steadied himself ready to strike. Then dropped his fists. "You are not worth it. As much as I'd like to punch you, you are not worth it! You are corrupt! You line your own pockets with temple tax. Fear of losing Rome's favor blinds you from seeing Yeshua as King. You burden the people with hundreds of additional laws, oral interpretations. Laws! Laws! Laws! Jacob's face reddened and he inched closer to Caiaphas. "You expect everyone to keep laws you never keep yourself." *He stood so close. Just one good blow.*

In disgust, Caiaphas backed away and acted as though he brushed Jacob's dusty fingerprints from his robe.

"Your wife and daughter will live with me. You will agree to never see them again."

Shocked, Jacob whirled back around and faced his childhood friend, fists clenched.

"Never! You will stay away from Abigail—*and* my daughter. This conversation is over!"

Caiaphas cocked his head and chuckled wickedly.

"That's it!" Jacob said. He launched his right fist and hit the mark, Caiaphas's scar. The priest stumbled backward, a look of shock across his bloody brow. Quickly, he used the inside of his flowing robe to wipe the blood from his eye.

"I swear, if you do not leave my wife alone, I will give you more than a black eye." Jacob turned to leave.

"Then your daughter will see her mother stoned," Caiaphas seethed. "I will see to it myself. False witnesses will be used."

Jacob froze. He stood on the threshold, the gold handle of the large, ornate door in his hand. He swiveled around and glared at the priest. His square jaw trembled. "You wouldn't dare!"

Caiaphas threw his head back and laughed mockingly then stared at Jacob and with a calm stern voice he answered, "You know I have the power. And I *will* do it."

"You sniveling, disgusting pig!" Jacob wanted so much to throw Caiaphas to the floor and beat him until he cried for mercy. His arm muscles tensed, ready to strike, but he breathed deep and tried to remain calm. "My daughter will never see that happen!" he gritted through clenched teeth then slammed the door behind him and stomped down the portico past the garden.

"Guards! Guards!" Caiaphas's shrill cry sounded like a woman. "Stop him!"

At the door the porter stepped in front of him. In fierce anger, Jacob flung him aside and fled outside. With two powerful jabs, he sent the two palace guards tumbling backwards down the steep stairs. He scanned the large open area. No time to cross. His eyes followed a small dog creep past and out of sight. He pursued the same path and disappeared into the perfect hiding place, a dark, shadowy alcove. He waited. The rotten garbage and excrement that attracted the dog oozed over his toes. His stomach churned. *What have I done?* A few minutes passed. He heard men's deep voices.

"I saw movement down here. He's got to be here, somewhere!"

His eyes scanned the darkness. Two shadows moved closer to his hiding place. *They are going to find me.* He held his breath. His heartbeat pounded in his ears. A mangy dog only a few feet away growled a low guttural warning. Jacob wanted to slap the creature for giving them away.

"It's just a wild dog! One of the guards said. He threw a stone and it plopped at Jacob's feet. The dog's growl intensified. "You fleabag! I will run you through with my sword."

"Clumsy oaf, you'll slash your own foot." The other guard scoffed and threw another rock. The dog yelped and bolted past the guards. They moved close enough for Jacob to grab their swords. *Bad idea!* Their foul body odor mixed with the odor of the excrement at his feet and he felt his stomach lurch. He held it back until they passed then added to the stench at his feet.

Minutes later he heard their sandaled feet tromp up the temple steps in the distance. One mumbled, "Caiaphas knows where he lives. We'll get him—tomorrow, when it's daylight."

Jacob slipped from his hiding place, splashed through numerous puddles to clean his feet, and wound his way in the dark, narrow maze of dwellings. *YHWH, help me! What shall I do? Where shall I go?*

There. In the distance, was a slight flicker in the upper room where he parted with Yeshua's followers to go home to Abigail and Jerusha. Peter! One of Yeshua's closest confidants! He'll *know what to do.* A few stars broke through the clouds above. Flashes of his daughter's facial expressions at the harlot's stoning darted through his mind. *She will not see her mother stoned. I'll take them away from here.* He rapped the secret signal. Tap, tap, tap. Wait. Tap, tap, tap. He stumbled through the doorway.

"Oh, Peter, help me!"

"What is it, Jacob? Whatever could have you so upset?" Peter looked up and down the street to see if his friend was being followed then blew out the lamp he carried.

Jacob trembled in the moonlit room. Peter guided him past the sleeping men. Light from the upstairs lamp shone on the stairs.

"Come. We can talk up there." Jacob stared at the men. If only he could sleep so peacefully. In the far corner of the upstairs room, Peter sat on a stool across from him and put his hand on his shoulder.

"Whatever has you so distraught, Jacob? It is not like you to be this way."

Jacob rubbed his face with his hands. There was no other way to present this.

"Peter, I hit Caiaphas!"

Peter's jaw dropped.

"You did what?"

"I hit him. Bloodied his face. I—" Jacob put his head in his hands to control himself. He did not want to weep in front of Peter, especially now when his tears would be from anger as well as heartbreak. He took a deep breath and blurted, "My brother, I was so angry. I caught him with Abigail—in bed!" Peter stood up, his face red.

"The scoundrel! He deserved it, Jacob. As a man, I can tell you, he deserved it. But the position he holds, hitting the high priest of the nation, well that is different."

"What am I going to do?" Jacob crumpled to the floor, his head in his hands. His shoulders shook. He could hold it back no longer. Loud sobs erupted. He felt Peter's two large hands cover the top of his head. After several minutes, a calmness settled upon him, and he looked up.

"I lost control. I can never forgive myself for being so foolish. He told me if I didn't allow Abigail and Jerusha to come live with him and agree to never see them again, he'd have Abigail stoned for adultery." Peter lifted him from the cold floor.

"Sit here on this bench and rest. It seems that you and Yeshua have a common enemy."

Jacob leaned his head back against the wall and closed his eyes, his lips parched, his throat dry. He heard Peter moving around the room.

"Here, drink." Peter handed him a goatskin bottle full of fresh water. "Drink deeply."

The stench of garbage and excrement rose from his feet. The puddles evidently didn't wash away the filth as he had hoped. Jacob glanced down. Peter knelt before him with a bowl of water and a cloth.

"No! I don't deserve such service."

"Yeshua taught us the greatest in the kingdom is servant of all. My friend, it is an honor to serve you. You would do as much for me." Humbled, Jacob leaned back against the wall again and closed his eyes. He felt the soothing strength of Peter's hands rub the filth from his toes. Clean water washed over his feet. He heard the window shutter open and the splash of the old water on the ground outside.

"Now my friend, let's talk about what you should do with this circumstance you find yourself in. You must work this through yourself. I cannot tell you what to do, but if YHWH forgave King David for his adultery, you must forgive, too."

"Forgive Abigail, yes! Caiaphas, *no!*"

"And you—do you want YHWH's forgiveness for hitting the high priest?"

Jacob slumped forward, his head in his hands, his fingers spread through tangled hair.

"I am not sure I can forgive myself."

"YHWH forgives and his mercies are new every morning. Go back to your house. You will be safe there for now."

The self-condemning thoughts fled. Jacob stood to his feet, ready to return home. Peter placed his hands on Jacob's shoulders.

"I will be praying for you. You will find your way."

Jacob bowed his head and sighed, then looked up in his friend's eyes. "Yes, I will find my way."

Chapter 8

J acob entered the same gate, sat on the same bench, smelled the same pomegranate bushes. Hours earlier, he felt the excitement of giving the special purple cloth to his wife and daughter and telling them that he had found Mashiach. Yeshua, my friend, Mashiach ben David, the long awaited King. What would *he* do?

"YHWH, help me," he cried. The words echoed across the garden. Movement behind him caused him to turn.

"Abigail." The early dawn cast shadows across her face and hid her dark brown eyes.

"Would you leave Jerusalem?" Jacob almost begged. "Would you go away with me?" Guilt for putting them in this position gripped his inner being, and he hated to sound so desperate, so vulnerable. His eyes lingered and drank in her beauty, but she refused to look at him. Why did she refuse his love? She looked down.

"No," she answered. "You are following a group of people who will get us killed." Jacob groaned and turned his back. Her words sounded so cold, but he asked her to leave everything, everyone she knew, and follow him to some unknown place. Why would she say yes, except that she loved him and wanted to be with him? But maybe she didn't want him as her husband anymore. He summoned the courage to ask the most important question.

"Do you love Caiaphas?" He waited. Silence. When he turned around, she was gone.

"Why? Why? Why does she have to be so difficult?" He slammed his fist against the wall. Numb to the pain in his knuckles, he dropped to his knees. What would he do now? He stared at the colorful tiles and remembered his last visit with Jerusha before he left.

"I have no other choice," he mumbled, "Abigail won't leave with me, but I will take Jerusha."

The blood from his knuckles mixed with tears and dripped onto the tiles. His chest tightened. His stomach churned.

Stone her! Stone her! Then you can keep your little girl with you! the inner voice screamed.

"No!" he groaned. A battle raged.

Stone Abigail. Keep your little girl.

I can't. Jerusha loves her mother.

She'll think the mean priest did it. She won't blame you.

I love Abigail.

She doesn't love you. Give up. Stone her. Jerusha won't see it. You can protect her.

I can't. Not now. I struck Caiaphas. She'll be in danger.

He won't hurt Jerusha.

I can't take that chance. I must let her go. I must let them both go.

Jacob dropped his head.

"Give me strength to trust them to your care," he whispered. The other voice stopped. His shoulders slumped. He turned and wound his way through the garden and momentarily hesitated at the pomegranate tree. He touched its dark green leaves and raised his tired swollen eyes. Rosy pink clouds on the horizon spoke to him of a new day, one without his wife and daughter. *I will come back!* he vowed.

***

The afternoon sun shone bright. Peter was right—the guards never came. Caiaphas had more than a bruised face—his pride was bruised as well.

This worked in Jacob's favor and gave him more time. A servant from the palace, a disciple of Yeshua, brought word to Peter that Caiaphas met in secret with Ananus, Caiaphas's father-in-law. They plotted Jacob's demise. He had till the morrow before they came for him. As much as Jacob wanted to stay and use his wealth and influence to fight for Abigail and Jerusha, wisdom prevailed. He breathed deep. The smell of fresh rain. He patted Peter on the back and walked him to the courtyard gate.

"I am leaving Jerusalem. I plan to travel with Luke across the Jordan River to Perea to make a place for my family. I will be back. Abigail may change her mind when Yeshua sits on his throne. Luke knows of some families there that are of our faith. For a few days, I'll hide in a tunnel beneath the city while I make arrangements for Jerusha. He assures me I'll be safe there. I need your help, though. Who do you know whom I can trust to keep a watch on Jerusha and Abigail while I'm gone, someone with character, someone trustworthy with my money?"

"I know just the right man. You have seen him at our gatherings. His name is Stephen, a Hellenist Jew but accepted by the Sanhedrin. He lives near here and is persuaded that Yeshua is the Mashiach."

"Yes, I know of this man. Yeshua and I have talked with him in the synagogue. Would you ask him to meet me. Luke will show him where I will be."

"Of course," Peter answered, then stopped and stared at the ground for a minute. "Traveling alone is dangerous. At least you will have Luke. Still dangerous, though. Be careful and watchful. You know what to do."

"We will travel mostly at night, staying away from the thieves, marauding zealots, and patrolling Roman legions."

Content with the plan, Jacob opened the gate for Peter and stepped outside into the street.

"The sewage smell is better today. The shower must have washed the streets clean."

Peter slapped his back.

"You also smell better."

Jacob laughed. It felt good to laugh. It helped to ease the empty void he felt about leaving his wife and daughter.

"I will instruct Stephen about Jerusha's future." A purple butterfly landed on his arm. He peered at it for a moment. "I will talk to Jerusha tonight. I need your prayers. She may not understand why I am leaving, but my hope is that Yeshua restores the kingdom soon, then Abigail couldn't deny that he is the Mashiach. Maybe then she will not be afraid. Maybe . . . Jacob stopped speaking and wondered if that would be enough for her to come back to him, to love him again. Maybe she loved Caiaphas? He had not seen her dimpled smile in a long time. Peter interrupted his thoughts.

"I understand," he said, "Shalom, my friend."

"Peter!" someone yelled. "Peter! It's Peter!"

Jacob watched children gather around his friend and pull on his arms. Peter looked back and nodded.

"He has his work and I have mine," Jacob said, his thoughts now on Jerusha as he slipped back into the courtyard. *I must finish her gift and prepare to leave.*

He went to his bedchamber to retrieve the unfinished box and opened the creaky door. Abigail stood in front of the window, the light shining through her dark hair, her eyes cold, distant, uncaring. His eyes darted from her to the bed.

"Why?" he asked and clutched her arm as she tried to cross the room in front of him. She struggled against him.

"Let me go!"

Releasing her arm from his grip, he grabbed the door and slammed it shut then placed his muscular frame between her and the door, arms crossed over his chest.

"We need to talk." He longed to grab her, smother her with kisses. Her long, thick lashes against her blemish free skin, the curves beneath her robe awoke a deeper desire. "Why, Abigail, Why?" he spoke in a softer tone, now.

"I am afraid, Jacob. I am so afraid. This Jewish cult you follow will get us killed. You put Jerusha and me in so much danger. She believes everything you tell her. I tried to tell you—to tell you to stop. You would not listen. Caiaphas listened. He understands my fears. He agrees with me. I feel safe with him. He said he would protect us."

Jacob wanted to promise safety, but in a jealous rage he sinned, and it cost him everything and everyone he loved, probably what Caiaphas wanted all along. Rubbing his fingers through his thick, scruffy hair, he suddenly knew. It was a trap; Caiaphas's way to get rid of him. He played right into his hands.

"I hit Caiaphas in defense of you, He seeks to arrest me."

Abigail's eyes widened. "You hit the high priest? Jacob, don't you know—"

"I know. Caiaphas is a scoundrel, a thief who stole my wife to satisfy his own lust—and a man who pretended to be my friend from childhood. He's a coward—using his power for—oh, forget it. You feel safe with a coward. And I—I can only promise my love," he hesitated and looked deep in her eyes. "Do you—do you still love me?"

Abigail's eyes brimmed with tears. "I do not—" She hesitated. "I do not know. I only know I am afraid." Jacob thought for a while about grabbing her and demanding her to go with him, yet he knew that was not an option. If only he had not fallen prey to Caiaphas's trap, he could stay and woo her love back. But he had allowed jealousy and anger to blind him. Now he had no other choice but to give her what she wanted.

"Will you feel safer if I leave? A divorce?" Jacob asked.

"Yes," she answered. "I've been thinking about this for a while. This will be hard for Jerusha. She will miss you, but she will be safe." Jacob squeezed his eyes shut.

"Then I will give you your divorce. You must leave tonight, though, before the soldiers come to arrest me. I will not have Jerusha frightened by their presence here. She must not know that her father hit the high priest—or that her mother slept with him. Caiaphas will take you in. I am sure of it. I am not sure how safe you will be with that conniving coward. But know this: I will always love you." He opened the door and moved out of her way.

Abigail fled past him. Her fragrance lingered, and he flung the open door against the wall, then stomped across the room and retrieved Jerusha's unfinished box from the table next to the bed. He wanted to throw it. He wanted to throw anything to relieve the anger—anger at himself, anger at Abigail, anger at Caiaphas. He gripped it tight in his hands, looked outside, and saw Abigail. She stood under the jujube tree by the iron gate.

A longing stirred, a longing to be in the garden, the special garden where he often spoke to YHWH as he worked. He turned from the window and left their bedroom, glancing back one last time at their bed.

"I love you, Abigail," he whispered.

Outside, he pulled up his workbench in the garden and started carving. His nimble fingers smoothed the sharp edges of the box.

"Love hurts so much," he mumbled. When a butterfly flittered past, he stopped his work and scanned the garden.

"Where is my Jerusha? I haven't seen her for a while. Why hasn't she come to see me?" The box fell to the ground and he picked it up still mumbling, "Maybe she senses the tension between her mother and me." Across the garden, he heard tiny steps quicken their pace and he looked up. Jerusha stood in front of him. Her eyes blinked back tears. "Well, well, whom do we have here?" he said. She plopped her arms to her side.

"I saw Mother crying. Why is she so sad?" Jacob gathered Jerusha in his arms and sat her on his lap.

"Sometimes, Jerusha, people feel sad. Don't you feel sad sometimes?"

"Yes," she answered. She saw the box. "What are you making now?" she asked and jumped down.

"Wouldn't you like to know, my little lioness," he said. "Maybe tonight you'll find out."

"Tonight? You'll tell me tonight? I want to know now."

"Come here," he said. He drew her close. "No matter what the future holds, never forget that I love you." She fiddled with her fingers then wiggled out of his arms and yelled, "Don't!"

He watched her scamper away and disappear into the dwelling.

"Tonight is our last good-bye," he whispered. "What has happened? She never wants to be with me. Will she miss me? I will miss her."

His large, weatherworn hands trembled. The shofar blasted from across the city.

"I will need your strength," he prayed

"I am with you, my son, even in the darkness."

***

That evening he found Jerusha in her room on her bed. The light in her emerald eyes gone. A darkness, a sadness, an almost pouty mouth greeted him.

"Jerusha, will you come for a walk with me in the garden? The stars are bright." She shrugged, and he lifted her complacent body. Arms dangled at her sides. He carried her down the portico to the garden and set her feet on the blue and white tiles. A gentle breeze blew threw her long, black hair. The lamp-lit pathway cast shadows on her bare feet, so tiny for a ten-year-old. Butterflies fluttered from their resting places. She ran to catch one and quickly returned, the butterfly resting in her palm.

Just what she needed to cheer her troubled mind.

Jacob pointed to the stars. "It is written that YHWH knows all the stars by name. Look how many stars there are." She slowly counted, one, two, three . . .

"Too numerous to count. That's how many thoughts he has toward you. Come, let's sit in our favorite spot." Distracted by the butterflies, she tripped. Jacob caught her just before she hit her head on their bench where a ripened fruit was cut open and ready to share with her. When Jerusha saw it, she squealed.

"Ah, that is my Jerusha. Look at those dimples. That is what I wanted to see."

Jacob savored the picture of her as she counted the many seeds inside.

"Here," he said, "let's just eat it." His red-stained fingers lingered on her face as she looked up. He gazed into her smiling eyes. "I remember the day you were born. Your emerald eyes shined big and bright. You are such a miracle." He looked down at his robe folded on the bench, the tzitzits carefully placed inside. He breathed in a deep breath and exhaled, trying to keep his emotions under control. He could not let her see his sadness; the tears that threatened to overflow. With a soft, gentle voice he spoke.

"You will be leaving with your mother tonight. I will not be living with you anymore." Her mouth turned down in disapproval.

"Don't say that. It makes my heart beat fast. I never want to leave you. I love you." He placed his robe in her lap.

"I am giving you my robe. When you cover yourself with it, when you dance with it, when you finger the tzitzits, remember me. It might be hard for you to understand why we must separate. I cannot explain the reasons why." He wrapped his arm around her shoulders. "You must trust me. I am doing this because I love you so very much, and we will see each other again."

She started to speak. He placed his hand over her mouth.

"Just listen." He reached under the bench and pulled out the box he had made. It was wrapped in purple cloth, the gift he had bought for her on the last trip.

As she unfolded the cloth, he said, "This is to remind you of my deep and unending love. It is a treasure box to put your pendant in when you are not wearing it. I have put pomegranates on the outside. They remind me of our fun times together. They also remind me of you." He placed the box on the bench.

He picked up an uncut pomegranate and placed it in her hands. "I've noticed recently that it is hard to get inside your heart to that tender part. Much like the tough skin of a pomegranate, you seem to be protecting yourself. It is like you are holding a secret inside, guarding something. Do you want to talk about it?" She strongly shook her head. Her hair flopped back and forth over her face. "I don't know what has happened," he continued, "One thing I do know. I've planted many seeds of my love in here." He touched her chest. She cringed and drew back. He grimaced. "One day the covering will be taken away." He took the pomegranate from her hands and cut it open. "When you see the red juice of the pomegranate, remember that you are royalty, your heart will forever beat with the blood from the tribe of Judah." He laid the fruit aside, picked up the gift. "Now, open the box."

Jerusha fumbled with it. He took it from her hands and opened it. Her eyes widened. "What is that?" she asked and pointed to the bronze relief on the bottom. He placed her small, fragile fingers on the relief and applied just enough pressure for it to unlock and pop open. She gasped. A crystal clear jasper stone glittered in the moonlight.

"A jewel for my jewel."

Jerusha's black eyelashes blinked back tears.

"This jewel is to remind you that one day you, like the jasper stone, will shine and sparkle in the light of YHWH's unshakeable love."

She closed the box. He felt her tiny, thin arms wrap around his neck and squeeze with all her might. The box fell to the ground. Jacob clung to her and savored the softness of her hair against his cheek. He gulped. He never wanted to let go. Suddenly, she pushed away from him. He saw terror in her eyes.

"Father," her voice quivered. "I can't tell you." She grabbed the robe and slipped off the bench. "I can't tell you." For a moment she closed her eyes and moved her head back and forth, then briefly glanced into his eyes. "I can't." He saw the tears that threatened to overflow and watched her frantically duck under the bench and retrieve the box.

"You will hate me forever. I can't tell you," she squeaked and ran like a monster chased her, dust flying from under her bare feet. The butterflies flitted overhead. The tzitzits flopped in the wind. He longed to run and swoop his troubled daughter in his arms and never let her go.

"Oh, YHWH, help."

He threw his head back. Squeezed his eyes shut. Drops came anyway and ran into his beard.

"Help my daughter. She is hurting so much. You know what she is afraid to tell me. You know. You know what it is. It hurts so much to let her go." The wind rustled through the trees. "She is yours now," he groaned. "She has always been yours."

***

Jacob watched and listened from the upper bedroom window. Torches cast dark shadows across the courtyard below. The song thrushes and crickets that normally sang nighttime songs were quiet. Abigail and Jerusha touched the mezuzah on the doorpost as he had seen them do a million times as they entered or left the dwelling. His two beloveds departed. The iron gate clanged behind them. Jerusha's tiny leather sandals pitter-pattered on the dusty path.

"Where are we going?" she asked Abigail. Jacob heard his little one's deep and heavy breathing. In the moonlight he saw one of the tzitzits dangle from the bundle she carried, her small fingers wrapped around it. Her shortened stride and heavy load slowed her pace and made it impossible to stay up with her mother. Abigail waited, the few belongings she carried balanced on her hip and a lamp in her hand.

"You will see," he heard Abigail answer. "We are moving to a new house."

Jerusha scrunched up her nose. She coughed and gagged. Jacob groaned. The garbage and sewage scent again.

"Why do we have to leave *our* house? Why can't we stay with Father?"

Abigail shuffled her load to the other hip and shoved Jerusha along. Jacob turned and walked away. He couldn't bear to watch anymore. A black shadow moved behind him and a sharp pain shot through the back of his head. He heard Abigail's words, the last ones he caught of their conversation before he blacked out and slumped to the floor.

"He is sending us away. He has given me a writ of divorce."

Chapter 9

"I don't understand," Jerusha said as she trudged along beside Abigail.

Silence. She glanced up and hoped to read her mother's body language, her facial expressions. She knew her mother well enough. The tormented look, the grim set in Abigail's mouth silenced her many questions. She would ask them later when Mother's mood changed.

The duo wound their way through the shadowy streets. A gust of wind blew around a corner and extinguished the lamp Mother carried. A gloomy darkness crept over Jerusha. An unnerving fear of the unknown ate at her stomach. Father's words penetrated her foggy mind. *"No matter what the future holds, just remember that I love you."*

Moments later they stood in front of Herod's palace. Jerusha wondered if she could find her way back in the dark and run home to her father. Heavy fog and the growling dogs in the shadows persuaded her to cast that thought aside. At that very moment the porter opened the door as he did so many times in the past. Only this time he welcomed them in the dark, a lamp in his hand.

"Caiaphas is expecting you. We have everything ready."
Jerusha moved closer to mother.

"We are living here?" she asked.

"Yes," Abigail answered.

Surprised, her eyes and nostrils widened as she sucked in the
pungent air. *How can this be happening? This can't be true. Father
wouldn't do this to me.*

"Follow me," the porter asked.

"No!" Jerusha refused to move, buried her face against Mother's
side and tried to hide beneath her arm. "I am not staying here!" The
large roon swallowed her muffled whine.

Mother ignored the remarks and tried to coax her to follow the
porter. Jerusha stiffened her knees.

"Now what do we have here—a little girl refusing to obey her
mother?" Caiaphas spoke with poised authority as he entered the
room. Jerusha heard her mother gasp and looked up and saw her
mother staring at a woman next to Caiaphas. It was his wife, her arm
intertwined with his like she owned him. Jerusha remembered her but
wondered why Mother was so surprised.

"What shall we do with such rebellion?" Caiaphas continued.
"I am sure when the little one is given a chance to think about her
actions that she will honor her mother as the Torah commands."

Jerusha held her breath. She felt the blood rush to her head and
she gripped her mother's cloak for fear of passing out. A picture formed
from her memory of Caiaphas on that scary day. His face. The stone
in his hand. The angry cries. This man, the one standing in front of
her, the one in whose house she stood, was the one who pushed the
woman off the cliff. Why hadn't she seen this before? Backing away
from him, she recalled his words, "Stone her! Stone her!" And Efah's
threat of stoning rang loud and clear in her thoughts, too.

Towering above, Caiaphas now peered down with pompous eyes.
His wife squinted through narrow slits, like a cat ready to pounce.
Jerusha wondered why she glared so intently. She remembered that in
the past when she was very little, this woman, Efah's mother, would feed
them a meal of delicious delicacies and laugh and converse with her
mother and father while Jerusha watched their son from across the table
and dreamed of marriage. That was before Efah forced his way with her.

Those days with their two families seemed like a dream from ages ago. In the last year, all the visits happened without Father, mostly when he traveled. Reluctantly, Jerusha moved forward. Her knees wobbled and she clung more tightly than ever to her mother for support.

"That's better little one." Caiaphas stepped toward her. "You're trembling. Don't be afraid."

Don't touch me, she screamed silently, retreated a few steps, and hid behind mother.

"What are *they* doing here so late at night?" his wife asked. Jerusha peeked out from behind Mother's cloak. The woman stared at her Mother.

Of course, she admired her beauty. Many in the marketplace, both men and women, noticed. Jerusha felt proud to be with her and looked up. Her mother blinked her long, thick eyelashes and caressed Jerusha's head, undisturbed by the other woman's stare.

"Darling," the priest answered his wife, "you were just saying the other day that we needed new servants for the kitchen. I've acquired their services. Jacob has given Abigail a writ of divorce, cast her off like a dirty rag. We could not just let our friends beg on the streets, now could we?" Mother's caress stopped.

"No, of course not. The kitchen is a perfect place for them," his wife answered.

"How dare you treat us like this!" Abigail responded. "We are your friends." She pulled Jerusha close to her side.

"Oh, how wrong you are. You *were* our friends. You are now our servants." Caiaphas motioned to another servant who stood attentively awaiting his orders. "Take them to the quarters behind the kitchen." The other woman, his wife, moved across the room, stopped under the archway that opened to the portico, turned, and addressed Caiaphas.

"Don't take long, Caiaphas. I'll be waiting for you in our chambers."

"Caiaphas," her mother cried, "are you going to let her do this? You said you would keep us safe."

Caiaphas drew close. The stench of his breath mixed with the incense in the room sickened Jerusha. In a low whisper, he spoke in Mother's ear.

"Oh, you'll be safe enough. I would never allow anyone to harm or kill you. I have need of your services. I'll call for you when my wife is occupied or gone. Herod's kitchen will not be the only place that will require your service." Jerusha never saw him treat her mother like this before and did not understand what his words meant.

"I thought you loved me," Abigail pleaded. Caiaphas grasped Abigail's chin.

"I do love you. I love your beauty. Too beautiful for a man like Jacob." Jerusha had heard her father tell her mother that he loved her, but what is this talk of Caiaphas's love? It made no sense.

He released her face and turned away. His long, black robe brushed across Jerusha's face. She snuggled deeper under mother's arm and clutched the folds in her robe. The suffocating panic she experienced over and over when the boy touched her resurfaced. She wanted to flail her arms and legs, kick and run away, but it happened only in her imagination. In reality, she stood paralyzed, her feet frozen to the floor.

Mother peeled Jerusha's arms off and knelt down in front of her and tucked a few strands of loose hair back in her radiyd, the head covering she always wore in public. Jerusha saw confidence in her dark eyes.

"Don't be afraid. I will take care of you." The light from the lamp reflected off the crown hidden deep in the lion's mane of the pendant that dangled from Jerusha's neck. Caiaphas turned and saw sparkles on her face.

"What's that?" he asked.

Jerusha grabbed it. Emboldened by her mother's promise of protection, she spoke with confidence.

"It's mine. My father made it. He says I should never forget who I am—that I'm royalty—I'm from the tribe of Judah. I will dance before the King one day." The words flew from her mouth before she remembered whom she addressed. When she saw Mother roll her eyes, she gulped.

Caiaphas came toward her.

"You? Royalty?" he said with a mocking curve to his mouth. "Look at those eyes. Those eyes don't come from a pure bloodline. You're no more than a simpleton, a half-breed. No better than a Samaritan." His eyes fell on Abigail. "Now your mother's eyes, those dark eyes speak of a true Hebrew of royal lineage. Too bad she must now serve me. She would have been a regal wife to the high priest had she not married your father, that half-breed. She is now good only for servitude."

"How dare you talk to me and my daughter like that. Why are you acting like this? I thought you cared about me, about us?" her mother cried.

He chuckled. "I do. I'm giving you a place to live, aren't I?" He turned his eyes upon Jerusha. "Now about this king you refer to—who is he?" he demanded.

"I don't know, yet. My father says I will meet him someday. When I find him, I will know him. He will be like my father. He will like my dancing, just like my father likes my dancing." Speaking of her father gave her courage. She relaxed and walked over to Caiaphas. "Would you like to see what my father made for me?" she said and held out her pendant.

He hovered. His jaw jutted out.

"Take it off!" he commanded. That familiar sensation that she awoke with all too often at night gnawed at her stomach again and twisted it into knots. "You are not royalty!" he boomed. "I know your father. His eyes are lighter than yours. It's only because of his wealth and influence in this city that I associated with him at all. He is a traitor! He follows those who speak treasonous words against Rome. Take it off!" he repeated.

Jerusha felt Mother move closer and try to slip the pendant off her neck. She clenched whitened knuckles around it, but Abigail tugged it free from her grasp and handed it to Caiaphas.

"Why—why did you take my pendant away?" One tiny, rough point in the lion's mane caused a slight prick in Jerusha's skin. She stared at the blood in her palm, numb to the pain. Stunned and confused, she watched teardrops fall into the blood, curled her fingers over the wound and rubbed her nose to stop her sniffles. "Why does he call Father a traitor?" she asked.

She watched her mother stare at the priest, then look down at her and back up to the priest, as if she expected him to explain.

"Idol!" The priest's shrill cry echoed across the room and down the hallway. Jerusha's shoulders jerked beneath Mother's hands. She glanced up and saw the pendant fly through the air. It glittered as it traveled across the room and plopped in the fire. *No!* she tried to scream. Her throat tightened. Nothing came out. Every muscle tensed up. She held her breath and looked at his red face and eyes that pierced, then back to her pendant in the fire.

"I will not have idols in my house!" he shrieked.

Jerusha collapsed.

***

The room was dark when Jerusha awakened. Shadows flickered on the wall like towering dark monsters, their pointed claws grabbed at her from all sides. She froze beneath the scratchy cover. *If I don't move,* she thought, *they won't see me.* She held her breath, afraid every sound she made would draw the monster's attention. *They mustn't see me! They mustn't hear me.* She drifted back to sleep and spiraled down into that dark, scratchy place that she had visited so many nights since Efah forcefully hurt her with his touches. No way out! Stuck forever!

She grasped at the webs wrapped around her face and fought the itchy yarnlike strands that held her tight and kept her from moving. She strained her eyes to see the distant speck. A light. A faint light. She had seen it before. Each time it flickered, then disappeared.

"Please! Please!" she begged. "Don't leave. Father! Where are you? Help me, Father! I can't get out! Help me! Someone help me!" The monstrous darkness swallowed her words. She choked and grabbed at her neck for her pendant.

Jerusha heard her mother's voice whisper the words from the pendant.

"Arise, Lord. Let your enemies be scattered. Let all who hate you flee before you." She opened her eyes. The golden flecks in the lion's mane danced on the wall and left an ever-so-faint impression of a crown. She reached for the image.

"My pendant," she moaned.

"We will not be his servants. I will not allow it." Mother's voice sounded determined, her fragrance lingered close. "At least I was able to retrieve this from the fire," she comforted.

The pendant touched Jerusha's bloody palm. She winced. "I'm sorry," her mother whispered and kissed her hand, then curled Jerusha's sweaty, trembling fingers around it. "Forgive me. I will not allow anything else to happen. I'll talk to Caiaphas. He will listen to me." Jerusha heard and closed her heavy eyes again. Mother snuggled close. She'll fix it. Tomorrow.

***

Someone shook Jerusha's shoulders. Confused and groggy, she recoiled like a caged animal, eyes widened in fear.

"Hurry," the servant compelled. "The high priest wants to see you." She felt Mother move and rolled over, but Mother grabbed both arms and jerked.

"Get up! Maybe Caiaphas has come to his senses. Quick! We must go!" Jerusha slid off the mittah and stumbled to get her balance. Mother straightened her robe.

"Where are we?" Jerusha asked. The only light in the tiny room came from a lamp on a small ledge in the wall. The wick burned low. The smell of olive oil lingered.

"Herod's palace," her mother reminded.

Like flashes of lightning, Jerusha's memory returned. Her father's good-bye. Living in this horrible place. Her pendant thrown into the flames.

Without the intimidating presence of the high priest, her anger flared like a raging fire throughout her body. Every muscle tensed up as she remembered his accusation. Pain seared through her palm as she clenched her fist. "Ouch," she cried. Startled, she looked down at her pendant and remembered what her mother said the night before. She would not let anything else happen. She would fix it.

Idol! The priest's judgment boomed into her memory. She fumbled to hide the pendant inside her girdle.

"Please hurry!" the servant urged them out the doorway. She stepped beneath the lintel behind mother.

"This is the biggest kitchen I have ever seen," she said. When she heard the grinding millstone, she stretched her neck to look behind her to see where the sound came from. A donkey's large, brown eyes stared at her from under the archway to her right. Attached to the upper stone, he clopped round the lower stone. Some women gathered flour from the mill, moved to the other side of the room, added water and other ingredients, and knelt before a large slab and slapped the dough, their tunics tucked in their belts. Two others slid readied dough onto a huge slab and place it in the bread oven. Red-orange sparks flew from the oven and hit the women's arms. They slapped at the embers that smoldered on their radiyds. The smell of fresh bread awakened Jerusha's hunger, even amidst the odors of hot, sweaty bodies and donkey dung.

She heard a bleat from across the room to her left. Another archway opened into a separate part of the large kitchen. Several goats stood in a line tied to an iron loop. Women sat on stools, one at each goat, and milked. She saw through an open door on the far side of that room outside a herd of goats and sheep grazed. In the distance a vineyard grew alongside an orchard with a variety of trees, probably olive, pomegranate, and fig.

"This way," the servant motioned. The other servants kept their heads down and busy with their tasks. They seemed not to notice Jerusha and Abigail. Perspiration rolled down her face.

"Mother, it's hot in here," she complained. They moved through the immense room and stepped out into a portico that led to another building. They hurried along the blue and white mosaic path. The cool air on her wet brow cooled her hot body. She panted.

"Stop!" she said, "I can't keep up. You are going too fast." The servant waited at the door of the building, then pushed open two, tall wooden doors with gold reliefs. When they stepped through the doorway into the beautiful courtyard garden, Jerusha's stomach knotted up. This was the place. Efah brought her here. The flowers, which brought such pleasure to others who walked these paths, awoke familiar and sickened feelings—the shame, self-hatred, and condemnation that harassed, especially at night, when she found herself grasping strand after strand to get free from that dark ball of neverending pieces of yarn, string, and sticky gunk.

The multicolored mosaic path wound around the gurgling bronze fountains and pools surrounded by well-manicured flowering shrubs and luscious green plants. In the distance she saw him. Efah. He stood next to the secret place, his father by his side.

Caiaphas dismissed the servant with a wave of his hand. The suffocating panic that she might be left alone with the boy constricted her throat. She gasped for air. Not able to breathe deeply, her short breaths quickened. The son and his father stood erect with an aloofness and superiority that made her cower.

"Never forget who you are. You are royalty." She twisted to look behind, so sure her father must be there. All she saw was the gentle rustling of the pomegranate bush in the morning breeze.

"Caiaphas, have you reconsidered your decision? We are your friends. We should be allowed to stay here as your guests, not your servants," Abigail spoke with great confidence.

"Your duties will be to keep the fires stoked in the kitchen oven, the fires going beneath the bath floors, and the bedchambers warm." His grin broadened at Abigail. "You will also scrub tiles and serve meals, only to me, my wife, and my son, privately, of course, when we stay here. We can't let our friends see that you have fallen into hard times, now can we?"

"Caiaphas, this is absurd!" Abigail yelled.

He completely ignored her outcry and called two soldiers who stood at attention at the door.

"They have been assigned to you. They will follow you everywhere and take turns standing outside your sleeping quarters at night."

"Take them to the kitchen," he spoke to the soldiers. "And if they escape I'll have your heads."

He dismissed them with a wave of his hand. The son swirled around and walked away without a word, not even a "hello."

"Humph! He acts like he doesn't even know me," Jerusha retorted. *How dare he treat me as a simple servant girl. Doesn't he know who I am? I am royalty. I am from the tribe of Judah.* She stood tall and straight, like the lioness her father adored.

"Come Jerusha," Abigail said, "We are leaving this place. We will find some place to go." The soldier stepped in front of them.

"Halt!" She turned the other way. The other soldier blocked them, too. "You will go with us." His deep loud voice sounded like father when the matter was settled.

***

Jerusha stayed with mother, like a shadow, everywhere, the two soldiers never far away. They started in the kitchen. She held new tinder and watched Mother place it in the oven, the old coals so hot it took her breath away. Numerous sparks popped like glowing rubies in the air. Abigail shielded Jerusha.

"Get back," she yelled.

Red blisters formed on Mother's hands and arms.

"I want to help!" Jerusha cried.

"Stay back."

Later in the afternoon she carried a small pile of kindling and tried to keep up. Mother slowed down and waited. It was a long way to the fires beneath the bath floors. She wanted so much to be up above in the fresh air.

"Mother, this time, when we go back to the kitchen, could we go through the portico? I don't like this dark place."

Abigail grimaced. "Oh, Jerusha, look at the scratches on your hands." She stopped, put down her pile of wood and wiped Jerusha's face. "Do I have black soot on my face, too?" she asked. Jerusha nodded in agreement. "We are a fine pair, aren't we? I should have listened to your father. He was right about Caiaphas. I don't know why I didn't see it."

"Don't worry, Mother, Father will come and get us," Abigail sighed.

"No, I fear he won't."

Jerusha's stomach tightened. Was Father angry at Mother? Or maybe he was angry with her? Mother's words sounded so final, like she knew something that Jerusha didin't know. What could it be?

On their return trip to the kitchen, they plodded up the steep, narrow, spiraling stairs to the ground floor. At the top, Jerusha breathed in the fresh air and rubbed an itch on her nose.

It was the first time she had heard the song thrushes. Fountains gurgled in the distance. They sounded so refreshing, then she heard a snicker and groaned. It was him. He strolled toward her. A beautiful girl, older than she, with clear blemish free skin hung on his arm.

"Look at you," he laughed, "Black soot is perfect. Blend in with that ugly, black mole." Jerusha touched her face and glanced up at mother.

"Don't talk to my daughter like that," she said.

"Too bad she doesn't have your beauty." He veered the young woman away and continued his stroll.

"Don't listen to him. Your father and I like your beauty mark. It makes you special." She wiped the soot and tears from Jerusha's face. "I wonder what happened to your father?" she added. Jerusha saw a tender faraway look on Mother's face. "Come, we must scrub the asla." Jerusha wondered why they must clean the toilet and looked up at the two soldiers who accompanied them. One towered high above like a giant in Roman armor. Praetorian guard? Father despised the Romans.

They guarded Caesar in Rome and the Prefect in Jerusalem. Usually rude and cruel. *What has this soldier done to be assigned the lowly task of guarding me?* Because his waist was at eye level, she stared at his sword, then tipped her head back to look up at his eyes. Hmm. She saw a flicker of kindness there. She glanced over at the other one who was a little shorter. He looked mean. Light and darkness. She was determined to know more about the taller one.

***

The stench of the asla gagged Jerusha. There were many holes in one long, marble slab with flowing water running beneath. She held her nose and helped mother knock loose the extra feces that the water had not washed away.

"Let's rest," Abigail said. *Finally*! Jerusha sat for a while on the marble seat and rubbed her back.

"Here, let me help you." She heard a deep voice and looked up. The giant stood beside them. The shorter soldier was gone. The taller one took the cleaning tools from their hands.

"I'll finish for you." His words were the first spoken in kindness all day.

"Why are you helping us?" Abigail asked.

"Yeshua, a Jew from Nazareth, healed the centurion's servant."

"You are a follower of Yeshua?" Abigail asked.

"In all my campaigns across the empire, I have never heard or known anyone like him. This man—this Yeshua. There is something about him. His words pierced my heart. He says to love your enemies. Do good to those who persecute you."

"My father likes Yeshua. He is a friend, but he does not like Roman soldiers. He says they are mean." She stepped up on the marble slab and peeked under his bent-over form and looked into his eyes. Something in his eyes. He winked. "You are not mean. Why do you help us?" He rose up and even though she stood on the slab, he still towered over her.

"I am tired of fighting. I have heard of your father."

Jerusha clasped her hands. "You have heard of my father? Have you met him? Do you know where he is? Why he does not come and get us?" She couldn't believe her good fortune. Well, Father would say that it was YHWH watching over them.

"Thank you for helping us," Abigail curtly responded and cut the conversation off. She stood tall and straight. "I think we can finish now." Jerusha saw anger in her eyes, the same anger she saw when Father talked about Yeshua.

"As you wish." He handed them the scrubbing tools.

Intrigued by this giant with shoulder-length blond hair and blue eyes, Jerusha gathered her courage. "What do we call you?" A broad grin spread from high cheekbone to high cheekbone.

He hesitated, then spoke with a deep drawl, "Call me Yogli."

***

That evening they cleaned up the best they could with a small bowl of water and put on fresh clothing supplied by Caiaphas. Jerusha's stomach growled with hunger. She longed to grab the bread that lay on the platters of fruit and meat and gobble it down. No food for them until they served the guests, hundreds of them. Tonight she and her mother were chosen to serve the high priest and his son in their private quarters. The other servants served over one hundred guests in the two main triclinium. It was a new word Jerusha had learned that day, a Roman word for a room that contained a dining table with couches on three sides. Always questioning, she wondered if Father would scowl if she knew a Roman word. She snuck a grape from the fruit platter and plopped it in her mouth before anyone saw.

"Here, you carry this." Mother handed her a lightweight basket with bread and picked up a large mosaic bowl full of fruit in one hand and a mosaic platter with lamb in the other. With a rumbling stomach, Jerusha followed behind with the bread. They wound through the garden alongside the pools. Jerusha yearned to get in the waters and be refreshed. Some men conversed waist deep behind the waterfalls that splashed into one of the pools surrounded by lush greenery. She kept her head down. She only saw Father's upper torso naked once. Accidently. He never disrobed in front of her. These men were like Efah.

One temple guard opened the large ornate door and led them down a hallway lined with white marble columns. He rapped on the double door at the end and opened it at the priest's request.

Caiaphas stood alone in front of the fire that burned in the corner. It reminded her to find a hiding place for her pendant when she got back to her room. Mother placed the bowl and platter on the table and reached for the bread basket from Jerusha. Caiaphas ran his finger down the side of her face.

"I will send for you tonight."

"Don't touch me," Abigail responded and jerked away.

Caiaphas grabbed her mother's arm and slapped her face.

"You belong to me Abigail, and you will do as I say." Mother glared at him. Jerusha's heart beat fast. "Guards, take them back to their quarters."

That night her stomach twisted in knots again. Numb, she just looked at the food. When mother coaxed her to eat, she shook her head.

"I'm not hungry." She collapsed on her mat in the darkness of their room, beaten down, worn out, and used up. Afraid to go to sleep, afraid that she'd get trapped in that dark, disgusting ball again, afraid she'd never come out, she snuggled closer to mother.

Suddenly the guards threw open the door.

"You," the temple guard, the shorter one, pointed to Mother. "Put these on and come with us." He tossed a clean tunic and robe at Abigail.

"Must I dress in your company?" Abigail said.

He ignored her plea and stood in front of the door. Yogli, the taller one who said he knew her father, turned his back. Mother crept to the dark corner and slipped out of her dirty garments into the clean ones.

"Mother, I want to go with you."

"You must stay here," Mother's voice muffled through the garment that slipped over her head. "Be brave. I'll be back soon," she said after her head came through the opening. Jerusha glared at the temple guard, who devoured her mother with his eyes, then grabbed her arm and jerked her through the doorway. Mother glanced over her shoulder, her weak smile not too comforting. She watched the three of them leave while the door slowly banged shut on its own, but the keys jangled and the lock clicked.

Alone and in the dark, Jerusha rushed to the corner and rummaged through the wool bag and found Father's robe and snuggled beneath it on her mat. She grasped the girdle that held her pendant in one hand, and with the other hand, she squeezed her fingers around one of the tzitzits on her father's robe.

"Will I ever see you again, Father?" she whispered, "Do you know about Efah's touches? Is that why I now live in this horrible place?"

Her eyelids grew heavy. Not able to stay awake any longer, she drifted asleep. She heard Father's voice. "No matter what the future holds, my little lioness, never forget I love you."

"I won't forget. I love you, too, Father," she mumbled. "Someday, I know you'll come for me."

He winked.

"You will come," she whispered, "I know you will come."

Chapter 10

Three Years Later

J erusha looked at the scars on her hands from the sparks that
dropped from the many fires she attended the last three years. She
wiped tears from her cheeks with calloused fingers. She and Mother
had been servants of the lowest sort, given the most back-straining,
filthy, and tedious jobs. Only when a special guest arrived were they
allowed the privilege to serve the high priest and his sons their meals.
Their tattered and torn clothes were removed and replaced with
a more appropriate attire for the occasion, only to be taken away
afterwards.

Sometimes, a fresh set of clothing was left for only Mother. In the
late evening hours, Jerusha would hear them summon Mother to come
to the high priest's quarters. Many times the following morning, she
would soothe a swollen bruise over her eye with cool water. Jerusha
never asked what happened. It was better not to speak of it. The
cramped quarters where they slept reeked of their own body odor,
among other unavoidable smells.

Her body's painful passage from childhood to maturity left her with curves like mother's that seemed to draw more attention than she wanted from Caiaphas. His stares unnerved her.

Numb, she stared into space. A fresh set of clothes for her lay on the mat. She had been summoned to serve the wedding feast for Efah. Ever since his betrothal to that beautiful girl who walked with him in the garden that day, she sunk lower and lower into despair. As his slave, he cast her off, like a woman's dirty cloth, sticking his nose in the air. She still hid the secret from Mother about what happened with him in the garden. Mother suffered enough at the high priest's hands, without the worry over her encounter with his son.

During these last three years, Efah mocked her, stripped her of her dignity with his looks, and then completely ignored her, acting like she didn't exist. Her greatest fear, that he would catch her in the garden again and force her to submit to his demands, never happened. She couldn't understand why she was not comforted by that fact, but every time she thought on these things, she only felt confused and troubled.

One part of her hated the thought of his touch; the other part felt drawn to him in a strange way. What's wrong with me? He doesn't want me. He doesn't love me. When she heard of his betrothal to another, something inside of her died. The news left her hopeless. She wondered if any man would ever want her, a woman defiled, to be his wife. Her only hope, that one day he would love her, died with his betrothal. Now they summoned her to serve at his wedding.

Methodically, she dressed. "Hurry," Mother had urged. "What's wrong with you? Why aren't you ready? They are coming. I can hear the music." Emotionless, she moved down the lavishly decorated hall to help with the festivities. The servants talked excitedly and rushed about preparing the wine and food. Even Mother smiled in anticipation of their arrival. Upon stepping into the great hall, she approached Mother, numb and lifeless.

"I can't do this. I feel sick."

"If you don't comply with Caiaphas's demands, you will pay a price. Stand over there in the shadows. Maybe he won't notice you aren't serving. If he motions for you, please, for your sake, obey."

Jerusha hid in the dark corner, hoping for the night to end without being called. Unfortunately, when the procession came through the door, Caiaphas and Efah saw her. They both devoured her with their eyes like a piece of meat. She cowered. Sickened by their looks, she tried to retreat to her quarters. The high priest caught her arm.

"Where are you going? My son and his wife must be served."

"Yes, sir," she replied and dropped her eyes to the floor. The last three years of servitude had humbled her. She no longer thought of herself as royalty. Her father never came for her.

Left a slave, to serve the one she hoped would one day love her, she bowed to the priest's request. Pouring Efah's wine, she closed off another part of her heart to love. No one would hurt her this way again. Not her father. Not the son of the high priest. Not any man.

***

A few months later Jerusha and Abigail were permitted to go to the temple under the watchful eye of Yogli. Since he kept his distance, Jerusha felt safe enough to challenge her mother's new interest in Yeshua. "I don't understand why you attend those foolish meetings, Mother. Yogli said Yeshua was crucified. His followers are doomed to be arrested. Maybe killed. You could be killed! Yeshua didn't restore the kingdom like Father thought he would. Those men are no more trustworthy than him." She glanced over at the giant, who stood next to the ornate pillar in Solomon's porch. The other guard, the temple guard, had other duties today.

Abigail grabbed her arm and yanked her behind the large marble column. "Hush, you are the one that's going to get us killed. Like I told you before, I've seen a difference in them. Watch for yourself how the slaves who are Yeshua's followers serve the high priest. They are kind, gentle, and obedient, even when he beats them. When I asked why they serve with such joy, they told me about Yeshua. They said he is resurrected like your father told us, that his kingdom is not of this world. It sounds strange, but there must be something to what they say or they would not serve with such joy and peace under these circumstances. It has made me want to learn more. But I won't risk taking you to the meetings."

"Well, that's good because I would not go!"

"You sound so much like me when your father tried to talk about Yeshua. That's why we are at the temple today—I want you to hear for yourself Peter, the fisherman. He denied knowing Yeshua the night of the crucifixion, but preached with power on Shavuot. Three thousand men from all nations repented and accepted Yeshua as their King."

Jerusha watched Caiaphas from across the temple courtyard. His eyes made her uncomfortable. She was glad she was not at the palace alone with him. That same old, creepy feeling crawled up inside. A warning. Get away.

She averted his gaze. Looking into his eyes made her feel dirty.

"Look at him dressed in his fine clothes all puffed up." Like Efah, he never acknowledged her existence, except with his filthy looks. She and Mother served him in silence, afraid to even speak in his presence.

Abigail urged her closer to Peter.

"I want you to be able to hear."

The crowd pressed in on them.

"Get out of the way!" Someone shoved her to the side and she watched him clear the people out. So this was where her other guard was today. Bullying other people around. Caiaphas's dirty work. The religious leaders paraded through the crowd. Caiaphas led the way. She heard her mother's voice like it came from a distant land.

"Is that the beggar that usually sits by the gate, the crippled one, the one we pass each time we come to the temple?" She felt her shoulders shake. "Look! Pay attention!" Jerusha awoke from her stupor, momentarily forgot about Caiaphas, and slowly turned her attention to the commotion around the fisherman.

Stunned, she answered, "It *is* the crippled beggar. He is walking!"

"Men of Israel," the fisherman began to speak, "the God of Abraham, Isaac, and Jacob, the God of our fathers, has glorified his servant, Yeshua Christos."

"That is the Yeshua your father knew," Mother whispered in her ear.

"It is in his name that this man stands before you today," the fisherman continued. "You crucified him, and he has been raised from the dead and he has been sent to you first, to bless you by turning each of you from his wicked ways." The captain of the guard grabbed the fisherman.

"You are under arrest," he bellowed and dragged him through the crowd. He didn't care that he knocked Abigail to the ground as he passed.

"Mother!" Jerusha gasped. "Mother, let me help you," she said and bent down to take her elbow. The crowd pushed against them as the mob tried to follow the guards. A man stepped to the other side of Abigail and pulled her up. He smiled politely and disappeared.

"Did you know that man?" Jerusha asked.

"Yes, I've seen him at Peter's meetings," her mother answered. "Let's go," she added as she coaxed Jerusha along. "I so wanted you to hear him. There's something about him, something about his teachings that gives me hope for us. We'll try to come to the temple again tomorrow. Maybe he will be back. "

"But Mother, he has been arrested."

"He teaches that with YHWH all things are possible," she replied.

"Like Father coming to get us?" Jerusha scoffed. Mother kept moving and ignored her sarcasm.

***

That evening Jerusha lay on the mat and thought about the day's events. *Why had the high priest taken the fisherman away? He healed a crippled beggar. Is that a crime?* His words vibrated with a spiritual authority beyond the understanding of a mere fisherman. A quick glimpse of his eyes, soft, in contrast to the shady, steel-eyed fishermen she had known, radiated a kindness, a gentleness, a peacefulness that reminded her of father. Even while the fisherman was being arrested, it seemed more like his enemies scattered before him. He carried himself like royalty. Not the cruel, prideful arrogance of Caiaphas. Just a quiet confidence.

Finally, she drifted off to sleep. In the darkness, she felt a hand slip down the front of her robe and touch places reserved for her and her future husband. She pushed the hand away. It returned again. And again she pushed it away. Her mind, a fog from deep sleep, couldn't seem to find reality. *This can't be happening. This is a dream.*

She jumped from the mat. In the shadowy, flickering of the night lamp she recognized his face. It was the high priest. She commanded herself to be confidant like the fisherman. She tried to stand erect and challenge him; instead, she dropped her head and muttered.

"What are you doing?" She slowly backed into the corner of the small room and clung to the wall.

He motioned with his hand.

"Come, lie down. I won't hurt you. I've mistaken you for your harlot mother."

"Where is my mother?" she asked, repulsed by his stinging insult.

"She must have gone outside to the garden—for some fresh air," he spoke, his eyes narrowing.

Jerusha remembered. Mother snuck out again. *If he finds out, she'll be arrested. Why did she have to go?*

With her back and head completely up against the wall, she started to creep toward the doorway. Moving along the wall, her hand felt the entrance to the secret opening that she had created to hide her precious box and pendant.

Trapped, she weighed her options. If she stayed against the wall and the high priest came to her he might find her treasure. If she moved any closer to him, he would grab her before she could escape. He must not find Father's gifts! She squeezed her eyes shut and whispered the words on the back of the pendant.

"Arise, Lord. Let your enemies be scattered. Let all who hate you flee before you."

A little more humiliation. A little more shame. What did it matter? I'm already ruined. A husband won't want me anyway. Sickened by what she had become, she started to move away from the wall toward the man who had stolen everything. She clenched her hands and wanted to strike him with all the force she had within. Having seen his agility in the past, she knew there was no escaping.

Instead of fighting, she closed her eyes, hung her head in submission, and waited for the inevitable, ready to do whatever she had to do, to keep him from finding her treasure.

"Father, where are you?" she mouthed silent words. Her memory flashed back to the comfort of his arms when he shielded her from Caiaphas's ugliness the day the harlot was stoned. "Where are you?"

Father's gentle, firm look quieted her thoughts. She lingered in the darkness. "Not all men have such hatred." With closed eyes she reached out to Father's image, stumbled and fell onto the mat. Her eyes popped open and darted back and forth in the shadowy darkness. He's gone! Caiaphas left! Relief flooded her being.

She scampered to the open door and checked both directions. Only the guard.

Why? Why did he leave?

Mother's words from earlier in the day drifted into her thoughts, "*With YHWH all things are possible.*"

Chapter 11

Weeks Later

"Mother, I want to go with you to hear Peter tonight," Jerusha pleaded as she grabbed her mother's sleeve. "I cannot stay here alone. Please! Caiaphas might come when you are gone."

"You are right. The danger of you staying behind is far greater than the danger of being caught with Peter." Abigail lovingly cupped her daughter's chin in her hand. "How very beautiful you've become."

Jerusha looked down. The only time she felt at all beautiful was when she was given new clothing to wear to serve the high priest's fancy guests. "Beauty doesn't matter. Not here."

Jerusha pulled out her comb and ran it through her hair. Their clothing was that of servants, but Mother was determined that she be clean and well-groomed whether serving tables or going to hear Yeshua's disciples. Thankfully the rains came this week and filled the mikvah bath on the roof.

She placed the comb and brush on the indented ledge above the bed. She was tired of the hard limestone slab that was so unlike her soft bed at home. At least it was wide enough for the two of them to share. Mother did her best to keep it soft with goatskin sleeping mats and a larger quilt that her midwife friend gave to her.

Jerusha's stomach growled. She thought of the lentil stew and bread she passed up. She couldn't eat, not when she thought her mother would leave the palace without her.

"I was hoping for you to hear Peter. I think you will be inspired! His words carry such power, such love. He is not afraid of the Romans or the Sanhedrin. He continues to speak of Yeshua as King and how his kingdom comes not with observation but is within you. I've seen him heal and deliver in the name of Yeshua Christos. These people are different—so different from any Jew I have ever known. I don't know why I didn't see this before. Your father tried to tell me. I should have listened to him."

"Father abandoned us," Jerusha replied, the bitterness obvious in her voice. She braided her long hair so that it hung over her right shoulder then walked toward the small, round sufrah table and ran her fingers over the smooth leather. "Why would you believe his lies now?"

"Jerusha, your father was forced to leave because I wouldn't listen to him. It was my fault."

"I blame him!" Jerusha no longer tried to hide the rage that built inside. She pounded her fist on the leather and the metal rings on the sides clanged against the wall. All of Father's words about love and Yeshua were lies. If such a king existed, why did she work as a slave for a religious man with lust in his eyes? "I'd stay here if it weren't for my fear of Caiaphas," she muttered through clenched teeth.

"Don't be bitter. Look at how Yogli and the others have treated us—with kindness and love. Something emanates from him that gives me hope. Death or arrest, I'm driven to know more. Are you sure you want to go?"

Jerusha poured water from a clay pitcher into a basin which sat on a special wooden table acquired for them by Yogli—a gift that would have been discarded had he not intervened. She wondered sometimes if Father had paid him to be so kind to her and Mother. She rubbed her fingers over the blue and yellow ceramic tiles, some broken, but the beauty still evident and splashed her face. She reached for the towel on the wooden peg. Her hand brushed over the crack, the secret hiding place for her pendant.

"I would rather risk death than being caught again with Caiaphas—that pig. He makes my skin crawl." She dried her face and neck, not able to remove the dirty feeling that lingered from his touches. The memory of the son's touches surfaced, too. *No one can know. No one! They will blame me.*

"Then get your cloak. We must hurry." Jerusha kept her eyes down, afraid Mother would ask questions—questions she couldn't answer.

Three staccato taps on the door. Jerusha gasped.

"Don't be afraid. It's Yogli."

Abigail cracked the door open and peaked through the small slit.

"Move quickly," he whispered. "We have only a few minutes before the other guard returns." He glanced above to the flat roof where the night guard watched over the slave quarters and the garden.

Abigail opened the door wide and took Jerusha by the hand. In the darkness, Yogli did not appear as friendly. The soldier's steely eyes assessed her, his square jaw firm and set. She eased her way passed his tall bulky form. What if Yogli double-crossed them? What if someone paid him more than Father?

"Can we trust him?" she whispered, after they moved a little farther ahead.

Her mother nodded and motioned her to be quiet. He led the way back inside the vast palace to a narrow stairway in the back of the kitchen.

His muscular arms grasped at a nearly invisible crack in the large stone wall, pulled it forward, and slid it over.

Jerusha glanced at her mother, a question in her eyes.

"A secret door," she whispered.

The flicker of the lamp in the kitchen revealed five or six others inside the passageway who stood a few stairs down in the dark. Jerusha's heartbeat quickened. With the help of Yogi, she stepped down the first deep stair. Abigail followed. The stone door ground shut behind her.

"It's so dark in here I can't see your face or my hand," Jerusha whispered.

Abigail guided her fingers to the wall behind them.

"If you keep your hand on this wall and make small, careful steps, you will find your way to the bottom without falling. Count the stairs. There are twenty-four."

Jerusha crept in silence and dragged her palm along the cold, damp stone. She stopped at an occasional mossy splotch and cringed. *Yuck!* A few more steps and a creepy critter ran across her hand. She gasped in the dank, musty air and shuddered. Panic threatened to erupt. Several more stairs lay ahead. A cobweb brushed her cheek. Frantic, she wiped it off and reached for the wall. Secure again with it under her palm, she continued. "If I counted right, I have two more stairs," she whispered. She heard water rushing. It was lighter now. With the last step beneath her feet, someone moved a large bush back.

"You made it," they whispered and took her hand.

"Mother, where are we?" she asked.

"Behind the large waterfall outside the palace."

Jerusha breathed deep, her senses awakened by the fresh water and flowering plants. She let the water wash over her fingers and followed a narrow path that came out from under the waterfall. *So many stars are out tonight!*

She followed her mother and Yogli down one street and then another. Each time someone came into view, they ducked into the shadowy darkness. When they arrived at the gathering place, three staccato taps on the door gave them entrance. She stepped into a small room lit with two lamps. It was like entering into another world—the warm greetings, the smiles, the peace—so different from the grim, fear-infested palace where she lived. Unlike the temple where the women had their own court, in this place, the men and women conversed with each other like an extended family meeting under a covered booth at the Feast of Sukkot.

"Abigail!" A woman waved and made her way toward Jerusha and her mother.

"Who is she?" Jerusha asked.

"She is the midwife that birthed you. Her name is Chaya. We have become friends at these meetings. Do you remember her?"

"Oh, yes, I remember. She is Timon's mother. I thought she looked familiar." For the moment, it was a relief to enjoy friendly faces rather than cowering beneath the demands of guards and doormen.

The midwife hugged Abigail.

"I'm so glad you made it tonight. It has been awhile. I've missed you."

"It's not easy getting away from the palace," Abigail answered. "I brought my daughter tonight." The midwife's eyes widened and she grabbed Jerusha's hands.

"So this is my miracle baby. You have grown so much these last three years. You're so beautiful, much like your mother." Jerusha pulled her hands away, shrunk back and touched her black mole. "My son will be here tonight," Chaya continued. "I don't know what's taking him so long. Do you remember Timon? He worked in your father's workshop. You know, he has been keeping it up since your father's been gone."

Jerusha didn't say what she was thinking. Timon probably needed a job. Who wouldn't grab the opportunity of running Father's famous woodworking shop? And what did she mean "since your father's been gone"?

Jerusha wanted to escape this conversation and averted her gaze across the crowded room. She eyed the stranger who helped her mother up that day in the temple when they visited with Peter. The dim lamplight in the darkened room gave just enough reflection on his face for her to be sure it was him.

"Mother, who is that man talking to Peter?" She noticed Mother's embarrassed look. *Probably my rudeness to the midwife. Oh, well.*

"That's Stephen," Abigail said.

When Jerusha turned her eyes toward him, she noticed him glance her way. *Oh, no!* She dropped her eyes, but her curiosity won out, and when she looked up again, she saw him slip away from the fisherman and move toward a crippled, gray-haired woman, not far from Jerusha. He squatted down in front of the woman and poured a few coins from a pouch into his hand. Even though she was uncomfortable with his close presence, she drew near enough to see him place the coins in the woman's palm, wrap her fingers around them, and mumble some words she couldn't hear. When he arose, he turned directly toward Jerusha.

"I have been wanting to meet you since that day I saw you in the temple with your mother," he said. With tender caution he took her hand in his and continued, "I know your father."

She stared into his eyes, unable to speak, unable to move. Her typical questioning mind went to work. *Who are you? How do you know my father? Where is he? Is he all right? Why doesn't he come and see me?* She was so absorbed with her quest for answers, she didn't hear the loud pounding on the cedar door that gave entrance to the small room.

The door flew open and a collective gasp went up from the people in the room. Instantly Stephen released Jerusha's hands and swished past her toward Peter, an apparent attempt to protect him. When he glanced back at the doorway he grinned.

"Timon! We're glad it's you, not the soldiers. Who is this you have with you?"

Jerusha backed away. She felt the cold, rough limestone against her hands as she tried to hide in the darkened corner, a quiet place where she could watch and be alone. She moved her head to see in between the people's heads. *Timon?*

He was older, of course, with a full beard and more muscular, taller. He stepped over the threshold with a woman in his arms. His muscles bulged even through the robe. The woman was tiny in stature; her gray hair hung lifeless and disheveled, her radiyd half off her head, her eyes red and swollen.

"Don't be afraid," he spoke softly, his voice much deeper than she remembered. The old woman appeared to be as light as a piece of lamb's wool. He knelt with ease in front of Peter.

"She came to my house. She's dying. Christos is her last hope."

The fisherman laid his hand upon the woman. Others gathered around. As they prayed, Timon stroked the woman's hair; her sobs soaked into his cloak.

Jerusha stepped a little closer; the shadows from the lamp flickered on her face. *It is him. He's changed so much since I was little.* She watched him slowly help the woman stand.

"I have no more pain," her frail voice trembled.

He wiped her tears, his strong, calloused fingers nimble and gentle. Still on one knee, he held his arms out, an obvious protective move to guard against an accidental fall or stumble.

Jerusha remembered Timon's politeness to her mother, his offering to carry the waterpot from the well home while she tagged along behind and jabbered a thousand questions.

"Thank you—thank you for bringing me here," the woman said. He rose up; his tall stature towered above the smaller figure.

"My pleasure," his voice much deeper than she remembered. And with a slight bow, he gave the woman a wink. His long, thick lashes accented dark eyes that fell on Jerusha who stood in the shadows behind the woman. Their eyes locked. She noticed his black brows arch slightly. *He's mocking me. Or flirting?* Heat rose in her face and she covered her black mole. He grinned a lopsided smile with a slight nod. Jerusha backed into her darkened corner again, relieved when Stephen made his way through the crowd and broke her view of him.

Both of us have changed. He never looked like that at me before. Of course, I was a little girl. She looked down at her curvy body and wrapped her cloak tighter.

She noticed Peter stood on the far side ready to address the people. Chaya and her mother moved toward her, Timon not far behind. She watched him greet those around him, his cheerful countenance contagious; the smiles and joy spread from one person to the next as he conversed.

Jerusha felt a hand on her elbow. Stephen. *Oh! Good!* A distraction that took her thoughts away from Timon.

"Please may I assist you?" he asked and led her to an opening on the floor with enough space for them all to be seated.

She glanced past him to look at Timon again, who pulled his gaze away from the older woman he talked with and turned, his dark brown eyes upon her. That twinkle in his eyes! A warmth spread through her body. *Oh, no. He is coming over here.*

Flustered, she sat with the other women on the floor. This was the first time she really cared how she looked. She didn't look up, but felt Timon's presence as he found a spot next to his mother. Stephen sat next to Jerusha, leaned over, and whispered in her ear.

"When Peter is finished speaking, I will explain about your father."

"Oh! How could I have forgotten about Father! Not that he hasn't forgotten about me," she responded. He smiled. Irritated and annoyed, Jerusha rolled her eyes. *Men! I want nothing to do with any of them.* She glanced at Timon and back to Stephen. *How could he just drop the statement, "I know your father," and calmly sit down? Doesn't he know I haven't seen my father in three years? I don't trust him. I don't trust any of them.*

The fisherman's voice boomed.

"The Sanhedrin has threatened us. We are not to speak in Yeshua Christos's name or we will be arrested. Of course, we must obey YHWH, instead of man. We know that his kingdom is not of this world. His kingdom is within us."

What? These men! How can a kingdom be within you?

". . . through much suffering you enter into his kingdom."

Well! If the kingdom is about suffering, I should be a queen.

Her thoughts drifted back to when she was with Father. *"Never forget who you are. You are royalty . . ."*

"I'm not a little girl anymore, Father. I don't believe your stories," she whispered in reply, as though he could hear her now. She glanced back at Peter, scanned the room, and observed everyone's faces. Her mother's eyes glistened.

Her father's words echoed from yesteryear in the garden the night he sent her away. "You must trust me," he had said. *No, Father. You are a traitor. You left me,* she argued silently. *You follow this strange and unusual King. That's why Caiaphas hates you. I almost hate you as well. Deserting me. Leaving me to live a life in fear and servitude to him.*

Timon startled Jerusha. His voice boomed loud and clear.

"Let us pray to our father!" He stood now beside his mother, his arms extended.

Another man across the room shouted.

"Yes, let us entreat our father. He will help us!"

Others joined them and raised their voices in unison with them.

"Sovereign Lord, who made heaven and earth and the sea and everything in them, who through the mouth of our father David, your servant, said by the Holy Spirit . . ."

Jerusha pulled on her mother's sleeve.

"Who is this father they are praying to? Are they praying to David? He can't help them. Foolish men!"

Her mother sat still, eyes closed, chin lifted, unresponsive. Jerusha felt wet drops on her hand. She looked over at her mother, and even in the low lamplight she saw glistening tears drip from her jawline.

"Mother? Are you all right?" The volume of the prayers increased, and Jerusha guessed that her voice was lost in the sound.

". . . for truly in this city there were gathered together against your holy servant Yeshua, whom you anointed, both Herod and

Pontius Pilate, along with the Gentiles and the peoples of Israel, to do whatever your hand and your plan had predestined to take place. Look upon their threats and grant to your servants to continue to speak your word with boldness."

Jerusha looked up at Timon now standing beside Peter whose words continued to flow and mix with the others, ". . . while you stretch out your hand to heal . . ."

Somehow, among the growing noise in the room, she heard her mother's voice.

"Forgive me, Father. I have sinned against you and your son, Yeshua Christos."

Peter's voice rose above the others, ". . . and signs and wonders are performed through your holy servant Yeshua."

"I have never heard prayers like this in the synagogues." Jerusha continued to pull on her mother's sleeve and her mother's voice joined with the people.

"Take my life and fill it with your Spirit." The sounds ebbed and flowed spontaneously in beautiful, unorchestrated reverberations that made her shiver. After awhile, the walls rumbled and shook, the floor vibrated. Jerusha scooted back so that her back was entirely against the wall. Yogli wobbled beside her, using his large spear to keep himself balanced. Jerusha instinctively looked for the doorway. She wanted to escape but there were too many people between her and the doorway.

"What's happening?" she shouted to no one in particular.

"I am not sure," Yogli answered in his deep voice.

"It's an earthquake!" a young girl cried from across the room. Jerusha saw a mother pick up her daughter and run outside. The heavy cedar door banged against the wall. She held the baby in one arm, squatted, and placed the palm of her hand on the ground and yelled.

"It's not an earthquake. It's perfectly still out here," she laughed and hugged her daughter. "It's not an earthquake!" she yelled again.

Inside the room Jerusha felt the vibrations of the floor. Lamps shook, the wicks vibrated eerie shadows on the wall. Peter widened his stance and extended his arms to keep his balance. The quaking stopped. Nothing damaged. Nothing misplaced. Faces full of awe and glory tipped upward.

"Hallelujah," Abigail softly said, tears still flowing unbidden. Her eyes were closed in reverence.

Chaya giggled just a little. Jerusha looked at the two of them. *Are they mad?*

Timon, now beside her, chuckled softly.

"He is here."

"Hallelujah!" Peter shouted. "The Spirit of the Lord is here! He is with us, as he promised!"

Jerusha hugged her cloak and scooted a little closer toward the door, away from her weeping mother and giggling midwife—away from Timon who unnerved her both by his presence and his obvious faith in Yeshua.

The elderly woman stood up and lifted her hands, then clapped in rhythm to the old familiar Jewish celebration hymn. Someone handed her a tambourine, and she slapped it slowly at first, then built up the meter until people stood to their feet and formed circles of dance and stepped in rhythm to her tambourine. Her crackled voice sang out the words of Moses' and Miriam's song: "The Lord reigns! Forever and Ever!"

Round and round they went, some to the left, others circled to the right, hands raised, voices full of laughter and song. Something deep within Jerusha stirred—something she had forgotten. Dance.

Chaya finally pulled back from her circle, laughing and crying at the same time, and stood near Jerusha. Jerusha stood to her feet behind her.

"What just happened?" she asked. "What's wrong with you?"

"Oh, Jerusha, the Lord has answered our prayers," she said and hugged her tight and long.

Jerusha rested her cheek against her shoulder.

"Why haven't you answered my prayers?" she spoke quietly to this invisible King. "Why haven't you sent my father to rescue me? Are these more worthy?" Her eyes blurred. She tried to blink back the salty teardrops, but they trickled down her cheek into the corner of her mouth. Toughen up. This is senseless. She pushed away and rubbed her face with the back of her hand. "How am I ever going to hear what Stephen has to say about Father now? All this noise—this jubilation—

this commotion," she mumbled in disgust. It was so loud in the room, she knew no one heard her.

Mother now stood beside her, arms raised in surrender, eyes closed; tears streamed down her face. Stephen knelt, arms uplifted. Jerusha shook her head in disdain.

She watched Yogli lean over and reluctantly tapped her mother's shoulder.

"We must get back to the palace." He turned to Jerusha. "We must go."

Stephen looked up.

"We'll talk again. I have much to tell you about your father."

Jerusha nodded. Something about these people reminded her of Father. Memories of his words and his laughter flooded back to her. She smiled just a little and then stopped herself. What if it was all a lie? Quickly, her defenses flew upward, and she guarded her heart from thinking any further about her father. It was easier to think of him as gone forever. Even better, not to think of him at all.

Chapter 12

The cool evening breeze rustled the silver-green leaves of the olive trees that covered the mount and soothed Jerusha's nerves. Stephen had finally summoned them to come. *Two weeks! About time!* He sent word through Yogli and arranged for a few hours reprieve from their palace duties.

She and her mother stood on the ridge and looked across the Kidron Valley. An orange globe descended in the distance behind the white limestone wall and spread a fuchsia glow across the horizon. She heard her mother whisper, "It is so beautiful. It reminds me of your father. How I miss him. We came here sometimes and watched the sun set."

Jerusha moved from the stony path and leaned against an old olive tree, its trunk twisted and deformed, and admired her mother's beauty. Her mother's countenance had changed so much since that night when the room shook. Along with a quiet, peaceful glow she had never seen before on her mother's face, Jerusha had watched her converse in the marketplace with such confidence about Yeshua, the King, whom she once despised. She no more cowered in fear. She no longer scorned Father.

The guard stepped from the shadows. Jerusha jumped and slapped her hands over her heart. "You scared me. I forgot you were there," she said.

She heard Stephen's voice from a distance. "Shalom," he said as he climbed the last stretch of path to the level ground where they waited.

"Stephen, thank you so much for arranging this," Mother smiled. "Anything you know about Jacob will be a blessing!" Her dimples deepened.

"It's an honor to serve you." He took her mother's arm and walked her toward a large flat rock and looked at Jerusha. "I'm so sorry it's taken me so long to meet with you again. I'm sure you have many questions about your father." He tried to give the customary greeting kiss. Jerusha recoiled and moved past him to her mother. She noticed he hesitated momentarily, head cocked, and eyed her with an assessing look. Finally, he spoke and pointed to the rock.

"Please, be seated." Jerusha felt mother tug her arm.

"Come, sit next to me," she urged. Jerusha obeyed, her gaze still fixed on Stephen.

Yogli separated himself and sat on a large rock, out of earshot. He appeared to be guarding their meeting, and Jerusha wondered again what made this man so kind. Why did Yogli care to help them at all? Is Yeshua's love so great that even a Roman soldier succumbs to its power?

Stephen retreated to another rock across from the women.

"I met your father soon after you left with your mother to live with the high priest," he said quietly. "Even though I had seen him many times in the crowds before Yeshua's death and resurrection, it was only after he risked everything for you and your mother, that I knew for sure that he was one of us."

Jerusha crinkled her brow. *Risked everything?*

"The night you left, he was taken to the palace and flogged."

Mother gasped.

"What? Why?" Jerusha asked. Mother cringed and grasped her hand.

"Luke, Caiaphas's physician and one of us, treated him and took him to a secret tunnel below the city. While he recovered, he instructed me about his plans for you and your mother."

"But—"

He raised his hand to stop her from speaking.

"Please, I know you have many questions. Let me finish."

"He loved you and your mother. When the high priest coerced her into—well, into coming to the palace to live, that old scoundrel threatened your father and said he would have her stoned if your father didn't agree to let you and your mother live with him. He doubted the high priest had honorable intentions toward your mother, but hoped for the best. He never knew you became his servants. He expected that the high priest would make you both part of—well, part of his family, I suppose. To keep your mother from being stoned, Jacob had to agree to never see either of you again."

They both gasped.

"Did you know about this?" Jerusha asked Mother, her tone raised.

"No," she responded quietly. "The only thing I knew was that your father gave me a writ of divorce—at my request."

"At your request? Why?" Jerusha asked.

"Because I was deceived. I was afraid his beliefs would get us killed. I believed Caiaphas loved me and—"

"Loved you? Mother! Are you out of your mind?"

"Perhaps I was out of my mind." Abigail's head dropped and tears dropped onto her lap. "I believed we would be safer with him, even though he had a wife. How foolish I was. I didn't know of his threats or that your father talked to Stephen." She looked at Stephen now.

"Why didn't you tell me about this?"

"He asked me not to tell you."

"Why would he do that?"

"Because he thought you would tell Caiaphas and put us all in danger. He planned to come back, when the time was right, when he heard you were ready—were one of us—and take you out of Jerusalem. I watched your heart soften toward Yeshua, our King, over these last years. I knew, by the Spirit, the night the room shook, that you'd surrender to him. That's why I approached Jerusha and told her I knew her father. It was time."

Stephen stood and approached the women. He squatted down in front of them and looked toward the horizon. He took a deep breath before he continued.

"The night Jacob left Jerusalem—" he said, 'no one must know that I have spoken to you about this. Keep me informed. I'll be back soon.'"

"Father told me to trust him, that he *had* to send me away," Jerusha said, "and that he *loved* me. What kind of love is that? How dare he leave me with a self-righteous, arrogant—" she stopped suddenly. The familiar churning in her stomach, that same old nauseating feeling that twisted and turned inside, tore at her insides.

Strangely, Jerusha felt no animosity toward her mother, only sadness for the terrible hardship and division in her family. Besides, Mother had already paid a high price for her foolish trust of Caiaphas. Anyone who saw her eyes bruised from time to time could gather that her life was not easy.

"I never saw your father again after that night. We talked until dawn. He told me many things about you and . . ." he hesitated and looked tenderly at Jerusha, "your father made me promise that if for some reason he was unable to return, when you came of age, I would contact you and arrange for your marriage to one of us."

"What do you mean *one of us*?" she interrupted. "That's the second time you have used those words." She jumped to her feet, stomped her foot and blurted, "Never mind! My father has no right to arrange my marriage. He left me! I hate him!"

Stephen now stood face-to-face with Jerusha and peered into her eyes.

"Although I don't know why he has never contacted me again, I know that wherever he is, he longs to be with you."

She slumped to the rock and buried her head in her mother's chest. The garden echoed with the sobs that had been pent up for three years in her secret prison.

Stephen's shadow passed over Jerusha's face as he stepped away from them and went over to talk to Yogli. She heard his whispered words, carried by the wind into the distance. The leaves rustled. The doves cooed. The evening shadows crossed the garden path and enclosed them in darkness. She looked up with tearstained cheeks and saw him beneath the olive trees. He stood next to the soldier and waited.

Abigail lifted Jerusha's face to gaze into her eyes.

"Please forgive me for all the pain I have caused you. If I hadn't listened to Caiaphas's lies, we would still be living with your father." Grasping her hands, she continued, "Your father did the only thing he could do. Caiaphas gave him no other choice."

"I don't believe that," Jerusha retorted. She broke free of her grasp, stood, and walked away. The city lights sparkled in the distance like fireflies. "If he loved us, he would have found another way. Why didn't he just take us away with him?" Her words echoed across the valley. A soft breeze carried her mother's scent, frankincense, an oil given to her by father. It was the one thing that Mother kept from him when they went to live at the palace.

Abigail followed Jerusha to where she stood, looking over Jerusalem. "Jerusha, if you are going to hate someone, hate me. I am the one who caused your pain. I told you, Jerusha, I wouldn't go with him. If there was another way, he would have taken it. He loved you so much. He loved me, too, even though I pushed his away." She stared up at the stars. "Where are you Jacob?"

Yogli signaled them. "We must go," he said.

The full moon cast enough light to see the path. Stephen helped Abigail and Yogli helped Jerusha down the rocky slope to the bottom. After awhile, the path widened and the men walked behind the women. Jerusha glanced up at her mother; the beams on her face revealed a calm. *Where does such peace come from?*

"What did Stephen mean, 'one of us'?" she asked. Her body quivered from the cold air.

Abigail shared her outer cloak to protect from the cool, damp mist that soaked her tunic. When Jerusha's teeth stopped chattering, Abigail spoke.

"Stephen, myself, and many others believe that Yeshua, who was crucified and arose from the dead, is the Mashiach, the Messiah. He is adding to us daily those who are willing to surrender all that they are and all that they own to follow him and obey his teachings. Even some of the priests have become one of us."

"Is this the Yeshua we knew?"

"Yes."

"What kind of King allows himself to be crucified?" Jerusha mocked.

"One that loves, even his enemies. One that comes to serve, not be served. One that humbles himself to show the way," Abigail continued. "One who forgives, even those who crucified him."

Yogli helped them back into the palace through a side entrance unnoticed. He escorted them down the corridor to the kitchen, more nervous than usual, fidgety.

"What's wrong with him?" Jerusha whispered, "He is troubled about something."

"I have noticed it, too," her mother responded. "I can't imagine what's got him so disturbed."

When they got to the door to their room, he stopped before he opened it, then turned toward them. "Come with me," he said with a stern, dark countenance.

Jerusha's heart thumped faster. She glanced at mother, who had stopped and stared intently at Yogli's eyes.

"Is this necessary?" Mother's voice sounded weak and fatigued.

"Yes, follow me."

Mother breathed deep and released it.

"If we must," she said.

"I don't trust him," Jerusha said.

"Please, I'm too tired to argue. We will go with him. He's been a good friend and never betrayed us."

"How do you know he hasn't? Maybe he is the reason the others have gotten arrested. Maybe he's a spy."

"Jerusha, I know you have trouble trusting, and I am partly to blame for that. But he wouldn't risk getting caught with us in another part of the palace if he didn't have a good reason. Now come on," she said. Mother grabbed her hand and pulled. Jerusha stumbled forward. They walked across the kitchen and out the back door that opened into the animal shelter.

The horses neighed and snorted. Jerusha had come many times in the past years to nuzzle her face against the beautiful, white thoroughbreds. She patted their rumps.

"Shush. It's okay. It's just me," she said and walked around to their heads and rubbed their noses. The soldier stopped and waited with her mother at the far end of the shelter.

"Please hurry," he said.

Jerusha eyed the soldier carefully. *What kind of trap does he have waiting for us?* She plotted in her mind a way of escape, if necessary, and then followed them out of the shelter. They crossed into an area that she and mother had never been allowed entrance, the outer courts of the soldier's quarters. Yogli looked around and knelt down by a bush, removed a rock, and pulled a parchment from a hole beneath the rock. Jerusha stood a distance away and watched him give it to her mother.

Men's voices in the quarters got louder as they approached. Jerusha ducked behind the armory and watched Yogli yank mother behind the bush. *Why would he risk bringing us here? He's in danger, too, if we get caught.* The Roman soldiers passed; their hobnailed sandals echoed a frightening alarm.

Yogli slipped from the hiding place, helped her mother stand, and approached Jerusha. She saw mother slide the parchment into her cloak and pull her radiyd over it and cover the bulge. The soldier motioned to her to follow. She willingly obeyed this time.

"I've hidden this parchment for a while. I should have given it to you a long time ago. Forgive me. I hope it brings you the hope you so deserve," he said.

"What is it?" Abigail asked.

"You will see. I will leave you to read it with your daughter alone. I recovered it from Caiaphas's fires one night. I fear he has had many such parchments burned. I'm sorry I didn't give it to you sooner."
He disappeared into the darkness, as they were near enough now to quietly make their way back. She knew he stood nearby.

Once inside their room, Jerusha's curiosity burst forth.

"What is it, Mother?" She rubbed her arms to warm herself. The brazier fires in the corner had gone out and the reddish orange embers gave little light or heat.

The lamp, which never went out, glowed from the ledge above the mittah, their shared bed. Somehow they got enough oil to keep the lamp burning day and night, a reminder of YHWH's constant care. Abigail removed it and placed it next to her on the mittah, where she sat down. Spear-shaped figures bounced on the walls.

"Come, sit with me." She patted the space beside her. Jerusha nestled close, smelled her mother's frankincense, the expensive oil given to her by her father before they became captives, then she watched and listened to the stiff parchment crackle a bit when her mother unrolled it.

"Be careful with it, Mother." Jerusha touched her arm. Abigail stopped, then unrolled a little more until the scroll lay open in her hands. "What does it say?" Jerusha sked.

"It's too dark to read. Here," she reached for the lamp, the only light source in the room, and handed it to her daughter, the scroll rolling back up. "Hold it up so we can see." Jerusha took it with one hand and held it high over the writing and leaned in close. Her eyes stung a little from the smoke of the burning olive oil. She noticed her mother's hands, now free, trembled as she uncurled the partially burned scroll.

In the flickering light they read the words out loud together, "Abigail and Jerusha . . ."

"It is a letter to us," Jerusha spoke with surprise.

They continued reading, "I pray and trust that you will get this letter. I know Caiaphas will have spies guarding against you having any contact with me."

"Father?" Jerusha asked, the lamp wavering in her hand.

"If you hold that still," her mother spoke, a slight tremor in her voice, "maybe we'll find out."

Jerusha steadied her hand, and they bent down again over the parchment and continued reading together. "If you receive this, know that I have gone to prepare a place for us. I will come again to get you."

"It is from Father!" Jerusha said. "Does it say where he is?" She strained her eyes to read the previously burned portion to find the answer. The scorched letters smeared together. "It's useless, Mother. I can't make it out. It's too burned. Why hasn't he come? It's been such a long time. Is he dead?"

Her mother's silence caused Jerusha to look over. She saw sorrow in her eyes, charcoal smudges on her face from the parchment, and a trail of tears moved through the dark smears and dropped onto the back of her hands. The letter fell to the dirt floor and rolled up at her feet.

She waited in silence, not sure what Mother was thinking. Just when she was about to ask if she was all right, she heard her tender voice.

"Jacob, I am so sorry. Wherever you are, I'm ready to follow you to the uttermost parts of the earth. I just hope it's not too late."

Jerusha ached inside. She replaced the lamp on the ledge, wrapped her cloak tighter around to keep out the chilled air, and snuggled next to her Mother, who had curled on her side and clutched her cloak, too. This time they slept on the hard stone and placed the sleeping mats over them.

It was too late at night to get dung to refuel the brazier fires. Jerusha wished she had been more dutiful. Yuck! Even after this long time of service, the task repulsed her. She felt mother shiver.

"Regrets. So many regrets," Abigail moaned. After awhile, Jerusha tried to bring comfort, her eyes heavy with sleep.
"Maybe we can escape and look for Father. If he's still alive, we'll find him."

Chapter 13

"Just a few more days, Mother," Jerusha said, raising her voice above the marketplace noise.

"Don't talk of our plan in public," her mother warned with scrunched brow.

Accompanied by the guard, they searched for the woman who sold herbs needed for the Pesach meal, the yearly Hebrew feast that celebrated the Israelites' deliverance from slavery in Egypt. This celebration was Jerusha's favorite. She believed *this* story told by Father; all good Jews believed it. The plagues. The parting of the Red Sea. Miriam's dance. A good day for their escape. Surely, YHWH will make a way for them, too.

Tambourines jingled in the far side of the marketplace opening. Jerusha peered through the shoulders of the men in front of her. A young girl twirled around, arms lifted high, in the middle of a circle of older children, who laughed and sang. Jerusha swayed with joyful anticipation of freedom. Maybe she'll find Father. If not, at least she'll be free again. The musical jangles mixed with the sound of hundreds of bleating lambs the herdsmen brought to sell.

She felt a slight nudge on her leg and turned. The small, nappy-headed creature begged with innocent, dark eyes. A man in a colorful robe pulled on the rope around its neck and knelt down to examine it for any blemish. The herdsman stood beside him, waiting. She never liked this part. The lamb's death. His blood. Poor thing. One spotless lamb needed for the sacrifice in the temple for each haburah, a fellowship of families that partook of the meal together, usually in someone's home. Stephen made arrangements for her and Abigail to gather with him this year, a part of their plan to escape the palace and the city. Of course, Yogi must be their guard that day.

She felt her mother's protection, much like she had felt as a small girl in the crowd a few days before Pesach, keeping a close watch, the tight grasp of her hand as she squeezed between two men with their backs to them who barely acknowledged their presence as they passed by. So much pushing and shoving in the crowd. The population of Jerusalem swelled with Jewish pilgrims coming to the holy city, maybe a million or more. She gazed at their tents that dotted the hills outside the city wall as far as she could see.

Yogli towered high enough above their heads to keep track of them. Jerusha stretched her neck to look behind. His eyes caught hers and then looked behind her to the Roman soldiers positioned at the gate. Three more days, on Pesach or Passover as the Greeks called it, she'd walk out. She smiled at him. He nodded, kindness in his eyes. She would miss him after they left the city.

Her mother conversed with the woman and exchanged a few coins for the herbs. They moved from the crowded marketplace up a steep hill. In the west, the sun was setting and the road seemed to glow in front of them. Jerusha always liked this time of day. She couldn't be sure, but this seemed like the same path that led to her old home. *Yes. It is. There's the grove of olive trees that I rested under on the way home with Father from the Gihon spring.*

"Mother, why are we going this way back to the palace?"

"I wanted to see our old house. See if there's anything left of our old things. See if your father left any evidence of where he might be found. Maybe another letter."

When they entered the courtyard twenty minutes later, the old gate creaked open. Jerusha felt a rush of excitement. Startled by a slight movement among the pomegranate bushes in the evening shadows, she knew they weren't alone and stopped.

"Shalom? Is someone there?" Jerusha called. Behind the dark green leaves, a frail woman rose. "Who are you?"

"Don't you remember me?" she answered, her voice quiet, kind, a little familiar. "I knew you when you danced here with your father." Jerusha's mother now approached the woman. "Naomi! It's been such a long time. What are you doing here?"

"I have come here ever since the night you left and they took Jacob. I always feared this King he believed in would get him in trouble, but I came after his arrest to take care of this place until he returned. He said he'd be back. Three long years it's been."

"Oh, Naomi, you must believe in Yeshua. He fulfilled all the prophecies. His kingdom has come. He's ruling now, even though we can't see him."

Jerusha cringed and nudged her mother.

"You'll get us killed speaking like that," she whispered.

Naomi smiled.

"I have great respect for you, but I can't believe. Yeshua was just a carpenter from Nazareth. You should be careful whom you talk to about this. There are rumors that soon many will be arrested because of him. I won't give you away though. You are my friends."

"Oh, it is so good to see you. Thank you for taking care of this place. You are a loyal servant and friend. Do you have food and a place to live?"

"Yes, I live with my family now. I come here when I can just like I told your husband I would. Who is he?" she pointed to the guard.

"He accompanied us today to the market. Excuse me, I need to talk to Jerusha alone." Her mother tugged on her cloak and moved out of hearing distance to speak to her. "You do understand that we can't tell her about anything—that we are slaves—that we plan to escape . . ."

Jerusha interrupted, "Or that you believe in this King."

"Yes, I took a risk saying that, but she needs to know the truth. Look how loyal she's been, even knowing what your father believed. Hear heart is tender to receive the truth."

"Well, she needs to hear the truth from someone else. Right now we need to concentrate on getting out of the city alive."

"Naomi knows better than to ask too many questions. She knows if I want her to know something, I'll tell her."

"Mother, I want to leave. This place brings back too many memories of father. I long to see him, to find him. Can we leave now?" She watched her mother glance around the courtyard. The guard waited at the gate. Naomi stood in the darkness under the decorative door mantle. Jerusha's eyes strained to see in the darkness.

"Mother, what's that?" she asked. "Do you see that tiny white sticking above the mezuzah?"

They both rushed to the doorposts. Jerusha pulled out a small piece of parchment and held it up in the open courtyard so the full moon shown on it and read her father's scribbles. "I'll be back," her voice quivered, eyes blurred. She crumpled on the bench.

"Remember when we left that night Mother, we touched the mezuzah. He knew we'd be back one day and left this message for us to find. Where are you, Father?" She felt her mother's hand on her shoulder, glanced up, and saw her motion to Naomi to leave them. The gate creaked and she disappeared.

Abigail sat beside Jerusha and took her hands.

"I don't know what has happened to your father, but tonight the secret meeting is at Stephen's. Maybe he'll have more answers for us. Let's go. We won't find anymore answers here." They left the dark dwelling behind, their memories awakened, their questions unanswered.

***

Unlike the previous meeting places, they came to a beautifully carved cedar door guarded by a porter who unlocked it for them. Stepping inside they found a spacious courtyard surrounded by several buildings and porchways. Decorative pillars supported the roof beams, and delicately carved lintels were displayed above the doors. This was like a palace compared to the overcrowded single rooms illuminated by a small, high window and a few small wall lamps where the secret meetings had been held in the past.

Large candelabras provided enough light to see the faces of the people seated across the courtyard on stools. They talked and smiled in subdued conversation surrounded by beautiful and well-cared-for shrubs and flowers. On the far side of the courtyard Stephen laughed as he conversed with the men whom Jerusha had learned from previous meetings to be the other leaders of the Yeshua followers.

Jerusha and Abigail retired with the other women in an area surrounded by flowering pomegranate bushes. The fragrant red blossoms awakened memories locked away behind a wall. The smell nauseated her as she closed her eyes and remembered the terrifying moments with Efah. *No, please, no,* she had pleaded. *It hurts.* The pomegranate bushes that brought such delight when with Father now only brought guilt and shame.

"*My little lioness, I have something to give you.*" She remembered staring at the small box he held in front of her. "*I have put pomegranates on the outside—they remind me of you . . . a protective covering has grown around your heart.*" He had cupped her chin in his hand and raised her face so he could look deep into her eyes. "*One day the covering will be taken away and you will remember again who you are, from the tribe of Judah. You are royalty.*"

She shivered and wrapped her cloak tighter. *If I find Father, he must not know what I have become.*

A man's loud voice caused her to look up to see what was happening.

"Our widows have been overlooked in the daily serving of food!" he said.

A purple butterfly fluttered in front of her and landed on the red pomegranate blossoms and drew her attention away. *Let them argue among themselves. The butterflies congregating among the bushes are a more inviting attraction.* One lone butterfly broke from the crowd, landed on her lap, and spread its wings. It seemed to beckon—come, fly away with me.

"I envy you, little butterfly. So beautiful and free."

A wisp of wind stirred the bushes and the butterflies scattered, a flurry of color across the courtyard. Momentarily, a blue butterfly stayed on her hand, then lifted its wings in a good-bye gesture. It joined the purple butterfly nearby on the lintel and drew her attention to Stephen who stood next to Timon, his head bowed in humble submission along with the other five men.

Jerusha listened.

"You have been chosen because you are men full of the Holy Spirit." She glanced away, but not before Timon looked over and saw her. A lopsided grin spread across his face.

Embarrassed, she dropped her chin and fiddled with her fingers. Peter's encouragement continued, "We will devote ourselves to prayer and to the ministry of the word, confident that YHWH will move mightily through you, for the scripture says he supports the fatherless and the widow." His prayer boomed loud with authority. "Empower them with your wisdom from on high."

The whole assembly agreed, "Amen. So be it!" and gradually dispersed, a few at a time.

The two women waited to speak with Stephen. Disturbed by his delay, Jerusha watched him pull a few of the leaders aside, and they ducked into a room just off the courtyard.

"That's strange," she commented to Mother. "What is he doing?

"Oh, he's probably getting instructions about the widows."

"He looks like he's talking about us. He keeps looking over here," she said.

Peter nodded as Stephen talked. Determined to find out what they plotted, Jerusha rose and moved a little closer so she could hear what was being said.

"I agree," Peter said. "Now is the time. If you wait any longer, you will miss the open door." They wrapped their arms around Stephen. While they prayed, Jerusha moved back to stand with her mother, who waited eagerly to talk to Stephen.

"Does he know of our escape plan?" she asked.

"Yes, he knows. He's the only one I confided in. He agreed that Pesach would be the perfect time to leave the city unnoticed. And he promised to talk to Luke to find out where your father was last seen and arrange for our safe passage there." Jerusha saw Stephen stop Timon at the large cedar door before he left. While the two men stood under the lintel and conversed. The porter held the door open.

"What are those two planning?"

"Jerusha, you are way too suspicious of people. They're probably just talking about the widows." Unable to trust no man and convinced she had reason to believe Stephen was up to something, Jerusha ignored her mother's reprimand.

"Here he comes."

"How are my two favorite ladies?" Stephen's jovial demeanor unnerved Jerusha.

"What have you heard from Luke about Jacob?" Abigail asked.

"Not much more than I've told you in the past. When Jacob left here, his plans were to travel to Pella. Luke does know of a family that met Jacob, but they haven't seen him for years."

Jerusha watched mother's dimples disappear.

"Does Luke think he's still alive?"

"He doesn't know. He has no word either way."

"We'll find him," Jerusha said, trying to comfort her mother, even though her stomach churned at this unsettling news.

"I will accompany you back tonight. I have some business with Caiaphas. He still doesn't know I am a Yeshua follower. It's important that I hide my identity. I hear rumors in the palace sometimes that helps protect our meetings from being exposed."

***

Stephen's somberness on the way back to the palace troubled Jerusha, but she kept silent, not mentioning it to her mother. While hiding in the bush, they watched him enter the palace through the main entry. The soldiers seemed to know him well. When Stephen was inside, Yogli led them around the back behind the waterfall and up the now familiar dark passageway. When he pushed with his broad shoulder against the stone door, a sliver of light broke through the darkness and momentarily blinded Jerusha.

A deep, unfamiliar voice cried out from the kitchen, "Halt! You're under arrest!"

At that moment a flash of silver in the darkness came into her view. Her eyes, now adjusted to the light, widened. A muscular man with a sword had come around the heavy door. With the full force of the man's weight, he sword scabbard came down on Yogli's head. He crumpled to the stone floor. Blood covered his eyes from the wound. Jerusha shrunk back inside. One soldier jerked Yogli out of the doorway and she heard his body scrape across the kitchen floor as he dragged him out of the way. The other soldier's tall, dark presence blocked their entrance. She saw his hobnailed feet at the top of the stairs.

"We know you're in there. We've been watching you for weeks. Your outings have just come to an end. I am your new guard. This traitor will be flogged and thrown in jail. Maybe taken to Rome." The women gasped. Jerusha thought of running down the stairs and out the back. Too late!

The other guard, who smelled like leather, perspiration, and ale, reached into the darkness, grabbed her arm and yanked her into the light. She heard her mother cry out.

"Don't hurt her. It's my fault," Yogli moaned. Jerusha's feet hit his bloodied face as the guard dragged her through the kitchen, and she glanced back at Abigail, who scampered up the stairs behind them and stared at Yogli. "I'm so sorry, Yogli. It is my fault," Abigail said as another guard yanked her away.

"Leave him alone. He's going to pay. The insubordinate traitor!"

Jerusha's guard dragged her like a rag doll down the portico and threw her on the cold tiles of her room. The other guard threw her mother on top of her, and she watched her roll and hit the wall. The heavy cedar door slammed shut. Keys jiggled in the lock. She peeked through black stands of hair. Her mother lay motionless, quiet.

"Mother? Are you all right? Wake up!" She scrambled onto her knees and shook her mother's shoulders. "Wake up!" Abigail's eyes blinked open as they heard the sound of a whip crack against flesh.

"Yogli?" Another crack. Jerusha covered her ears. And another. The giant groaned between each crack of the whip. She scrambled to the door and tried to open it.

"Stop! Stop!" she pounded until splinters tore her skin.

"You can't stop it." Her mother groaned.

"Mother!" She ran back to her. "Let me help you." They staggered to the mittah and collapsed.

"We are trapped! We will never get out of here. We will never find Father. We will never be free." She felt mother stroke her hair in the darkness. The chilled air soaked into her robe.

"YHWH will make a way where there seems to be no way. Just believe, Jerusha. Just believe."

Chapter 14

Jerusha held her breath through most of the awful flogging. When the horrendous punishment stopped, she got up and stirred the embers of the brazier in the corner to warm the chill in the room. Her mother kept her hands busy, too, and rolled out the soft, fur mats on the mittah and swept the floor with their broom.

"How did they know?" Jerusha said quietly. "Who gave us away?"

"I don't know. Yogli is the only person in these courts that has truly been a friend to us."

Jerusha shuddered. "Do you think they will send him back to Rome? I hear—"

"Hush now," her mother said softly. "We will pray now for Yogli, for it is all we can do.

I am more concerned about what Caiaphas will do with us now that he knows."

Jerusha's eyes widened, her heart raced. What will Caiaphas do?

"I am sorry," her mother answered. "I should not have said that. I am—I am just so shocked, so upset. We will be all right." Her halfhearted smile troubled Jerusha. "Here, come lie down." Her Mother patted the mat beside her. "Things will seem better in the morning. Every day is a new beginning."

"We need a new beginning. Our plan to get out of here is ruined now." Jerusha filled the lamp above the mittah with olive oil and crawled in beside Mother and covered herself with her robe.

"You said, 'Just believe.' How do I believe? Every time a flicker of hope springs up, something comes along to put it out."

Jerusha felt Mother reach out from under her robe and pat her leg.

"It will happen, Jerusha. It will happen." Her voice sounded tired. "Yeshua Christos's father desires for you to know him—to become his child—to know his Son." With each phrase, her words slurred together. "He will reveal him to you." Sleepy and worn out, she barely got the last phrase out. "Just as he revealed him to me." Within seconds Jerusha heard her mother's deep and heavy breathing.

She closed her eyes, too.

Mother believes. Father believes. I want to believe. A picture formed. *From the back, he looked like Father, long colorful robe, long dark hair. He held the hand of a little girl dressed in a sparkling white gown; her black hair flowed down her back past her shoulders. They walked barefoot in a meadow of various shades of green grass splattered with a rainbow of different flowers seen across the horizon. As they walked through the grass, colorful butterflies filled the atmosphere around them. The young girl dropped the man's hand and skipped after the butterflies. Her hair bounced as she twirled around and around, her arms extended, hoping to touch just one of the blue, yellow, or purple butterflies. The man picked her up and lifted her into the air. She giggled and returned safely to his arms. From her mittah, Jerusha giggled, too. So did he. He lifted her again—higher this time! Again the girl giggled and simultaneously Jerusha giggled, too. Another giggle from Jerusha. The next time, as he boosted her ever so high, she stayed in the air and morphed into a purple butterfly, beautiful and free. In the mittah, Jerusha spread her arms out over her mother and smiled. "My little butterfly," the man said. She moved in free-flowing circles across the meadow, dipping and fluttering from flower to flower. The man turned to leave. Suddenly she was again a little girl with the purple butterfly in her hand.*

"Don't leave me," Jerusha's words echoed in the darkness. She stared at his back as he retreated across the green meadow.

"I'm not," he responded and continued to walk away. "I'm always watching you."

"Don't go! Don't go!" she pleaded. The butterfly flew away and she reached toward his disappearing form in the distance.

"Wake up," her mother shook her shoulders. "You are dreaming." Jerusha sat up.

"I'm his little butterfly."

"Whose butterfly?" her mother asked. "I don't know what you're talking about."

"Oh, Mother, I think it was Father, but I'm not sure. I couldn't see his face. He kind of looked like Yeshua. It may have been someone else. I was little again and he tossed me up and caught me, and I turned into a butterfly and I flew across the meadow and—and it was so real. Why do you look at me like that?"

"For just a flicker of a moment I saw that same sparkle in your eyes, the same carefree joy, the same radiant smile that has been absent for so long. Jerusha, I am sorry. It was just a dream."

The smile faded from Jerusha's face as she looked around the room and remembered where she lived and whom she lived with.

"We have overslept. We must hurry. Caiaphas is receiving a special guest today and we must prepare for him," her mother said. She quickly straightened her hair and placed the veil in place. "Caiaphas left fresh clothes for us."

Jerusha moved slowly wishing she could slip back into that place in her dream where she was a little girl who giggled and played with butterflies. She sighed and trudged behind her mother as they left their quarters.

The guest arrived in the afternoon, reclined with Caiaphas in the courtyard garden, and drank the wine they had left for them earlier. He had received similar guests through the years, always from the Sanhedrin. This one was no different, dressed in his robes of nobility and leisurely eating and conversing with him.

When Jerusha entered the courtyard with the bread and fruit, the guest leaned on his forearm with his back to her. His ornamental cloak shielded her from seeing his face, although she recognized his voice. She hesitated but a moment before proceeding, at Caiaphas's command, to serve them. She kept her eyes down.

"What is Stephen doing here?" she asked her mother after she had left the courtyard. "Do you think he's the one who gave us away?"

"I don't think he would do that."

"I don't trust him. Why didn't he tell us he was a part of the Sanhedrin? Does Peter know?

"I'm sure he does. They have no secrets."

"We need to warn Peter, just in case he's a spy. He may be telling Caiaphas where the secret meetings are. I don't want to get arrested," Jerusha whispered and glanced around to be sure no one else heard.

"After last night, I'm sure he already knows about us and the meetings. He's probably been watching us for a long time."

Stephen returned numerous times over the next several months. Each time he ignored them, not acknowledging that he had any idea who they were. During those months, the women were unable to get away and talk to Peter about what happened to them the night their guard was arrested. It was too dangerous to send a written message.

One evening Jerusha saw Stephen pour coins into Caiaphas's hands and was certain that he plotted their arrest. Later that night, a servant called for her mother to go to another area of the palace. Jerusha was left alone, without a companion as she returned to their room.

A shadow moved behind her. Her heart thumped loudly in her chest and she paused. The shadow stopped, too. *If I can just get past the courtyard gate, I will be safe.* She took off and ran as fast as she could down the corridor. Almost there. When the she passed the gate, someone grabbed her arm and pulled her close. Caiaphas!

"How unfortunate for us that your mother rarely leaves you alone. Neither of you are of use to me any longer. I have arranged for another man in the Sanhedrin to experience your delicate services. Tell your mother to pack only the things you came with. You leave tonight. I have sold both of you."

"Sold us?" she inquired. "To whom?"

His mouth curved up slightly on one side. "To someone who needs your services. You and your mother will make good concubines for him," he laughed. "I really don't care what he does with you." As she struggled against his grasp, he shoved her away. She landed on her side on the tile floor, once again feeling the sting of being discarded and humiliated.

His black robe swooshed over her face as he passed by and forced her head down with his foot. He smashed against her face against the cold stone floor and laughed wickedly, then walked away. She glared up at his back and mouthed the words, "I hate you," through gritted teeth and watched his dark silhouette disappear into the shadows.

Trying to get up, she tugged at her garments now tangled in her feet. Unintentionally, this brief struggle with her clothes provided the necessary moment she needed to calm herself or she would have run after him and smacked him in the back or worse, slapped his face. Once standing upright, her immediate concern turned toward mother. She rushed to the servants' quarters to give her the news. There Abigail was bedding down for the night. She grabbed her shoulders.

"We've been sold. We leave tonight! Caiaphas said to take only the things we came with."

Hurriedly retrieving her treasure box from its hiding place, she opened it and removed the pendant. She carefully rubbed her fingers across the delicate carvings her father had engraved on the pendant and recited the words on the back. "Arise, Lord. Let your enemies be scattered. Let all who hate you flee before you." The old melody formed that she had sung so many times as a child. It had been years since she had looked at the pendant. She smiled. The golden crown hidden in the lion's mane still sparkled in the lamplight.

Slowly the words and another melody came together in her thoughts. "I am the lion of Judah. Deep within my inner most being dwells the Holy God of all Israel. I am the lion of Judah." Where did that come from? I don't remember hearing that before. "I am not a lion. The man in my dream said I'm a butterfly," she whispered.

"What are you mumbling about?" her mother asked. Jerusha looked up.

"Um—oh, nothing."

A moment later Father's words encircled her in an echo from the past.

"My little lioness, you are royalty. You are from the tribe of Judah."

"Father, where are you?" she whispered and placed the pendant back inside the box, wrapped the box in the purple cloth, and hid it inside the girdle she'd made from old rags. Tying the bulging girdle around her waist, she hoped to hide it beneath her head piece.

Caiaphas must not find her treasure box, the one thing she owned that gave her worth.

Her thoughts drifted back three years to the night she had come to live with him. How scared she was winding down the dark pathway getting farther and farther away from Father, the only man she felt safe with. At first she dreaded nighttime. Falling asleep nearly always caused her to sink into that horrible place. Eventually in her dream she found the light in the darkness. If she'd look up, far in the distance between the layers, she'd see a distant flicker above her head, a blinking light reflecting off the lion's crown. She'd scratch and claw her way through strand after strand of yarn, string, and sticky gunk.

Reaching out for the pendant, she'd awaken empty-handed, at first disappointed; then she'd smile, knowing the pendant waited for her in the wall. Whatever happened tonight, her pendant, her treasure, hidden safely next to her beating heart, spoke of hope for tomorrow. Leaving these slave quarters behind, she'd find a way to escape the slavery that lurked ahead.

Her father called her a lioness. Why? Her heart longed to be free, like the butterfly. Who was the man in her dream? Where was Father? Was he alive? As usual, she asked so many questions—all without answers. At least she was leaving this horrible place. Mother said every day is a new beginning. Only YHWH knows what lies ahead. She looked at Mother, who stood at the door ready to go.

"We're leaving, mother! We're finally leaving! Like you said, 'tomorrow's a new day.'" Abigail dropped her things and hugged her tight. The rhythmic thud of the guards' sandals against the tiles grew louder and louder outside the servants' quarters.

Chapter 15

Jerusha wrestled with her veil to make sure it covered the bulk protruding beneath her robe.

"Where do you think we are going?" Abigail shrugged her shoulders. "I don't know. I'm just glad we're leaving this place. Anywhere will be better than here."

Someone pounded on the door. Startled, they hurriedly picked up their few belongings. The guard's keys jangled in the lock and the door flew open. A grim-faced guard blocked their exit, sword-in-sheath by his side, his legs spread shoulder-width apart. He pointed to the guard behind him.

"Follow him," his gruff voice and the fierce look in his eyes alarmed Jerusha. Her heart pumped vigorously with excitement and maybe a little fear. This was her last departure from this room, never to serve Caiaphas and his son again. But where were they going? She shuddered, scanned the room, then brushed by her mother and extinguished the lamp, the one they kept burning continuously since their arrival, a constant reminder of YHWH's care. Sandwiched between the two guards, they marched like soldiers through the large, wide-open kitchen. The aromas of leftover lentil stew and fresh baked bread for the next morning reminded Jerusha she hadn't eaten, too troubled by the interchange between Stephen and Caiaphas, coins given, probably a sign of betrayal. Maybe their arrest. Her stomach growled in protest. As they made their way through the torch-lit corridor to the main entrance of the palace, she and her mother hurried to keep up with the soldiers. The last time she crossed this threshold, she clung to her mother. Tonight she led the way, the first one behind the guard, Abigail next, followed by the last guard.

Jerusha felt eyes watching. She stopped and glanced around. There in the shadowy corner she saw him—Efah. He smirked. She pursed her lips together and tightened her jaw. Caiaphas stood across the room by the fireplace, the same one he had thrown her pendant in that first night. The wood popped and crackled. She felt the girdle around her waist and knew her treasure was snug and secure.

"Hypocrites! If the people only knew how perverted and corrupt you are! Rome's puppets!" She whispered softly enough so the guards could not hear her words, but loudly enough to vent her anger. When the guard yanked open the heavy cedar door with gold reliefs, she turned her back on both of them, she hoped forever. The force of the night air blew her robe back

"Stop your mumbling!" the shorter guard commanded as he shoved her through the doorway. Jerusha lifted her chin and stepped over the threshold, never to look back. The others followed, and the big ornate door slammed shut. Once outside, she breathed deeply of the night air. The first guard led the way. With long legs, he pounded his hobnailed sandals down the tiled steps at a quickened pace and never looked behind him to see if they could keep up. Following the well-conditioned and fit guard proved exhausting, especially for her mother. She had aged over the years, the heavy, backbending work taking its toll on her body.

"Here, Mother, let me help you," Jerusha said and took the small bundle from her arms. "Hurry," the guard prodded. Exasperated, Jerusha stared up into his menacing eyes and kept walking but slowed down in defiance and tried to give her mother a reprieve. The guard shoved both in the back.

"I said to hurry!"

Hungry dogs growled from a dark corner.

"Shut up, you mongrels!" the guard yelled.

Jerusha heard Mother's heavy breathing. "Are you all right?" she asked.

"Yes, I'm fine," she answered. A thick fog hung over the streets and prevented the travelers from seeing too far ahead. Jerusha juggled the bundles from one hip to the other and grabbed her mother's elbow, just in case she stumbled. Out of breath and gasping for air, they finally stopped. The guard clanged on the gate and yelled for someone to open it. "Mother," Jerusha wheezed, "this is Stephen's dwelling. Are we *his* servants—or maybe—maybe under house arrest?" The iron gate creaked open. Several smiling servants greeted the women.

"Shalom! Come in. Come in. We've been expecting you." The guards turned about-face and quickly left, much to Jerusha's astonishment. She watched their shadows disappear into the darkness and heard their swords thump against their armor as they tromped in unison back down the path. Anxious, she looked around the courtyard. An eerie mist hung over the pomegranate bushes. In the shadowy lamplight the scarlet blossoms looked like splotches of blood against the dark green leaves. Trying to relieve the tension in her chest, she breathed in deeply and exhaled in a long, jagged breath. The puff of breath lingered in front of her in the cool air. She cocked her head and listened to a deep, familiar voice that came from the other side of the courtyard.

"It was imperative this was done tonight," Stephen said. "I wanted them out in time for the next gathering." The words sounded muffled, maybe behind a closed door. Jerusha lifted the front of her robe with both hands so she wouldn't trip as she tiptoed closer to the voice. The next words boomed clear and distinct.

"When is the next one?" he continued. "I was told it was tomorrow. Will it be here?" *Traitor!*

"Yes, it's tomorrow at Luke's place. We've had to be more careful, so we changed it again," Peter answered. Jerusha cringed and tiptoed back to Mother. She fidgeted, then cupped her hand around her mother's ear and whispered, "I wonder why Peter has not been arrested?" Her eyes widened to a new revelation. "Stephen is using

Peter to find out where the followers meet! We must find a way to talk to him alone and soon."

The door creaked open and a sliver of light cast a man's dark shadow across the blue-and-white-tiled path that led to the courtyard. The shadow moved through the fog until he stood in front of the women. Jerusha watched a grin spread across Stephen's face.

"I see you have arrived safely," he said. Jerusha wiped the nervous sweat from her palms on her tunic and asked, "Would it be possible for us to meet with Peter alone?" An unexpected quiver in her voice caused her to glance down, afraid her eyes would give away the terror she felt. Her stomach churned. "I will ask Peter if he will be able to join you. I must leave and attend to another matter." She glanced up and saw him look at them in deep thought.

"Please, will you excuse me?" he asked. After they nodded, he crossed the courtyard to speak again to Peter.

"Attend to another matter, indeed," she whispered to Mother. "Does he think we are fools?" They watched the especially long conversation with Peter. Stephen shook his head like he didn't agree with him. Finally, he strode across the tiled floor with long strides, his silken cloak flapped in the breeze that came from the opened cedar door to the veranda. A porter stood guard there as if awaiting further instructions.

"He has agreed," he announced over his shoulder and hurried over the threshold and disappeared into the fog. Jerusha stared at the porter while he closed and latched the heavy door. When Peter approached, he pointed to the bench beside the pomegranate bushes and cleaned the moisture off with his sleeve.

"Please have a seat," he said. "What can I do for you?" He placed his hand under Abigail's forearm and helped her be seated. Jerusha remained standing and glanced around the courtyard to see if they were alone. She pointed to the door and blurted.

"Quick, you must follow him! He's a traitor. He's informing the high priest about where the followers meet. He may be going now to summon the guards to arrest us." Peter eyed her carefully.

"And you heard him say these things you accuse him of?" he asked. "No, I never heard exactly what was said to the high priest," she stuttered. His tall stature and confident demeanor intimidated her.

"But he met with him numerous times these past months. We've heard the rumors that many of our friends have been arrested during that time. It must be him that gave away their secret meeting places. Did you know he is in the Sanhedrin?" "Yes, I knew," he answered calmly. "There are things you don't know, and I do not have the freedom to reveal them to you. You must receive the information from Stephen himself." "You won't follow him to see where he's going?" "No, I'll not humiliate my friend by checking up on him. I trust him. He's a man full of the Holy Spirit and wisdom. Now, will you excuse me," his words stung like a reprimand. His crinkled brows and turned back as he left the courtyard spoke an even stronger disapproval. Abigail tried to stand. Her knees buckled and she landed with a thud back on the seat.

"What have I done?" she whispered and leaned her head into Jerusha's waist, who still stood in front of her and stared at the door through which Peter had left. "I have accused an innocent man," Jerusha felt the warmth of her mother's breath through her robe. "I know Stephen well. He would not betray us. Why did I think otherwise?" "Stop it!" Jerusha yelled. Her disrespectful tone caused her mother to look up. "We're not wrong!" she yelled and stomped her foot. "This man is a traitor. Peter should have listened to us. He's deceived. I've never trusted him and never will." She swung around. Her robe swooshed in her mother's face and she felt a tug.

"No, Jerusha, Peter is right. We've accused an innocent man."

Jerusha tuned back around and shook her mother's shoulders.

"Why do you believe him?" she yelled, then gasped and backed away, ashamed of how she acted.

"Because," her mother started to answer, then she stopped. In the silence Jerusha heard the song thrush in the distance. "I'm sorry, mother," she whispered. Abigail pushed off the bench, her body obviously tired and achy, and stood straight, her dark hair hidden behind the radiyd. She stared directly into Jerusha's eyes. Peace. Jerusha felt it. Peace. Her mother spoke clear, quiet, and slow.

"Peter is a trustworthy man!"

Jerusha looked away. She clenched her fists. Every muscle tightened. "No man is trustworthy!" she spewed.

Jerusha thought she heard someone clear his throat and looked through the fog in the direction of the sounds and saw a figure by an ornate pillar across the courtyard. Whiffs of air blew the fog away to reveal a young boy, who stood tall and straight. Moonlight broke through and shone on his face.

"If you will follow me, I'll show you to your quarters," he said. Jerusha felt her mother's movements beside her and pulled her eyes away from the boy. A wave of guilt passed over her for yelling at her mother, but she just stood and watched her mother pick up her belongings and start to follow the boy down a torch-lit corridor. Even in the shadowy darkness, the tiny blue and white tiles beneath their feet beckoned her to follow. She stayed behind, though, and stared at the door. *Fools! Left me alone with no guard. I can escape. But where would I go?* She shrugged her shoulders, grabbed her belongings, and hurried to catch up.

"Wait for me," she cried. Partway down the corridor, the boy hesitated and then opened one of the double doors, twice his height, and stepped inside. Jerusha's leather sandals clopped on the tiles, and she almost skid to a stop behind Mother, who stood under the beautifully carved lintel. She leaned around her mother and looked into the room. Her jaw dropped. The bedchamber was furnished with two beds with purple silk pillows obviously arranged to give the bed an inviting beauty, delicately painted tiled tables with blue bowls of fruit, blue platters of bread, and a wineskin bulging with wine

"This is your sleeping quarters," the boy said.

"You mock us," Jerusha spoke.

"No, I would never do that," he answered. "We were instructed to prepare this room for you. We worked on it all day." "We?" "The servants," he answered.

"Why are you serving us? We are servants, too."

"I'm not at liberty to discuss that with you. Clean tunics hang on those pegs and there's clean water for bathing over there. Please go in," he coaxed. "It's prepared for you." Reluctantly, they entered. He left them standing in the middle of the room, gawking at the ornate furnishings.

"Mother, what's going on? Could we be Stephen's concubines? Remember what Caiaphas told me. He said we'd make good concubines, and Peter said Stephen had something to tell us."

"No!" Abigail spoke firmly. "I told you. He's an honorable man. He would not do that to us." "He bought us as his slaves. He can do whatever he wants with us!" she retorted. "No!" Abigail swirled around to face her daughter. "I'll hear no more talk of this. He's an honorable man." Jerusha's cheeks burned at her mother's rebuke. Silently, she turned her attention to the room. The comfortable surroundings made her keenly aware that she stood there in her old garments, dirty and hungry. Mother freshened up for bed, changed her old garments for the new, and chose a bunch of grapes from the bowl. She sat down and patted the bedcover.

"Come," Abigail beckoned. "Eat some bread. Drink some wine." Jerusha folded her arms and turned her back.

"You hurt only yourself by your stubbornness," Abigail added.

Jerusha retreated to the corner and rolled out her old bed mat, wrapped her old cloak around herself, and curled up for the night. Her stomach still growled. She would not be Stephen's or anyone else's concubine. She'd rather be arrested, thrown in prison, or even die. No one would do what Caiaphas and Efah had done. Not ever!

Chapter 16

At dawn, Jerusha awoke to a soft rap on the door. She yawned, stretched her achy arms above her head, and rolled over. Shivering in the damp air, she wrapped her cloak tighter around her shoulders, sat up cross-legged on the dirty sleeping mat, and slipped her arms into the cloak.

"Who's there?" she asked and glanced around the room. It was even more beautiful in the early morning dawn, the multicolored mosaic pillars on each side of the door sparkling in the light. She closed her eyes and breathed in a sweet fragrance that came from the far side of the room. She got up from the tiled floor, moved to the latticed window, and peeked through the square openings. The garden outside the window held an array of colors; orange, scarlet, and white blossoms were splattered among the rich, deep-green and silver-green leaves. The sun reflected off one lone, purple butterfly near the window that sat on a colorful tiled bench. *Oh! You're so beautiful! Phew!* She stuck her nose in the underarms of her dirty clothes soaked with sweaty body odor and looked up. The unused bath water glimmered in the yellow and white ceramic bowl on the table beside her mother. She watched mother rise from the soft cushions, slip into her cloak, and walk barefooted to the tall, ornate double doors.

"Who's there?" she asked. A child's voice answered.

"My uncle sent me. I'm sorry if I woke you." Abigail opened the door and peeked out. Jerusha could see through the small opening a young girl. Three, maybe four years old. The bright-eyed child smiled and summoned with a wave to follow.

"Just come as you are," she said. "He returned a few moments ago and wants to meet with you—now—before he goes to sleep. Please hurry!" she urged and motioned again with her hands. "It must be important." "Tell him we'll be right there," Abigail answered and shut the door.

"See, we are his concubines," Jerusha spoke and wiped the sleep from her eyes. "I told you he is not trustworthy. I'm glad I rejected his bribe gifts. I'm glad I'm not clean or well dressed." She swaggered across the room and waved her arms. "Hush! I told you I will not listen to such talk," her mother replied and straightened her radiyd. "He is an honorable man." In the early morning hour, the doves outside their window cooed and entreated Jerusha to yield to her mother's wisdom. She refused.

***

Jerusha looked at her mother, who moved with dignity across the courtyard in her new silk garments. The odor from the fragrant oils she had used permeated the air as she passed by. Her eyes smiled above the new radiyd that hid her face. So beautiful! Not Jerusha. She rolled her eyes and dawdled in her tattered, smelly garment, her radiyd barely in place over her nose and turned-down mouth. "Did they not leave a clean garment for you?" Stephen asked. He stood beside a marble pillar and moved toward them. "Is my appearance not acceptable, sir?" she mocked, satisfied she caused a slight raise in his brow. He continued, "I thought the widows had prepared a new garment for you. Were you not pleased with what they made?" His eyes looked kind and gentle as he now stood before them, his arms spread in a gesture of concern. She ignored the kindness she saw in his eyes. *Traitor! Spy!* she thought.

"I paid no attention to your bribes, even though my mother partook of all your dainties." She saw Abigail turn her head with that look she got as a child when she was disrespectful. Jerusha shrugged.

"Look at her—dressed—clean and ready for you." "I can see you misunderstood my intentions," he said and moved away. "Humph!" She crossed her arms in defiance. "I don't think so." She watched him lean back against the pillar, cross his arms over his chest and raise one hand to his chin in contemplation. A tug on his tunic by a young boy pulled his attention away from her, and he squatted down to speak to him. She heard giggles and stepped away from Stephen and followed the tiled path around the gurgling fountain. Even at this early hour, she saw several children laughing as they played with homemade toys; boys with wooden sheep, girls with stick dolls. Some of the children reminded Jerusha of her early years with her father as they chased the butterflies from plant to plant. One small girl clutched her hands together.

"Look, I got one," she said to Stephen. "Be careful not to squeeze too tight," he said. "It's better if you let it go." She looked behind her to another area of the courtyard. Older women guided the fingers of young girls as they taught them the intricate rhythm of weaving on looms. Other children watched intently as women sewed with wooden needles, making new garments. She thought of the clothes left for her in the room and almost regretted not wearing them. But no. Her smelly clothes showed Stephen where she stood. She looked up and watched her mother gravitate to the far corner of the courtyard. Older girls held babies and entertained those too young to participate in the weaving and sewing. Others nursed. Are all these his wives? She never heard whether he was married and raised her eyebrows at her next thought. Maybe some were reserved as concubines, their duties performed at night. When Stephen finished speaking to the child, he waved at Abigail and Jerusha to follow him. They left the crowded courtyard and entered another room off the veranda. Her growling stomach reminded her that she'd not eaten. Eyeing the meat, fruit, and bread on the tables, she wished she'd partaken privately of the meal left for them the night before in their room.

"I will not accept his dainties now," she whispered to herself and bolstered her resolve. "Please, let's eat," he said. "I'm hungry and we

have matters to attend to before I retire for some much needed sleep."
He poured water over his hands from the cleansing pitcher and offered
it to the women. Abigail accepted. Jerusha declined. He ignored her
denial.

"Please join me," he entreated as he moved to the couches
around the food table, stretched out, and leaned on his left elbow and
forearm. Again she declined and moved as far away from the couches
as possible. Stephen's brows peaked as he again ignored her denial and
waited respectfully for Abigail to make herself comfortable before he
spoke the traditional thanksgiving offering.

"Blessed art Thou, Jehovah our God, King of the world, who
causes to come forth bread from the earth." A slight tap at the door
interrupted the uncomfortable trio. Stephen rose and opened the door.

"Shalom, my friend!" He greeted Timon with the customary kiss.
"I'm sorry we didn't wait for you," he said. "I wasn't sure you'd return
in time. I'm so glad you're here to celebrate with us." Jerusha backed
further into the corner, determined not to be his concubine either.
She recoiled behind her radiyd and covered her face. She finally
glanced up. Their eyes met briefly before she looked down again. He
was dressed in a silken robe, not the everyday wool tunic that he'd
worn at Stephen's dwelling the last time she was here. This intrigued
her—and troubled her. He nodded and removed his headpiece, then
turned to wash his hands.

"We have accomplished much these last months, but there are
many widows and orphans that still need help," he said and placed
a torn piece of bread in his mouth and washed it down with a sip of
wine.

"God will provide," Stephen replied and reclined again on the
couch and placed some bread in his mouth. "Now let's give our
attention to these ladies." He smiled and pointed to Timon, who by
this time had stretched out on the couch across from him. "I have
summoned him here for a twofold reason. I admire and trust him. Full
of the Spirit, he serves the widows and orphans with integrity and
honor." Why does he brag so much of this man? Jerusha mused from
her hiding place in the shadows. *I won't be his concubine either*, she
thought valiantly with upturned chin. The familiar churning in her
stomach tormented once again. The increased secretions in her mouth

signaled a wave of nausea that threatened to overtake her. She closed
her eyes, gulped, and begged her body to submit to her control. *Don't
throw up.* She gulped again. *Don't throw up.* She squeezed her eyes.
Don't throw up. She watched Stephen stand and pat Timon on the
back and continue.

"The first reason I've summoned him here is to be my witness." He
picked up two scrolls with gold seals from a nearby table and handed
one to Abigail. "Your debt is paid. I give you your freedom." Her
mother stared at the gold seal on the scroll.

"You bought my freedom?"

"Yes. When I heard from Caiaphas about Yogli's arrest and
flogging, we decided to use Caiaphas's greed to our advantage. Many
of us gave toward our offer to buy your freedom. We only wish Yogli
could have been saved, too. We heard they took him to Rome."

"Oh, no!" Abigail cried. "He was so kind to us. After his arrest, I
prayed nightly for him. Jerusha and I will forever be grateful for Yogli's
kindness. It tore us apart as we listened to each strike of the whip."
She glanced down at the parchment in her hands. "I'm—I'm most
grateful for this," she stuttered and clutched the scroll to her heart.
"But I do not deserve such generosity and love."

Jerusha, still hidden in the shadows, looked at her mother. Her
eyes darted from her to Stephen.

"What about me?" she asked, her voice quiet and filled with fear.
"What about my freedom?" Her voice began to tremble and grew
louder with each word. "Am I not worthy? Am I too dirty? I suppose
you want me for a concubine?" He kept his distance.

"No, Jerusha. I don't want you for my concubine. Yeshua Christos
our King gave his life for you. That makes you valuable—of worth
beyond measure," he spoke softly and extended the scroll. "I give
you your freedom, too. Your debt is paid." She stiffened. Her gaze fell
on Timon, who had risen from the couch and now stood beside her
mother, a short distance behind Stephen. Her eyes flashed between
them. "Please accept your freedom. I promised your father to watch
over you. He would want you to be free, free to choose." "Free to
choose? Free to choose what?" She froze, unwilling to accept the scroll,
afraid of what it would mean. Stephen placed the scroll back on the
table.

"The first reason for Timon being here today is to be a witness to your freedom. The second reason is because of the promise I made to your father. I know you want to travel to Pella to search for him. I, too, want to find him, especially for you and your mother's sake. But I fear something may have happened to him. He wouldn't have left you and your mother here for this long. Something has prevented him from coming. He may be in jail or worse. Everyone I have talked to, who has traveled that region, has not seen or heard from him. It's as if he's disappeared off the face of the earth. If he could be in Jerusalem, I know he would be here. He loved you so much. It's for this reason that I want to present Timon to you. I promised your father to follow through with his plans, if he was not able to be here. He wanted so much for you to be protected and loved by someone that was one of us, knowing that the King's love would flow through that man. I tried to tell you about this that evening with your mother on the Mount of Olives. Because of the covenant I made with your father, and because he's not able to be here, I present this man for your husband." He pointed to Timon. "He has accepted my offer." She stared at Stephen's back as he grasped Timon's shoulders with both hands and spoke, "On behalf of her father, I speak the traditional betrothal. "You shall be my son-in-law." Stephen withdrew from Timon and stood beside her mother. Jerusha wanted to run away. This can't be happening. Father wouldn't do this. She felt trapped, unable to escape. Somber and reserved, Timon approached. She looked into his eyes. Gentle. Compassionate. He reached into his robe. She jerked back and bumped her head on the wall, but noticed he held a wooden box. It looked like the one her father gave her, the same pomegranates carved around the bottom.

"Your father gave this to Stephen. He told him that you would know that this came from his hands. I extend it to you as proof that your father has approved this betrothal. I have placed a gift of my own inside the box."

Jerusha grabbed her girdle and felt for her treasure box. Yes. It's still there. He reached out for her hand. Back against the wall, she couldn't move any farther away, so she allowed him to place the gift in her shaking fingers.

"By this, you are set apart for me according to the laws of Moses and of Israel." Breathless, she stood, her eyes fixed on the box. It looked like it came from Father. She tried to fight back the sickening nausea that sought to overwhelm her again and laid her head against the wall. The spots in front of her eyes faded into darkness and she slid down into Timon's arms. She felt the box slip from her hand and thud to the floor. Darkness swallowed her.

Chapter 17

Jerusha opened her eyes and saw elaborately carved cedar beams on the ceiling.

"Where am I?" She whispered. She felt the silken pillows beneath her head. Still groggy and not coherent, she turned on her side. "Father, where are you?" A sliver of light shone through the white-latticed window on her face and she squinted against the brightness. Grabbing the cool, wet cloth that had fallen from her forehead, she sat up, and swung her bare feet onto the cold tiles. A little dizzy because she moved too fast, she placed her head in her hands and waited for it to pass.

She smelled frankincense. Her mother must be near. She scanned the room. There, by the fire, Abigail knelt and mumbled words, indistinct and unclear, her silhouette calm and beautiful. *There's that peace again.* Ever since that night at the gathering when the room shook, her mother had an uncanny confidence that everything would be all right. She said it was because of her King.

Jerusha wasn't convinced. Where was this King when Caiaphas and his son had their way with them? Where was this King when

Yogli got arrested? Where was this King when they were betrayed by Stephen? Trustworthy? Honorable? Maybe. Her mother said they were—both of them —Stephen and the King.

Now fully aware of her surroundings and why she was there, she glanced at her old garment that hung on a peg beside Abigail and grasped for her girdle. Her rough, calloused fingers snagged the soft fabric of the tunic under her hand, the luxurious gift that she had rejected the night before. Her eyes caught sight of the girdle on the table. She stood, examined the gold embossed trim around her sleeves and crossed the room to touch the rough texture of the old one. Tattered and torn as it was, she identified with it. Uncomfortable with her new attire, her eyes followed the shaft of light that now filtered through the lattice and shone on the scroll's gold seals that lay on the table three feet away, exactly where Stephen laid it.

"Is it true? We are free?" she asked her mother quietly.

"Oh! Jerusha! You startled me."

"Sorry."

Abigail stoked the fire with an iron poker.

"I was praying for you. I didn't see you get out of bed. How do you feel?" she asked, her voice quiet, subdued.

"I think I'm fine," she said and rubbed the sleeve of the old robe against her cheek. "Maybe a little afraid. Is it true? We are free?"

"Yes, Stephen gave us our freedom." Her mother stared into the flames.

Jerusha rushed to her mother's side, knelt, and tilted her mother's face towards her.

"Mother, look at me. Let's leave this place. Let's go back home," she begged. "Our old house is empty. We can go there. Maybe Father will still come for us." Mother peered with a blank stare. Jerusha continued, "Or we could try to find him. If we're free, we can do what we want." Her eyes followed her mother as she rose, moved to the table, and picked up an object that was next to the scrolls hidden from her sight, behind the girdle.

"Remember this?" she asked.

"Oh! I forgot—Timon. We're betrothed?"

"Yes," Abigail answered. "Your father gave Stephen instructions about your betrothal if he didn't return." Jerusha stood and moved closer to Mother, who handed her the box. She rubbed her fingers on the pomegranate engravings on the outer edge.

"It looks so much like the one Father made for me. How can this be?"

"Your father loved you so much. He must have prepared it especially for you. There's no way Stephen or Timon would know to make this. They have never seen your box or pendant. Are you starting to see now that Stephen is trustworthy? He's just following your father's request to take care of you. And he and Timon take such good care of the widows and orphans."

"All the women and children in the courtyard?" Jerusha asked.

"Yes, they stay here until a relative or friend takes them in."

"He must think I'm a fool. Accusing him. Defying him. Rejecting his offer." She paused and swished around. "I'm still not sure I trust him. Why would he care about us?"

"Because of your father," her voice trailed off. Jerusha watched Abigail take her old girdle from the table, pull out her treasure box, and hold it up. "I remember when your father made this." She held it to her nose. "The smell of the acacia reminds me of him. He loved to work with this wood."

"Mother, you're acting so strange." She cupped her hands around her mother's hands, her father's treasure box in their hands. "Father may still be alive. We have to find him." She pointed to the other box on the table. "He may not approve of this betrothal."

Her mother swallowed hard. Her eyes brimmed with tears.

"Jerusha, while you slept, a letter came from Luke." She placed the treasure box on the table next to the other one and took Jerusha's hands.

"What did it say?" Jerusha asked expectantly.

Mother's long, black lashes squeezed shut.

"The letter came from a family that knew your father after he left. It said that Jacob was arrested by the Romans and forced to row for the Roman fleet. The ships were in port on the island of Crete when a great earthquake hit. No one has heard from him since."

"Oh, no!" Jerusha cried.

Her mother's dark eyes lingered at the fire for a while before continuing, "They believe he died in the earthquake."

"No! It's not true. I don't believe it!" She grabbed her mother's shoulders. "Tell me it's not true."

"I can't. The truth is that we really don't know for sure what happened to him. What we do know for sure is that he was on the island of Crete when the earthquake happened and the Roman fleet was destroyed. It would be a miracle if he's still alive," her voice quivered. "Come here."

Jerusha surrendered to her mother's embrace and laid her head on her shoulder. She felt the softness of her mother's cheek that rested against the back of her head. Convulsing sobs came. She didn't think she'd ever stop crying. Her hot tears soaked into Mother's robe. "Jerusha, I'm sorry—so sorry—for both of us. What good is freedom without your father to share it with?"

***

Jerusha, dressed again in her old garment, waited for her mother in the courtyard, her treasure tucked again in her girdle around her stomach, her few belongings in a bundle under her arm. Stephen agreed with them that they needed time to grieve, and their mourning period should be at their old home.

She heard children's giggles, dropped her bundle, and walked around the fountain but kept hidden behind a pillar. Her betrothed sat on the ground with children climbing all over him. "Again," one child begged.

"You want more?" Timon's deep voice echoed. "More tickles?" he said and grabbed the boy and rolled him over. She watched the boy's face turn redder with each giggle. "How about you?" Timon reached for another child. "I think you need a good tickling, too."

Too much laughter for her. Not today. She noticed the charming twinkle in Timon's eyes, though, and blushed. More giggles. She smiled and backed away, not wanting to disturb their fun.

She tiptoed backward toward a bench. *Whoa!* A large stone flew out from her feet. Thud! A flurry of butterflies fluttered out of the pomegranate bush. Her radiyd flopped to one side and snagged on the branches. *Humiliating!* She struggled to loosen it and make her escape unnoticed. *Too late.* The bushes rustled and a chubby face peeked through the deep green leaves.

"Do you want to be tickled, too?" the little one asked.

"Oh, no," Jerusha moaned and rolled her eyes upward. She motioned with her forefinger over her lips, "Shhh."

The bushes flopped closed, and Jerusha heard the high-pitched voice holler.

"Sir, over here, I think she needs a tickle."

Jerusha jerked on her radiyd, tried to get up, and slipped. Her tunic worked its way up to her waist and she yanked it down with both hands. A pomegranate branch stuck up between her legs. *Double humiliation!*

When she looked up, Timon peered over the bush. She grabbed the end of her radiyd, covered her black mole, and felt a flush rise up her neck as she watched a lopsided grin spread across his face. He stared down at her and pulled on his full, dark beard.

"Well, who do we have here?" he asked with that same charming twinkle in his eye. "I think we've found a beautiful butterfly resting in the bush," he continued. Four or five faces peeked over the bush as the children gathered around to see. The sound of their giggles rippled through the courtyard. "May we be of assistance?" he asked with a slight bow.

Jerusha shook her head.

"Just go away!"

"As you wish, little butterfly. We will allow you to free yourself." Compassionate eyes winked, and he motioned with his arms. "Come, children. Let's see what we can do for the widows."

She watched them follow him across the courtyard, their curiosity too hard to contain.

"Who's she?"

"What's she doing here?"

"Do you know her?"

"Why did you call her a butterfly?"

"You ask too many questions," he answered and glanced back over his shoulder.

"Jerusha! How did you get down there?" her mother stood on the tiled pathway beside the bushes.

"I decided to play in the dirt, Mother."

Her mother sighed. "I saw your bundle over there and came looking for you. Let me help you with that radiyd." She unhooked the cloth from the branch and offered her hands to pull Jerusha up. "Stephen is waiting to take us home. He and Timon are our escorts."

Jerusha brushed the soil from her robe and straightened her radiyd.

"Do we have to go with them? Can't we go alone? We know the way."

"No, it's getting too dangerous to be alone in the streets unattended by a male escort, especially after dusk. The walk is too long. It will be dark before we arrive," she answered. "Come on. I left my things over there by yours."

Chapter 18

Embarrassed, Jerusha refused to look at Timon, who now stood next to Stephen at the gate. She felt his eyes on her. She stepped past him and walked beside her mother through the open iron gate held by Stephen and rushed out into the street. *Humph. Betrothed.*

The two men carried the women's bundles and followed them down the steep hill. Jerusha put her hand over the area of her radiyd that hung below her eyes and covered her nose. "The streets smell worse than ever. We need rain." Her mother gagged and covered her nose, too.

The sun was setting behind their backs. The men's dark shadows merged with the women's as they wound down the steep hill.

Home. Three long years since she'd slept in her own house, her own bed—the house and the bed that her father provided for them. Darkness enveloped them. Jerusha wrapped her old cloak tighter. "Mother, will Stephen and Timon stay with us tonight?"

"Yes, until the others come in the morning." Jerusha knew she meant the other family members, to bring food and mourn with them, the tearing of clothing, ashes on heads, groanings. She wondered what Father would think of all this? *What if he's not dead?*

In the distance, one lone light moved toward them. Closer and closer. "Naomi," Abigail called to her, then stopped to greet her. "I'm so glad to see you. How did you know?"

"Stephen told me. I'm so sorry for your loss. I have prepared a meal for all of you," she said and gave the lamp to Stephen, who held it high for them to see.

While Naomi set the table and carried water, Jerusha stole away for a bath in her parents' room. Her mother kindly heated the water in the kitchen and brought it to her, then gave Jerusha one of her old tunics to wear. The tunic was beautifully made and, even though it was old, it seemed new to her and fit her perfectly. She hoped it wasn't too cheerful for a daughter in mourning. After her bath, she combed her long, dark hair, scented the tips with an old bottle of mother's oil, and put on her mother's old radiyd.

***

Later, she and Abigail waited for Stephen and Timon to join them at the table her father had made. Her mother seemed lost in thought. Strange. She rubbed her fingers along the carved design on the edge. There it is. The dent she made with her small tool. He always let her be his helper. She smiled. "I wasn't much help, Father," she whispered.

"I'm sorry, Jerusha, were you talking to me?" her mother asked.

"No, I was just remembering how Father allowed me to help with his projects and always fixed my mistakes, my messes." She chuckled, closed her eyes, and tried to remember his face. Such a long time. Being here, it felt as if he stood right beside her, holding her hand.

She opened her eyes. A purple butterfly sat on the table ledge. "How did you get in here?" she asked. "You're not usually out at night." A little girl again, she cupped her hands around the critter, stood, and carried it to the open window. "There you go. You're free, too!"

Just then Stephen and Timon appeared from the guest rooms, and the five of them sat down to eat Naomi's delicious cooking.

The pomegranates were fresh, of course, and the fish was broiled to perfection. Jerusha hadn't tasted this type of olive oil in a long time. She dipped her bread into the bowl before each bite, and savored the flood of good memories that flashed before her. The men talked to her mother and Naomi about some meeting that Jerusha did not care about. She easily ignored them all and tried to enjoy this moment. She was finally home.

How many times had she dreamed of returning to this table? And here she was the daughter, not the servant, and certainly not an object of a man's lust, to be used at will. She closed her eyes and pushed those thoughts out of her mind. Tonight belonged to her—to her freedom. *No slave thoughts!* Jerusha realized that tonight she was not summoned to serve anyone nor did she have to wait until the guests left to eat her own dinner. It was a good feeling, and she looked at Stephen with some gratitude.

After they ate, the men retired to the guest rooms. "I'd like to go to the garden before I come to bed," Jerusha said to her mother.

"Of course," Abigail answered. "Naomi already lit the courtyard lamps."

Jerusha helped to clear the table and clean the dishes. It was wonderful to put her hands around the familiar plates and goblets. When the last bowl was put away, her mother walked Naomi to the gate where her son met them to walk his mother home. Abigail sent her off with enough food for the two of them to enjoy the next day in their own home.

Jerusha smiled, proud of her mother's kindness, then walked the pathway to the courtyard and stopped at the fountain to look up into the sky. Clear. No clouds. Bright stars. Full moon.

Her mother walked up behind her.

"Beautiful, isn't it?" she whispered.

"I could see it all with my eyes closed," Jerusha said and looked at her mother, surprised at her dimpled smile. "I know every inch of this garden. I miss Father. I've always missed him, even when I was mad at him for leaving, I missed him," Jerusha's voice caught just then.

Her mother touched her cheek.

"I know, Jerusha. I miss him, too. I'm going to my room. Maybe you should sleep with me tonight. I'll wait up for you."

"The moon *is* beautiful," Jerusha said and gazed at the starlit sky. "On nights like this, I would wonder where Father was and imagine him standing under the moon thinking of me."

"I have had many nights like that, too," her mother said, then lightly kissed her forehead, turned, and walked away. Her frankincense hung in the air.

Jerusha removed her radiyd, felt the gentle breeze, and shook her hair free, unhindered on her shoulders. She moved to the bench where she sat with her father as a child and envisioned twirling around and dancing before him, his infectious laughter ringing in her ears and causing her to twirl even faster.

"I love you, Father," she whispered.

Dance. It has been a long time.

She stood. Hesitated.

A breeze encouraged her forward. Quietly, she slipped off her sandals, stretched out her arms and spun around and around, eyes closed, along the tiled path. It felt good. Free. Suddenly her hand whacked someone.

"Father?" Her hair splashed across her face. She opened her eyes. Shocked, she looked up through dark strands. "Timon!" That infuriating, lopsided grin! "What are you doing here?" she asked and stared into smiling eyes.

"I'm sorry to startle you. I had come to enjoy the full moon, too. It was only after you spoke, that I realized you were standing behind the bush. It didn't seem appropriate to interrupt. I was turning to leave when you whirled around and bumped me. My apologies," he said.

"You seem to have a knack for finding me in the most ridiculous moments," she muttered.

"I'm sorry," he said softly. He turned to leave. She rushed to get her radiyd from the bench and replace it. She turned around. His long, striped robe gently brushed against the bush at the end of the path.

"Wait!" she yelled. Still adjusting her radiyd, she ran to the corner. He stood in the lamplight by the fountain in the courtyard, his fingertips in the gurgling water, his back turned away from her.

"Please don't go," she said.

He turned, his face somber.

"I know you miss your father. I'm so sorry," he said.

She smoothed her radiyd around her hair.

"Toda." She stepped closer. "I want to ask you a question. I cannot talk of it to my mother. I can't encourage false hope. Do you think my father could still be alive?"

He stared at her for the longest time, his eyes tender, gentle.

"Anything is possible with our King."

"Your King," she said bitterly. "I knew Yeshua. He was only a kind man, not a king."

"No, Jerusha. He's your King, too. Yeshua's father hasn't revealed him to you yet. One day you will see and believe." He took her hands into his own and her heart raced.

"So rough. You've had too much abuse," he said.

She yanked her hands away and covered her black mole, her eyes still fixed on his dark brown pools.

"I want you to know I will not force you to marry me. You're free—free to choose. I will wait for your decision." She watched him turn to leave, then stop and swirl around to face her. "As I told you yesterday," he continued, "I left a gift for you in the box. When Stephen extended his offer to be your betrothed, I took some time to pray and think. I never wanted to be betrothed to someone who wasn't one of us. When you were little and I worked with your father, I saw a joyful and lighthearted little girl. However, lately I was not sure about you, but Stephen assured me. Tonight when I saw you twirling around and around, you reminded me of the little girl in your father's shop, carefree, joyful." He hesitated, thoughtful. "My gift to you came from a dream, you know."

She stared at him.

"A dream? About me?"

"Would you like me to tell it to you?" he asked cautiously.

"I don't know. Why would you have a dream about me?"

"Because Yeshua, our King, loves you—and he loves me—and he loves your father."

"Why does everyone talk about him like he's a king? He doesn't love me. No god or man has ever loved me—except maybe Father. And I pushed him away. Now he's gone." She blinked back tears and turned her back to gain control. He came and placed his hands on her shoulders, then spoke, a gentleness in his tone.

"Jerusha, not all men are like Caiaphas."

She swished around and faced him, fire in her eyes.

"Why did you say that? What do you know about Caiaphas? And how he treated me?"

"Only what Stephen observed in the palace. And these calluses and scars." He took her hands in his.

"You sound so much like my father," she said quietly and removed her hands. "When I saw a woman stoned, he said, 'not all men have such hatred.'" She sniffed back tears. Her throat became so thick that she coughed. Finally, she said it. "I—I don't believe *either* of you." She wiped the tears from her cheeks. She wanted to slap him. Why? He hadn't hurt her. She stared, motionless. Tears? In his eyes?

He waited in silence. One drop ran down his cheek. He didn't move. Another drop. And another. She reached up and wiped the next one before it reached his beard.

"Why do you cry?" she asked, her voice soft.

"Because . . . because you don't believe you are worthy of love. You're so afraid. You have built a wall around your heart to protect yourself."

"I've never seen a man cry, not even my father," she hesitated, uncomfortable. "Do . . . do you still want to tell me your dream?"

"Only if you want to hear it."

"Yes, yes, I want to hear it."

He directed her to the bench where her father used to work. Jerusha sat with ample space between them. Both of them stared at their own feet crossed in front of them. Timon cleared his throat, then began.

"In my dream, I saw you twirling and dancing before the King, then bow before him. When you arose, you turned and wore the most beautiful pendant on your neck, a lion face with a crown."

She gasped. "A lion face? With a crown? How did you know? Did Father show you?"

"I didn't know. He never showed me any such thing. I saw it in the dream." He looked down at his hands in front of him and formed his fingers in the shape of the pendant. "In the middle was the most unique jewel I'd ever seen. Every detail was inscribed in my mind." He tapped his temple with his forefinger and took her hands. "When I awoke, I knew this was going to be my betrothal gift to you. I didn't trust myself to make such a beautiful gift, so I went to the craftsman and he made every detail as I remembered it. Have you looked inside the box?" She heard the excitement in his voice.

"No, I'm sorry I haven't," she answered, her hands shaking. His touch awakened a new feeling in the pit of her stomach, something never experienced before. Different from Caiaphas's touch. Different from his son's touch. Different even from Father's touch.

"Well, I just want you to know you can keep the gift whether you marry me or not."

"I . . . I . . ." she stopped. "I can't wait to see it."

A strong breeze rustled the pomegranate bushes and lifted a familiar fragrance into the air; sweet, not nauseating like at the palace.

"Well, if you don't mind, I'd like to talk with you again tomorrow before I leave?" he asked.

"Yes, of course," she answered. This time she smiled at the lopsided grin that spread across his face. "We'll talk in the morning, then." He disappeared into the darkness. She must hurry. The box waited to be opened. Tonight!

***

"Jerusha, you look flushed." Mother stood by the brazier and warmed her hands. "What's taken you so long?" Jerusha sat on the mittah, several layers of lamb's wool with woven pillows made by the widows on top, compliments of Stephen. The flames from wicks sticking out of the olive oil lamps cast a soft glow in the room. The fire in the brazier crackled.

"I have been with Timon. Don't worry mother. I know we weren't to be alone together. It just happened. Nothing to worry about. Where's that box?"

"What box?"

"The one Timon gave me."

Jerusha saw her mother's eyebrows peak.

"Oh, Mother, please. It's not what you're thinking," she scolded her.

"The box is sitting on the table over there."

Jerusha rushed to the table and picked it up.

"What's going on? Why all the interest in the box now?"

Jerusha went back to the other mittah. Her hands trembled. The lamp on the ledge above her head flickered a soft light on the box. She rubbed her fingers over the pomegranate engravings, then closed her eyes and tried to quiet her pounding heart. *"I am the lion of Judah."* Her eyes popped open. *"My little lioness."* She looked down. A majestic lion with a crown engraved on the top. *Father?* She opened the box. A purple butterfly glittered in the soft light.

"Oh, Jerusha. It's beautiful!" Her mother now stood next to her.

Jerusha picked it up and held it close to the lamp. It shimmered on her face. She turned the jewel in the light and saw tiny engravings.

"I can't read what it says," she said.

"You will have to wait for morning and hold it up in the sunlight," her mother said and sat beside her on the mittah.

"Timon told me I was free to choose. He won't force me to marry him. And he said I could keep his gift, this jewel, no matter which way I decide."

"I have always liked Timon. I was the one who encouraged your father to mentor him. Did you know that?"

Jerusha looked up, her face flushed. "No. I thought that was father's idea since I didn't turn out to be a boy."

Abigail smiled at that. "And how grateful we were that you were *not* a boy! YHWH knew how much we needed you, our own little girl. You brought us so much joy, Jerusha. And Timon—Timon is a good man."

Jerusha put the jewel back in the box.

"I don't know what to think about any man," she said and placed it back on the table. Her father's treasure box lay beside it, and she swung the wooden cover back on the gold hinges. The lion pendant lay in the bottom.

"Timon is different than Caiaphas, Jerusha. He will treat you with dignity. He already has by offering you freedom and this gift, unconditionally. Caiaphas degraded you. You were his slave, his possession to serve his every whim. Timon will honor you."

Jerusha laughed.

"What is honor to a man? Give me a gift? A little food? Some fancy clothing in exchange for service at his table *and* in his bed?"

"Timon is not like that. Neither was your father. I just couldn't see it at the time. I was deceived."

Jerusha glanced down at the pendant.

"Father *was* different." Jerusha caressed the box and then the pendant. "I loved everything he made, especially this pendant. A lion with a crown. I never understood why he called me his little lioness. I just accepted it. I wish he was here now so I could ask him—so I could ask him about Timon."

"I long for your father, too. Jerusha. If I could go back and change things, I would. It's my fault that he's not here for us. I rejected him. I rejected Yeshua as King. I so regret that decision. Don't make the same mistake I made. Timon's a good man. I've watched him. I think he's fallen in love with you."

"Me? How could he love me? He just feels sorry for me." She slapped her hand on the table. "I will not accept his gift. Then what will he do? Have his way with me like—" she stopped. Mother must not know. No one must know, especially Timon. She did not tell father and she would not tell him either. *I'm ruined, dirty, unworthy.*

"No one can love me," she added in a whisper. "I cannot even love me." And she blew out the lamp.

Chapter 19

Jerusha dressed in her old robe, covered her head with her radiyd, threw the ends over her shoulders, and left her room with the jewel Timon gave her in hand. He at least deserved her thanks, even if she wouldn't accept his exquisite gift.

She tucked a strand of her jet-black hair back beneath the drab radiyd and strolled through Father's house, sickened by what she saw. In the darkness the night before, she hadn't noticed how run-down her childhood home had become. Naomi had kept up the inside fairly well, but the outside was clearly too much for her. These years without care left it in ruins. Unloved. Just like her. The bushes were large and overgrown, and bore less fruit. Jerusha sighed. No doubt Mother would have most of this mess cleaned up by the end of the week, even in this period of mourning.

The sun filtered through the dust stirred up by her sandaled footsteps on the colored-tiled walkway. She stopped and picked up a piece of broken tile and tossed it aside. It clanged against one of the marble pillars that lined the veranda. The marble pillar leaned out awkwardly. The ground beneath its base was eroded away and the roof it held up pulled from the wall. She walked around the unstable structure.

"Ouch!" Thistles, that had grown up between the once well-manicured bushes pricked

her toes and she quickly stepped back onto the tiles farther down the path where it seemed more

safe. Across the way in the courtyard, she heard mother's cries, along with others that mourned and covered her ears.

"I—can't—take this," she yelled and stomped her foot. "Father's gone! What's the use of throwing ashes on your head or moaning like a sick cow. His house is in ruins." Her words

echoed in the empty corridors. Above the women's shrill cries in the courtyard, she heard a man's deep voice.

"Jerusha!"

"Timon!" Of course it would be him. She straightened her radiyd and smoothed her robe as he ran toward her. When he caught up, he turned to walk beside her, his breathing a little increased.

"I was on my way to your father's garden. May I accompany you?"

"Well, we're both going the same direction," she said and threw out her arms and let them flop at her side. "It would be foolish to not walk together."

"I'm sorry if I intruded on your solitude." He cleared his throat. "You are mourning."

"I don't want to talk about that," she quipped. "Look at this place. It's in ruins," her voice trembled. She squeezed her eyes shut. Tears threatened to overflow. *Not here. Not now.* She swallowed and waved her hand toward the courtyard. "It doesn't matter to Mother. She wants us to move back with Stephen after the mourning period. 'Too many memories here,' she said. 'Too painful.' She's told him she wants to be his bond servant, help take care of the widows and orphans."

They strolled past the mourners and stopped at the fountain. "Like everything else, this needs cleaned and repaired, too," she said and held one hand in the dirty stream that flowed into the slimy, moss-covered tiled basin. She squeezed the other hand tight around the jewel and glanced at Timon, who also held his fingers in the water, his eyes on her. Uncomfortable, she wiped her hands on her robe and bumped his arm as she turned away and hurried up the path to the garden, to sit on Father's bench, a safe place.

Timon rushed ahead and opened the iron gate.

"Jerusha," he said and waved his arm in a slight bow as she passed.

"You hold the gate for me?" She felt a warmth in her neck rise and tightened her radiyd around her face. Three years of servitude, mostly to men, made her uncomfortable with Timon's gesture, sure he wanted something from her—only slaves serve for nothing.

"Your throne awaits," he said and winked. "May I?" he asked, and extended his hand to take her arm, a slight arch in his brow.

"You're mocking me," she said and brushed past his hand.

"Not at all," he responded. She felt a wisp of air as he moved around in front and blocked her path.

"Jerusha, look at me." He lifted her chin. "You are royalty."

Jerusha gasped. "That's exactly what Father said! It's unnerving how much you talk of the same things."

She went around him, past the bench to the wall and fiddled with one of the broken branches of the dried grape vines, the jewel still enclosed in one fist.

"Look how many thorny vines have worked their way through these," she said and changed the subject. "My father wouldn't like this. He cut away the weeds and pruned the vines every week."

She opened her fist and let the sun's ray shine on the jewel in her hand, then picked it up and held it to the light and stared at the tiny etchings. "I wanted to read these scribbles before I gave this back."

He came from behind and placed his hands on her shoulders. She smelled his manly presence, the ointment in his hair. Her eyes flittered from the jewel to his strong, wide shoulders enlarged in his shadow on the wall. She froze, her palpitating heart sending a new and different sensation through her body.

He bent down and spoke in her ear. "Does this mean you are not accepting my marriage offer?" he asked, his breath warm on the cloth of her radiyd.

"I—I don't know what it means," she answered, her hands shaking from his close presence. "I suppose it means you can't buy my service."

"I don't want your service, Jerusha. I want your love."

"Well, then you can't buy my love either."

"If I could buy your love, it wouldn't be true love."

He reached over her shoulder and pointed to a space on the wall between the vines. "Look!"

She raised her eyes and squinted at the squiggly lines dancing on the white limestone. "My—little—butterfly," she read and gasped, then swung around and shook the jewel before Timon's face. "Why did you put those words on this?" she asked, fire in her eyes.

"It was in my dream. I made it exactly like the one in my dream." He smiled that infuriating lopsided grin again.

"But, those words were in my dream, too!"

He took her hands and gently enfolded the jewel in her palm.

"Jerusha, a lot has happened to you in the last few days. You need time to mourn. I do not know why both dreams had those words in them. I suspect it has something to do with your father and our King." He cupped her face in his strong hand. "Please, just keep the jewel. Think and pray about it for a while longer. In time it will become clear."

Flustered, she turned away.

"I'm sorry I snapped at you," she mumbled, then walked around the bench and stared at the jewel. "I just do not understand. I thought I knew what I wanted, but these words . . . how did you know?" She paused, deliberating. She pictured Timon as a teenage boy working beside her father in the workshop in the lower city. And now, this dream. What would Father say? "I will keep it—for a while. But please, you must leave me alone so I can think."

"Take as long as you need. I know this place holds many memories."

She pulled her radiyd over her mole and watched him walk away. When he rounded the corner his toe kicked a pomegranate that lay on the ground and it rolled onto the path in front of her. Jerusha rushed to pick it up. So many memories from the past splashed across her mind. With the jewel in one hand, the pomegranate in the other, she strolled through the garden along the narrow pathway until she came to Father's bench, the one thing in this house that needed no repair.

She threw the end of her radiyd behind her back, laid the jewel on the bench, and dug her fingernails into the tough pomegranate skin, trying to tear it open.

"Father, you cannot be dead. I need you." The fruit flopped out from under her fingers. Exasperated, she plopped on the bench and closed her eyes, still gripping the fruit. A memory formed in her mind—a little girl counting seeds, her father's stained fingers wiping red juice from her chin. She smiled. "You told me I had a protective covering around my heart like this fruit," she spoke softly to him, barely above a whisper, as if he could hear her now. "You were right. But I couldn't tell you my secret," she continued to speak to the invisible figure. "If you knew what I had done, if Timon knew . . ."

She paused and remembered the little girl who ran from her father. She talked so softly that she could not even hear herself. But the words needed to be said, and they needed to be spoken here, on this bench. "I wanted to crawl on your lap, but I was afraid you would know how dirty I was. I trusted him, Father, but Efah forced me, hurt me. I tried to stop him, but he threatened that if I told, no man would love me or want me for his bride. Caiaphas touched me, too," she choked and gagged. "Scum! I hate them both!" she screamed and threw the pomegranate at the wall. It splattered open, its red juice running to the ground. "Please Father, come back!" she begged and crumbled to her knees, her face in her hands. "I cannot cry again. I have cried so much," she moaned and grasped the jewel that had fallen to the ground. Her chest tightened. Her eyes burned. The tears came, at first a trickle, then more and more and more.

After awhile she wiped her cheeks with the back of her hand and blinked then moved her eyes to the right and to the left. *It's still there on the wall. A vision?* She blinked again. *Still there.* She watched a scene unfold before her eyes. Strong weatherworn hands slipped radiant white sandals, covered with white pearls and sparkling diamonds on a woman's feet. In an instant the picture morphed into a groom presenting his bride on a balcony, large double doors behind them. A multitude of people below worshipped in song and dance but paid little attention to the bride and groom, so they turned, went back inside, and left the people to their celebration. Again the picture changed to the bride in a knee-length, pure white gown. Barefooted, she twirled and danced before the groom in the bedchamber.

"Jerusha?" Stephen spoke, his voice soft, gentle.

Surprised, she looked up, the image on the wall gone.

"What are you doing here?" she asked.

"I've come to share the vision I had while in prayer. May I help?" He offered his hand. "You had a vision, too?" she whispered, too quietly for him to hear, then grasped the jewel that sparkled next to her and allowed him to help her stand.

They walked along the winding path. His presence felt strange, like being with Father. She knew to wait for him to speak. Much like Father, she could tell he contemplated what to say, choosing his words carefully.

"I saw you in a white, knee-length tunic with many chains wrapped around your body. When you danced, the chains began to fall off." He stopped and faced her. "Jerusha, even though you are free from being a slave to Caiaphas, you're still in bondage."

She crinkled her brow and waited before she responded, "What do you mean, bondage? I'm not in bondage."

"It's not physical chains that hold you captive."

She fiddled with the butterfly jewel, still not looking up. "Sometimes, I'm in a dark place—at night—in my dreams. It feels so real. It's always the same place—no light—trapped inside a ball of yarn, string, and some kind of sticky substance. I scratch and claw at the strands to escape. I see a light above my head but I can't reach it. My hand feels my father's pendant—in the gunk—but I can't move and wake up mumbling the words, 'Arise, Lord. Let your enemies be scattered. Let all that hate you, flee before you.'"

Stephen stroked his dark beard, his brow drawn together in deep thought.

"The light you are reaching for is Yeshua Christos, our King." He hesitated. "Would you mind telling me what your pendant looks like?"

"It is made from acacia and is a lion's face with a golden crown in the mane."

"The lion of Judah."

"How did you know that is what's engraved on the crown?"

"It is written in the Torah, 'Judah, your hand shall be on the neck of your enemies.' And, 'Judah is a lion's cub.' It also says, 'He crouched as a lion and as a lioness.' Your father has left you quite an inheritance."

"Maybe that's why he called me his little lioness."

He grinned and pointed to the butterfly in her hand.

"Is that the jewel Timon made for you?" he asked.

"Yes, I do not understand how he knew to put the same words on it that were spoken to me in my dream. He says he had a dream, too. Oh, this is all so confusing. Butterflies! Lions! Dancing!"

He took her hands.

"One day, you will understand. For now, know that when you feel trapped, when you feel afraid, when you feel alone, say out loud, 'It is written, Arise, Lord. Let your enemies be scattered. Let all who hate you flee before you,' then take a step of faith and dance, even if you don't feel like it, dance to your heart's content. One by one the chains will fall off. Your destiny, the King's plans for your life, will unfold."

"Father said I would dance before the King, but I do not know him. You both believe Yeshua is the King. How can that be? He is just a man, like you." Jerusha remembered his playfulness with the children. "A kind, humble man, but not a royal King that rules over his enemies. I do not understand."

Stephen smiled then. "You will. Your eyes will be opened soon."

They walked in silence to her room. When they got to her door, she stopped and laid her hand on his wrist.

"Please, will you ask Timon to meet me in the garden before you leave?"

"Yes, I am sure he will want to see you."

"And Stephen, toda, or as the Greeks say, thank you. You've been so kind," she spoke over her shoulder as he walked away.

Chapter 20

B ack in her room, she opened the new box Timon had given her. There, in the bottom, she noticed a pomegranate relief, like the one in the old box.

"Do you suppose there's something beneath this one, too? Let's see," she said and pressed on it. "How did Father do that?" she pressed again. Nothing happened. "Hmm." She tried one more time and pressed harder. When she released it, the bottom loosened and it popped up. She tipped the box over and the false bottom fell into her hand along with a scroll, cracked and yellowed.

When she unfolded it, it broke into several pieces. She laid the false bottom on the table, picked up a piece of the scroll that fell to the floor and carefully pieced it together with the others. Unlike many young Jewish girls, her father taught her to read Hebrew and she deciphered the writing with no trouble.

Jerusha,

If you are reading this, it means something has happened to me. I have not been able to return to Jerusalem, and you are now betrothed. Do not be afraid, my little lioness. I have chosen Timon for you to marry, and he will pay the mohar. Open your heart and love him. I have complete confidence that he will love, cherish, and protect you. I have provided your dowry. You will make a beautiful bride. Never forget who you are, my daughter. My blood runs through your veins. You are royalty, from the tribe of Judah. I pray your journey has not been too difficult. Yeshua is the King. One day you will dance before him in his kingdom. I have always loved you and your mother. I always will.

Your father, the one that adores you.

Wet drops plopped on the parchment from her face.

"I love you, too, Father."

She laid the letter on the table and picked up the butterfly jewel, Timon's matan gift. *What did Timon say? He saw me dance before a King. A pendant with a jewel.* She opened the other box and rubbed her finger over the lion's face. *There—an indention.* She laid the jewel on the lion's nose. Perfect. After a little push, it snapped in place.

She slipped the pendant around her neck.

"I must talk to Timon."

"Jerusha," her mother called from the doorway. "Why do you wear your necklace now? We are in mourning."

"Mother, I've decided to accept Timon's offer. I have so much to tell you, but there is no time. I must meet him in the garden before he leaves. Will you come? Stephen will be with him. They leave today. The two of you can be my witnesses."

She grabbed her new garment that hung on the peg.

"Hurry! Help me change. And can I use some of your oil?"

"I'll get it from my room," she said, a smile curving on her lips.

"Oh, and Mother, could you ask Naomi to prepare water for a mikvah."

A short time later, Jerusha, sat on the mittah dressed in the new gold embossed
garment, the old one thrown on the floor at her feet, her pendant around her neck.

"You look like a queen."

Jerusha looked up at mother.

"Am I doing the right thing?"

"What is your heart telling you?"

"It's a little afraid."

Abigail sat next to her. "I assure you, Jerusha, you have nothing to fear. Timon's a good man. I see love in his eyes." She turned Jerusha's face to look in her eyes. "I think maybe you're feeling something for him, too?"

"Mother, I'm so confused. I don't know what I feel."

"Don't be afraid to love, Jerusha, and be loved," she took her hands and pulled her to her feet. "Come. They'll be waiting."

***

The temperature dropped a little by the time Jerusha and Abigail reached the garden. The sun's decent on the horizon cast a soft glow. The two men waited at the gate, their few belongings packed and sitting next to them on the ground. Jerusha smiled at Timon's sudden uncomfortableness as he opened the gate. He fumbled with it clumsily. She wanted to laugh, but nodded with a grace and dignity foreign to her and held her head high, unlike the slave that served Caiaphas.

Their eyes met and his mouth slowly formed that now charming lopsided grin that she was growing to love. He stumbled a little, but recovered and offered his arm. "May I?" he asked, a twinkle in his dark eyes. She took his arm and they walked together while Stephen and Abigail followed.

The late afternoon sunrays filtered through the olive trees on their faces.

"The trees have grown so much," she said.

"As have you," he responded. "I remember seeing you here when I came with Mother."

"I don't remember seeing you here. I saw you mostly at Father's shop in the city."

"I'm not surprised you did not see me. You never left your father's side. Paid no attention to me," he chuckled. They stopped by her father's bench. He turned and took her hands. "I've had my eye on you for a long time. You look especially beautiful this evening." She reached for her mole. He caught her hand. "Please, don't. I like it."

"You do?"

"Yes, it adds a unique and enchanting touch to your dimpled smile."

When Jerusha grinned, he added, "It's quite attractive, especially after I've been scorned by your fiery eyes." They both chuckled.

She saw him glance at the lion's face on her chest and looked down. The golden crown in its mane and purple butterfly jewel on its nose glittered in the evening sun's rays that broke through the tree limbs.

"That's the pendant I saw in my dream. Have you decided to keep the matan?" he asked and lightly touched the jewel in her pendant. She nodded. "And my offer of marriage?"

"Yes," she spoke softly and kept her head down. "There's much I still don't understand—about Yeshua, about my father, about our dreams." She raised her head and stared into his eyes. "Or about my feelings about love." She blinked shyly. "But one thing I do know. I accept your offer."

She sat on the bench and continued, "I found a letter from my father in the box you gave me. He must have put it in there before he gave it to Stephen. He approved of this marriage." Timon's eyes were on her. Steady. Unmovable. So serious. She stuttered, "I'm ready to be your wife."

He stared for what seemed like the longest time, then sat beside her and took her hands.

"Jerusha, you have scars both on the outside and the inside. These," he rubbed the top of her hands, "will fade over time. But those on the inside. . . ." She sucked in her breath. *He's going to reject me.* She closed her eyes and listened to the thumping in her temples and tried to calm the nausea in her stomach. "The scars we can't see," he continued, "can only be healed by Yeshua, the King."

"Does this mean you don't want to marry me?" she asked and stared at her hands.

"Jerusha, look at me," he waited until she raised her head and peered into his calm, gentle eyes. "It means I'll walk with you through the difficult healing—as your husband. I love you. But you will need Yeshua's love, too. My dream showed you dancing before him. One day you will be completely free. But I, like him, love you just like you are. It's for your sake that I want your freedom." He hesitated. "Shall we tell them?" he asked, his endearing grin returned as he pointed to Abigail and Stephen, who stood back to give them privacy.

She nodded.

He stood. "Abigail, Stephen, may I present my betrothed." He swooped his hand toward Jerusha and bowed, then looked up and winked. She smiled.

"My friend, do you have wine to share with your betrothed?" Stephen asked.

Jerusha admired Timon's fluid movement and broad shoulders, his striped robe rippling in the slight breeze, as he strode past Abigail and Stephen to the garden gate. He rummaged through his belongings and found a small, bulging wine skin.

"Just for this occasion," he answered, a cup in the other hand.

Stephen laughed.

"Bring it here."

Timon's grin and jovial manner warmed Jerusha's heart. She cocked her head to the side.

"Were you so sure I would accept your offer?"

He chuckled. "It is good to be ready." He handed Stephen the cup. When he opened the wineskin it deflated a little. He tipped it up and let the red liquid flow into the cup, his eyes on Jerusha.

"My friend, she's beautiful, but the cup runs over," Stephen laughed.

Jerusha saw her mother cover her mouth. She, too, choked back a giggle and watched Stephen pull a scroll, the contract, the ketubah from the inside of his robe. He stood before the two betrothed with the cup in one hand and the scroll in the other, her mother slightly behind him. He offered the cup. After Timon, then Jerusha, drank from it, he said to Jerusha, "You drank from the cup. Do you accept this ketubah?"

She glanced briefly at Timon and nodded. Stephen slapped Timon on the back.

"I accept you, on behalf of her father, Jacob, to be her betrothed. What YHWH has joined together, let not man separate."

The two witnesses accompanied them through the courtyard to the entrance gate. Timon set his bundle down and gently pulled Jerusha close. She stared at him, a flutter in her stomach.

"I won't see you for a while. I'll be busy preparing a place for us. When your mourning is over and I have everything ready, I will come for you."

"I will be ready," she whispered. He drew near and kissed her cheek.

She glanced at Abigail and Stephen. Their backs were turned. When she looked back at Timon, he winked, picked up his pack, and motioned to Stephen to follow.

Jerusha felt her mother's arm around her waist, and they watched the two men walk down the hill. The children who played in the street pulled on the men's arms and laughed at the funny faces Timon made. He turned around and winked at her one more time, and then he was gone.

Chapter 21

Jerusha stood at the iron gate. The shade from the jujube's green canopy cooled her sweaty brow. A paralyzing grief gripped her thoughts while she watched Abigail and Naomi nail boards to windows, sweep tiles, and pack the few belongings left behind three years ago when Caiaphas arrested her father. She not only grieved over the loss of him, but the loss of her childhood home. If only she could stay, but the thirty-day mourning period passed, and Mother wanted to help Stephen with the widows and orphans.

She glanced up at the blazing, unseasonably hot Av sun and wiped her face with the sleeve of her tunic, covered her eyes with her hand, and scanned the horizon. The temple glistened in the distance, gold against white stone. Their home was high enough to see the sacred place and beyond the Kidron Valley, the Mount of Olives. Every day she came to look for him. She longed to be that little girl again that ran to greet him—have him catch her in his arms and swing her up over head.

The only male figure she saw coming was Stephen, holding a rope with a donkey that tagged along behind. A few children braved the heat to play in the dusty streets. The women would wait until evening to fetch water. The men were busy in shops or at the temple. Stephen wound his way through the narrow maze of square rooftops below and climbed the last steep slope to give his aid in moving them back to his house.

"Shalom," he greeted her and tied the donkey to the tree, then turned to stand beside Jerusha and looked out over the city. "The temple is beautiful, but Yeshua prophesied its destruction. One day, when the city is surrounded by armies, we must flee. Until then, we urge our neighbors to come into his kingdom. We now carry YWHW's presence within us. We are his temple."

Jerusha cared nothing about this prophesy. Without father, life felt empty. A future with Timon meant nothing without him here to give his blessing. A letter was good, but his presence would mean so much more. She looked at Stephen, the only father figure in her life, now.

"You are a good man," she said. "I have grown to trust your wisdom." She spoke with the same respect and honor she gave father.

The children's giggles and laughter drew her thoughts to the last time she saw Timon, his playful antics with the children as he left her home. She chuckled beneath her breath and smiled. They seemed to love him. She thought she might love him, too. Mother said she saw something in her eyes when she looked at him. The same look her mother said she had when she married Father.

After loading the donkey, she and Mother left with Stephen. Jerusha walked alongside him. The donkey, weighed down with their belongings, trailed behind. Mother and Naomi walked ahead and chatted. She looked back one last time before they wound around the corner at the two-story structure with boarded windows and locked gate.

"If Father's alive—if he comes home—how will he find me?" she asked Stephen.

"If your father is alive, nothing will keep him from finding you," he answered.

"Do you think he's alive?"

"It's not been revealed to me, yet. Anything's possible. Your father would want you to enjoy your life with Timon. If Jacob is alive, he will find you," he paused, "if he's not locked up in a Roman prison somewhere like many others."

"Oh, Stephen, it makes me sick to think he may be suffering." Exasperated, she added, "Maybe he *is* dead.

"Alive or dead, your father is with Yeshua Christ in his kingdom."

"Where is this kingdom?"

"His kingdom is not of this world. It is within those of us who believe and affects the kingdoms of this earth everywhere we go, just like our Yeshua, our King, did when he walked this land."

"Sounds confusing."

"If you keep seeking, it will be revealed." She dismissed his kingdom talk.

"Stephen, thank you for allowing me to ask about Father. I can't talk to Mother. She's hurting too much."

They wound down the hill and back up a small incline in silence. A tiny girl, about four years old, came running through the gate. Dust flew up from her bare feet.

"Stephen," she yelled and broke their solitude.

"Sarah," he answered and swooped her up in his arms. "Do you remember Jerusha?"

The girl ignored his question and pointed to the donkey which stopped obediently when he dropped the rope.

"Can I go for a ride after you unpack him?"

"Of course. I wonder if Jerusha would like to take you. Shall we ask her?" Jerusha saw the girl's big, black eyes peek over his shoulder, then turn away.

"I know her. She's the one Timon called a butterfly."

"He did? Why would he call her a butterfly?"

"I don't know. She looked funny. A branch stuck between her legs." Embarrassed, Jerusha covered her face with her radiyd and looked away. When she turned back, she watched Stephen whisper in the girl's ear, tweak her nose, and set her feet on the ground. A group of children of all ages and sizes, male and female, exploded through the gate.

"Here they come," Sarah said and scampered to get out of the way. She dodged the rambunctious herd, jumped on the bottom ledge of the iron gate, and rode it as it swung back and hit the limestone wall that surrounded the courtyard. The orphans surrounded Stephen and asked question after question. Sarah waved at Jerusha and called above the noise.

"Do you want to ride the gate, too?"

Jerusha laughed. "Maybe the donkey," she answered, her troubled thoughts swept away by the children's joyful conversations with Stephen and Sarah's carefree enthusiasm.

Stephen started handing the children goatskin bags filled with water and other items to take inside. The midwife and other widows who heard the ruckus came to help Abigail and Naomi.

While unpacking a pouch of grain and feeding the donkey a handful, Jerusha saw Sarah's tiny shadow sneaking up with arms and hands outstretched like a bear. She smiled and let spindly fingers poke her ribs.

"Tickle, tickle," Sarah said and giggled.

Jerusha dropped the grain and swirled around. "You better run," she teased. "I'm going to get you."

Sarah screamed and tried to run, but Jerusha grabbed her and began tickling.

"Stop, stop," she said, barely able to breathe. Jerusha laughed, quit her tickling, and swung the lightweight child with tiny bones onto the now unpacked donkey.

"There! No more tickles for you or me."

Sarah looked down with her big, round eyes and thick, black lashes, the most prominent feature on her thin face, and blurted in childlike trust, "I like you."

Jerusha tapped the girl's short, pointed nose.

"I like you, too. Ready for a ride?" Sarah raised her head high and nodded a big yes, her petite, square chin almost hitting her chest. Jerusha nudged the stubborn beast, turned it and led it up the hill to a small olive grove a few yards away, around a tree and back down the slopping path. Sarah hugged the donkey's neck.

"Do . . . you . . . like . . . Timon?" She asked. The donkey's plodding jarred her words.

"Yes. Do you?" Jerusha answered and looked back to be sure she wasn't slipping off.

"I *love* Timon," Sarah answered. Jerusha's heart warmed to Timon's influence in the girl's life. She remembered his deep laughter, twinkle in his eyes, and unending patience as he played with the children in the garden.

So caught up in her own pain, she never noticed, or cared to notice, the honorable qualities he possessed: his tenderness with the widow he brought to Peter for healing, his humble desire to serve. He had held the gate open for her. Such a simple gesture, but even the memory thrilled her! *How could I have been so blind?* A longing for his return tugged at her heart. She, too, loved Timon, not as a little girl loves, but as a grown woman.

***

"Here comes another one," Sarah announced, dressed in her best tunic and robe, her hair partially braided across the top of her forehead like a crown, the rest hanging loosely around her shoulders. Strangers to Jerusha, but friends to Stephen, they arrived one at a time through the gate and approached the festive table where she sat with Mother and watched Timon's mother and other widows serve fruit trays, bread, and roasted lamb.

"We want to honor your betrothal tonight." After three years of slavery to Caiaphas, their service made her uncomfortable. Who was she to be served in such grandeur?

She looked up at the stranger with gentle eyes much like Stephen's and Timon's. "Shalom," he greeted. His full, gray beard was down to his chest. His tan, weatherworn hands held a small object wrapped in gold silk. "May I?" he asked with a slight bow. She nodded. He unfolded the cloth. The golden folds fell around his hand and revealed a clear jasper stone in his palm. Jerusha cupped her hand over her mouth.

"I've had this jewel since I met your father years ago."

"You knew my father?"

"Oh, he acquired my services to help build a place for you to live in Perea. When the Romans came and arrested him, he gave me this jewel to keep until he returned." She laid her hand over her mother's arm and glanced over at her. The lamplight shined in her dark eyes, but Jerusha saw sadness behind her long, curly eyelashes, a watery brim threatening to overflow.

"My husband died in an earthquake on the isle of Crete," Abigail said, a lump in her throat.

"I heard. I'm sorry for your loss. Many nights I've laid awake and pondered the possibility of him being alive, only to give up such thoughts. That's why I came tonight. He would want your daughter to have this stone. He was keeping it for her wedding day." Jerusha held her tongue. She wouldn't reveal her doubts about father's death in front of mother. It may create a false hope. He must be alive but to tell Mother would torment her even more. Instead, she asked, "Why do you do this for me?" A tough shell around her emotions prevented her from even a tiny tear forming. No crying! She must be strong for Mother.

The old man answered, "Isaiah prophesied many years ago, 'Lift up your eyes and look around; all of them gather together, they come to you . . . you shall surely put on all of them as jewels and bind them on as a bride.' We all come to you this evening as representatives of your father and the King."

"You're too generous. I don't deserve this." She watched him twirl the ends of his beard in his fingers and contemplate what to say.

"Your father shared many times his concern about you. He talked of a protective covering around your heart—how you ran from his presence, afraid to get too near. You and your mother were always on his mind. He prayed for you numerous times."

That night, after insisting on helping with the cleanup, she sat in her room, the one Stephen provided, and stared at the gifts brought, mostly by strangers, spread across her mittah. Why? She never saw such love.

One older woman brought a jewel from her own wedding attire. "I have no daughter to pass this to," she said. Her face radiated a joyful countenance. Her toothless smile spread wide. Jerusha sighed happily and moved to the open window.

She heard the children's giggles fade as they moved past her door and down the corridor to their sleeping quarters. These last few months she had come to covet the joy and peace in this house. *I wonder what it will be like to live with Timon.* Her stomach knotted up. *If he rejects me, I wonder if I can come back here.*

Chapter 22

The cooler temperatures of the month of Tishri, September and October, signaled the pilgrimage to Jerusalem for the annual seven-day Sukkot or Feast of Tabernacles. Jerusha touched the customary circlet of coins attached to her radiyd that spoke of her betrothal in public. It was the fifteenth day of the month, the first day of the celebration. She sighed, her thoughts on Timon, and bent over and dusted her robe with her hands.

"Watch out," her mother cried. She felt the edge of a lulav that everyone who celebrated the feast, carried. The unopened palm branch brushed her cheek, and she rose up just in time to prevent a poke in the eye.

"Sarah," Abigail said, "you must be more careful. There are too many people in the streets to be waving that carelessly around." Jerusha noticed a little pout to Sarah's downturned mouth. The little one convinced Stephen to allow her to go with them to the temple. Sarah told everyone that she hoped to see Timon.

The three generations of females, accompanied by Stephen, walked among the throng of people, most holding palm fronds, leafy branches, and poplars. Jerusha scanned the many temporary sukkot booths built from palm branches that lined the streets and stood upon rooftops of the dwellings and looked for a glimpse of Timon. Next year they would build their own sukkot for the celebration at the home he was preparing for her. She smiled at the thought of her own home.

As they neared the temple, the shrill cries of rams and goats being slaughtered almost stopped her in her tracks. Father taught her, of course, that the Feast of Sukkot included morning sacrifices. She stared at Sarah's big, bright eyes and remembered the lamb she took to the temple with her father as a little girl and how she cried when they took it away, how he lifted her in his strong arms.

A shofar blasted and jarred her thoughts from Father. The crowd parted and the temple's Water Gate swung open. *Caiaphas!* He led a procession through the streets, dressed in that black ornate robe she'd grown to hate, the phylactery on his forehead. Other members of the Sanhedrin followed along the outskirts and listened to the musicians play joyful tunes on flutes and timbrels and nodded their approval. How she loathed that pompous flair and that same arrogant lift to his chin. Caiaphas carried a golden pitcher a hundred yards to the Siloam pool, filled it with water, and handed it to his son. *Hypocrites!*

Sickened, she turned away. A small crowd gathered around Stephen and listened. She heard his pleas to come to the sukkot at his dwelling, to hear how Yeshua Christos came as the lamb of YHWH.

"In him you can drink of living waters." A few listened. Most scoffed.

Sarah wiggled her way beneath his arm, and he stroked her head. Jerusha watched and listened as the tiny one pulled on his robe, looked up, and asked a question, then another one. "You ask too many questions," she remembered father saying. Startled by a guard's loud shout from the temple steps, her thoughts returned to the present unsafe environment. She leaned into mother.

"Why does he risk all of us being arrested?"

"Stephen loves his people. Like Yeshua, he wants all to enter the kingdom."

Jerusha shook her head in disbelief.

"Come along, Sarah, leave Stephen to his teaching," she called.

"I like to listen," she said.

They moved along with her mother into the temple and watched Caiaphas strut up the steps and pour out the water on the altar.

"Please, Lord, save us," he prayed. "Hear our prayers." He continued reciting psalms and told how YHWH's shekinah glory, that cloud of fire, made itself known in the wilderness on sukkot. Ugh! She couldn't stomach any more and started to walk away, then stopped.

"Is that Timon?" she asked her mother and pointed to a man standing beside a pillar. Her heart quickened. They both placed their hands above their brows and shaded their eyes from the late afternoon sun that glistened through the many palm fronds the worshippers carried.

"See, Mother. He is talking to that crowd gathered around him."

Sarah tugged on her arm. "I want to see Timon. I miss him. Don't you miss him, Jerusha?"

"Out of the way!" a Roman soldier cried. "Move out of the way!" Several cohorts of soldiers marched through the scattering worshippers, an obvious attempt to intimidate and squelch any troublemakers from instigating an uprising. Sarah dropped her lulav and clutched Jerusha's robe. A legionary on his strong steed blocked Jerusha's view of Timon, and she lost sight of him.

"He's gone. I can't see him now."

Mother pulled on her arm. Jerusha picked up Sarah, wrapped her legs around her waist, and followed to the Court of the Women for the lighting of four golden candelabras. The Roman intrusion troubled Jerusha. So much unrest. Never as a little girl did she remember their presence among the worshippers in the temple. She remembered seeing a few soldiers here and there outside the temple gates but not within the temple courts.

As the priests poured oil into the golden bowls, she looked again for Timon and saw a small skirmish by the temple gate. She watched the soldiers drag a man through the crowd. *Timon?* The man jerked loose and quickly darted away. *That's not him. He's too scrawny. Timon's shoulders are much broader.* She breathed a sigh of relief and turned back to see the priest torch the bowls. The flames roared into the air and lit the darkening sky. The smell of burning olive oil permeated the air. They stood close enough to feel the warmth of the flames. She glanced at Sarah and watched her eyes widen.

The sun was now hidden behind the limestone wall, an orange haze across the horizon. A man lifted and rattled a tambourine. Quickly a circle formed. Jerusha rehearsed in her mind the exact steps Father taught her as a child. Voices lifted softly in song, then increased in volume and intensity as the men leaders danced.

"Happy is every man on who guilt rests,
he who having sin is now with pardon blessed."

"Come, Jerusha," Abigail interrupted her thoughts. "We must prepare. Many are gathering with us tonight. Among those celebrating Sukkot, no one will discern that we gather to celebrate and worship our King and eat at his table." They backed away from the dancing and slipped through the crowd to make their way to Stephen's large house, the place that had now become their home.

"There is Stephen over by the gate," Abigail pointed, her other hand on Jerusha's shoulder. "He is waiting for us."

Jerusha set Sarah's feet on the ground, took her hand, and they moved against those coming for the celebration, down the steps and winding among the many makeshift booths, some with only men inside, others with families or empty, their worshippers most likely a part of the celebration in the Court of Women.

A father led his little girl outside the sukkot and lifted her to his shoulders. He laughed at her enthusiasm, waving her lulav in hand above his head. Jerusha smiled. How she missed those days. The noise quieted as they drew nearer Stephen's house, and Jerusha's thoughts turned again to Timon. When would he come?

Long branches now covered the entrance to the lamp-lit courtyard. Sarah joined the other children as Abigail and other widows instructed the orphans what to do. Everyone worked together to put the finishing touches on the food preparations. Jerusha carried the wine and bread from the kitchen and placed them on the table beneath the branches that covered the normally open courtyard. Stephen did quite a good job erecting the booth, especially with as little time as he had on his hands. Such a large booth was needed—Stephen had a large family!

"Shalom," Stephen greeted the guests at the iron gate with a kiss and ushered them all to the sukkot.She found a bench on the far side away from the table, outside the sukkot, and looked up at the stars. Even from this distance, one-half mile away, the light from the temple candelabras shined in the darkness. It reminded her of the light in her dream, just out of reach, but so bright. "Yeshua Christos," she spoke, "Stephen says you are the King and the light of the world. My father believed in you. He said I would dance before you one day."

She heard her mother's laughter above the flutes and tambourines and looked across the way at the women, mostly widows, gathered by the table, some serving, some dancing, joyful in the midst of tribulation. Many had been arrested and released. Worse, a few watched their husbands and sons killed before their eyes. They definitely found light in darkness—how else could they sing a tehillah, a song of praise. Like it says in the Sefer Tehillim, the Book of Psalms, "You turn my mourning into dancing."

Timon's mother radiated with joy and peace. One of the boys did an outstanding flip as he danced then somersaulted into Chaya's knees. She laughed a belly laugh that made Jerusha envious. She hadn't laughed like that since being with father as a little girl.

What gave the midwife so much joy? Her husband was falsely accused, tortured, and killed by Romans. Widowed. Barren. Some in the community mocked her for raising Timon alone. Somehow YHWH provided. Jerusha remembered her stay in the palace. She understood well what it meant to be mocked by the religious, the look in their eyes, the wagging tongues, the threats!

She sighed. Timon, an orphan, was her betrothed. How ironic. She remembered how the children teased him in the streets in front of her house. "You don't have a father! You don't have a father!" they tormented. At the time, she turned a deaf ear to their cries. What did that matter to her? She had a father.

"Timon, I'm so sorry I didn't care," she whispered. Memories of his playful laughter with the orphans crowded her thoughts. Of course! He understood. He loved them. A sickened feeling crept into her stomach. *How calloused I've been. Selfish! Only cared about me.* Tears flowed down her cheeks. "YHWH, help me," she cried. "Show me the way."

"Jerusha," her mother called and waved for her to come. She rose and joined the celebration, a heaviness in her heart.

She watched as Peter took the cup of wine and spoke, "Yeshua said this is the new covenant in my blood, shed for you." Many times she had seen them partake of this meal together, these followers of Yeshua Christos. Peter continued, "Do this, as often as you drink it, in remembrance of me," then passed it to Stephen, who took a drink, and he passed it to the next; each in turn took a drink.

As the cup went from hand to hand, Jerusha remembered what Father said: "Without shedding of blood no man can stand in the presence of YHWH, not even the high priest." She thought of the little lamb he took from her hands to be sacrificed at the temple. "Someday you will understand, my little one." *I understand, Father, that I am too dirty to ever stand in his holy presence or dance before him.* Her mother had told her how Yeshua hung on the cross, the perfect lamb of YHWH, his blood shed for her. It is too late for me. He cannot forgive me. I am not worthy. The thought of Yeshua, her father's friend, bleeding for her that made her sick to her stomach.

Never before did she feel such need for cleansing, but when the cup came to her, she passed it on as she had done many times in the last year. Her mother sat across from her, and Jerusha noticed a single tear drop roll down her face.

Peter then took the bread and said, "Yeshua Christos, on the night when he was betrayed, took bread, and when he had given thanks, he said, 'This is my body given for you. Do this in remembrance of me.'" Jerusha again remembered her father's friend, Yeshua, and how kind he had been to her as a child. Mother told her that Caiaphas crucified him. "For you," she had said, "for your sin, for the sin of the world. Just believe."

"King David brought the ark of the covenant to Jerusalem and danced before it," Peter said. "The Levites declared, 'Arise, Lord. Let your enemies be scattered. Let all who hate you flee before you.'" She placed her hand over the pendant that hung beneath her tunic. She was waiting for her wedding day before displaying it openly for all to see.

"If King David danced before the Lord because he knew the Lord's presence scattered his enemies as the ark moved into Jerusalem, how much more reason do we have to dance and praise since the temple veil is torn and—like the ark of the covenant—we now carry his presence within us and scatter the enemy everywhere we go."

"It doesn't look much like the enemy is scattering before you to me," she whispered. "You were arrested and beaten." Just then she looked at the people around her, faces that radiated peace and joy.

The people erupted in spontaneous praise. A young girl started playing a flute. Many tapped tambourines to the beat. Abigail and the others formed a circle around the table, held hands, and danced. The music rose to a crescendo, her mother and some of the others let go, raised their hands and twirled, while others clapped. Many love songs from the Psalms blended into harmonious worship to their King. Jerusha smiled. Stephen took her hands and lifted her to her feet.

"Dance, Jerusha, dance."

Jerusha allowed Stephen to lead her to the outer edges of the circle. He stepped aside then, and Jerusha swayed to the music and watched Mother, more beautiful than ever, her dancing eyes and dimpled grin. Father would be pleased. She closed her eyes and lifted her hands and for a few moments twirled around and around and around. Laughter rose in her belly. A small giggle burst forth.

Harlot, the accusation boomed into her thoughts. *What will Timon think when he finds out about your secret?* She stopped. *He'll reject you. He'll cast you off.* That old suffocating panic gripped her throat and knotted her stomach. She gathered up the bottom of her robe and ran to her room.

A slight breeze from the white-latticed window blew the dwindling flames in the brazier. She stirred the embers and rubbed her hands together to warm her fingers. A chill ran down her spine. Lightning flashed in the distance. Rain. A few drops splattered on the tiles outside the window.

She pushed aside the dark thoughts and for a few moments allowed herself to feel again the freedom of that little girl loved by her father. "I danced tonight," she said, then ran to the wooden chest in the corner and opened it.

Beneath a few other articles of clothing she pulled out her father's robe, held it to her face, and breathed in his fragrance that still lingered. She fingered the blue, knotted tzitzits on the corners. Royalty. "Father, you are wrong," her voice caught. "If you knew—if Timon knew." *I must tell him before the wedding.* Her stomach twisted in knots. "I think I have fallen in love with him, Father. The only man I have ever loved, besides you, and I will probably lose him, too." Kneeling on the cold tiles, she slumped against the chest, buried her face in her father's robe, and sobbed.

Just believe.

I can't!

After awhile she heard a light rap on her door.

"Jerusha? Are you all right? I saw you leave. May I come in?"

"Yes, Mother, come in."

The door creaked open, and Abigail knelt down beside her on the tiled floor and enveloped her in a warm embrace. Her mother's radiyd fell off her shoulders and landed on Jerusha's chilled toes.

Abigail whispered into her hair.

"You are so tormented."

Jerusha sat back on her knees and opened her eyes. Her mother kept her head down and fingered the now worn, blue cords on her father's robe, then lifted it up around Jerusha's shoulders and stared into her eyes for the longest moment. "I need to tell you something. I hope it helps. You may be very angry with me when you find out." Jerusha sat up straighter, her hands in her lap.

"What are you talking about?" Abigail ignored her comment and continued.

"I never told you before because you were so young. But you are getting married now, and it is time you know the truth."

"Mother?"

"Please, Jerusha. This is difficult. Wait to speak until I am finished. You were so angry with your father and at times seemed to blame yourself for his leaving us. I tried to tell you it was not his fault. Nor was it your fault. But what I never told you was that I committed adultery with Caiaphas."

"What?"

"I was so deceived. I am sorry Jerusha. Because I believed Caiaphas's lies about Yeshua, I hurt you and your father. Your father could have had me stoned, but instead, he put me away privately. Only Caiaphas knew of my sin, his sin. That is why I am so grateful for Yeshua's forgiveness. When I heard he prayed from the cross, 'Father, forgive them. They know not what they do,' I knew he was the Mashiach, the King. I will forever be thankful for his sacrifice for me.

He made a way for me to come to his Father and I accepted his free gift of eternal life with the Father, his Father. Yeshua's blood cleansed me."

For some reason Jerusha was not angry with her mother. Instead, her thoughts went toward herself and what her father told her that without shedding of blood no man can stand in his presence. She believed her mother had found peace and wanted the same for her. How could she not believe that? She walked in such joy.

"I do forgive you. I want what you have, Mother. I want forgiveness. I want joy. I want peace."

"Just surrender to him, Jerusha. He loves you." Jerusha thought of Yeshua's smiling face when he threw her up in the air as a child. She sucked in her breath. The dream! It was him! He is the one who called her 'my little butterfly.' He is the one who said he was always watching.

"Mother, you are right. Yeshua is more than a man. He is the Mashiach, the Messiah we have waited for. He is the Christos, the anointed one. Just think, he was with me in the flesh as a child." A warm tingle flowed through her body. "And he is with me now in Spirit." She smelled the fragrance again of her father's robe. "Father, I know the truth. I know who he is. I believe," she said and burst into tears. Joyful tears!

That night, after her mother left her room, she looked out her window at the starry night. "Yeshua, I know you have accepted me and love me as I am. But will Timon? What will he do when he finds out about Efah? Help me to tell him. He deserves to know."

Chapter 23

Six Months Later

I t was late afternoon when Jerusha looked out the window of the bedroom that she and her mother shared to take in the view of the Mount of Olives. The winter rains had softened the ground to allow the dormant seeds buried beneath the hardened earth to open up and push through the fertile soil, exposing many new plants to the sun's warmth and energy. Spring's vibrant shades of green against the cream-colored olive tree blossoms on the mount meant Timon's return may be close.

She enjoyed the fragrant, white almond flowers that surrounded Stephen's home in the early spring. Now the grape vines with their long, flexible stems and lobed leaves donned the wall outside her window with tiny flowers that would soon develop into a cluster of sweet grapes. Bees hummed delightfully from blossom to blossom. One day soon Sarah would pull a fistful of sun-ripened grapes from the vine and pop them into her mouth.

Jerusha had grown fond of her guardian, Stephen, and his garden of flowers, vines, widows, and orphans. She smiled. The same flowers she saw outside, along with scarlet pomegranate blooms, lay in a basket in Jerusha's room, ready if Timon came, to be laced in her hair by mother. The larger scarlet flowers a striking contrast against the tiny white flower. She breathed deeply of their fragrance. It had been rumored that Timon may come tonight. She had already bathed in perfumed water, just in case, and lit the lamp in her window an hour ago.

She watched the sun's orange glow hasten its departure behind the white glistening city wall. A myriad of lamps sparkled like stars and lined the pathway before her eyes. Jerusha's heart leapt. *Timon!*

She ran to the door and yelled down the corridor, "Mother, they are coming! Please, I need your help."

Abigail rushed into the room and hugged Jerusha then grabbed the basket of flowers on the bed and moved them to the table.

"Here, be seated," she said and pointed to a chair. "We must have you ready when he comes."

"I'm scared," Jerusha said and rubbed her throbbing temples.

"All brides are apprehensive," Abigail answered, her nimble fingers working the flowers through Jerusha's hair with expertise, a craft she learned while serving Caiaphas's wife. When she was finished, Jerusha stood and let the old garment fall from her shoulders to the tiled floor. Her lion pendant glittered in the lamplight.

Abigail helped slip the white, silk tunic over her head.

"I should have had you put this on first," she said and straightened the flowers again in Jerusha's hair. "What was I thinking?" She grabbed the ornate robe that hung on a peg next to the radiyd and held it open as Jerusha slipped her arms through the openings, then she carefully placed the shimmering bejeweled radiyd over her hair and wrapped it around her face. She stepped back and took in Jerusha's beauty.

"Oh, your father would be so proud of you. You look like a queen, the royalty he always spoke over you." She lightly kissed Jerusha's cheek and left the room.

Of course, Jerusha could not see herself. She quickly dabbed oil onto her arms and hands and rubbed it in. *He's coming!* Her throat went dry and she grabbed a ladle of water from their pail.

The sound of jubilant laughter and music in the distance got louder and louder. Jerusha dropped the ladle into the bucket and moved to the window. She wondered where Timon would take her—where their home would be. It wouldn't be long now, and she would see it for herself! The shofar blew.

"The Bridegroom comes," Stephen announced. She shivered in the cool evening breeze. Her heart raced.

"I haven't told Timon the truth," she groaned. *What will he do tonight when he finds out I am not pure? How will he handle not having the traditional blood-stained sheets the wedding guests expect to see hung outside our bedchamber after we consummate our marriage? Will he reject me? Will he have me put away silently like Father did Mother? Would he actually have me stoned?*

Her chest and shoulders rose as she inhaled a large breath of the night air, then slowly released it through her mouth. Ghostlike apparitions floated across the garden and disappeared.

Years had not dulled her memory of that day long ago when Caiaphas's shrill voice screamed, "Stone her!" as he stood above the cliff and looked down at the helpless woman.

Timon's not like Caiaphas or Efah. I must tell him. He deserves to know the truth—that Efah forced me—that I couldn't stop him. She stood in her wedding attire and trembled. *What if he doesn't believe me?* All the thoughts that she had tried to force back for months tumbled forward, forcing her to look, to think, to remember. She felt sick.

The wedding party journeyed close enough for her to see him now. He led the procession, euphoric, almost like a triumphal champion, his stature lean and strong with a kingly air. He caught sight of her standing in the window. Their eyes met for a moment before she slipped into the shadows, embarrassed by the love radiating from his dark eyes. *After tonight will he still love me?*

Her hands shook as she fastened her radiyd in place and lifted her bejeweled robe just high enough not to trip as she crossed the room and journeyed down the portico to the courtyard. In the flickering lamplight and radiant full moon, a multicolored array of butterflies led the procession. It was as if they knew she was coming and made plans to announce her arrival. Butterflies fluttered through the air as she moved past their nighttime resting places and landed on the red flowers in front of her, bowing before their queen.

Outwardly, she moved with a majestic grace and dignity that did not reflect the inner turmoil of a woman fearful of her betrothed's rejection. Her glimmering radiyd hid her disheartened countenance and moonbeams sparkled in her eyes. She stopped near the dark green pomegranate bushes, where she'd spent so many hours watching the butterflies enjoy their freedom. The melange of brilliant blues, yellows, and purples always cheered her darker thoughts.

Timon entered the courtyard, his eyes beaming with a joyful exuberance. He approached with a slight nod and a bow. His appearance mesmerized her. She barely moved or breathed and gazed into his eyes and drank deeply of the love that emanated from his dark pools. Enchanted by his presence, she forgot about her secret.

Stephen pronounced the wedding blessing. "Our sister, may you increase to thousands upon thousands; may your offspring possess the gates of their enemies." She glanced at her mother and saw a tear trickle down her cheek. Standing next to her was Sarah. She giggled with glee.

Jerusha left with Timon and moved with the joyful crowd through the lamp-lit streets toward her new home. This trip was so different from the gloomy, fear-filled journey to Caiaphas's palace that had been forced upon her as a little girl. Instead of hiding in the dark, silent shadows as she had wound her way to some unknown destination, she was now carried along a lighted pathway by a jubilant celebration toward a wedding feast prepared in her honor.

Timon enticed her to join him in dance. She swayed to the music with him. Captivated for the moment, the lighthearted, carefree little girl within unveiled herself and danced before her husband, laughing and twirling with an elegant poise of royalty.

Carried along by the crowd, she kept her eyes on Timon and paid little attention to the twists and turns that led to their destination. Suddenly, she looked up at her mother, who stood at the open gate, her dimpled smile spread wide, her dark eyes twinkling. Father's house? She looked back at Timon.

"Your chuppah awaits," he said.

"I don't understand?"

"Your father left an inheritance. I've restored it—my gift to you. I hope you are pleased."

"Oh, Timon, I *am* pleased!" Jerusha walked through the gate and stopped underneath the twisted trunk of the old jujube (sidar), its branches a green canopy overhead. "I said good-bye to Father many times while standing under this tree." She moved to one of the limbs that hung down and separated the leaves from the thorns, carefully picking the ripened dark red fruit. "It's strange. I've wondered if someday he'll come back. I can't believe he's really gone forever." The music stopped. She saw Stephen motion for the wedding guests to follow him inside. Alone with Timon, she glanced up. Timon came from behind and placed his hands on her shoulders.

"Anything's possible," he whispered. She closed her eyes and tried to calm her racing pulse. *Is it possible you will love me after tonight?* She moved away from him to the doorpost and touched the mezuzah.

"Father left a message here that said he'd be back."

Timon wrapped his arm around her waist. "I know you miss him. Come inside and see what I have done with the house," he said and wiped a tear from her cheek.

She stepped over the threshold.

"Oh, Timon! It is beautiful! The lamplight glimmered on the purple and blue tiles that lined the walkway of the veranda that led to the courtyard. She stopped by the marble column and laughed. "No broken tiles to throw?"

"It has been cleared of all potential weapons," he said with a wink. "I've seen the fire in your eyes."

"Afraid of me?" she teased, brushed past his arm, then glanced back coyly, wrapped her arm around the marble pillar and spun around. He grabbed her other arm and gently pulled her close. She blushed.

"My only fear is that you won't love me," he said. She felt his strength. Her heart quickened and she desired to kiss him and tell him she did love him. Before she could answer, he relaxed his grip. "Our guests are waiting." She heard the music grow louder in the garden and he released her. "I'm sorry to be so bold."

He led her through the portico into the courtyard. The fountain, once filthy, now ran with pure, clean water, its tiles sparkling in the moonlight. He opened the gate to the garden and bowed.

"My queen, your throne awaits," he said, that lopsided grin spread wide. This time Jerusha felt like royalty. She took his arm and walked on the purple and blue tiles into the garden, every bush trimmed, no thorns in the blossoming grape vines.

"Oh, it's more beautiful than when I was a child. I love what you've done. I love—" she stopped and looked into his eyes. She knew he waited for her to finish the sentence.

"Come, my queen," he teased, then winked and seated her in grandeur beneath the canopy next to him. She reveled in the merrymaking as the guests arrived and partook of the feast he had arranged. She was completely enamored with her husband's attentive gaze and didn't want to leave. But true to custom, she and Timon attended to each guest with love and a gaiety Jerusha thought she'd never experience again. Several hours later he leaned over and whispered in her ear.

"Come away with me," he nodded toward their private chamber. She smiled in agreement.

Once inside their bedchamber her fingers fumbled with her veil as she removed it and revealed her glittering pendant beneath for him to see. The purple butterfly jewel on the lion's face sparkled in the lamplight along with the golden crown in its mane, etched with the words, Lion of the Tribe of Judah. She placed the veil on her husband's shoulders and made the common declaration at Jewish weddings.

"The government shall be upon your shoulder."

He drew her to himself.

"My little butterfly. I've known I loved you since that night I saw you in the garden moonlight without your radiyd, arms stretched out, twirling in childlike abandonment." She rested her head on his chest. "I refrained myself from laughing when you scrambled to replace your radiyd and left it cockeyed on your head." She giggled and gazed up at his dark eyes. "You were beautiful even then," he spoke softly and caressed her cheek. "The day you wrestled with the pomegranate bushes and tried to hide; again your radiyd ajar, cheeks blushed in embarrassment, your green eyes glaring up, determined not to let me help. I knew I wanted you for my wife."

She blinked and looked down. "I, too, have fallen in love with you," a flush rose in her cheeks. His embrace stirred something wonderful and new. "Your concern for the orphans, your gentle touch with the widows, reveals a man I can trust." Tears glistened in her smiling eyes. "I feel safe in your arms." She sensed his desire to love her fully and moved away and stood by the window and breathed deeply of the fragrant blossoms on the terrace below.

She wanted to please him, to enjoy the fullness of his love, to give herself to him, but fumbled with her robe's clasp. He wrapped his arms around from behind, gently helped unfasten it, and removed the robe from her shoulders. It fell to the floor. Her soft tunic rippled gently in the slight spring breeze and she shivered a little.

"Don't be afraid," he whispered. "I love you." His hand slipped beneath the tunic.

She stiffened.

"Stop. I can't do this. I'm sorry. I can't do this," she snatched her robe from the floor, covered herself, and ran to the bed. "I have disgraced you."

"Jerusha, what are you talking about?"

"I have—" she stopped. "I am—I am—not worthy. You will not have the bloodied sheet to put outside the door," she said and choked back tears. She saw his puzzled look and flopped on the bed, her sobs echoed outside the garden, unheard by the festive crowd. She knew the witnesses watched for evidence of their consummation and she waited for his retaliation, his rejection. Several minutes passed. The bed sheet moved under her leg and she sat up.

"What are you doing? She asked and wiped the sniffles from her nose on her sleeve.

"I will not let my bride be humiliated."

She watched him drag the sheet across the room and prick his finger with the knife that lay beside the pomegranates on the table. After wiping his blood on the sheet, he rushed to the door and opened it. She heard the loud music from the celebration. He threw the sheet outside and slammed the door shut.

"There! They have their evidence."

She stared, her mouth gaping.

"Why would you do such a thing?"

He moved back to the bed, sat down, and took her hand.

"Because I love you. You are my wife. Nothing will change that. We have a lifetime to know each other. Please tell me what happened."

"I—I cannot tell you," she rolled on her side away from him, covered herself with her robe and curled into a ball. She felt him get up and heard his robe brush by their bed as he moved across the room and blew out the lamp.

Chapter 24

Jerusha awoke enveloped in darkness. Curled in a ball, perspiration ran down her back. She clutched her pendant to her chest and rubbed her face softly into Timon's robe, tucked closely around her neck and shoulders. She reached out from under it and touched his lean, muscular build. He faced away from her. She groaned, saddened by her inability to fully give herself to him and blinked back tears of frustration and confusion.

What was she going to do? She rubbed her fingers across her pendant. The engraved words in the gold crown in the lion's mane spoke of her royal inheritance. She drifted back to sleep.

"I'm dirty. I'm not who you think I am!" she screamed and spiraled fast and faster downward. "Help me. Someone help me." Strong hands grabbed her shoulders. She saw the light but couldn't reach it. She heard Timon's deep voice in the distance.

"Jerusha, wake up."

"No. No. No," she moaned and clawed at the strands around her face.

"Yeshua, help her," she heard Timon cry. "I'm here, Jerusha, don't be afraid."

The light above her head became larger and larger with each tug. She pulled herself closer and closer to its brightness. Suddenly, she was totally enveloped in a shining brilliance so intense she could hardly open her eyes. The all-encompassing light emanated from the face of the One sitting on the throne. Translucent creatures hovered around him, their melodious voices singing "Holy, Holy, Holy" grew to a crescendo. A rainbow of vibrant color encircled the throne. Instantly, she fell on her face before the royal seat. A slight tap on her shoulder and a swoosh of air passed over and caused her to glance up.

The One on the throne held a girl on his lap. It's me! Jerusha watched the girl who sat unhindered by a radiyd smile up into his face, which was covered with a cloudy, shimmery mist. This free-spirited, laughing, young girl was fully engaged in conversation with One who adored her. Jerusha listened more intently, "My little butterfly, don't be afraid to fully receive and enjoy your husband. He is my gift to you." He lifted her down and she spun pirouettes around his throne. With each spin the scene faded.

She awoke on her side cradled in Timon's arms and wondered what happened. It felt like a dream. Maybe a vision? No, it seemed more like a real place? Whatever happened, it filled her with great joy and peace. She smiled in the darkness and listened to Timon's rhythmic breathing. His hand lay across her waist. His breath warmed her neck. She lifted his fingers, kissed his palm, and rested it on her chest, her hand over his.

"You are my gift," she whispered. Aware she stirred his manly passion, she closed her eyes, relaxed in his arms, and waited.

***

The golden slice of early morning sunlight shone on her face. She opened her eyes and squinted as she peered around the room. *I am married.* She saw Timon beside the window, his back to her. He slipped a fresh tunic over his head and allowed it to drop across his broad shoulders. She wondered why he had not responded to her gesture of love. She knew he had been awake and obviously stirred. *She wouldn't blame him if he was angry.* His robe fell from her shoulders as she rose from the bed.

He turned, deep in thought.

"I see you are awake," he said, and motioned toward the table. "Come, enjoy some nourishment." A bowl of plump figs, several clusters of green grapes and dark red pomegranates sat in a colorful tiled bowl in the middle of the table. She struggled to wrap his large, striped robe around her shoulders and glanced up.

"May I be of assistance?" he asked, his dark brows burrowed together in concern.

"No, I can get it," she answered. The sun shined through the opened white-latticed window and warmed her toes as she approached, dragging his robe on the purple and blue tiles. That endearing, lopsided grin widened across his face.

He reached out and enveloped her in his strong arms. For a fleeting moment she drew comfort from his strength. Her face buried in his chest, she smelled the fragrance of his fresh tunic, but not sure why he rejected her offer of love the night before, she stiffened and pushed away from his embrace.

"I'm not hungry," she said and turned her back. Her hand swiped across the table edge. She looked down and saw his dried blood.

"I appreciate what you did for me last night," she said and kept her eyes on the blood, afraid of what she might see if she looked up into his eyes. Her heart pounded.

She felt him circle around her stiffened body and lean against the table, his presence so close she heard his breathing.

"Do you remember what you screamed in your sleep last night?" he asked.

Uncomfortable with his question, she reached for a pomegranate and fumbled it onto the table. It rolled away and she caught it just before it fell off. A flush rose in her cheeks. She wondered why she always acted like a bumbling idiot around him and stuttered.

"Uh . . . no."

A protective covering has grown around your heart. I don't know what's happened to you—one day the covering will be taken away. . . .

He carefully took the pomegranate from her hands, picked up the knife, and cut it open. He laid one half on the table, sunk his teeth into the juicy pulp, then wiped the extra drops that ran down his chin with the back of his hand.

"You said, 'I'm dirty. I'm not who you think I am.' Were you talking to me?" he asked.

She stared at the other piece of fruit.

I've planted many seeds of my love within your heart.

"I—I don't know. I may have been talking to Father."

His red-stained fingers touched her cheek and slowly brushed away the single tear that trickled down her face.

"Jerusha, what are you hiding?"

She closed her eyes and savored the tenderness of his touch, then glanced up at his concerned gaze.

"I do have something to tell you, a secret I've never told anyone. You deserve to know," her voice quivered. "You may not want anything to do with me after I tell you."

He looked directly into her eyes, no playful twinkle, no lopsided grin, and with deep sincerity quietly whispered.

"Nothing you say will change my love for you."

Afraid she might not have the courage to continue, she slipped away from his attempted embrace, moved to the mittah and sat down. Fiddling with her fingers and keeping her eyes down, she began her story.

"When I was a little girl I frequently traveled to Herod's palace with my mother and I developed a friendship with Caiaphas's son, who visited there often with his father. I even had hoped that when I got older, Efah would be chosen for my betrothed. One day—"

She unveiled more and more details, sickened by the memories, but finally looked up at his reddened face. He slammed his fist down on the table. Greatly startled, every muscle in her body froze as she stared at his enraged expression that glared back. *He hates me.* The silence lengthened between them.

Finally, her words tumbled like a waterfall over a ledge.

"I'm sorry. I'm so sorry. I don't blame you for being mad. I should have stopped him. I just couldn't. I tried. I really tried. Please—what are you going to do? I told you that you wouldn't want anything to do with me. I'm so sorry!" She threw herself on the mittah. The tears burst forth in uncontrolled staccato bursts.

Immediately, Timon rushed to her side.

"I'm not angry with you," he spoke softly but loud enough to be heard over her cries. She felt his strong hands lift her and hold her tight to his chest. "I'm angry at them."

"You still want me as your wife?" she hiccupped.

"My love has grown stronger each day since the first time I saw you with arms stretched out, twirling around, unveiled in the moonlit garden. Nothing you say can change that."

She buried her head in his chest and rested in the safety of his embrace. This time she welcomed his caresses as he lifted her mouth to his. When he approached those delicate places she stiffened a little and then surrendered.

"I trust you not to hurt me," she whispered. She was enraptured by his gentleness and patience as their hearts and bodies blended, giving themselves to each other in oneness of true marriage.

Blinking in the late morning sunlight, she lay in his embrace and listened to the sound of his breathing until it gradually slowed and he fell into a deep sleep. Not wanting to awaken him, she carefully disentangled herself from his arms and legs and slipped out of the bed, her heart overflowing with admiration and love. She splashed water on her salty, swollen eyes. Music floated into the room from the continuing celebration in the courtyard.

Extending her arms in childlike abandonment she twirled around and around, dipping and swaying to the melody. *He loves me anyway. Timon loves me anyway.*

For the first time since being a little girl sitting on Father's lap she felt cherished, special—like royalty. She grasped the pendant that hung around her neck, walked to the window, and looked out over the city where she had been born. She remembered again Father's words. *"Your heart will forever beat with the blood of the tribe of Judah. My jewel, you are royalty."*

A quiet melody began to rise from the depths of her inner being. With the melody the words came. *I am the lion of Judah. Deep within my innermost being dwells the Holy God of all Israel! I am the lion of Judah.'* She felt again like the lioness Father adored.

Timon stirred. She turned to see him resting on his forearm with a broad grin.

"You never looked more beautiful or content," he said, a twinkle in his eye.

Slipping from the bed, he approached from behind and encircled her shoulders in a tender embrace. She hummed the newly formed melody and swayed in his arms.

After awhile, she whispered, "I desire to give you many sons and daughters."

"Today, it is enough," he spoke softly in her ear, "that you completely surrendered to my love."

Chapter 25

The seven-day consummation period passed. It was now time for Timon to present her publicly to the wedding guests without her veil. She stood erect, fully dressed in her bejeweled garment next to him.

"Are you ready?" he asked and smiled with a glint in his eyes that radiated his love. Her grin signaled her readiness. "Don't be afraid," he added. "You shine brighter than the pendant you are wearing."

Timon knocked on the door. Almost immediately, Stephen, who had been waiting outside for this moment, opened it. They stepped through the archway to greet the waiting guests. Cheers and exultation ensued as they made their way through the crowded courtyard stopping to exchange the customary kiss of peace with each guest.

Jerusha thoroughly enjoyed the dignity and security of her new identity. *He knows everything and still loves me.* She struggled to contain the giggles bubbling up within and remain dignified and reserved. Her spirit soared. She wanted to dance and laugh and sing.

"I sense that carefree child inside wanting to break loose and celebrate," he whispered in her ear.

"Wait until we are alone," she giggled. Unable to contain the joy, she twirled around once and bowed a curtsey with obeisance.

Lifting her demure eyes, she spotted Caiaphas and Efah standing behind him beneath the entry lintel. She sucked in her breath and rose up. Timon turned to see why. The pompous priest maneuvered his way through the guests toward them. The guests stopped chatting. Timon stepped directly in front of her and pulled himself to full height. His broad shoulders blocked the high priest's view of Jerusha.

"You are not welcome here," he spoke boldly.

"I came looking for Jacob. I'm sure that traitor would not miss his own daughter's wedding. Where is he?" Caiaphas demanded and waved his arms at the temple guards who followed. They marched around him single file, shoved the wedding guests to the side, and started a search of the house. Tipping over the tables, the soldiers clattered down the tiled veranda. Jerusha heard the echo of heavy cedar doors thud against the limestone walls and watched as they hacked with glistening swords at the dark green pomegranate bushes.

"He's not here," one guard spoke. She looked his direction and watched him fling her father's bench to the ground. The delicately carved edge landed in a puddle of mud. An anger stirred in her bosom. A flush rose to her cheeks. She moved from behind Timon and stood straight and tall before Caiaphas, Timon's hand resting possessively on her shoulder.

"How dare you treat Father's house like this. If he was here, he'd—he'd have something to say about all this!" she blurted with the courage of the little girl who felt like royalty again. Caiaphas's eyebrows winged upward. Was that a glint of fear she saw?

"But, but," she could hardly spit out the words, "but my father's dead." The words sounded so final. *No, it's not true,* her inner child cried. Tears threatened to overflow.

She turned her back to Caiaphas and looked up at Timon.

"That self-righteous pig will not see me cry!" she whispered, startled by the hatred in her tone. She pressed her cheek snug against her husband's muscular body, then turned and faced her worst enemy.

The sun's rays reflected off the butterfly jewel on the lion pendant and sent sparkles across Caiaphas's face. He stared through narrowed slits, his dark, beady glare fixed on Jerusha's cherished possession. Her fingers enclosed her father's treasured gift in her palm. She gripped it tight. He would not have an opportunity to throw it into the fire this time.

"Idol worshipper!" Caiaphas screamed and pointed to her pendant.

Timon stepped in front of Jerusha again.

"How dare you interrupt our wedding festivities with your uninvited presence and unfounded accusations! Get out!"

"Don't you know I have the power to have you arrested?" Caiaphas sneered.

"I said get out!" Timon spoke slowly through gritted teeth, his fists clenched at his sides. "You will not intimidate anyone in my home," he yelled and pointed to the courtyard entry.

Emboldened by Timon's words, she stepped out from behind his muscular build and stood beside him. Reaching for his hand, she intertwined her fingers in his and glanced at Efah. His smirk roamed down to her pendant that hung sparkling in the light for all to see. It had been awhile since she had seen his lustful eyes devour her like a morsel of meat. She covered her chest with her arm and leaned closer to Timon. He let go of her hand and wrapped his arm around her waist.

Caiaphas glanced around the room. Stephen and Peter moved forward and stood, one on each side of Timon and Jerusha. Others moved in closer as well. Jerusha heard her mother's voice urging Sarah and the other children to come with her and the sound of tiny footsteps echoed through the corridors. A door creaked shut.

Jerusha's stomach tightened, and she stared straight at Efah. *I'll die before I let you touch me again.* Her hands trembled and she felt Timon's strong fingers clasp her hand in his and squeeze, a protective signal that showed he knew she was afraid.

"You will pay for associating with this man and his harlot wife!" Caiaphas blurted. Jerusha's heart quickened. She remembered the stoning she saw as a little girl and Caiaphas's smug, hate-filled eyes glaring at the woman below. Surely Timon wouldn't hand her over.

She glanced up at him. His jaw, firm and set, spoke of his anger, too. Was he angry at her? Her thoughts of his blood on the bed sheet and his tender embrace from the previous day brought an assurance. He glanced briefly at her and winked.

She looked past him to Stephen. *What was he thinking? Did he believe Caiaphas?* He, too, appeared unmoved by the accusation. Her eyes moved back to Caiaphas. In the silence, his calculating eyes darted from face-to-face. She held her breath. Finally, Caiaphas made his exit. Efah and their small gentry of guards followed. The porter slammed the door shut.

Jerusha turned and looked up at Timon, surprised by the soft twinkle in his eyes. She knew for a woman to talk so boldly to any man in front of other men brought disgrace on her husband. She had reprimanded the highest religious authority in Judah.

"I'm sorry," she whispered. Her dark lashes blinked back tears. "I've caused you such embarrassment in front of our family and friends."

"I'd like to give him more than a tongue lashing," he said and tapped her nose lightly and pulled her close to his chest. Relieved, she smiled, but a familiar shame and condemnation crept over her heart. The others in the room surrounded them. An older man with a long, gray beard broke the silence.

"The high priest lacks wisdom and love. In days gone by it was not so. Things in Jerusalem are changing." She heard the low murmured cries for deliverance and peace. She wondered what the future held for her and Timon. Would they survive here? Maybe Timon would be better off without her. One by one the guests departed. Stephen, the last to leave, cupped Jerusha's chin in his hand.

"Jacob would be pleased with you," he said, then patted Timon on the shoulder. "And you, too."

"Oh, Stephen, you've been like a father to me. I'm so grateful for all that you've done for us," she answered and looked up at Timon. He nodded and clasped hands with Stephen. They stood under the ornate lintel and watched him walk in the shade of several olive trees and depart. The large iron gate clanged shut.

Jerusha turned and walked with a purpose, Timon following, along the winding tiled pathway. Together they lifted the bench from the mud and cleaned the mud splattered on the pomegranates carved on the edge, her most favorite part. She scooped water from the puddle with her palms and poured it over the smears.

"I was so mad at Caiaphas," she said.

After a long silence, Timon spoke, his tone soft.

"I know you don't want to hear this, but we must forgive him and Efah."

"No!" she snapped. "I will never forgive them. I hate them."

She plopped on the ground near the puddle and looked at her bejeweled garment smeared with mud. Caiaphas and his son ruined her wedding, threatened her friends, heaped humiliation upon humiliation. Wasn't it enough what happened in the palace? Did they have to spew their poison on every part of her life? Evening shadows crept across the courtyard. The handmaids lit the lamps. Timon reached down, set the bench on the ground, and lifted Jerusha to her feet.

"Come, my beautiful wife." He wiped dirty specks from her cheeks with his finger. "You are not alone. We'll face this together," he said and kissed her lightly on the forehead. "I hate them, too."

"You do?" she stared up into his eyes. He nodded, then closed his eyes. "Help us forgive, Yeshua—like you forgave from the cross those who crucified you," he whispered. He took her arm and led her through the garden to the bedchamber. Standing in front of the window, their fingers intertwined, they looked out over the city at the lamps twinkling in the darkness.

"He'll have us arrested. He'll find some way to make a complaint against us. He'll say we broke the law. It's always by the law. He'll call us blasphemers, idolaters, adulterers. He'll trump up false witnesses. I may be stoned!" Jerusha's voice squeaked, revealing her greatest fear.

"Stop!" he said and grabbed her shoulders, half shaking her. "Whatever happens, I love you and I will do everything in my power to protect you."

"Timon," she said wide-eyed, "Maybe we should leave Jerusalem." He thought for a moment before answering.

"No, Jerusha. We cannot leave. Stephen and Peter need me here to take care of the widows and orphans."

Weak from the intense emotions, she collapsed against his chest. He picked her up and carried her to the bed. She felt the soft pillows beneath her head and the warmth of his cloak around her shoulders as he tucked it under her chin.

"Rest now," he said and kissed her on the cheek. The fragrance from the pomegranate bushes under their window wafted in the air. He slipped into bed, reached out, and pulled her close. His hand brushed her chest.

"Don't!" She pushed him away, turned over, and curled on her side. "I'm sorry," she said. A tear trickled down her cheek. Again she tumbled down into that horrible, dark place, unable to receive his love. *What's wrong with me?*

All night Jerusha tossed and turned, mumbling indistinct replies to apparitional demon-like creatures. She'd awaken bewildered, pulse racing, and stare into the darkness afraid to go back to sleep. Lying on her side, she'd feel Timon's strong arms pull her into his body and hold her tight.

"It's all right. You're safe now," he'd whisper in her ear. She'd relax and drift back to sleep.

Early in the morning she crept from the mittah and approached Timon who stood before the window, peering out at the terraced garden. She laced her fingers in his and they watched the ghostlike fog float along the garden pathway among the pomegranate bushes near the ground.

"I'm sickened by how many sleepless nights you must have endured while living with Caiaphas." He raised his right fist and pulled it back ready to hit something. "I envision beating him merciless," he grimaced and dropped his fist to his side. "I'm vexed by hatred." He leaned his head against the window shutter. "What shall I do?"

A cool, damp mist blew gently across their faces. She saw him take a deep breath and exhale, his shoulders relaxing a little. Then suddenly, he came to attention.

"I need to move quickly. I must catch him before he leaves for the day. Prepare to leave," he commanded rather abruptly.

"Where are we going?"

"I must fetch the daily bread for the widows and take it to Stephen," he answered and continued to stare out the window. Not sure if this sudden visit to Stephen was necessary, she scrunched her brow, but moved slowly to fetch her cloak.

Chapter 26

S tarving dogs scavenged for scraps of food in darkened corners the closer they got to the market. Several times when the dogs bared their teeth and snarled from the shadows, Timon jumped in front to shield her. She wondered at his jittery behavior and yet savored his safe guardianship, a feeling new to her, but one she had longed for since Father's disappearance.

The sun had fully risen by the time they entered the wide-open marketplace. Traders were unpacking heavy loads from camels. Men and their sons erected booths laden with fruit, bread, woven cloths, or pottery to sell. The aroma of bread baking in the city ovens was a welcome scent. Within no time the bread was purchased and they were quickly en route to Stephen's house with as many loaves as they could carry.

"You are especially sullen today," she said breathlessly, with a concerned crinkle in her brow as they traveled hurriedly toward their destination. She thought he might be thinking about the events of the previous day, but by now she convinced herself that it was better to forget everything that Caiaphas had said and pretend it never happened. When she awoke she had squelched the turmoil in her stomach, a survival tool she'd acquired while living in captivity. The inner twisting and turning had resurfaced again as she watched Timon's restless agitation.

"When we get to Stephen's house I would like to meet with him alone," he finally said without looking down. "I have some important matters to discuss with him." She winced at his apparent dismissal. His foreboding glower silenced her many questions. As they neared the dwelling, she saw Mother waving.

"Jerusha! Timon!" She yelled. When they reached the entrance, she opened the iron gate and took the bread from Jerusha. "Shalom, my children," she greeted with the traditional kiss of peace. "Sarah saw you coming and ran to tell me. She and the other children are waiting inside."

Sarah yelled their names and ran full speed toward them, her tiny sandals flopping on the tiles. Timon swung her high in the air. She giggled with glee. The two were a picture of her happier times with Father. She smiled down at the other children who quickly surrounded them.

"Do it to me! Do it to me!"

"I want to fly like Sarah!"

"Me, too! Pick me!"

They each took their turn. Jerusha slipped into the garden to talk with Mother.

"I saw the glower on Timon's face when you approached. Why did you come here today? I thought you two would want to be alone."

Jerusha blushed. Her mother had talked to her about the wedding night before she married, and she knew what she meant by her subtle comment.

"Mother!" she spoke with a raised pitch. "You are embarrassing me."

"I'm sorry, Jerusha," she patted her hand. "Yesterday was quite an emotional day. Caiaphas ruined a perfectly beautiful wedding feast. If your father had been there . . ." her voice trailed off. "Never mind. Tell me more about why you've come."

"Well, Timon said he needed to bring bread, but I think it's more than that. He's been especially solemn today."

The children interrupted and came running. "We're hungry!"

Abigail laughed. Her dimples warmed Jerusha's heart. For some reason, today she looked older, but still so beautiful. She touched her dark mole and remembered how as a little girl she wanted to look like her. Now she saw a beauty inside that she desired to replicate. *She's so caring and kind.*

"Everyone find a place on the ground," Abigail said. "We'll eat in the garden today." She handed Jerusha some of the bread, and they walked among the children, tore small pieces off the larger loafs, and dolled it out to the children.

"After we eat and the younger ones take a nap, we'll go to the Gihon Springs to fetch water. It's such a warm day maybe you can tickle your toes in the water, too," Abigail promised.

"Mother, that reminds me of when I went to the springs with Father. He always let me ride the donkey."

"He spoiled you," Abigail joked. Jerusha chuckled.

"Look, Jerusha!" Sarah yelled and pointed. "A purple butterfly landed on your hand. The other day I waited and watched until I saw one come out of its chrysalis."

"My father taught me about the chrysalis," Jerusha answered and watched the butterfly flitter away. "Maybe I can share with you sometime about what I learned," she offered. The movement of a shadow over the pomegranate bushes caught her eye and she saw Timon following Stephen down the portico.

"Excuse me, children. I have something I need to do. I'll try to be back in time to fetch the water." She ran a little to catch up with Timon, but he disappeared behind the cedar door before she could catch him, so she stood outside the door and listened.

"What's this about?" she heard Stephen ask. "There's quite a fire in your eyes."

She heard a fist slam on the table and her shoulders jerked.

"I hate them! What they have done is inexcusable," Timon yelled.

"I assume by them you mean Caiaphas and his son."

"Yes." The seething in his voice frightened Jerusha. "I'm not at liberty to share what has been revealed to me. Just know it's deplorable, and it involves my wife."

"I remember the lust in Caiaphas's eyes every time she entered the room," Stephen said. "Hold still so I can wipe the blood from your knuckles." Jerusha heard Timon wince. "It sickened me," Stephen continued. "And I was so glad to get her and her mother out. I only wish it could have been sooner. So, why are you confiding in me?"

"You are one of the wisest men I know. How do I combat the rage—the outright hatred that burns inside?" Timon asked. "More than once I've imagined choking him until he begs for mercy."

Jerusha glanced down the corridor to be sure no one was coming. After a few minutes of silence, she heard movement inside. She peeked through the crack in the door. Stephen placed his hands upon Timon's shoulders and looked directly into his eyes.

"Do you remember how much Yeshua has forgiven you?"

"I have not done what Efah and Caiaphas has done."

"Maybe not, but could you ever repay Yeshua for the debt you owed?"

Jerusha groaned inside for Timon as he hung his head.

"No."

"Then you must forgive them. These revengeful and tormenting thoughts will grow worse until you do. Yeshua's love will be blocked from flowing through you. Your beautiful, new wife, the one you want to protect, will suffer the most. Your freedom and hers depends on your surrender to his ways."

"I don't know if I can do that."

"Our King never tells us to do something that he doesn't empower us to do. Choose forgiveness instead of revenge. He'll do the rest."

Jerusha heard a loud pounding on the entry door to the courtyard. Fear tingled down her spine and without thinking she pushed the door open and flew into Timon's arms.

"Someone's coming!"

"Stay here!" he commanded. "It may not be safe."

She stood under the lintel and watched her new husband and Stephen run down the portico and followed at a distance. When the large, ornate cedar door flew open and banged against the limestone wall, she jumped behind a marble pillar. A tumultuous crowd swarmed inside.

"Blasphemer!"

Jerusha crept out to see who the accusation was against.

Timon stood face-to-face with Caiaphas. The fire in her husband's eyes and the clenched fists revealed his readiness to strike.

No, she cried inwardly and ran toward them, willing Timon to hear her. *Don't strike him. He's the high priest. They'll kill you. It's me they want.* The words stuck in her throat, but her feet flew toward her husband.

Before she reached him, the temple guards pushed Timon aside and grabbed Stephen. Timon stepped out and placed his hand on the chest of the guard.

"Stop!" The guard looked at the high priest who motioned to wait.

"Caiaphas, you are the high priest. You have the authority to stop this. He's done no wrong," Timon pleaded.

The small crowd roared in protest around them.

"Blasphemer! Blasphemer!"

A man from the Synagogue of the Freedmen nodded a signal to another man who stood near Stephen.

The man nodded back, then pointed to Stephen.

"I heard him speak blasphemous words!" The man's eyes wildly darted about, person to person. "*Many* blasphemous words."

"No, that's not true!" Timon shouted. Jerusha wiggled through the crowd and stood beside Timon. He placed his arm around her.

"I told you to stay in the room," he whispered.

"I'm your wife and stand with you," she said with more confidence than she felt. The frenzied crowd shoved them aside and dragged Stephen out the courtyard gate and down the hill. Caiaphas followed behind, a smug, self-righteous tip to his chin showing his pious approval. Timon ran to the gate with Jerusha right behind him. Sarah squeezed in between them and Timon swooped her up in his arms. The other orphans and widows gathered around, too.

Caiaphas turned.

"My hands are clean," he announced with a pompous flair. He laughed contemptuously and whirled around, his priestly robes fanning a circle behind him. "He'll have a fair trial, though, with many witnesses," he called loudly for all to hear and followed the hate-infested mob, who growled their accusations like mad dogs against Stephen.

"I didn't expect him to come against Stephen," Jerusha said. "I thought he'd come after us." She saw Sarah's eyes widen.

"Where are they taking my uncle?" The tiny one's voice quivered.

"I'm not sure what's happening, Sarah, but we must all be brave," Timon said and looked at Jerusha.

"Go," she said and reached for Sarah, who clung to Timon's neck.

He pealed Sarah's arms off, gave her to Jerusha, and kissed them both on the cheek. She saw him glance behind her and turned to see his mother with Abigail and the numerous widows, mostly the old and frail that gathered around them, the smallest orphans held in their arms, and the toddlers cuddled beneath their cloaks.

"Where are all the men servants?" he asked.

"They probably followed the crowd, curious about Stephen," Chaya said. "Go. We'll be all right."

Timon nodded. He kissed Jerusha's cheek once more. "Please Jerusha, this time do as I say. Stay here. Get everyone inside and lock the gate after I leave."

Jerusha nodded in agreement and watched him run down the hill. She could feel her heart pound in her ears. She took Sarah inside the gate and locked it. I must not let her know how scared I am.

"Why did they take Stephen?" a young five-year-old boy asked. His chubby arms pulled on Jerusha's cloak.

"Where did Timon go?" Another orphan boy, taller and thinner but still shorter than Jerusha, chimed in. She patted the younger one's head and glanced at her mother in silence, unable to answer. Tears threatened to overflow. She felt Sarah's tiny palm touch her cheek and gently pull her face around to look into her eyes.

"Will they come back?" she asked. Numb, Jerusha froze as Abigail took Sarah from her arms. She heard the other widows call the troubled children into the garden and the sound of Stephen's cedar toy chest squeak open. Fortunately, the two boys forgot the questions and ran into the garden.

"I want a toy," they both cried simultaneously.

"I want down," Sarah asked, no longer interested in the answer to her question. She ran to the large loom where an older widow began her daily weaving. Jerusha, eyes glazed over, watched the young girl stare at the warp as it moved up and down.

"Can I help?" Sarah asked.

Abigail wrapped her arm around Jerusha's shoulder.

"Come with me." She led her away from the noisy children to a bench in the far corner of the garden.

"I'm so scared," Jerusha spoke in a whisper. "What's going to happen to Stephen? And Timon?" She sat with her mother in silence for a few minutes and wiped the wet drops from her cheek with the back of her hand. Her stomach rumbled and churned. "Mother, I'm so angry," she whispered. A burning rage grew within and caused her whole body to tremble. She jumped up.

"I can't just sit here and do nothing. This is all my fault!" She waved her arms in a circle and flopped them at her sides.

"No, Jerusha, it's not your fault!" Her mother answered sternly.

"Yes, it is! Caiaphas threatened everyone that had anything to do with me that he would have them arrested. I shouldn't have yelled and challenged his authority. I should have kept my mouth shut. Mother, I hate him! He's ruined my life! Just when I think I'll have some happiness, he shows up and turns my world upside down again. Stephen and Timon are in danger because of me. I must go after Timon. He told me to stay here, but I can't. I just can't! He's in danger!" Jerusha noticed her mother's eyes widen as she stood and grabbed her shoulders.

"What good will it do for you to go after him and put yourself in danger? It will just cause him more trouble," she pleaded.

"I have to, Mother. It's *me* they want. I'll persuade Caiaphas to let Stephen go and take me."

"No, Jerusha!" Abiah's yelled. "You're not thinking straight!" She shook Jerusha's shoulders.

"Let me go!" Jerusha said and twisted free. "I'm going to find Timon and Stephen before it's too late." She fled down the tiled path, her mother in pursuit. The older women's slower gait allowed the gap between them to widen.

"Jerusha, come back!" Abigail yelled.

Jerusha's fingers fumbled with the lock on the gate.

"There, I got it," she said, flung the gate open, and ran down the hill. "I'm sorry, Mother. I have to find them," she yelled and kept running.

Chapter 27

She knew where they were taking Stephen. She must hurry. In no time she caught up with the crowd gathered outside the door to the Chamber of Hewn Stone. Breathless, she pulled her radiyd high around her face. She knew her blue-rimmed green eyes would draw attention if anyone looked her way, but they were too involved with their murderous threats against Stephen. Her quick, deep breaths behind the light wool cloth warmed her face and she tried to slow her racing heart.

"Excuse me," she squeaked to some men. "May I get through?" Their eyes were not on her, so she wiggled between them, ducking under their extended arms that pointed to the action ahead. Suddenly, she felt a huge hand wrap around her mouth and yank her close. A gruff but familiar voice whispered in her ear.

"Don't scream and draw attention to us, and I'll let you go." Her heart jumped to her throat. She looked up, stunned to see Yogli! She jumped with excitement and surprise. "Yogli! Oh, they didn't send you back to Rome?"

Someone shouted and Yogli looked that way, always on guard. It was then that she saw the scar across his right cheek—a lifetime reminder of the night he was caught and flogged—for helping her and Mother. How often she wondered what happened to him. Peter and Stephen had received no word, but the kindness in Yogli's eyes revealed a man with no bitterness.

"What are you doing here?" she asked. He still had a grip on her arm.

"The question is, what are *you* doing here?" he asked. "This is no place for a woman, especially you," he reprimanded.

"I must get to Timon. You remember him, don't you? From Peter's meetings? The midwife's son. We're married now."

He narrowed his eyes and crinkled his brow, then let go of her arm. "So I've heard."

Jerusha rubbed her arm, sensing that Yogli questioned her motivation. "You don't like Timon?"

"I know Timon would not approve of you being here."

"I'll go with or without you," she stated flatly.

"You always were a little stubborn and snippy. I think that's what kept you alive in that horrible existence in the palace. You'll need my protection in this crowd. If I don't, Timon will never forgive me."

At that moment, the rambunctious crowd jostled them, and Yogli protectively stepped in front of Jerusha. She was face-to-face with the spear that was strapped to his back.

"Follow me and stay close. Hang onto my cloak so I know you're still behind me."

She sniffed as they shuffled forward until they broke through the crowd.

"Timon!" she yelled and rushed into his arms. He looked down at her, then up at Yogli, who now stood behind her.

"When are you going to learn to do what I say?" he scolded. Timon nodded at Yogli. "It is good to see you." Then he looked down at Jerusha. "Did she put you up to this?"

Jerusha jerked her head up.

"Timon, I need to talk to Caiaphas. I'm the one he wants. I may be able to persuade him to let Stephen go and take me instead."

Exasperated, he shook his head and looked at Yogli.

"Please—will you continue to keep her safe?" he asked. He posed the question with a confident tone of a close friendship. Jerusha heard a loud slap and snapped her head around.

Stephen stood in the middle of the crowd, the soldiers keeping most of them at bay, all but one man who laughed and mocked. Blood trickled from Stephen's mouth and down his chin. Jerusha wrinkled up her nose at the stench of a man who stood next to her in a ragged and dirty robe and looked up at Yogli.

"He's from the Synagogue of the Freedmen," he whispered.

At that moment, the smelly man broke through the guard barrier and smacked Stephen with his fist. Stephen staggered and glanced up at Jerusha, his eye blackened and swollen, refusing to fight back.

Jerusha's hands flew to her face in horror. *Oh! Stephen, this is all my fault. You shouldn't have helped me.*

"Timon, I've got to stop this," she looked up at his reddened face. He appeared to not hear what she said. Suddenly, he burst through the barricade, grabbed the arm of the abuser, and twisted it behind the man's back.

"Why do you strike a man before he's tried?" He twisted harder. "This man is innocent! If you strike him again, you'll have me to answer to!" Timon threw the man to the ground. He turned and stood nose-to-nose with one of the guards. "And you! Why do you allow this injustice?" he yelled.

The crowd laughed and shoved Timon aside. He stumbled and fell back into Yogli. He looked at Jerusha as he regained his balance and stood.

"I never wanted to believe the evil rumors about Caiaphas because he is the high priest. But after what you told me and the way the sly fox has turned this crowd into a frenzy against an innocent man, I see now that he deserves to die," he spewed.

"I tend to agree with you, but Timon, please. Don't say such treasonous things in public. It could get you killed," she pleaded and gripped his arm. The grinding sound of the huge cedar door to their left drew her attention away from him. Thirty or forty guards tromped through the opening.

"Get back!" one yelled. "You're not allowed in here. Only the witnesses to be heard by the Sanhedrin." He grabbed Stephen, tied his arms behind his back, and dragged him inside. "You! A guard pointed to the man who had accused Stephen. "And you," he pointed to Stephen's other accuser. "Come with me! The rest of you stay outside."

Jerusha saw Timon motion to Yogli, who stood behind her. Yogli took her arm and nodded. Timon sneaked behind the crowd and tried to get inside. A guard jabbed the butt end of a spear in his belly, shoved him back and held him at bay with the tip now bearing down on Timon's chest. Jerusha gasped and looked up at Yogli. He put his finger to his lips, an obvious sign for her not to scream.

"I'll run you through the next time you try that," the guard threatened. Timon jerked the spear from his hand, but two other guards overwhelmed him and threw him to the ground.

"You are NOT going to save him, you Hellenistic dog," one of them spit out the words through broken teeth. A slimy substance ran down Timon's beard. He wiped it with the sleeve of his robe and scrambled to get up. The guards thundered inside and slammed the heavy door shut. The crowd rushed to get in and trampled Timon underfoot.

Jerusha saw him roll over toward her. Face down, he protected his head with his arms. Yogli held onto her with one hand, bent down, and yanked Timon's robe from the back and raised him to his feet.

"Follow me and I'll make a way out of this mess," he said. "Keep her between us," he told Timon. With his massive breadth, he led the way through the jostling crowd, Jerusha sandwiched between the two men. When they exited the mob, they stood before another chamber entrance on the inside of the temple.

"Toda," Timon said.

"Stephen is my beloved friend, too," Yogli said, his voice deep and heavy with concern. His massive height towered over them. He looked down with gentle eyes not typically seen in a soldier with his huge build.

"Of course," Timon said. A tinge of guilt passed over Jerusha when she saw the displeasure toward her in his eyes.

"I'm sorry, Timon. I had to come." She felt the mob closing in, heard their murmurs against Stephen, and knew it would not be a fair trial. She stared at their murderous expressions.

"What's wrong with these men?" she cried.

"I've heard a man named Saul has great influence in the city, even with the high priest," Yogli answered. "And he hates Yeshua's followers."

"Yes, it's true," Timon replied. Jerusha was beginning to see that this trial was bigger than Caiaphas's hatred of her.

"Move over for the Sadducees!" Someone in the crowd yelled. The mob parted like the Red Sea, and three men dressed in black robes with phylacteries around their foreheads passed through the crowd toward the door. Timon nodded to Yogli, took Jerusha's arm, and the three of them slipped behind the jeering men. Jerusha heard one of the religious leaders grumble that they must stop this movement among our people, stop those who follow this false King and believe in this false kingdom. She glanced up at Yogli.

"What are they talking about?" she asked. He motioned her to be quiet.

They moved along with their backs to the wall toward the closed door, Jerusha in the middle. When the guards came outside to protect the three Sadducees, the trio managed to slip inside and hide behind a large marble pillar.

Jerusha peeked out and in the middle of the large chamber she saw Stephen, his hands tied behind his back. The guard slammed him face down to the decorative tiled floor. He looked so alone, his garments torn, his face beaten. Above him, she saw most of the seventy council members of the Sanhedrin seated in a semicircle.

"There's Caiaphas," she said and pointed. He walked past Stephen to the opposite side, swished his robe around and sat, ready to preside over the proceedings. She wanted so much to run out and plead for him to take her instead of Stephen, but she was beginning to sense something else at work.

Who is this Saul that Timon and the soldier mentioned? What did he have to do with this?

"Timon, I don't understand what's happening," she said and pulled on his arm and looked up. What she saw in Timon's eyes worried her. He almost didn't notice her presence.

"I'd like to wipe that smirk off his face," he grimaced. "In the past, Stephen sat among these same men and ruled. Now he's the one on trial," he gritted his teeth. Jerusha saw disgust in his eyes to the apparent injustice. His hardened expression troubled her.

She watched Stephen, the man who had taken her father's place in her life, the man who had bought her out of slavery and provided a home for her. His face, beaten and bruised, radiated a shining peace. He glanced around the room and nodded slightly at a few whom she knew had surrendered to the King. She presumed most present at this council were staunch supporters of the high priest.

"He's guilty. Maybe this growing rebellion will stop after he's stoned," she heard the voice of one of the three Sadducees escorted by the guards behind her. Another one replied, "He speaks blasphemy and works magic." Their voices grew louder as they moved closer.

Timon motioned to her and the soldier, and they crept with him to another hiding place. She glided quietly between the two men, across the hall to a huge ornate pillar. She heard the guard's loud footsteps as they approached. Her pulse quickened, but she kept her position behind Timon, eyes down, and held her breath. She saw the bottom edges of the Sadducees' black robes pass only inches away and heard the guards' hobnailed sandals clump up the stairs that led to the upper floor where the Sadducees would take their places among the council.

At that moment, the mob charged the door and swarmed into the outer portion of the chamber. Jerusha noticed a few of Stephen's servants mixed in the crowd. Numerous guards locked their shields to keep them from descending upon him.

One by one she heard false witnesses testify.

"This man speaks against this Holy Place and the law," one said.

Another deep voice growled.

"I heard him say that this Nazarene will destroy this place and change the customs of Moses."

"They are liars," Timon yelled and rushed under the archway to get to Stephen. Jerusha tried to follow, but Yogli grabbed her arm and held her behind the pillar.

"Halt," the guard warned Timon and placed a spear on his belly.

"I want to testify," he demanded and pointed at the assembly.

"I want to testify, too," she looked up at Yogli. He shook his head and tightened his grip.

"No other witnesses allowed," the guard said and gruffly pushed Timon against another pillar.

Timon waited for the guard to turn his back, then shoved his way past and ran into the middle and stood next to Stephen.

"You are accusing an innocent man!" he shouted. The crowd roared behind him, some in favor, some opposed to his statement.

"Look at his face," Jerusha heard Timon insist. She glanced around Yogli's girth and saw Timon point to Stephen.

"I've never seen a guilty man with so much calm. He looks like an angel. That should speak of his innocence."

"So peaceful," she spoke softly.

Caiaphas stood and shouted.

"Guards, get this scum out of here."

"Oh, no! What will they do with Timon? Arrest him? Maybe scourge him!" She tried to pull free from Yogli's grasp, but he held her tight.

"Stop! You're going to bring attention to us, then we'll all be arrested. Timon won't like that!" he whispered. She pursed her lips together and took a deep breath, ready to dispute his argument when she heard Timon shout.

"When they bring you before the authorities, do not become anxious about what you should speak in your defense! For the Holy Spirit will teach you in that very hour what you ought to say." She knew those words were for Stephen. She relaxed a little.

"What's happening to Timon?" she asked Yogli, unable to see around him.

"Shhhh. I can't see Timon, but Caiaphas raised his hands to quiet the crowd," he answered.

She heard Caiaphas clear his throat.

"Pig!" she gritted her favorite name for him between clenched teeth, still in Yogli's grip. The giant soldier grinned down at her and shook his head slightly. "Feisty as a mountain lion, you are."

"We will give him a chance to speak for himself," she heard Caiaphas say in his self-righteous nasal tone. "Are these things true that they accuse you of?"

Jerusha quietly prayed, "Yeshua, you are Christos, the King of heaven and earth. Don't let them take Stephen. He's a good man. The orphans and widows need him."

"What's wrong with me that every man I love gets ripped from my life?" she mumbled, thinking now only of herself. She heard a loud scuffle and looked to her right.

"If you do that again, I'll arrest you!" the guard spoke gruffly to Timon and threw him against a pillar. She breathed a sigh of relief. They let him go.

Yogli pulled her from behind the pillar and motioned Timon to follow. She looked Timon's way and could hardly keep up with the elongated stride of the soldier as they hurried down the hall, his grip on her arm tighter than ever. She saw Timon jump to his feet and maneuver his way through the raging mob. *Timon!* She reached out for him with her free arm, but lost sight of him when she and Yogli turned the corner into an alcove.

"Stay put!" This time the soldier spoke sharply to her, his giant body towering over, his gentle eyes stern. She nodded.

He moved a short distance away and waited for Timon. When he reached the corner, he yanked him to the right into the alcove with Jerusha.

"Come with me. I know a secret passage that leads to the other side," Yogli said.

Jerusha grabbed the front of Timon's cloak.

"Timon, don't do that again," she pleaded.

Timon's eyes twinkled for a fleeting moment. He nearly smiled. "Now you know how I feel."

"Come on, you two," Yogli said, his voice deep and guttural. They followed him up the stairs and ducked beneath a tiny opening. When they came out the narrow passageway, they were on the other side by the door that led outside. Unfortunately, another crowd gathered inside this doorway, too.

Jerusha looked down from the upper floor at Stephen. He looked at the crowd who had just beaten him and peered into the eyes of his judges. *He's such a gentle man,* she thought.

"I've grown to love you like a father," she whispered.

"Hear me, brethren and fathers!" He nodded in respect to the council. "The God of glory appeared to our father Abraham and gave him the covenant of circumcision. Abraham became the father of Isaac, and Isaac the father of Jacob, and Jacob the father of the twelve patriarchs who in their jealousy sold Joseph as a slave into Egypt."

Jerusha smiled, her eyes closed. *I remember this story, Father. Slavery. Betrayal from his own brothers. You said I was destined to rule like Joseph. What they meant for evil, YHWH meant for good.*

The Sanhedrin listened to Stephen's oratory, unable to dispute his wisdom. He continued, "Later they disowned Moses, saying, 'Who made you ruler and judge?' Our fathers were unwilling to be obedient in their hearts, turning back to Egypt saying to Aaron, 'Make for us gods who will go before us.' They also took along the tabernacle of Moloch and the star of Rompha, false images which were made to worship."

Stephen's fatherly eyes rested on Jerusha. She groaned inside. *I never showed him the appreciation he deserved.* She tried to express it in that brief exchange.

He glanced around the semicircle and continued.

"Our fathers had the ark of the covenant. David asked that he might build a dwelling place for the God of Jacob. However, the Most High does not dwell in houses made with human hands as the prophet says, 'Heaven is my throne, and earth is my footstool of my feet; what kind of house will you build for me?' says the Lord. 'Or what place is there for my repose? Was it not my hand which made all these?'"

She placed her hand over the pendant made of the same wood as the ark.

"Arise, Lord. Let your enemies be scattered. Let all who hate you flee before you," she whispered.

"You men who are stiff-necked are always resisting the Holy Spirit," Stephen continued. She saw his eyes lock with Timon's and knew he was pleading for him to yield to the power of forgiveness. She glanced back at Timon and saw a darkness in his eyes that clouded the gentleness and love that shined through him on her wedding night.

The change she saw scared her. *Is this what hatred does?* She watched him look away from Stephen, unmoved by his silent plea, and glare at Caiaphas.

"If he harms him, he'll pay," she heard him say. "I'll hire the Sicarii to secretly assassinate him—or take him out myself. That would be more satisfying."

"You are doing just as your fathers did," she heard Stephen's voice rise in pitch and loudness. He spoke with godly authority, like a lion to his prey. She wondered at his boldness. "They killed those who had previously announced the coming of the Righteous One, whose betrayers and murderers you have become."

"Caiaphas is the one who deserves death," Timon growled. He dropped Jerusha's hand. She looked down at his clenched fists, then up to his face, and followed his eyes to the guard's spear. She knew what he was thinking. *No!*

Suddenly a man moved in front of him and she saw his hidden dagger. *A Sicarius!* Timon noticed, too, He grabbed the man's shoulder and stopped him. She knew he wanted his dagger. Jerusha sucked in her breath.

"Timon, no!" she grabbed his other hand. He stared at her with such hatred she cowered back and looked up at Yogli behind her for help. He furrowed his eyebrows and pulled Timon around.

"Use your head," Yogli pleaded. "Jerusha needs you to stay alive. For a few denarii they'll assassinate him in secret. They hate anyone in bed with Rome." Jerusha wasn't sure revenge by the Sicarii at a later date was a good idea either, but at least it would give Timon time to calm down. This was not the man she had grown to love.

"How dare you accuse us! You're the one on trial here!" Caiaphas railed. Jerusha jerked her head around to see him pointing at Stephen, who appeared unmoved by his outburst.

"Behold, I see the heavens opened up and the Son of Man standing at the right hand of YHWH," Stephen decreed and pointed up.

"I don't see anything," Jerusha whispered, but she knew Stephen didn't lie.

"Do something, Yeshua!" Timon yelled. "If you don't, I will!"

Many of the Sanhedrin covered their ears.

"We will not hear any more of this blasphemous talk!" Simultaneously, the restless mob rushed upon Stephen and cried, "Stone him, stone him!"

"No!" Timon screamed. "He's innocent!" Jerusha felt the pull of her arm by Yogli as he jumped into an alcove and shoved her against the wall to keep her from being trampled by the throng. Timon hesitated, but then left them and followed close behind the crowd. Timon stopped in his tracks. She caught his eye and followed it to Stephen as they dragged their battered friend past. In those brief seconds, Stephen mouthed the words, *"Forgive him."* Timon visibly trembled all over. *"No!"* he shouted, his fist raised. "I'm ready to fight this whole mob—even die for you. I will never forgive! What good will that do?" He screamed, but his words were drowned out by the snarling mob. Startled by his outburst and the ugly look in his eyes, Jerusha backed away.

Yogli placed his hands on her shoulders and whispered, "He feels helpless. He'll work through this. Don't be afraid. Yeshua, the King, dwells inside and will win this battle. A battle you fight, too, eh?"

She looked up into his kind eyes.

"Yes, I've fought this for many years. I hate Caiaphas!"

"I know. I watched your torment from a distance and asked Yeshua to help you forgive. Perhaps today you will find it in your heart to forgive—like Stephen said just now. It's time."

"No! I can't! I swore I'd never forgive him. Never! Do you understand? Never!"

As soon as the grumbling crowd past, Jerusha cried, "They're taking him to the stoning pit!" Yogli released his grip, and she rubbed her arm. "Let's go."

Timon ran back to Jerusha and grabbed her shoulders and shook her. "You're not going! Do you hear me? You're not going!" He shoved her against Yogli. "Don't let her follow me!" he commanded and ran after the crowd.

"Timon!" she cried and tried to run after him. Yogli grabbed the back of her cloak and pulled her back in the alcove, pinned her arms to her sides, and lifted her body up, her tiny feet kicking the air. "Let me go!" she kicked his chin. "Please," she said, her voice quivering, "I can't lose Timon, too." He gently released his grip. She slumped against the tiled wall and slid to the cold floor, her knees to her chest. Sobs exploded from her chest. Head against the wall, she hid her face behind her radiyd. Finally, she looked up at her guardian, who stood legs apart in front of her, his arms at his side ready to snatch her if she moved.

"I never dreamed you would be my guard in this way," she said, her voice scratchy and broken.

"Come," he said. "Yeshua has spoken. He wants me to take you to the stoning. YHWH's ways are not my ways," he said and offered his assistance, his hand under her elbow as she struggled to get up. "I know a shorter route. We must hurry!"

Chapter 28

Yogli led Jerusha through the city gate at a quickened pace. Finally, they caught up with the crowd. Out of breath, she glanced up at Yogli.

"I know you risk Timon's wrath by bringing me here," she said. "He won't be happy with you or me." She touched his arm. "Toda."

"If I had not heard Yeshua tell me to bring you, I would have taken you safely home. What happens is in his hands."

As they neared the ledge that overlooked the pit, the voices grew louder and she noticed a man, dressed in a silk robe, many cloaks lying at his feet. He sat high on the side of the hill.

"Who's that?" she asked.

"That's Saul, the man I told you about earlier. He's a devout Jew taught by the prestigious rabbi, Gamaliel."

"Look, there's Timon," she said. Yogli nodded, took her arm and led her around the outer edge of the crowd and started to climb the hill opposite Saul. "Where are you taking me?"

"I promised to bring you, but we'll stay far enough away to keep you safe," he said.

"I want to be with Timon."

"You want to be with him, but he doesn't want to be with you. Yeshua didn't say to take you to Timon. He said to take you to the stoning. Why? I don't know," he said and shook his head, "But as I told you before, his ways are not our ways." Exasperated and yet thankful, she went with him without an argument.

He led her up a steep path to a flat rock, waist high. Her hands trembled as she placed them on the rough limestone and pulled herself over the hump. He guarded against a fall from behind and when she was set, he easily jumped up to stand close at her side. Her eyes fell on a narrow, winding path to her right that led to the bottom of the stoning pit. *Maybe I can get to Stephen or Timon when he's not looking.*

"Blasphemy!" a man yelled, a large, round stone in his fist.

His accusation was echoed by many others within the crowd. They were surrounded by a sea of angry faces, pointing fingers, and loud accusations. Afraid of what she might see, she kept her head down and stared at the ground. *I don't know why I try to act brave. I'm really a coward.*

When she finally got the courage to look, she saw the man from the Synagogue of the Freedmen throw Stephen over the ledge. *Oh! Why did I look now?* She heard the thud of his body hit the jagged rocks below and grimaced. She could see the top of the limestone walls that surrounded him, preventing him from escaping, but was unable to see where his body lay. Stones started flying.

She heard Timon's voice over the loud curses. Her eyes scanned the crowd. *There! That's him looking over the cliff!*

"No! You're stoning an innocent man!" he screamed and pumped his fists in the air wildly.

"Ugh!" She groaned. She quickly climbed down off the large rock, wrapped her arms around her waist, bent over and gagged her stomach contents on the ground. The smelly liquid splashed on the bottom of her cloak. She wiped her lips with the back of her sleeve. Yogli lifted a small goatskin bottle from around his neck and offered it to her.

"Toda," she said, breathless.

She sloshed the water in her mouth and spit the water on the dusty ground, being careful not to hit her sandaled feet. She looked across the hill. Most of the people around them had already left their lofty view and ran closer to the ravine for a better view.

Caiaphas climbed up on the opposite hill and stood beside Saul. The pious hatred she saw in the priest's cold eyes made her shiver, even though the late afternoon sunrays beat down on her head and shoulders, usually a comfortable warmth. Today she felt a heavy chill.

"I'd like to stone *you*, you evil, self-righteous pig." She shook her fists in his direction and handed back the goatskin bag to the soldier. Out of the corner of her eye she saw Yogli cover his mouth to mute his chuckle. She dropped her head, embarrassed by the outburst. *This is no way for my father's daughter to act.* She clenched her fists at her side, quieted down, and took a deep breath. Suddenly, a familiar, slimy twisting rose from her belly.

"Where's Timon?" she gasped and scanned the crowd, "I don't see him."

"There," Yogli pointed, "near the middle, in the front, by the man with the dark brown cloak. He's a Sicarius. I've seen him slip a dagger in the side of a man and disappear unnoticed. Usually some poor man gets the blame," his words trailed off, knowing it was not conversation for a woman to hear. "I'm sorry, Jerusha, my soldiering days overcame my wisdom from above," he whispered.

She paid no attention to him or his apology. Her eyes were fixed on Timon. She saw him cup his hand around the fellow's ear like he was speaking some secret. The man raised his eyebrows, smiled, and shook his head up and down.

"Oh, no, he's making an agreement with the Sicarrii," she said.

"Get out of the way!" A man shoved Timon aside and hurled another stone below at Stephen.

"Blasphemer!" he taunted, his voice echoing off the stone wall.

Timon stumbled but remained standing and moved closer to the edge.

Down below, a shadow moved across the limestone wall. A man's figure stood, slumped a little, but still standing.

"Stephen!" she gasped. In the past, she'd overheard the men and boys talk about the gruesome details of stonings, how they lay crumpled in a puddle of blood for hours, groaning in pain, until they took their last breath. Somehow, he gathered strength and stood. More rocks pummeled him.

"He's still standing," Yogli whispered.

She tapped Yogli's foot, and he gave her a hand to help her back up onto the large rock for a better view.

The shadow moved again and she saw him step out from under the ledge, his face bruised, eyes swollen shut, a red liquid mixed with dirt oozed from his nose and mouth.

She turned away, then heard him yell, "Yeshua Christos," and looked back at his bloody gaze as he lifted it to heaven crying, "Receive my spirit." He raised his arms, then dropped them weakly at his sides and fell to his knees. With a loud voice he cried out, "YHWH, do not hold this sin against them!" His head fell forward and his body slumped over.

"No!" she cried and started to run. The soldier grabbed her arm. "Wait!" She turned and beat his chest.

"Why? Why? Why?" She crumpled to her knees at Yogli's feet, her face in her hands. Her shoulders shook in convulsing sobs.

Stunned by Stephen's behavior, the crowd stopped throwing stones. No more yelling. In the silence, she heard the echo of her cries. *Timon?* She looked up and watched him shove the men aside as he moved along the ledge and ran down the hill to a small opening at the bottom. He charged toward Stephen, scooped up his limp body, and held him to his chest. His friend's arms dangled at his sides.

Caiaphas screamed, "Don't stop! Throw more stones!"

"He's dead!" Timon yelled and turned his back to the crowd, still holding the limp body. One rock hit his back, then another.

"Stop them," Jerusha cried to Yogli.

"Look!" A guard scampered into the pit. The stones stopped pummeling Timon's back. He jerked Stephen's chin and stared into his eyes. Next he placed his ear to his chest.

"It is true. He is dead."

Caiaphas stepped forward, both arms in the air, shaking his fists at the heavens. "It can't be true," he screamed. "No one dies that quickly in a stoning." The guard shrugged his shoulders and said flatly. "He's dead."

Jerusha heard the clunk and plop of stone after stone drop to the hardened soil. The stench of her stomach contents on the ground and the distant sight of Stephen's blood smeared on Timon's hands and chest nauseated her. She looked up at Yogli and saw him rub his eyes, an unsuccessful attempt to hide his tender emotions. A loud roar filled her ears. Gray dots appeared before her eyes and she crumpled at Yogli's feet and leaned her head into his sandals.

"Take me back," she said weakly, and her world went black.

***

Before she could open her eyes, Jerusha felt the dusty earth beneath her fingers. A strong arm and hand supported her back and head.

"Timon?"

"No, it's me, Yogli."

She must have fainted. She chided herself for being so—so fragile. Yogli helped her sit upright. The sun hung low in the western sky, casting dark, eerie shadows across the stoning pit, now empty. Voices murmured in the distance.

"Where is everyone?"

Yogli squatted on his haunches, his forearms propped on his knees, and stared into the pit with her. He flicked a small stick over the stone slab where she sat. Jerusha marveled at his patience. To look at him, no one would guess that he was so gentle, so kind. It's no wonder that Stephens and Timon trusted him implicitly.

"The murderers left when they saw that Stephen was dead. Timon and many Yeshua followers have taken our friend's body."

"Does Timon know I was here?" she asked and brushed the dirt from her lap.

"No. They carried the body out the other end. Timon never looked this way." A brief flash of Timon's dark, hate-filled eyes crossed her thoughts.

"He's bent on revenge. I saw it in his vacant stare. I'm afraid I've lost him, too."

Yogli's silence signaled he believed she may be right. Her hands felt heavy as she flopped them in her lap and took a deep breath. "I'm ready to go back," she whispered. "Mother will be worried."

She looked up. The orange disc cast its evening light across the plain homes. Behind them the temple was encased in the evening light, but dark gray clouds loomed above, threatening rain. Thunder rumbled in the distance, and she wondered if they'd make it back to Stephen's house before a cloudburst. Yogli pulled her to her feet and took her arm as they descended the small hill. Her legs felt weighted, and her feet slipped on the loose stones. She breathed in short gasps, a heaviness in her chest, then stopped.

"I don't understand why Yeshua had you bring me to the stoning," she mumbled between breaths, her head and eyes down. She felt him grasp her elbow and steadied her wobbly stance. A little dizzy, she slowly tipped her head back and lifted her questioning eyes. He rubbed his fingers through his scruffy beard and stared unflinching at her quizzical expression.

"As I said before, YHWH's ways are not our ways."

She rolled her eyes and looked away. A spark ignited.

"What about Caiaphas?" She retorted, "Don't you hate him for killing your friend?" She yanked her arm away. "I do! He's taken everything from me! Is that YHWH's ways, too?" She stomped farther down the hill with renewed strength, then turned and waited in silence, her hands on her hips. He lumbered closer and signaled her to keep moving. But even in the increasing darkness she saw the kindness in his eyes, almost a pleading for her to forgive, much like Stephen in the trial. Finally, he spoke.

"Caiaphas's judgment is in YHWH's hands," he said quietly. "I will not dishonor Stephen's death by letting hate fill my heart. Did you hear his last words? Have you not seen what hate has done to Timon? Don't let it destroy you, too."

Yogli spoke to her like a father would to a daughter. His demeanor always defied his staunch armor and Roman sword. She tried to recover herself. She straightened her shoulders and turned toward the city.

"Let's go," she said, a tremor in her voice. She felt his huge presence stop beside her and take her arm.

"I'm taking you a different way to avoid the watchmen on the city gates. I learned of a secret passage while in Herod's palace. It will be safer."

Chapter 29

I t was dusk and the wind rose slightly as they approached Stephen's dwelling. Jerusha heard the outer gate bang against the limestone wall. She wondered why Mother left it unlocked, grabbed her radiyd to keep it from flying off, and quickened her pace. The olive tree's silver-green leaves rustled behind her as she touched the mezuzah on the ornate cedar door. Its iron hinges creaked, and Jerusha jumped, uneasy with the fact that this door crept open unhindered, too. She looked to her left at Yogli, who stood, sandaled feet, shoulder width apart, hand on his scabbard, ready to draw his sword.

"Something's wrong," she said, "These doors should be locked. The evening lamps should be lit by now."

He stepped protectively in front and she followed.

"Mother, where are you?" she whispered and glanced around the shadowy courtyard, a whiff of pomegranate blossoms alerting her that they approached the garden. It was hard to see, but as far as she could tell, nothing was amiss. Panic rose, cut her breath off and constricted her throat.

"Mother," she tried to whisper a little louder and inched her way around Yogli. He turned and put his finger to his lips.

In the misty darkness, she tripped over the weaving loom that lay flat across the tiles, the yarn strands tangled and strung across her path. Maybe the wind knocked it over. She regained her footing, stopped, and picked it up. She wanted to call for Sarah and the others, but knew that Yogli was right.

The wind picked up and she felt a few leaves blow across her toes, and strands of hair escaped from her radiyd and whipped across her face. She could smell the rain. Lightning cracked the sky and the thunder followed. Jerusha put her hand out to feel for rain. She watched Yogli pick up the toy box that lay on its side and place it upright. A wind gust snapped the lid shut.

Mother! Jerusha grasped the front of her tunic and cloak, raised the bottom edges high enough for her not to trip, and ran the familiar path to Mother's room.

At her doorway, she felt Yogli's strong fingers grip her shoulder with an abruptness that jerked her around, and he signaled for him to go first. She yielded to his soldier's instinct and waited. Her heart thumped so loud in her chest she was certain anyone hiding in the darkness could hear.

Sword drawn, he crouched beneath the lintel and disappeared. When he returned, he nodded for her to go inside. She peered into a totally dark room, the shutters closed, no fire in the brazier. She felt her way along the wall to the mittah, where she sat and conversed with Mother numerous times. *Where is she?*

Yogli's gruff whisper from the doorway startled her.

"Stay here! I'll search the other rooms."

"I want to go with you."

"No!" She crossed her arms in stubborn defiance, but the serious look in his eyes calmed her.

"All right," she whispered. He ducked under the lintel and disappeared.

She crept to the darkest corner, kept her back to the wall, and pulled her radiyd high around her face. The coming storm rumbled in the distance and lightening lit up the room. She trembled and hoped he'd return soon. The storm grew louder, more intense with every thunder clap. *Why hasn't he come back?* Tears threatened to overflow, and she squeezed her eyes shut.

"Yogli, where are you?" she mouthed, no sound coming from her lips. A man's sweaty smell permeated the air in the room and she opened her eyes wide. Holding her breath, head against the wall, she moved her eyes back and forth and searched the room. *Was it Yogli or someone else?*

"They're all gone." The giant spoke from the doorway. She slumped forward in relief and wiped the few tears with the back of her hand.

"Where are they?" she asked and moved to the mittah. She flopped on the sheepskin and stared at the thin strips of moonlight coming through the latticed shutters across her sandaled feet. He brushed past, checked both directions in the veranda outside the room, then turned and stood guard. A little more at ease, he leaned against the door jam. Suddenly, she sat straight up.

"Caiaphas did this! They must have arrested Mother and the others, too. It's all my fault! I should have obeyed Timon and stayed here." Yogli's dark figure stood erect.

"What could you have done?" he said, his voice deep and strong. "You are not their savior. You are not Stephen's savior. You are not Timon's savior. There's only one Savior—King Yeshua Christos."

"Some Savior he is! Stephen is dead! Mother and Sarah are probably arrested! Timon's bent on revenge! Where is Yeshua in all this? Why did he let them kill Stephen? Doesn't he care what happens to those who love him?" She paused and listened. It was just the leaves rustling in the wind outside.

"First, Father abandons me and leaves me to serve a perverted pig—Yeshua's high priest nonetheless. Then, Yeshua allows the one who took Father's place to be ripped from my life. I begged him to save Stephen." She felt her mother's cloak beside her hand and lifted it to her face and savored the fragrant, familiar scent.

"Are you angry at Yeshua or angry at your father? Or yourself, perhaps?" Yogli asked softly above the wind that whistled through the lattices.

"Why would I be angry at myself? I haven't done anything to deserve this. Efah forced me. Where was Yeshua then? Where was

Father?" she answered, her last words muffled by her mother's cloak pressed to her face.

She remembered Yogli didn't know her secret and glanced up. The stoic look in his eyes revealed little about his feelings. Inwardly, she reprimanded herself for being so careless and wondered why she was so open with him. Yogli was a Roman soldier, a Yeshua believer, yes, but still a Roman soldier. Startled by the sound of male voices in the garden, she stood.

"There's no sign of the vermin!" someone said. It sounded like a man from the garden area.

Yogli ducked beneath the lintel and motioned for her to come to him and be quiet. Jerusha felt her way in the dark around the table between them, aware that the male murmurings and hobnailed footsteps grew louder. Yogli grabbed her arm and the two hid behind the open door, her body scrunched between the wall and the giant's large battle-ready stature. She closed her eyes, held her breath, and listened to the clang of sword scabbard grow louder, then diminish as the soldiers tramped past, down the portico.

"Any sign of them?" one yelled. The scuffled steps of soldiers coming from the other direction of the house echoed. "They're gone. They've been warned," one of them answered. "Caiaphas will not be pleased."

A rush of wind rattled the shutters open and blew an unlit lamp to the floor. The shattered pieces landed at her feet.

"Oh!" she sucked in a short gasp and wondered if the soldiers heard. Simultaneously, another flash of lightening lit up the room, and out of the corner of her eye she saw movement outside the window.

"Yogli, did you see that?" she whispered. Her heart pounded in her chest. She held her radiyd against the swirling wind and watched him slip with astounding quickness to the window and reach outside.

She heard a whimper. Yogli lifted a young boy through the window and covered his mouth and nose with his large hand. The youngster's widened eyes peeked out above his fingers. She recognized this orphan. It was Moses, the boy who stuttered, the one who saw his mother and father killed in a village outside Jerusalem. He wandered into the city, a beggar on the streets, until Stephen found him.

"Don't be afraid. I won't hurt you," the giant whispered. "But you must be quiet."

The boy nodded. The three waited in silence for several minutes.

"Stay here," Yogli said. "I'll check to see if it's safe."

Jerusha closed the shutters, gathered the trembling boy under her arm on the mittah, and waited. The sound of raindrops plopped a few at a time on the wooden lattices. In the distance, she thought she heard a baby's cry and wondered why a mother would have her baby out in this weather?

Moses tried to talk, but she shushed him.

After awhile, she heard Yogli outside the door.

"Come, we must hurry in case they return."

"Who?" Jerusha asked.

"I-I-I know," the boy stuttered. She looked down at him and back at Yogli.

"Ro-Ro-Roman soldiers," the boy continued. "A neighbor's slave warned us. Your mother and the uh-uh-uh-others are hiding in the ra-ra—they are hiding outside."

"In the ravine?" Jerusha guessed.

The boy nodded. Jerusha looked at Yogli. Panic gripped her heart. If she went to Mother, she might lead the soldiers to their hiding place. If she stayed, the soldiers might return and arrest them.

"What shall we do?" she asked. She saw in his eyes the calculating astuteness of a good soldier. He opened the shutters and peered into the darkness, his hand tapping his sword. The wind drove the rain against his face.

"I know this ravine. The waters are already high there from last week's rains. It will flood soon. We must hurry. They will need our help. The soldiers may be searching—or they may wait until the rain stops to continue their search," he said and grabbed the boy's arm. "You must be brave and lead us to them." He nodded. Yogli pointed, "Through the window. Now."

Yogli bent over and interlocked his fingers. The boy put one foot in his cupped hands and Yogli lifted him up and out the window. Jerusha gathered up her tunic and cloak and placed one foot in his hands, too. Up and over she went. Yogli followed, his large frame scraping the sides of the window frame.

"Which way?" he asked the boy. Lightning flashed and they all saw the soldiers simultaneously.

"Duck," Yogli said. They crouched down behind a few pomegranate bushes, motionless in the dark shadows. Five, maybe six, soldiers sloshed through puddles in the roadway and grumbled.

"Caiaphas can get his own guards out in this weather."

Puddles formed in the soggy ground beneath Jerusha's sandaled feet. Cold mud squished between her toes. The driving rain stung, and she covered her face with her radiyd and watched Moses motion for them to go left. He scampered down a steep slope a few feet away. She rose, picked up the bottom of her tunic and cloak, and followed, Yogli's hand beneath her elbow. Moses' dark figure slipped. He fell on his rump, slid, and grabbed the twisted branch of an old olive tree that grew in the side of hill. She looked down the precipitous path and hesitated. The streams of gushing water carved small river-lets around boulders before splashing over the edge into the turbulent waters in the ravine. Yogli stepped over first, took Jerusha's hands, and held her steady as she started her descent. She struggled with her footing in the slimy mud and loose rocks, but Yogli's strength kept her upright. Suddenly, the wind changed directions. It carried the sounds of babies' cries and children's whimpers.

"Yogli, I am afraid," she said. "They could drown. Don't worry about me. Get to them before it's too late."

"We'll go together," he answered. "It's not much farther." She saw him glance down at Moses, who held tight. The water now gushed over his feet.

"They're right there," he pointed below to where the flood waters rose. Jerusha saw her mother waist deep in the rushing waters with a baby in her arms.

"Mother!" she yelled. "Hold on, we'll help you!" Yogli aided Jerusha down to a secure place just above the water. She looked again. This time she noticed Sarah gripped her mother's arm with both hands against the turbulent current that flowed around her up to her chin. She gagged and coughed. Obviously too weak to hold on any longer, she let go and went under.

"Yeshua, save her!" Jerusha screamed.

At that moment, Sarah's arm popped up, and Yogli was already there. He grabbed her arm, swooped her up, and carried her to

Jerusha. Sarah buried her face in Jerusha's wet robe, coughing while Jerusha patted her back.

Yogli turned immediately to Abigail. They locked hands, and she climbed up the slope and out of the rushing water. Jerusha took the baby from her arms, and her mother collapsed in the mud. Sarah let go of Jerusha and clung to Abigail and cried uncontrollably. Jerusha handed the baby back to her mother, and she and Yogli moved along the slippery edge. One by one, they pulled the other five widows and twenty children to temporary safety of the muddy sloped banks. The women gently shushed them and held each one.

The rain let up, and the cries of the soaked children and babies echoed in the dark ravine. Jerusha rested her hand on Mother's shoulder and helped her to quiet Sarah. Her hair was icy cold and her little body trembled. Yogli stood behind her.

"I thank YHWH for the storm," Abigail said, her teeth chattering. "The thunder kept the soldiers from hearing the babies cry."

"His favor is on you," Yogli said. "The rain stopped the soldiers' search."

"Yeshua is good," Abigail said. "He watches over his children." Jerusha questioned Mother's wisdom but now was not the time to dispute it. They must get everyone home.

The muddy slope was too steep and slippery for the tired women and children to climb, so the weary travelers wound between the shrubs and rocks along the lower edge of the ravine until they came to a wide-open space. Jerusha looked down the hill at the temple court below. A few lanterns remained lit and barely visible. Most likely, somewhere inside, Caiaphas conspired to have them arrested. She seethed at the memory of his pious proceedings and false accusations against Stephen.

The cold night air settled on her wet cloak and she shivered, the baby whimpering in her arms as Yogli led them out of the ravine to safety. Her thoughts turned to Timon. He may already be in prison or holed up somewhere with the Sicarii. Sarah whimpered at her side and clung to her cloak. Jerusha pointed up the hill to her left.

"Just a little way to go and we'll be at my house," she softly told them, comforting them as she looked around at all of them. "I know everyone's cold. Think how warm you'll be when we get there. You'll shed those wet clothes like a caterpillar and cuddle up in warm, fuzzy sheep-skin covers. Won't that feel good?" Their chattering teeth and shivering bodies were their only response.

Yogli picked up Sarah and carried her in his arms. She whined a little, then rested her head on his chest. Jerusha shifted her little one to her other shoulder, then prodded the other children to keep moving, afraid the soldiers might return now that the rain had stopped. She would not speak of Stephen's death tonight. They had been through enough traumas for one day. It could wait until the morning.

The soaked travelers approached her father's house in trepidation. *Would they be safe here?* Jerusha motioned for everyone to be quiet. Yogli tried the gate. It was locked. Jerusha breathed a sigh of relief. No soldiers here or they would have kicked it open.

"I-I-I'm a good puddle jumper. I-I-I know how to get inside and unlock it," Moses offered. "St-Stephen showed me when we visited here to see Timon work on the house."

Jerusha's heart warmed. Somehow she had forgotten that Stephen helped Timon repair her father's house. And Moses, too, had helped. She never knew. Now Moses stood in front of her, his long hair clung to his cheeks, and his eyes pleaded for a "Yes."

"Let Yogli go with you," Jerusha answered. The giant placed Sarah in the arms of the widow who stood next to him. Jerusha watched Moses zigzag around the puddles, then look up at Yogli and jump. His sandaled feet landed on the other side of the muddy stream. He waved at the others and disappeared behind two large pomegranate bushes. At first, Yogli's head towered above, then disappeared as he bowed down to see where the boy went. When he stood, he shrugged his shoulders. Jerusha wasn't sure how to interpret his behavior, but it felt good to be home, safer somehow. Where else could they go with so many women and children?

A while later, she heard the lock jiggle and the gate creaked open. Moses ran out, a broad grin on his face, proud of his accomplishment. Yogli, his soldier mindset activated, insisted he go in first to be sure it wasn't a trap. Jerusha acquiesced, but a sense of well-being flooded her soul. A few minutes later, he waved them to come in. For now they were safe—back in Father's house.

Chapter 30

O ne of the older children lit a torch, and he and his friend proceeded to light the courtyard lamps. Yogli stopped him.

"No lamps. No fires. The soldiers may search here, especially if they think someone is at home."

Everyone groaned, including Jerusha. She wanted to warm her hands over the warm brazier flames. But Yogli was right.

The widows helped Abigail gather blankets and sheepskin covers for the children to stay warm until their clothes dried. Wet nurses immediately found small linens for the babies. Within minutes their cries ceased as they suckled and dropped off to sleep. The rain left the air warm and muggy, so the rest of the children stood in the courtyard, numb and dazed, as the widows rubbed their bare skin with dry towels and dressed them in new clothes. A large pile of wet clothes collected near the fountain. Two women brought goat's milk and tipped an earthen jar for each child to drink. Sarah sneezed, and Jerusha grabbed a dry towel and worked it through her hair while her mother dried the rest of her. This night would be hardest of all on Sarah—certainly one she would never forget. Jerusha didn't want to think about that now. She did not have enough loaves of bread for everyone, but she brought out all the bread that she and Timon had stored and tore off pieces so that every child had a bite to eat before they slept. The children were summoned one by one to large bowls of water so each one's feet was washed. Jerusha hoped that the traumatic evening would be washed out of their minds as easily.

Just then she spied Moses, out of line and oblivious to everyone else in the room but Yogli. What a sight!

"It's not nice to stare," she said to Moses, then glanced at the giant, the boy's object of attention, and back at the youngster. "Get some water and wash Yogli's feet, then show him to the room you stayed in when you were here. I'm sure you wouldn't mind if he slept with you tonight. Someone will bring dry blankets to your room." The orphan smiled, then scampered off for water.

It was barely eight o'clock, but thankfully, the children were too tired to protest being sent off to bed a bit early. She promised to tell them everything in the morning. The whole process was over in less than a half hour, and they trudged to the bedchambers assigned by Abigail, a widow in each room. Older orphans held the hands of the younger. Widows held babies. The women would attend to their own needs after the children fell off to sleep.

A few widows approached and asked about Stephen.

"I know you have many questions, but I can't talk now." Their eyes pleaded with her for answers.

She sighed deeply. They deserved to know. "They stoned him," she answered. Her voice caught as the pictures flashed in front of her. "We'll tell the children in the morning."

Jerusha bit her lip to gain control, then glanced at Yogli. "I'm sure you remember Yogli from Peter's meetings. He will remain here with us tonight?"

Her question was for Yogli. He nodded.

Tears sprang to the eyes of the widows, and Jerusha watched after them as one by one they slipped away in silence. She looked around and took a deep breath.

She saw movement under the olive tree. Chaya. Shadows flickered on her weathered face, concern for her son evident in her eyes.

"Where's Timon?" she asked. Jerusha couldn't let her know of the hate she saw in his eyes.

"He's with Peter and the others. They took Stephen's body for burial," she answered with a half-smile.

"Are they safe from Caiaphas's soldiers?"

"I think so, for now," She hoped she was right. She grasped the older woman's calloused hands.

"Yeshua, you protected us. Keep your hand on Timon, too. Bring him safely home." The words sounded hollow. Empty. She felt a greater need—for hate and vengeance. Even in her own heart.

"And Yeshua, show Jerusha the way to forgiveness," his mother added.

Was it that obvious? She wondered if somehow Chaya knew of Timon's hatred, too.

Jerusha glanced up and saw Moses carrying a ceramic bowl full of water, a cloth over his shoulder. The water splashed over the edge. Chaya dropped Jerusha's hands and moved toward him, but Yogli stopped her.

"Let me," he offered, bending down and taking the bowl from him. "Why don't you sit and let me wash *your* feet?" he asked the boy.

"Mu-mu-my feet?" he asked, a grin spreading wide across his face. "Are-are-are you going to wash her feet, too?

"I think he has plenty to do with yours," Jerusha interrupted. "Look at those muddy toes. I'll see you two in the morning."

"What about Chaya's feet?"

"I agree with Jerusha that Yogli has enough to do with your muddy feet," she answered and slipped quietly into the garden.

Jerusha listened to his giggles and walked past them, her feet tired and achy, her muscles tense and sore. The storm finally relented and a sliver of moonlight appeared between low-moving clouds and lit the tiled walkway to her mother's room. She rapped lightly on her door and peeked in. Abigail knelt on a rug, probably the colorful striped one that the widows made. She couldn't tell for sure in the dark. Mother's hands were in her lap with her back to the door as she mumbled. *Always praying.*

"Mother?"

Jerusha watched Abigail turn and shut the door behind her. The moon shone through the window and cast a soft glow on her face. In the daylight, her olive skin was smooth, except for a few fine lines at her temples that turned up, evidence of a continual flow of joy, something Jerusha coveted. Tonight, Jerusha stood for a few minutes and soaked in the peace that radiated from her mother's dark pools, then ran and collapsed in her open arms. Pent up tears soaked into Abigail's soft tunic, her gut-wrenching cries drowned as she stifled them in her mother's clothing. "He's gone, Mother. Stephen is dead. First, Father goes away. Now Stephen. All because of Caiaphas. I hate him!" she gasped between cries. "And the children. How could he dare arrest widows and children. What kind of priest does that?"

Mother stroked her wet hair for a while.

"It is written, 'Weeping may tarry for the night, but joy comes in the morning,'" she consoled.

Jerusha lifted her head. "Mother, you are still soaked to the skin." Jerusha grabbed a towel and set to work. "Now let's get you out of those wet clothes and wash your feet." Jerusha kissed her on the cheek, stood and helped her mother up.

From the peg next to the mittah, Jerusha handed her mother a fresh tunic with red stitches on the neck. Abigail shivered in the darkness as Jerusha lifted the heavy pan of water.

"Sit over here," she said and nodded toward the mittah. Abigail did not argue. She sat on the edge of the furry sheepskin cover, then stood and pulled it over her shoulders and rubbed, trying to get the warmth to soak into her mother's tired frame. As soon as her mother's feet were washed, Jerusha emptied the water into the bushes outside her window. She returned with more water for her own feet. Oh, so cold! She wiggled her toes to loosen the caked-on mud. Finally, the two sat on the edge of the mittah and patted their feet dry. Jerusha extended a long blanket over both of their shoulders.

"Mother, I'm afraid I'm going to lose Timon, too. He's so angry, so full of hate. He's ready to kill Caiaphas or have him killed. The look in his eyes scared me." Abigail dropped to the floor to massage Jerusha's legs. She kept her head down and mumbled indistinct words beneath her breath, then she stopped.

"Tell me what happened," she asked, and patted her leg, a signal for Jerusha to let her mother massage her foot.

"Well, Yogli helped me find him and of course he was upset that I had come." Jerusha sighed. "I don't know what we would have done without Yogli. He appeared out of nowhere." Jerusha paused for a moment, remembering the scar on Yogli's cheek and the beating he took for her and her mother. Immediately her thoughts returned to her husband. "Mother, what I saw in Timon's eyes made me sick to my stomach! He was a man determined to kill, get revenge, not the man who earlier told me we must forgive." Her mother patted her other leg dry with a soft cloth and started working with the right foot.

"Yogli, with his large girth, made a way in the crowd for us to get inside the chamber. Mother, you should have seen Stephen. He was so brave. His eyes shined. So peaceful and loving, even toward his enemies. He even asked Yeshua not to hold this sin against them. He wanted the people to see the truth about Yeshua, but they screamed, 'blasphemer!' Imagine, Stephen a blasphemer? I thought it was because of me that Caiaphas had him arrested, but a man named Saul was there. I think he had something to do with it. Yogli says that Saul hates Yeshua followers."

Mother finished the massage and took another robe from the peg by the window and wrapped it around Jerusha's shoulders as she sat next to her again on the mittah.

"Yes, I've heard that Saul is dangerous to those of us who accept Yeshua as King. I think it was him that influenced Caiaphas to go door to door and arrest us—one of the soldiers mentioned orders and someone named Saul. We escaped just in time tonight. Only Yeshua knows how long we'll be safe in Jerusalem."

Jerusha's stomach tightened. "I hate Caiaphas for what he's done. I hate Efah!"

"Efah? Why do you hate him?"

Jerusha gasped and covered her mouth.

"What are you hiding?" Abigail asked, then paused and stared at the floor before she continued. "When you were small, your father and I talked about it numerous times. We could tell something happened. You changed. Cut off your love. Became hardened, sometimes timid. It is time you told me what happened."

"Oh, Mother, he touched me, forced me to do things a little girl shouldn't have to endure."

Abigail's back straightened. "When? When did this happen?"

Jerusha did not want to throw guilt onto her mother. Not tonight.

"Does it matter when? It happened. And I was afraid to tell you, afraid to tell Father, afraid you would blame me. I had to tell Timon because it affected our marriage bed. That's why he came to Stephen's house today. He didn't know how to handle the burning hatred he had for Caiaphas and Efah. He knew he should forgive, but couldn't. Then they arrested Stephen and—and I can't forgive them either."

Her mother lifted her chin and stared into her eyes for a long moment.

"Jerusha, the same evil you saw in Timon, I'm seeing in your eyes. It has not been your fault what happened to your father and Stephen, but if you continue to hate and not forgive, it will destroy every relationship you have, especially with Timon."

Jerusha closed her eyes and saw Stephen's gentle eyes pleading with her to forgive. "Do not hold this sin against them." His words pounded against the hate.

"I can't," she whispered. Abigail still held her chin and mumbled words to Yeshua. Jerusha turned her head away.

"I can't forgive, I just can't." She rubbed the back of her neck and scrunched her shoulders.

"Yes, you can," answered her mother, her tone strong and confident. Jerusha slipped to her knees and laid her head in Mother's lap.

"Yeshua, help me," she groaned. "Help me love my enemies. Timon said all things are possible with you. Take this hatred," she pleaded with every fiber of her being. "I choose to forgive."

She heard a voice in her thoughts, Yeshua's voice—clear, distinct.

"Forgive who?"

What a strange question for him to ask.

"Caiaphas and Efah, of course. They are the ones that destroyed my life," she spoke angrily. "Help me forgive them. Help me forgive them."

"Who else?" his voice—gentle but firm—came again. She waited and remembered.

"Myself? I must have done something to make them think they could do that to me."

She felt her mother's tender touch.

"Jerusha, it was not your fault." Abigail tried to sniff back the tears, but Jerusha knew her mother. She knew her cries. "It is my fault. I was the one that believed a lie and gave into temptation and put you in that situation." Jerusha looked up. Her mother's tearstained face had so much remorse. "I know—Yeshua forgave me. And somehow I am learning to forgive myself. Will you please forgive me, too? The last thing in the world I ever wanted to do was to hurt you!"

Jerusha reached up and wiped her mother's cheeks with the sleeve of her tunic.

"Yes, Mother, I forgave you a long time ago."

"And your father? How do you feel about him?"

"I love him, of course."

"Why have you been so angry?" her mother asked.

"I don't know," her voice quivered. "I've—I've had no control of my life." She stared at her mother, "They forced me. I swore no man would hurt me like that again. Where was Father when I needed him? Where was Yeshua?"

"Jerusha," her mother spoke tenderly. "Let it go. Let go of the hate. Let go of the questions. Trust Yeshua. It is the only way to find peace. Forgive them."

Let go? Trust? Oh, how can I trust? Yeshua help me. Jerusha could not voice her thoughts, but Mother's words triggered more tears, and she cried for several long minutes. Worn out and tired, she finally stopped. In the quiet, she heard her name called. She lifted her head and rubbed her eyes.

"Timon?" she whispered, then turned to see. He stood under the ornate lintel. His broad shoulders filled the doorway. Shadows on his face, she couldn't see into his eyes and wasn't sure who greeted her, the man that loved her in the wedding chamber or the man that pushed her away at the stoning. She glanced back at Mother and waited.

His shadow moved across the wall as he approached. She closed her eyes, breathed deep of his manly scent and gathered the courage to look up. His eyes radiated the same warmth that she saw on her wedding night. He knelt in front of her and stared into her eyes. Abigail got up and made herself busy fetching water and straightening the room.

"I love you," he whispered.

"And I you," she blinked. A single tear escaped and rolled down her cheek.

"I have forgiven Caiaphas and Efah," he said and gently wiped the tear away. "When I held Stephen's body, I looked down at his face." Timon's voice broke. He sighed deeply and continued, "Even then, he looked peaceful. His last words, 'Hold not this sin against them,' echoed in my thoughts. How could I not extend the same love toward his persecutors? As I wept on his chest, the hate and revenge melted away. A peace came and I thought of you and had to get home. Jerusha, please forgive me. In my desire to get revenge, I pushed you away. I am so sorry."

She rubbed her hand across his cheek.

"I forgive you," then hesitated and cocked her head slightly. "Let's go to our room." He stood and helped her to her feet and dipped a slight bow to her mother. When he looked back at her, she saw the old twinkle in his eyes. He took her arm and escorted her out the door.

"I saw the stoning," she continued as they walked down the portico, her hand in the crook of his arm. He stopped, lifted her chin, and looked into her eyes.

"Oh, my Jerusha. Dear Jerusha. I should have known you'd have your way. I did not wish for you to see such a terrible thing."

"It wasn't like that, Timon. Really it wasn't. Yeshua told Yogli to take me."

"Well, I can't argue with Yeshua," he said and continued walking. "I can't argue with Yogli either. When I came in he was on a cot, sleeping at the gate."

"He's been incredible, all day," Jerusha mumbled. "Such a dear friend to us all." She looked up at Timon. "We watched from the hill. I saw you whisper to the Sicarii and thought I was losing you, too. I was so angry." She stopped inside their bedchamber, leaned against the table, and looked up. "Something's happened. After seeing you I feel so different."

That endearing lopsided grin spread across his face, and he drew her close, his embrace tender.

"I like what I see," he said, then lifted her chin and kissed her, at first gently, then passionately. He picked her up and carried her to the bed. "You have finally come out of the dark chrysalis," he said as he laid her gently on the soft cover. Without unforgiveness blocking her love, she smiled and willingly yielded to his touches and gave herself fully to him.

For a while she rested in the peace and safety of his arms, then the replay of Stephen's stoning and her narrow escape from the soldiers circled in her thoughts over and over.

"Timon, what will happen to us? To the children and widows?"

"I don't know," he said and tightened his arms around her waist and snuggled his face in the back of her neck. "I left some of the other men at Stephen's to watch over his body and to let us know if the soldiers return. I also stationed some men outside our home here to watch through the night if they come here. Of course, Yogli is sleeping just inside the gate. You can believe no one's getting past him. And we have to trust Yeshua. He's kept us safe so far."

Chapter 31

Jerusha awoke before dawn, nestled in the soft sheepskin cover of her own bed, Timon's scent in the air. She heard a light tap on door and Sarah's sweet, soft voice call.

"Timon? Are you awake?"

"She'll want to know about Stephen," he spoke quietly to Jerusha, climbed from the mittah and reached for his cloak.

"Yes, Sarah, we're coming," he said loud enough for her to hear. Jerusha lit the lamp at the bedside table while Timon dressed, then unlatched the lock and opened the door. In the shadowy light, she saw Sarah rush at him, wrap her tiny arms around his waist, and hold tight.

"It's not like you to be up so early," he said and patted her head. He gently unwrapped her arms, squatted, and stared into her eyes.

"I couldn't sleep," she blinked back tears and then her words tumbled out. "We hid from the soldiers. Abigail brought us here. I'm afraid. Will the soldiers take me like they took my uncle? What happened to him?" Timon glanced back at Jerusha and scooped

Sarah up in his arm. "Don't worry, Sarah. You are safe here with me."

"And my uncle? Will he be safe here, too?" Timon rubbed his eyes, but not before Jerusha saw a tear run into his beard.

"Why are you crying?" Sarah asked and touched his beard with tiny fingers. Jerusha wiped tears from her eyes, too, then watched Timon gently push the hair back from Sarah's face and pull her head into his chest.

"Because your uncle is gone."

"Where did he go?" she asked and fiddled with the edge of his cloak opening, a slight whimper in her tone.

"To live with Yeshua in his kingdom." He stroked the back of her head.

"He won't be back, will he?" her voice cracked. "Just like my mother and father."

"No, he won't be back."

She stuck her face in Timon's chest, her tiny body shook. The wracking sobs continued for several minutes, then she quieted.

"If he loved me, he wouldn't go live with Yeshua. He'd stay here with me," she stuttered between hiccups. "He's just like my mother and father. He doesn't love me. Yeshua should tell him to stay with me. He knows I don't have a father." She burst into tears again.

Timon looked at Jerusha, with an empty stare. He never talked of his father's rejection, but she heard Chaya mention it one time with Mother. He tipped his head back and squeezed his eyes shut, his brows scrunched together, an attempt to control his emotions. When Sarah's cry softened, he whispered in her ear, a catch in his throat.

"Sarah, Stephen loved you very much. He didn't want to go away. His life was taken by some mean men. He is with Yeshua now. Someday we'll be together again."

"I want to be with him now. I love him."

"I know, Sarah. We are all sad and will miss him." Suddenly, her head popped up.

"I hate those mean men," she blurted with an angry glare at Timon.

Jerusha groaned. She saw herself in little Sarah and wanted to help her not make the same mistakes she made.

"Oh, Sarah," she said and got up and moved closer. Timon embraced her with his other arm and pulled her next to him, and she looked up at Sarah's big, angry eyes.

"Hate only hurts you. It prevents you from loving others," she glanced at Timon, then wiped the tears from Sarah's face. "We want to always remember Stephen with love in our hearts.

The door creaked and Abigail opened it the rest of the way and peeked in.

"I'm sorry to interrupt, but the other children are asking about Stephen."

***

The children gathered around Jerusha and Timon as they walked into the courtyard. The little ones pulled on their cloaks and wanted to be held like Sarah. The older ones asked questions.

"Where is Stephen? Tell us what happened. Did they stone him?" Alarmed, Jerusha glanced at Sarah, who crinkled her brow.

"What do they mean stone him?" Her voice trembled. Her big eyes blinked back tears. The older boy heard and blurted, "It means they throw stones at someone until he is dead."

"That's enough of that," Timon reprimanded, "Now everyone find a place to sit and we'll explain."

Jerusha watched Sarah stare at Timon, her eyes big and round. He slid his fingers across Sarah's cheek and handed her to Jerusha. She carried Sarah on her hip as she walked among the children, patted heads, hugged shoulders, and made eye contact. Their innocence and hunger for love gripped her heart. They had each other, but they needed a father and mother, someone who listened and fought for their destiny.

Some of the young faces she didn't recognize. They must be the ones that ran to Stephen's house when the soldiers arrested their parents. Saul and Caiaphas wasted no time. Stephen isn't even buried, yet. She caught the empty, vacant eyes of one of the widows among the children as she walked past and sat on the bench behind the orphans.

Sarah wiggled on her lap and reached over to touch the red blossoms on the pomegranate bush. Her tug on Jerusha's arm drew her attention away from the other orphans, and Jerusha looked down at Sarah, who pointed to a chrysalis that hung on a branch, camouflaged among the dark green pomegranate leaves.

"You said one day you would tell me what your father taught you about the chrysalis," she whispered.

Jerusha smiled, held Sarah close to her chest, and leaned over to the hanging butterfly home, happy to distract her away from Timon's conversation about Stephen's death.

"See, how dark it is? That means the Creator's work inside is almost finished. Here, touch it very gently." She took Sarah's tiny fingers in her own and reached out to the hardened chrysalis. "The longer the caterpillar stays in here, the harder the shell becomes and the better its chances of survival. My father told me it is dark inside, but the caterpillar is not alone. Yeshua, its Creator, is working in the darkness to form it into a beautiful butterfly."

She stared at the chrysalis and thought of the many times she felt alone, abandoned by Father and his King. She smiled and shook her head in amazement of how her Creator had worked in dark times; the provisions, the changes he made in her. Somehow she knew he would take care of them now, even though the threat of the soldiers' return weighed heavy on her heart. How could she relay this understanding to Sarah?

"The chrysalis protects the butterfly," Sarah said, proud of her observation. "I don't like the dark. I don't like being alone," she continued, her lips pursed and mouth downturned.

"Yeshua promises to be with us always, even in those times. His Father is always watching, too," Jerusha said, trying to keep a positive tone to her voice.

The clamoring voices of the other orphans caused Jerusha to look up.

"What happened to Stephen?" An older orphan shouted. She saw the pain in Timon's eyes as he lifted a young boy and held him in his arms.

"I want to go home," a little girl pouted, then stuck her thumb in her mouth.

Timon put his fingers to his lips. The children quieted as they gathered around, some on the cold tiles, some on the ground among the bushes, their faces looking up eager to hear. She could see his struggle. He squeezed his eyes shut, took a deep breath, then looked at her with such agony that Jerusha rose to her feet. Sarah clung to her cloak.

"Stephen is gone," Timon said. "Like I told Sarah this morning, he went to live with Yeshua. You will now live here with Jerusha and me." No one spoke. The boy who earlier defined stoning dropped his head. The older children knew exactly what Timon meant. The younger ones just knew their beloved father figure was gone. That was enough. The sound of cries and whimpers grew, at first a few here and there, then a growing cacophony. Jerusha watched the widows pick up the little ones and wipe tears, both from their own eyes and the youngsters. She felt Sarah's face pressed into her cloak. The older children tried to be brave but most wiped tears from their cheeks with the back of their hands.

Suddenly, Sarah piped up.

"Don't be afraid. Don't cry. Yeshua is with us." She started to run from one child to the next. "Yeshua is with us. Yeshua is with us. Like the butterfly in the chrysalis, Yeshua is with us." Jerusha stared in amazement.

"Out of the mouth of babes," she spoke softly and looked at Timon, who stood with his eyes transfixed on Sarah. One by one the children stopped their crying. In the silence, an older boy, yelled, "I hate those men who took Stephen!"

Another one yelled, "I hate them, too. Someone should kill them."

"I'll throw a rock at them! See if they like it."

Timon waved his arms.

"Stop! Stop this now! Is this what Stephen taught you? Listen to me. I, too, wanted revenge, but I watched Stephen, bloody and bruised, fall to his knees and with his last breath beg King Yeshua not to hold this sin against them. We must honor his death by choosing to live in love, even love of our enemies. Stephen would want you to forgive."

"Timon!" Yogli yelled from the courtyard gate. "Soldiers are coming!" The children screamed and ran to hide, some down the veranda into their rooms, some behind bushes.

"Go to our room with Sarah and this time stay there!" Timon commanded Jerusha. "Yogli and I will take care of this." He rushed to the gate and yelled over his shoulder, "If you hear them come down the veranda, escape out the window, run through our garden, out the back gate, and find Peter or Luke."

A baby cried from the kitchen. Timon waved his arms at Abigail, Chaya and the other widows.

"Get these children out of the courtyard and be prepared to run out the back. Jerusha heard whimpers mixed with the clip clop of sandals as she scurried to her room.

"Yeshua, help us!" she cried as she shut and locked her door.

"Are the soldiers going to get us? Sarah asked, a tremor in her voice.

Jerusha wanted to assure her, but the words stuck in her throat. She slumped on the cold tiles under the window and waited. Sarah started to speak.

"Shhh," Jerusha whispered. "Be very quiet. If we hear the soldiers come, we are going out the window to find Peter." The quiet house was unnerving. Not even a baby's cry. The wet nurses sat in the dark corner of the room, their backs against the wall, wide-eyed as they rocked the babies. Minutes passed and then the lock jiggled. Jerusha sucked in her breath.

"Jerusha, it is me. Open the door."

"It's Timon!" Sarah yelled and ran to unlock the door.

She listened to Sarah fumble with the lock for several seconds, then looked up and saw the heavy cedar door swing wide and Timon sweep up the tiny girl high in the air. She giggled.

"Sarah, run and tell the others we are safe," he said and tweaked her nose. "They can come out of hiding."

"Yea!" her voice echoed down the veranda. "We're safe!"

"Timon, I can't take any more of this. I'm not sure how much longer I can hold up," Jerusha said and blinked back tears. He squatted and took her hands.

"It's over. We're safe."

"What! What do you mean? We're not safe!" She jerked her hands away. "We'll never be safe!" He raised her up and drew her to his chest.

"It may be hard to believe, but someone's been watching over this little butterfly. The Romans brought a decree just now that declared this household and those living here are under Rome's protection."

"Why? Who would do that?"

"It had a seal on the scroll from the signet ring of a Roman cognomen, Regulus from Perea. The waxed seal was a lion face and a butterfly."

"Father?"

"If it's not your father, it's someone who knows your father." He led her to the window, unlatched the shutters, and threw them open. "Look, Jerusha!"

She squinted against the late morning sun that warmed her face and breathed deep of the fresh rain-covered blossoms that permeated the air. Spring. New life! A purple butterfly that sat on the dark green pomegranate bush caught her attention. Sarah and her little friend were leaning into the pomegranate bushes, no doubt searching for another chrysalis or butterfly.

"This is our home now—our courtyard, our children, our ministry. Yeshua has made the way for us—and I know that Stephen would be pleased."

"Jerusha!" Abigail appeared in the doorway, breathless. "Yogli told me about the Roman decree and the signet ring. I can't help but think your father had something to do with this."

"But Mother, if it is Father, why hasn't he come back to see us?"

Abigail joined her daughter and Timon at the window. "That is the puzzling part. He loved you so much that if he could get home, I know he would. Something is stopping him. Either he's dead or something else has happened, jail or sickness. But that signet ring *has* to be from your father."

Jerusha leaned on the table and looked at her pendant then stared out the window.

"He never liked the Romans," she finally said. "He must have some connection with them or we wouldn't be under Rome's protection. But how? Why?"

"I'll tell you why," Yogli's deep voice spoke from doorway.

Jerusha gasped. "I—we didn't see you there, Yogli. Do you know something about all this?"

Yogli held his spear in front of him and leaned on it as though it was a walking stick. His large frame took up the entire doorway. "It's time you know the truth," he said. "Please, may I talk to you?" He looked around the room. "To all three of you, outside?"

Jerusha, Abigail, and Timon sat on the bench at Yogli's direction. The large man paced back and forth, and Jerusha noticed again how quietly he moved for a man of his size. He seemed to be gathering his thoughts. Jerusha leaned forward. "Yogli?"

Suddenly, Yogli was on his knee before her. "Jerusha, I am your grandfather."

Abigail's eyes widened. Yogli said, "Abigail, I am Jacob's father."

Abigail gasped.

"You are his father?" Abigail repeated.

Jerusha stared at Yogli. Timon's arm wrapped around her waist. She tipped her head to the side, then to the other side, inspecting Yogli as if it was the first time she ever saw him.

"Sometimes—sometimes you reminded me of him. Something about your eyes. And Father certainly has your build—and your large hands! But—but I thought I kept comparing you because I missed him so much."

"So many times I wanted to tell you, but I couldn't. I was afraid you wouldn't believe me. Or worse—hate me."

"Hate you? Why? I don't understand?"

Yogli stood, his massive figure towered above her as he moved beneath a nearby olive tree, shadows on his tanned face. *The scar!* Jerusha approached Yogli, reached up, and touched the scar.

"I never thanked you for what you did for Mother and me the night you were flogged. I am so sorry." She saw a brim of water in his eyes. Embarrassed, he shrugged.

"Tell me more," she asked. He cleared his throat.

"Years ago, I returned to Tarsus, our home, from a long campaign in the Roman guard to discover that Jacob's mother died." Yogli's voice cracked and Jerusha looked away as he struggled to gain control of his emotions. This certainly couldn't be easy on him. "I came home to find out my wife had died and my son had run away. He was only a boy—I could hardly believe he was there when I left and gone when I returned. But—Jacob never liked that I was a Roman tribune. It grieved me that his Jewish friends in Tarsus mocked him for it. I was immediately sent out on assignment again. The neighbor told me that Jacob ran away. I searched for him each time I came home. I paid people to investigate and find my boy." Yogli's eyes filled with tears and he looked away. "Only YHWH knows how much I love him."

Abigail put her head in her hands. "Dear Jacob, dear Jacob. All those years—I never knew."

Jerusha tried to process everything Yogli was saying. It seemed impossible, yet everything made sense now.

Yogli put his hand on an upper branch of the olive tree, stared up into the branches for a while, deep in thought.

"Then what happened?" Jerusha asked quietly.

Yogli sighed. "By the time I found him here in Jerusalem, you were already slaves to Caiaphas and he had fled the city. I asked for and was grateful to get the assignment to guard you and Abigail. I had no right to take ownership of you. I bought this home for my family when Yogli was a baby. He used to call it his enchanted castle," Yogli smiled at that. "He loved it here. I should have known he would return. But in reality I can see now that my own son disowned me. It's only now that I felt you needed to know."

Abigail spoke then. "Maybe not. Perhaps Jacob didn't disown you. Perhaps you were gone so long that he thought you were put in prison—or killed on your mission."

"The signet ring?" Jerusha asked.

"It is mine. Your father has the same ring and cognomen. He preferred to go by Jacob."

"So Father's had the lion and butterfly seal since he was born."

"Yes." He answered. She picked up the pendant that hung around her neck.

"That is why he made my pendant a lion and a butterfly. It spoke of my inheritance. Do you know what happened to Father?"

"No."

Jerusha stood to her feet. "I'll never stop searching for him. Do you think I'm being foolish?"

"I couldn't stop searching for him, Jerusha. And even though I've not found him, I've found both of you. If he's out there, you'll find him. You're like that flittering butterfly that doesn't look like she knows where she's going, but always gets to YHWH's appointed destination," he said, then grinned his approval. She paused and reflected on what she had just heard. She walked over to Yogli and touched his arm.

"Then—then you are really my grandfather?"

"Yes, but it might be best if you keep calling me Yogli. No one in Jerusalem knows me as Regulus. It needs to stay that way for your protection."

Abigail slowly approached Yogli. "You are truly Jacob's father?" she asked.

Yogli looked down at his feet and then into Abigail's eyes. "You are disappointed."

Abigail steadied herself and walked back to the bench to sit down. Yogli followed, but remained standing.

"Jacob never told me his father was a Roman soldier, but then, he would never talk about his family much either. Always avoided the subject."

"He was ashamed of it," Yogli said. Jerusha watched Mother stare up at Yogli for a minute. "My father bought our Roman citizenship in Tarsus. He felt it was the best thing—the safest thing—for his family at that time. So both Rome and Jerusalem were home to me as well."

"There is a resemblance," said Abigail. "And you have been so kind to us. How did an heir of the tribe of Judah become a Roman legionary?"

"It is a long story." Abigail motioned for him to sit down on the bench across from her.

"Please, tell us about it," she said. "We want to know."

"My father earned favor with Rome through his valiant fighting. His reputation earned me favors with governors and commanders. Thus, the favor that I pulled in for all of you here. I just returned from Rome. I wanted to give this as my wedding gift to Jerusha and Timon. As it turned out, it is both a wedding gift and a safe haven for Stephen's orphans and widows. Who would have thought all of this would have happened?"

"Incredible," said Jerusha. "And the signet ring?"

Yogli nodded. "Mine. Your father has one, too. His rightful inheritance from his grandfather—your great grandfather."

Timon whistled low. "Quite a story, Yogli."

Just then Chaya approached the three of them, dark concern in her eyes. Timon rose to greet his mother with a kiss and embraced her. "All is well, Mother. All is well."

Chaya dabbed her eyes. "Timon, I do want you to tell me what happened yesterday. But now Stephen's mother and Peter stopped in. We must go to Stephen's house to prepare his body. He must be buried today." Chaya looked at Abigail. "Do you want to go?"

"Of course," Abigail answered. "Jerusha, what about you?"

After seeing the stoning yesterday, Jerusha had no desire to participate in preparing the body for burial. "No, Mother, you and Chaya go. I'll stay with Timon and prepare the children for the funeral. Take Yogli and some of the older boys to carry the stretcher. We'll meet you at the bottom of the hill at the olive grove and follow to the tomb. Send one of the boys back to tell us when you are ready."

***

By the time the funeral procession reached the olive grove, the barefooted children with rent tunics were restless, but when they heard the groaning and the qinah of the lamenting women in the distance, they ran to see. Yogli, Moses, and two other orphan boys carried the stretcher, their eyes wide, tears spilling onto their cheeks.

"I will miss you, Stephen," Jerusha whispered, Sarah at her side.

"I will miss you, too," the little one added and wiped her nose with her sleeve. Jerusha and her little mimic stepped in behind the retinue of lamenters. She glanced down at Sarah, smiled at how much she imitated her actions, and took her hand. The other children trailed behind. Jerusha felt Timon's presence. Like a shepherd, he watched over them. No sheep would wander off today.

Many people followed and cried, dust flying in the air, clothes rent. It was obvious that Stephen was well known and loved. Most of the priests kept their distance, though. A few nodded their condolences as they passed.

At one point Jerusha looked up. Standing on a hill behind the people was Caiaphas and Saul, an evil glare in their eyes. She smiled at the peace she felt. No hateful thoughts. No clenched fists in anger. No twisting fear in her stomach.

They walked out the city gate toward the Kidron Valley to the burial site. After placing the body in the tomb, several young men stayed behind to share in the three-day watch. After those days passed, Abigail and Chaya would apply the final ointments and the tomb would be sealed.

The intense groaning of the lamenting women, who were paid by some of the Sanhedrin priests, bothered Jerusha. Stephen would want a celebration of his entry into Yeshua's kingdom, not this morose crying. *You have turned my mourning into dancing,* the words from the Tehillim ignited a plan in her thoughts. After the tomb was sealed and Abigail and Chaya completed the ceremonial cleansing on the third and seventh day, they would celebrate as Stephen had taught her to do in times of darkness. *Dance, Jerusha, dance!*

Chapter 32

The next morning Jerusha awoke with the warm sunshine on her face. She stretched and yawned, then crept from under the sheepskin cover, careful not to awaken Timon. She heard a light rap at the door. After she slipped her cloak on over her tunic, she unlocked the door and peeked out.

"Sarah, come in," she said and swung wide the large door.

"May I talk to you?" she asked with a bashful shrug, her eyes down.

"Of course, let's go to the garden," Jerusha answered.

Jerusha saw Timon stir. "Could Timon go, too?"

"Give us a few minutes and we'll meet you at Father's bench."

***

A few minutes later, Timon and Jerusha came into the garden. Sarah hung onto a marble column with one hand and twirled around it slowly, arms outstretched and eyes closed.

"Butterfly, butterfly, where will you land?" Jerusha asked softly.

Sarah bumped into them, and Timon lifted her high. Her giggle echoed among the early morning songbirds, a welcome relief from lamenting mourners' cries in the courtyard the night before.

Timon picked up Sarah and held her in his lap. Jerusha cuddled next to them on the bench.

"Now what's this about?" Timon asked.

Sarah twisted a piece of hair from his dark scruffy beard around her tiny finger for a few seconds, then looked up at Jerusha and bashfully back down at her braided creation.

"May I call you Ima? My mother is gone," she asked. "And may I call you Aba?" She looked up at Timon. "Stephen was the only father I can remember. You can take his place."

Jerusha blinked back tears. The loneliness in Sarah's tone brought back the empty sense of abandonment she felt while in captivity, the need to be loved—to belong. Even now she wondered where Father was. Dead? In prison? He had somehow been able to provide for her from afar, but she longed to touch him, hear his voice. She sighed. At least now she knew he loved her.

Jerusha tipped her head up and peered into Timon's eyes. He understood her longing, Sarah's longing too. An orphan himself, he carried himself with the dignity of a prince that had an inheritance, one who knew the love of a father. "Yeshua is the way to the Father," she had heard him say to the children earlier. Something inside stirred. She watched him cup Sarah's chin in his large hand.

"Yes, Sarah, you may call me Aba," he said. "I am sure Jerusha won't mind if you call her Ima, either. Will you Jerusha?"

"I would like that very much. Is there anything else, Sarah?"

Sarah shook her head.

"Very well. Then will you please ask the other children to meet me here as fast as they can? I have something to tell them," Jerusha said.

Sarah jumped off Timon's lap and scampered up the tiled path. Her black, wavy curls bounced to her waist, and her tunic rippled in the breeze as she disappeared around the pomegranate bush.

***

Jerusha watched the children with downturned mouths, sniffled, red noses, and slumped shoulders traipse into the garden and take their place on the ground in a semicircle before Jerusha and Timon. Sarah crawled onto Timon's lap.

"I love you, Aba," she whispered loud enough for Timon to hear, then looked at Jerusha, "and you, too, Ima."

Jerusha winked and whispered in her ear, "And I you," then sat upright and scanned the faces around her. Moses and the others looked so sad. A few older ones remained standing in the back. She stood to her feet and announced, "Please, sit down everyone."

Jerusha gently wiped a tear from Moses' eye. She kissed the heads of the older girls and caressed the tearful faces. Quietly, she made eye contact with each child. Their loss was so great, and that should be acknowledged before she shared what was on her heart. Timon followed Jerusha's lead and tousled the hair of the older boys and encouraged them, one by one. They were Aba and Ima to more than Sarah. Stephen had left them many children.

Jerusha picked up three-year-old Solomon and held him on her hip, kissed his cheek, and took her place in front of the children—*her* children.

"Children, today we all grieve because we will miss Stephen. He was a wonderful man and Aba to all of us," Jerusha's throat went dry and she wasn't sure she could go on. Hadn't Stephen been the guardian assigned to her by her own father? Wasn't it Stephen that brought her to Yeshua and to Timon? Jerusha bit her lip and swallowed hard.

"We all love Stephen. But I know that he would want us to celebrate with him that he overcame evil with good and now rules with Yeshua from heaven. Just like Yeshua, Stephen cried out to God to forgive those who killed him." Jerusha waited for those words to sink into the minds and hearts of the older boys, then continued, "I have a plan to yizkor Stephen's memory." Their blank, vacant eyes grieved her, but she continued. "When I was going through some dark times, Stephen encouraged me to dance. He said if I danced, the chains would fall off."

"When did you have chains on you? Were you in jail?" little Sarah asked. No one laughed. The children knew that Jerusha and Abigail had come from a terrible place, although none of them knew any details.

"That is a good question, Sarah. No, I wasn't in prison in chains. I had chains on me that you couldn't see, like some of you are feeling now, a heavy heart, no joy, a sense that I would never be happy again. Stephen's favorite mizmor says, 'you have turned my mourning into dancing.' So we have seven days to mourn. Now, as we mourn for Stephen I also want us to prepare for an evening where we remember Stephen with a melody of praise and machowl, the round dance. I remember his laughter when he taught me that dance."

"I can make a new flute out of a reed," one said.

"I'll make a new timbrel."

Sarah jumped up and pulled on Jerusha's hands. "You can teach us to dance the circle dance."

***

Peter and James came that week with provisions for the widows and orphans, gifts from their beloved friends in Jerusalem. Jerusha, Abigail, and Chaya organized the house and assigned rooms to the orphans and widows. Their clothing and household items that came from Stephen's house found their niche in square shelves carved into the walls and old wooden chests that Father had made.

The children, so open in their expressions of love for Stephen, came to Jerusha, especially when they found her alone in the garden.

One moment she wept with a child and the next moment she laughed with one.

For the next seven days Jerusha listened to children's laughter, scraping of wood with the chisel, and the thudding of the warp on the loom, all familiar sounds from days gone by in her childhood home. Timon sat on the ground barefooted with the boys and carved instruments. Some of the girls weaved colorful cloths to wave or tie in their hair. She taught Sarah and the little ones the circle dance. Each child had time alone with Jerusha or Timon to share their feelings about their loss. The mourning time passed, and the evening of their yizkor finally came. Jerusha greeted friends and family from all over Jerusalem to celebrate Stephen's victory.

Overwhelmed by the many people who loved Stephen, she stood with Yogli under an olive tree and listened to the adults closest to Stephen briefly give testimony to his impact on their lives. As mistress of the house now, Jerusha had to remind herself that her home actually belonged to Yogli at one time. She wondered, if her father was alive, what would he think about his return? Or Rome's protection of their home? As usual she had so many questions. She decided to lay them aside until another day. Tonight belonged to Stephen, her beloved father figure, who freed her from slavery to Caiaphas and wedded her to Timon.

As Peter recounted Stephen's life's work, the power and miracles that came from his preaching, her thoughts flashed back to Stephen's trial and what he saw when the heavens opened. Maybe someday she will see Yeshua again, this time in his glorious new body—on his throne beside his Father. She wondered what Stephen was doing now? Did he see them? Did he know they honored him and his victory into the kingdom? "I know," she said more to herself than to her father, "I ask too many questions."

She chuckled and focused on Timon as he shared the strength of Stephen's last words and challenged every listener to forgive. How she adored him now. Her father, a much better judge of character than she, chose him for her. Stephen told her. Again she wondered if her father was alive. She wanted him to know the many grandchildren she planned to birth in the future. Timon extended his hand toward her. It was her turn.

She stepped out from the olive tree, smiled back at Yogli and scanned the courtyard at the children's faces, whose eyes were all on her now. Could her words carry the same power as Stephen? How could she, a woman snatched from the dark chrysalis of shame, anger, and guilt, impact these innocent faces that looked to her for comfort? She gulped.

"Yeshua, give me the words," she prayed silently. In the long silence while she waited for the words to come, Timon took her hand and squeezed. Already, he knew her all too well and covered her with his loving support in those weak moments when she felt helpless like she did now. That's it! She knew what to say.

"Love," she barely got it out. Her throat constricted and she choked back tears. "Stephen loved. He especially loved you. He even loved his enemies. While he walked this earth, he displayed Yeshua's Father's heart, always reaching out to the orphans and widows. I will forever be grateful to my father for bringing Stephen into my life." Her nose began to run and she sniffed it back. *Why now? So embarrassing.* As always Timon was there in these situations. This time she was glad. She wiped her nose with the back of her hand. Other small faces that peered at her wiped their noses, too.

Timon spoke up now.

"Let us celebrate Stephen's life of love. Children get ready. You know what to do."

Jerusha and Timon sat on her father's favorite bench and watched the children, their children now, stand and recite a portion from the Torah that Stephen had taught them.

Others told their favorite memory of him. Moses stuttered, "St-St-Stephen s-s-saved my life. I lo-lo-love him."

"Oh, Moses," Timon said, "that's wonderful. He was so proud of you. He was proud of all of you children, even when you tested his patience." He looked at Jerusha and grinned. She knew he partly referred to her. "Now let's celebrate his life with song and dance."

Someone clapped, then clap, clap, clap, pause, clap, clap, clap.

The children's feet started to tap to the beat.

The younger girls ran to get their new timbrels—*jingle, jingle, jingle*. One pulled a flute from inside her tunic and started playing, at first a slow dirge, then gradually the beat increased. Timon led the boys with the reed flutes.

Jerusha and the widows formed circles with the older children. Arms on one another's shoulders, they moved to the beat, their feet crisscrossing in front, then in back. Sarah and the younger ones dashed under their arms into the middle, formed their own circle, moved the opposite direction, and giggled.

She remembered what Stephen had told her about dancing—"the chains will fall off"—and looked at the smiling faces in the circle. How right he was.

Someone handed Yogli a cymbal. Jerusha threw her head back and shouted, "For Yeshua, and for Stephen." Yogli crashed them—one, two, three! Jerusha chuckled seeing the large man crash cymbals together. The garden crescendoed in praise. Abigail and Chaya stood beside Yogli and lifted their hands and clapped in rhythm to the familiar Jewish celebration hymn.

"The Lord reigns!

Forever and Ever!

"The Lord reigns!

Forever and Ever!"

Jerusha unlocked her arm and made an opening for her mother and Timon. Abigail entered with Chaya. Timon laughed and kissed Jerusha's cheek as he connected with the circle and they continued their dance. Several new circles of Stephen's family and friends formed throughout the courtyard and garden.

Moses' flute hit a high note.

Crash! Yogli smacked his cymbals together and everyone sang again:

"The Lord reigns!

Forever and Ever!

The Lord reigns!

Forever and Ever!"

Jerusha broke away from the circle and went into the center: twirl, dip forward, twirl, dip backward. Sarah handed her a timbrel with long, colored strips of cloth. She swirled the timbrel in circles above her head three times, smacked the instrument, and twirled again. Everyone somehow knew to be quiet.

This time Jerusha sang solo, a melody she wrote to the words her father wrote on the back of her pendant:

"Arise, O, LORD!

Let your enemies be scattered.

Let all who hate you flee before you!"

The children trilled and danced around her and sang the chorus:

"The Lord reigns!

Forever and Ever!"

The meter quickened and Jerusha's feet leapt in rhythm to the tambourines. The children followed her, crouching down like lions just as she taught them. First to the left, then the right. At that moment, Father's words boomed into her thoughts, "My little lioness, you are royalty from the tribe of Judah. You will dance before the King one day."

Jerusha laughed with great joy, leapt into the air and landed in a squat, arms out to her sides.

Crash! Crash! Crash! Yogli beat the cymbals.

Silence.

Jacob's lioness stood and twirled, arms stretched out, and bumped into her father's bench. After a quick glance at Timon's twinkling eyes, she lifted her face to the sky and shouted.

"Yes, Father!" She twirled and raised her hands. "For the King!" She twirled again, away from the bench. "Now and forevermore, I dance for the king!"

Timon swooped her into his arms. "And you will dance for me, my beautiful wife." She blushed but kissed him as everyone backed away and left them alone in the garden.

Jerusha heard the children's giggles and looked toward the gate. Little faces peeked over the gate at Sarah, her head stuck in the pomegranate bushes. Most likely she looked for a chrysalis. A purple butterfly fluttered over her head.

Jerusha remembered her days with Father. *Where is he? Is he all right?* The questions started again and she looked up at Timon, her rock and strength. Whatever the future held, she knew he would be beside her no matter what. And she would dance. When darkness came, and she knew it would, she would dance before the King and any chains that held her captive would fall away. The King loved her and Timon loved her. Stephen's words echoed in her heart.

"Dance, Jerusha, Dance!"

Epilogue

The watchers blinked, pained by the explosion of light into their den of darkness. Strobe lights flashed slowly at first, then increased in magnitude until hundreds of flashes blazed and, for that moment, blinded the evil watchers.

"Yeshua's warriors!" cried one.

"AHHHHHHHHHHaahhhhhhhh!"

The dark-hooded creatures screamed and shrank back from the warrior angels dispatched by Yeshua. Their swords came at them with precision, calculated in perfect unison to every twirl the woman made in her dance. Whoosh! A heavenly beam pulsed from heaven's portal now opening over the city and pushed against the darkness coming against Yeshua's kingdom manifesting on earth.

The serpent-like leader glared at Yeshua's protective canopy that was beginning to form around the outer barriers of Jacob's dwelling high on the hill of Mount Zion. The strong frequency from the sound of the cymbals and instruments pulsated from the angel warriors' shields and spread a light barrier around the outer limits of the city.

"What is that?" the smallest fiend asked.

"I don't know!" the serpent snapped.

"Where will we go?"

"What is *that*?"

Confusion vibrated within the enemy's den of darkness, initiated by the music and dance from the garden gathering.

"AHHHHHHAahhhhh!"

The hordes of evil creatures crept closer one step, then slinked back four steps. On and on it went until they leapt into the air to swoop in between the shields before the angel army locked arms together. Each step to the music's beat in adoration to the King released fiery arrows from the bows of the heavenly archers against the attempted advancement of the enemy. Every arrow hit the backs of the retreating black-hooded creatures.

One high-ranking evil watcher yelled orders to another evil horde to attack. Before they could move, the woman's feet bounced, one, two, three and when she leapt, silver swords flew from beneath her feet and landed in the hands of a reserve angelic army, a backup that Yeshua released through her song. In the blink of an eye, they slashed through that horde of evil servants and more light broke through the darkness. Each twirl of the woman's dance released diamond-like sparkles into the atmosphere that filled the garden with a glorious fragrance.

"He is here! He is here!"

"The King is here! Retreat!"

"Retreat!" the evil minions screamed.

"NO!" the serpent-like leader yelled. He waved his arm at the hordes of evil, his followers. "Stop her! The time is short!"

No one stopped. Not one.

The serpent lifted his eyes and screamed at the backs of the cowards, "Destroy her love for Yeshua! Make her doubt his love for her. Now! Do it!"

Dance, Jerusha, dance.

About the Author

L inda Fergerson, a gifted storyteller and dancer, has a passion to see the Father's sons and daughters enter into their royal destiny. Dancing in initimacy with Yeshua helped break many of the chains of worthlessness, anger, and rejection that accompanied the sexual abuse she experienced as a child from a neighbor boy.

For several years she held "A Night with the King" meetings for women in her basement. After the women partook of a meal at the King's table, they stepped into His royal presence and listened as His sweet voice whispered love songs to their hearts.

Later, she ministered in Israel with Warring Dove International. She walked the shores of the Sea of Galilee, danced in Jerusalem, and had a divine encounter with Yeshua at Shiloh.

As Vice President of Women's Aglow in her hometown of Dodge City, Kansas, she gained a desire to see Holy Spirit-led worship and prayer overtake the city.

She founded His Writers, a writers group that prayed and interceded for editors, writers, and publishers to hear the Father's voice and bring forth the "child of promise" given to them that only they could birth.

Her greatest ministry is to her husband, Steve, and her three adopted sons, Samuel, Stephen, and Joshua.

She's available to speak. Some of the topics she speaks on are the following: Hebrew Dance, Intimacy with the King, and I Will Not Leave You Orphans.

To contact Linda Fergerson for prayer or speaking engagements email her at lfergerson1950@hotmail.com.